THE
PROSE WORKS
of
ALEXANDER POPE

Vol. I. The Earlier Works, 1711-1720

THE
PROSE WORKS
of
ALEXANDER POPE

Newly collected & edited by
NORMAN AULT

Vol. I. The Earlier Works, 1711-1720

GREENWOOD PRESS, PUBLISHERS
WESTPORT, CONNECTICUT

Library of Congress Cataloging in Publication Data

Pope, Alexander, 1688-1744.
   The prose works of Alexander Pope.

     Reprint of the 1968 ed. published by B. Blackwell,
Oxford.
     A 2d vol. covering the years 1721 to 1744 was not
published.
     I. Ault, Norman, 1880-1950. II. Title.
[PR3621.A8 1977]   824'.5   77-10892
ISBN 0-8371-9802-X

Originally published in 1936 by Oxford. Printed at the Shakespeare
Head Press and published for the Press by Basil Blackwell

Reprinted with the permission of Basil Blackwell

Reprinted in 1977 by Greenwood Press, Inc.

Library of Congress Catalog Card Number 77-10892

ISBN 0-8371-9802-X

Printed in the United States of America

PREFACE

THE extent of Pope's literary activities was far wider than is represented either by his own authorized *Works*, or by any subsequent collected edition of them. Throughout his life he indulged a fancy for irresponsible publication, and withheld his name—not always guilelessly—from many of his pieces. Much of his verse, for instance, though afterwards acknowledged by him or attributed to him, was first printed anonymously; and recent discoveries of a number of his poems which he himself had published in a way designed to conceal his authorship, further testify to this idiosyncrasy.

As with his verse so to a still greater degree with his prose—even allowing for the imposed anonymity of his contributions to the periodicals. No more than six of the forty pieces which compose the present volume were acknowledged by Pope on publication. Of the rest, some he claimed later as his own by including them in his *Works*; others were stated to be his by his contemporaries or have been ascribed to him by the scholarship of two centuries; yet others are now for the first time either definitely identified as his, or attributed to him with considerable—if perhaps differing—degrees of probability. Many of the pieces thus variously ascribed to him have never before been collected, others have never been reprinted in their entirety, while at least three of them could be read only in the original pamphlets of the utmost rarity.

Detailed evidence is given in the Introduction for the attribution to Pope of the prose works previously unidentified. These consist in the first place of two separate pamphlets of some importance, one being *The Critical Specimen* which is a satirical reply to Dennis's attack on Pope's *Essay on Criticism*, the other a burlesque sermon entitled *The Dignity, Use, and Abuse of Glass-Bottles*; and, secondly, of nine essays, namely, four from *The Spectator*, and five from *The Guardian*.

The Introduction also includes a good deal of new evidence bearing on the authorship, date, or circumstances of publication of the other pieces comprised in the present volume. These new facts will be found not infrequently to strengthen the case made by previous workers for attributions to Pope; though the fresh light they throw on the biographical occasions and historical background of other of these early works may necessitate some drastic revision of currently held views—such, for example, as that which supposes 'the battle of the Iliad' a comparatively brief and one-sided affair.

The collection into a single volume (with a historically critical Introduction) of so much that hitherto has been scattered or virtually inaccessible is a necessary preliminary to any attempt to establish a canon of the early prose works of Pope. To this end the works themselves, authoritative and presumptive, are reprinted in their integrity from the original texts and in their proper chronological order from 1711 to 1720. The later prose works, from 1721 to his death in 1744,will be similarly treated in a subsequent volume uniform with this: the two volumes together will thus comprise (exclusive of the correspondence) *The Complete Prose Works of Alexander Pope.*

In the preparation of this work I have become indebted for help to many friends; more especially to Mr T. J. Wise for the loan of several rare Pope pamphlets, as well as *A Letter from Sir J— B— to Mr. P—,* not to be found in our great libraries; to Professor G. Sherburn for photographs of *The Critical Specimen,* his copy being the only one yet located, though two others are said to be in existence; and to Mr L. F. Powell, Mr H. O. White and Mr C. H. Wilkinson for criticisms and suggestions.

N. A.

Oxford,
May 1st, 1936.

CONTENTS

[THE FEW pieces acknowledged by Pope himself have no asterisk prefixed to their titles below; one asterisk denotes those pieces which have been previously attributed to him, and two those now ascribed to him for the first time: references to the arguments in the Introduction for all these attributions being given in roman page-numbers.]

PREFACE	*page* v	
INTRODUCTION	xi	
A NOTE ON THE TEXTS	cxxvi	
**The Critical Specimen, 1711	xi, xxviii	1
CONTRIBUTIONS to *The Spectator*, 1711-1712	xxxiii	
**On the Desire of Distinction	li	20
**The Additional Graces	xlvi	27
**On Idleness	xlvii	32
*On Affectation	xliv	37
On a City and Country Life	xxxiv	42
*On Reason and Passion	xlv	44
*A Dream of the Seasons	xlix	49
*Proposals for News Papers, I	xxxv	56
*Proposals for News Papers, II	xxxv	59
**On the Love of Praise	lii	63
On a Fan	xxxv	70
On the Last Words of Adrian	xxxv	72
CONTRIBUTIONS to *The Guardian*, 1713	lvi	
On Dedications	lvii	76
*The Grand Elixir	lix	83
**On False Criticks	lxi	88
**On Easy Writing	lxiii	93
On Pastorals	lvii	97
Against Barbarity to Animals	lvii	107
A Receit to make an Epick Poem	lvii	115
The Club of Little Men, I	lvii	121
The Club of Little Men, II	lvii	125

**On a Dream of a Window in his Mistress's Breast
lxv 130
  On Sickness   lvii 134
**On Nature and Death   lxviii 137
**On the Origin of Letters   lxx 141
  On Gardens   lvii 145

*The Narrative of Dr. Robert Norris, 1713   xviii 153
  The Dedication of *The Rape of the Lock*, 1714 lxxii 169
  A Key to the Lock, 1715   lxxiii 173
**The Dignity, Use, and Abuse of Glass-Bottles, 1715
                                                  lxxv 203
  The Preface to *The Iliad*, 1715   xcii 221
*A Full and True Account of a ... Revenge by Poison,
   on the Body of Mr. Edmund Curll, [1716] xciv 257
*God's Revenge against Punning, 1716   cx 267
*A Further Account Of the most Deplorable Condition
   of Mr. Edmund Curll, 1716   xcviii 273

PROSE PIECES FROM *The Works*, 1717:
  The Preface   cxiv 289
  A Discourse on Pastoral Poetry   cxv 297

*A Clue to the Comedy of the Non-Juror, 1718 cxvii 303
*A Strange but True Relation how Edmund Curll ...
   was Converted from the Christian Religion,
   [1720]   cvii 315
  The Dedication of *The Iliad*, 1720   cxxiv 323

INTRODUCTION

THE earliest piece of published prose that can be attributed to Alexander Pope with any degree of confidence, is probably *The Critical Specimen*, a pamphlet dated 1711; for although the day and month of its publication have eluded inquiry, it almost certainly appeared before the 'few Spectators' which Pope confessed to have written, the first of which (if identified correctly) is dated November 16, 1711. But *The Critical Specimen* does not stand alone; it has many connexions with another pamphlet, *The Narrative of Dr. Robert Norris*, published nearly two years later, when *The Spectator* was no more and Pope was writing for its successor *The Guardian*. For this reason it will be convenient to depart from a strictly chronological sequence in this Introduction, and consider the two related pamphlets together, before proceeding to discuss Pope's contributions to the periodicals.

The Critical Specimen, 1711.

The Critical Specimen and *The Narrative of Dr. Robert Norris* are alike the outcome of the famous quarrel—then in its incipient stage but destined to be life-long—between Pope and John Dennis; and although this is not the place to retell that woeful tale, the events which led up to the publication of these two anonymous pamphlets, both attacking Dennis, must be summarized for the light they throw on the question of Pope's authorship. How or when the quarrel began is unknown, but it seems to have been due to a not inexplicable antipathy between a brilliant, sensitive, young poet and an ageing, uncompromising critic whose own poems and plays had met with little success. If we accept Dennis's account, written as late as 1729, a mutual friend, Henry Cromwell, had introduced them on Pope's first coming to town and at his instance; and they had met 'in Company' only a few times, when, after an interval, open hostilities broke out with Pope's derisive reference to him in the *Essay on Criticism*, 1711, as the typical author who is intolerant of correction. But although Dennis might seem to tell another tale, when, in the preface to his *Reflections . . . upon . . . An Essay upon Criticism*, 1711 (of which more anon), he complained that he had been 'attack'd without any manner of Provocation . . . by one who is wholly a Stranger to me'; a later remark in the same pamphlet shows that, whatever he may have meant by 'a Stranger,' he had been in Pope's company on one or more occasions: 'And I remember a little *young Gentleman* . . . whom Mr. *Walsh* us'd sometimes to take into his Company as a double Foil to his Person, and his Capacity.'

However irascible and cross-grained his natural disposition may have been, Dennis was, on the whole, an honest man; and there is every reason to believe that he was genuinely surprised at Pope's attack. On the other hand, however ready Pope was to resent and repay to the last drop of gall in his pen any injury, real or imagined, done to him (as this volume witnesses only too well), indiscriminate and unprovoked aspersion was emphatically not in his character, at least in these early days. One more attempt, therefore, to explain this much debated problem may perhaps be forgiven.

According to Pope's statement in *The Works* of 1717, the *Essay on Criticism* was written in 1709; but as the poem itself witnesses to Walsh's influence, and as Pope, towards the end of his life, once told Spence that he had shown it to Walsh in 1706 (Pope's memory for dates was latterly often a little erratic), it would seem that some draft of it was in existence before Walsh's death on March 18, 1708. However that may be, Pope's animus against Dennis had found a prior, though private, expression in a rhymed letter to Cromwell, where the following couplet occurs:

> And for a butcher's well-fed daughter
> Great D[enni]s roar'd, like ox at slaughter.

As this was written in July 1707, the origin of the quarrel

must be sought for still earlier. Thus we approach the
period of Pope's early visits to town in 1705 and 1706,
when, as a youth of seventeen or eighteen, rather countrified
in dress and manner, and lamentably handicapped in phy-
sique, but with a towering ambition and a wit above the
common, he began to frequent the coffee-houses under the
wing of one or other of his elderly friends—Wycherley,
Walsh, Cromwell and the rest, all alike vocal in praise of his
unprinted *Pastorals*—and so came at length into the company of the choleric and forthright Dennis.

> But *Appius* reddens at each word you speak,
> And stares, tremendous, with a threat'ning eye,
> Like some fierce Tyrant in old Tapestry!

In the complete lack of other evidence, it would seem that
these lines from the *Essay*, which constitute Pope's first
overt attack on Dennis, also explain it. Bearing all the
marks of having been drawn from the life, they look like the
outcome of an actual experience—a coffee-house encounter,
for instance, when, in general conversation, some chance
remark by the young poet, possibly quite harmless in itself
('But Appius reddens at each word you speak'), possibly
correcting something Dennis had said, unluckily roused
the fierce tyrant of letters to one of his characteristic out-
bursts of fury—an outburst forgotten the next day by
everyone but the discomfited victim. Some such personal
experience, whatever it was, seems alike necessary to explain Pope's early enmity, and to be implicit in his lines;
for it is very certain, from all we know of Dennis, that at any
fancied affront he would not be content to 'stare' silently,
and we have no reason to suppose his tongue was less vitriolic than his pen. With a brilliant but sensitive youth like
Pope, always conscious of his physical feebleness, such an
experience would amply account for any animosity he might
subsequently show. It would explain why, in the course of
his *Essay* when he had occasion to treat of writers who were
impatient under correction, he chose Dennis as their arche-
type, and sped that shaft at him, armed with a double barb,

at once identifying him with the hateful character of the
Roman tyrant and reminding him of the recent failure of
his tragedy *Appius and Virginia*.

Pope's *Essay on Criticism* was published anonymously on
May 15, 1711, and on June 20 appeared Dennis's rejoinder,
*Reflections Critical and Satyrical upon a late Rhapsody call'd,
An Essay upon Criticism*, probably the most outrageous abuse
of a young poet ever printed, in which Pope's bodily infirmities are gibbeted, his youthfulness mocked, and his
private character vilified, with a sustained brutality of
phrase only equalled by the epithets applied to his verse, of
which scarce one line is allowed to be passable except where
it had been stolen from an older poet and half-spoiled in
the process. But it being very difficult for a practised hand
to write thirty-two pages without a word of sense, so some
scraps of genuine criticism here and there interrupt the
even tenor of its scurrility (and of these, incidentally, Pope
admitted the justice, and was not too proud to take advantage in the second edition of his *Essay*). Space precludes
alike quotation from Dennis's pamphlet and any detailed
narrative of its effects on Pope, and our summary must be
of the briefest. We hear nothing of him for a few days after
its publication; but very soon he put on a brave face with
his friends, and later always maintained that his consterna-
tion was short-lived, even going so far as to say that the
pamphlet made him 'very heartily merry in two minutes'
time.' Nevertheless, being human, his thoughts within
five days of its appearance were running on schemes of
revenge, as is proved by his letters: he pathetically hinted
to John Caryll that a cudgel would be the best answer; and,
the same day (June 25), asked Henry Cromwell's opinion
'in what manner such a critic ought to be answered.' We do
not know what reply Cromwell made, but Caryll, it seems,
rather anxiously deprecated any kind of answer at all. And
Pope, who was ever on his best behaviour with the latter
grave and estimable gentleman (to whom he did not always
acknowledge his anonymous productions, and even, as we
shall see, on occasion disavowed them), sought to reassure

him on August 2 with the statement: 'I shall never make
the least reply to him.' Notwithstanding, someone did
reply to Dennis's attack, with a sixteen-page pamphlet,
now practically unknown and of the utmost rarity, entitled,
The Critical Specimen, 1711, and the balance of probabili-
ties strongly suggests it was Pope.

It is unfortunate that the exact date of the publication of
The Critical Specimen has eluded my search, but the pamphlet very probably followed hard on Dennis's *Reflections*, and
might well have been written, printed, and on sale before
August 2; in which case Pope could have equivocally saved
his face if Caryll had challenged him—a trick not unknown
to him subsequently. Apart from its obvious connexions
with *The Narrative of Dr. Robert Norris* published less than
two years later, which, as we shall see, suggest a common
origin of the two attacks on Dennis, the evidence pointing
to Pope's authorship of *The Critical Specimen* is comprised
of divers kinds—the witness of occasion, of subject and
method, and of matter and phraseology.

First, then, of the argument from occasion. We have
seen, in the foregoing brief summary of the antecedents of
The Critical Specimen, the place it presumably occupies in
the Pope-Dennis quarrel. A study of the pamphlet and a
comparison of it with Dennis's *Reflections...upon...An Essay
upon Criticism* prove beyond a shadow of doubt that it was
evoked by that attack on Pope, many passages of which it
satirically incorporates and reflects back again in disparagement of their author—the most interesting of these Reflections reflected being the use made of the 'Hunch-back'd
Toad' simile, presently to be discussed.

Secondly, of the argument from method and subject. The
pamphlet exactly follows Pope's early ideas of the conduct
of literary warfare, as explicitly described in the following
year in a letter offering his services to Caryll. On November
19, 1712, he wrote:

It was never in my thoughts to offer you my poor pen in any direct
reply to such a scoundrel, who, like Hudibras, need fear no blow but

such as bruise, but only in some little raillery in the most contemptuous manner thrown upon him, not as in your defence expressly, but as in scorn of him *en gaieté de cœur*.

The Critical Specimen, as the reader will observe, could not be described more exactly. It is neither a defence of Pope, nor a reply to the charges brought against him by Dennis, nor does it condescend to scurrilous recrimination; but like other pieces of the kind in this volume, it preserves an air of nonchalant gaiety, and quietly smothers its victim in ridicule. That, said Pope in effect to Addison (or said he had said, in a letter dated July 20, 1713, which repeats much of what he wrote to Caryll) is the way that Dennis should be treated.

Thirdly, of the argument from matter and phraseology. *The Critical Specimen* repeats a number of passages found earlier in Pope's correspondence (then unpublished), and contains in addition much material used by him elsewhere a little later. Only a few of these parallels,* however, can be noted here, the pamphlet being quoted first in each instance.

(*a*) How C[*hristophe*]r R[*i*]ch [having been shown a play by Dennis] intreated the Author with great Civility to acquaint him *whether it were one of your Tragedys or your Comedys*.

> Ask the same question . . . that Mr. Rich did of a modern play; 'Pray do me the favour, sir, to inform me; Is this your tragedy or your comedy?'
> *Letter to Cromwell*, Aug. 29, 1709.

(*b*) How he writ upon occasion two good Lines, being the most wonderful and surprizing Adventure in the whole Book.

> . . . Dodwell, who has done one thing worthy of eternal memory—wrote two lines in his life that are not nonsense.
> *Letter to Cromwell*, Nov. 1, 1708.

---

* Except in those rare instances where the original autographs were available, all quotations from Pope's letters throughout this Introduction follow the text of the Elwin-Courthope edition; other quotations of Pope's verse and prose follow the first editions unless otherwise stated.

(*c*) He had never read . . . that *Pegasus* wore *Bells* . . . wisely imagining *Pegasus* to be like a Millers Horse, that while he listned to their gingling he slacken'd his Pace.

I should be sorry and ashamed to go on jingling to the last step, like a waggoner's horse . . . to leave my bells to the next silly animal.

Letter to Caryll, July 13, 1714.

I really make no other use of poetry now, than horses do of the bells that jingle about their ears . . . only to travel on a little more merrily.

Letter to Caryll, Sept. 20, 1713.

(*d*) Of his Invention of a wonderful *Mustard Bowl* of a prodigious Size for the Players to make *Thunder* with.

With *Thunder* rumbling from the mustard-bowl.

Dunciad, ii, 226.

To this should also be added Pope's amusing footnote to this line (in 1729), and yet another reference in his *Prologue . . . to a Play for Mr. Dennis's Benefit, in* 1733:

And shook the stage with thunders all his own.

This gibe at Dennis's thunder has an added significance, insomuch that it does not seem to have been mentioned anywhere in print between its first appearance in *The Critical Specimen* and its reappearance in the *Dunciad* footnote, after which it became generally known; and also that the occasion of the Invention of the Mustard Bowl (according to an anonymous *Life of Mr. John Dennis*, 1734) was the performance of the ill-fated *Appius and Virginia* of which Pope had just reminded Dennis in the *Essay on Criticism*, and which is further ridiculed in 'Chapters' 16, 17 and 18 of this same pamphlet.

The foregoing three classes of evidence together establish a high degree of probability for Pope's authorship of *The Critical Specimen*, but there is more to be considered. First, however, let us glance at the negative evidence arising from the difficulty, if not impossibility, of naming another person who at this time was incensed against Dennis and was at once capable enough and friendly disposed enough to enter into the lists on Pope's behalf. It is true that Dennis had other enemies, but they were not Pope's friends at this date; for he had not yet met either Swift or Addison, and with Steele he was only just becoming acquainted. Furthermore, although a man may on occasion laugh at his own infirmities, it is hardly thinkable that a friend would have referred to Pope's physical deformity, as this pamphlet does more than once (to this point we shall return later). Nor would it be reasonable to suggest that someone not known to Pope, a stranger with a similar grievance against Dennis, should draw from Dennis's attack on Pope so large a proportion of his ammunition, when all the critic's work lay ready to his hand; or should be able so curiously to supplement it with material from Pope's private correspondence, not to mention other incompatibilities. Lastly, it is just worth noting in this connexion that the anonymous author seems once or twice to suggest that he is Steele, and in two or three other places that he is Swift; which suggestions, cancelling out, could only have been intended to mislead and can have no evidential value. Thus the lack of a probable, or even possible, rival claimant to *The Critical Specimen* leaves us with Pope's authorship as the only feasible hypothesis. But before we can consider its further confirmation in the unquestionable affinities existing between this pamphlet and Dr. Norris's *Narrative*, the latter must for a space engage our attention.

The Narrative of Dr. Robert Norris, 1713

The Narrative of Dr. Robert Norris is too well known to necessitate more than a brief account of the circumstances of its publication. Addison's *Cato*, for which Pope wrote the Prologue, was produced on April 14, 1713, with instant and overwhelming success; and, when published on April 27, quickly ran through several editions. Dennis, who had long nursed a grudge against Addison because of various criticisms in *The Tatler* and *The Spectator*, was apparently moved by his rage at the success of the play to write an adverse criticism of it, which, after some hesitation, he published under the title, *Remarks upon Cato, A Tragedy,* on July 9 (according to *The Evening Post* of that date). But an attack, however restrained, on one of the most successful plays of the period, and one, moreover, written by a man of unquestioned position in the literary and political world, was a very different thing from the bludgeoning of the anonymous and, for the most part, unknown author of a mere *Essay on Criticism;* and we may take it that a pseudonymous pamphlet which appeared within three weeks of the critic's *Remarks* with the alluring title, *The Narrative of Dr. Robert Norris, Concerning the strange and deplorable Frenzy of Mr. John Denn— An Officer of the Custom-house,* was not alone in making the implication that the poor man had taken leave of his senses.

This pamphlet has been very generally attributed to Pope in the past, with a few demurrers, of whom perhaps the most important are C. W. Dilke in the last century, and Professor G. Sherburn in the present. Dilke's case against Pope's authorship was argued without a knowledge of all the evidence since available, and may be passed over for that reason; but Dr Sherburn's opinion, recently stated in his admirable biography of Pope*, must command respect, and is not to be refuted save by chapter and verse. Briefly, he considers *The Narrative* to have been the outcome of a 'plot' by an unspecified number of people, in which, we gather, Pope and Steele were the prime movers, while Arbuthnot probably assisted, 'and some of Pope's Tory friends . . . must have helped to produce the pamphlet.' It is perhaps just possible that *The Narrative* was the result of multiple authorship; but as Dr Sherburn seems to have overlooked some evidence which militates against it, besides being not sufficiently critical of the evidence he does

---

* *The Early Career of Alexander Pope* By George Sherburn, 1934.

adduce, his presentation of the case is not conclusive. For example, it has long been recognized that the idea of *The Narrative* arose out of certain advertisements that were inserted in the newspapers from time to time over a number of years by a quack 'mad doctor,' one Robert Norris, offering to undertake the care, and 'by God's blessing' the cure, of lunatics; and Dr Sherburn, pointing out that one of Norris's advertisements was printed twice in *The Guardian* a few days after Dennis had published his *Remarks upon Cato*, comments on the significance of its appearance at that moment; and after saying 'This should mean that Steele was in the plot,' deduces that the 'conspirators' had inserted the advertisement to prepare the public for their forthcoming *Narrative of Dr. Robert Norris*. But this theory does not take into account all the facts.

It is unquestionable that Steele was deeply involved in politics at that particular time, not only in the controversy over the Demolition of Dunkirk, but also as a candidate for parliament actively engaged in contesting an election at Stockbridge, which he won in August. How much of July he spent out of London is not known; but it is very suggestive that from July 1 to August 3 every number of *The Guardian* has Addison's mark appended to it, which is generally taken to mean that Steele had left the conduct of the paper in his hands for that period. If Steele, therefore, had no time just then to spare for his paper in which he was really concerned, it is extremely unlikely he had time to waste on a whim like *The Narrative*. But Addison's management of *The Guardian* has, on the above hypothesis, a most unfortunate corollary; for if the insertion of Robert Norris's advertisement in that paper at that date is significant of any plot at all, as Professor Sherburn opines, it would seem that Addison's name must also be added to the list of 'conspirators' concerned in one way or another in the production of *The Narrative*. But the truth is that as regards either conspiracy or authorship the appearance of Robert Norris's advertisement in *The Guardian* for July 18, and 20, has no 'significance' whatsoever, simply because it was Norris's own advertisement, and one of several which began to appear simultaneously in other papers (in *The Daily Courant* for July 18, and 21, and *The Post Boy* for July 21, and 23), the reason for this particular bout of advertising being that the 'mad doctor' was notifying the public of his recent change of address from Snow-hill to Hatton-Garden, as is apparent from the advertisement itself which appeared for the first time on July 18 (and was continued intermittently for several months in practically the same words) as follows:

> Robert Norris, on Snow-hill, having had many Years Experience and good Success in the Cure of Lunaticks, is removed to the Pestle and Mortar near the middle of Hatton-Garden, where he hath a very convenient large House and Garden, Airy and fit to receive Persons of the best Rank of either Sex, with suitable Attendance. Any Person applying themselves as above, may there be satisfied, that the Cure shall be industriously endeavoured (and by God's Blessing effected) on reasonable Terms.
>
> *The Guardian*, July 18, 1713.

Lastly, seeing that *The Narrative* is dated 'From my House on Snow-hill,' it would appear that the author had not even seen these change-of-address advertisements, if indeed the pamphlet had not been written before they began to appear.

The other grounds on which this theory of multiple authorship rests have on examination as little actuality. Dr Arbuthnot is brought in to explain the presence of some (not very recondite) medical phrases. But if it is necessary for this argument to assume that Pope suffered from such mental obtuseness that, in spite of his medical friends and a quite obvious interest in medical things, in spite of having himself been in and out of doctors' hands all his life, he could neither have picked up enough knowledge for these details, nor have had initiative enough to look them up in a book, it would still be more reasonable to suppose that he had obtained this information in the course of ten minutes' conversation with a doctor—Arbuthnot or another—than that Arbuthnot should be made part-author of a pamphlet with which there is not the slightest evidence to show that he had any connexion. The remaining argument for multiple authorship seems to rest on Dr Sherburn's own statement: 'Pope had no great gift for such dramatic narrative: Steele and some of Pope's Tory friends had, and some of them must have helped to produce this pamphlet'—but that is opinion, not evidence. It is difficult to determine the precise limit of potentiality in a writer like Pope. Dennis, for instance, whose estimate of Pope's capabilities was even lower than Professor Sherburn's, did not think *The Narrative* beyond Pope's powers, and roundly accused him of writing it (*Remarks upon Mr. Pope's Translation of Homer* . . . 1717, pp. 91-92); Warburton, Pope's intimate friend and editor, thought it was a poor performance and semi-apologized for Pope's authorship of it; Ruffhead, Pope's first 'official' biographer—whether deriving his facts from Warburton or not—had no doubt of Pope's ability in the matter, and, without comment, said he wrote it; and it never struck Dr Johnson, as acute a judge of a man's literary capacity as need be, that it was too good to be Pope's, since he included it in his enumeration of the poet's works—but the cloud of witnesses need not all be summoned.

The case for Pope's sole responsibility for *The Narrative of Dr. Robert Norris* rests on evidence of a very different kind, some of which has never hitherto been presented. First in importance, naturally, are Pope's own confessions of authorship made in later life. And if it seems strange to any one unfamiliar with the problems of the Pope canon, that such an acknowledgement does not automatically end the matter, the explanation is that he, characteristically enough, had denied it soon after publication—as we shall presently see. Pope's implicit avowal of authorship was first made anonymously in the surreptitious edition of his correspondence in 1735 (where the letter in question is dated July 30, 1713), and was authoritatively repeated by him in the edition published under his own name in 1737 (where the same letter is dated July 20, 1713). The letter itself, while purporting to have been addressed and sent to Addison, was in fact a make-believe adapted from the letter to Caryll of November

19, 1712 (previously mentioned), in which he had offered
the services of his pen to his friend, who was then being
traduced in *TheFlyingPost.* In the apocryphal letter, Addison
takes the place of Caryll, and Dennis's *Remarks upon Cato* is
substituted for the newspaper attack; thus, after speaking of
Dennis, he continues:

> You may conclude from what I here say, that 'twas never in my
> thoughts to have offered you my pen in any direct reply to such a
> Critic, but only in some little raillery; not in defence of you, but in
> contempt of him.*

And to this passage he subjoins a footnote in explanation of
his meaning:

> * This relates to the Paper occasion'd by Dennis's Remarks upon
> Cato, call'd, Dr. Norris's Narrative of the Frenzy of John Dennis.

Whether or not the letter is apocryphal does not affect the
question; the point is that Pope deliberately wrote this note
implying his authorship of *The Narrative*, published it
anonymously in 1735, and gave it the authority of his name
on reprinting it in 1737. But that is not all. Pope directly
affirmed his authorship of the pamphlet a year or two later
in a conversation with Spence on certain pieces in *Miscellanies. The Third Volume*, 1732. It will be remembered that
that volume, like the earlier ones, had been edited by Pope,
who had placed *The Narrative* as the first item in it with the
three pamphlets on Curll (which Pope is believed to have
written) immediately following. The pieces included in the
volume are uniformly anonymous, and Spence having apparently inquired about some of them, Pope replied that a
certain one 'was written by Gay; that on Dennis, by myself.'
The last point to be made in regard to these avowals of
authorship by Pope, is that he has never been known to
claim a work by any other man, though he not infrequently denied his own. In view of these admissions of mature
age, Pope's early repudiation of the pamphlet can have little
weight, especially when one remembers that it was made to
his staid old friend Caryll, who, two years earlier, had de-

precated any rejoinder to Dennis, and had been reassured
with the words: 'I shall never make the least reply to him.'
It would seem that Pope was determined at all costs to preserve his dear anonymity, when, on October 17, 1713, he
reported to Caryll: 'As to the whim upon Dennis, Cromwell
thought me the author of it, which I assured him I was not,
and we are, I hope, very far from being enemies.' It is not
improbable that Cromwell (whose old friendship with Pope
seems to have ceased early in 1712) had thought himself
portrayed in the 'grave elderly Gentleman . . . a Grammarian,' who is made a slightly ridiculous figure in *The Narrative*, and had charged Pope with the authorship of it; whereupon Pope had characteristically denied his responsibility.
Nevertheless, that the writer was Pope and the 'Grammarian' Cromwell, finds further corroboration not only in certain descriptive details in the pamphlet itself, but also in a
previous letter to Caryll, dated August 14, 1713. This letter,
one suspects, was written on one of the rare occasions when
Pope was gravelled for something to say, or, rather, for
news of which his sedate old friend would approve. For this
reason, presumably, he refrains from speaking of his own
activities since his last letter (June 23), and Dennis's *Remarks on Cato* and the anonymous *Narrative* are alike avoided. He begins by saying at some length that he has nothing
to say beyond the old story of his affection for Caryll, after
which he goes on to describe the present distraction and inconsistency of his thoughts: how he is one moment soaring
above the stars with Whiston and the astronomers, the next
sunk in the very centre of nonsense with Tidcombe; now
recreating his mind with Steele at his wittiest, 'and now
levelling my application to the insignificant observations
and quirks of grammar of Mr. C[romwell] and D[ennis].'
The conjunction in a private letter of the names of these two
people, whose foibles were similarly ridiculed in *The Narrative* published a bare fortnight before, suggesting that
Pope's thoughts were still preoccupied with them, would
seem perhaps further to confirm both the identification of

his former friend as the 'Grammarian,' and his own responsibility for the piece.

Should additional proof of Pope's authorship of *The Narrative* be thought necessary, internal evidence is not at all lacking to corroborate his own declarations. The style, to a perceptive ear, is everywhere consonant with his acknowledged work in the same vein, and minor mannerisms and tricks of phrase could be cited, did space and patience allow. Two or three points of more general interest may, however, be permitted. In Pope's part of a joint letter which he and Gay wrote to Caryll (who was suffering from gout) in March, 1715, he says:'We desire you, in your turn, to condole with us, who are under a persecution, and much inflicted with a distemper which proves mortal to many poets,—a criticism;' which is clearly reminiscent of a passage in *The Narative*:

Doctor.   Pray, Sir, how did you contract this Swelling?
Dennis.   By a Criticism.
Doctor.   A Criticism! that's a Distemper I never read of in *Galen.*

Then, too, there is, in addition to its express mention, the use made of the *Essay on Criticism* in several places, notably in the further development of the 'tapestry tyrant' theme (p. 158), and in the new application to Dennis of the quoted couplet (p. 166) not previously associated with him—all of which appear rather oddly in a pamphlet ostensibly occasioned by Dennis's attack on Addison. Moreover, the whole thing is set in the key of raillery, rather than of abuse, exactly conforming to Pope's idea of the conduct of literary warfare already noted. And if we were compelled to believe the unsupported accusation made in *A True Character of Mr. Pope*, 1716, either by Dennis or Gildon (there is some doubt about the author at present), that Pope had at the outset 'teaz'd Lintott to publish [Dennis's] Remarks,' that could only show him still more deeply implicated in *The Narrative*. It would not, however, justify any other conclusion than that he foresaw in the publication of the *Remarks* a unique opportunity for a dual stroke such as his ingenious soul loved, and so may have helped to create the opportunity instead of merely seizing it when it came. For there can be little doubt that, with Dennis's outrageous abuse of him two years earlier still rankling in his mind, he exploited the opportunity to the utmost; and, under the pretence of defending Addison, revenged his old wrongs on his enemy by a further instalment of ridicule, the occasion of which effectually masked both his motive and his identity. But although there is no reason to suppose that Pope had any wish to injure Addison at this time (which was the gravamen of the above charge), that is not to say he would have been grieved had Dennis laid *The Narrative* at Addison's door. Addison, however, was adroit enough to circumvent this by an early denial of all responsibility for it in the following letter which Steele wrote to the publisher of the *Remarks*:

August 4, 1713.

Mr. Lintot,—Mr. Addison desired me to tell you that he wholly disapproves the manner of treating Mr. Dennis in a little pamphlet by way of Dr. Norris's account. When he thinks fit to take notice of Mr. Dennis's objections to his writings, he will do it in a way Mr. Dennis shall have no just reason to complain of. But when the papers above mentioned were offered to be communicated to him, he said he could not, either in honour or conscience, be privy to such a treatment, and was sorry to hear of it. I am, sir, your very humble servant.

Much ink has been wasted over this letter in the past, and many dark and incompatible meanings read into it, from moves in political intrigue to personal double-dealing on Addison's part; and on Steele's, anything, apparently, from a spiritless subservience to Addison to completely independent action—not to mention a part authorship of *The Narrative* itself.

But such speculations about the letter wholly disregard the occasion on which it appears to have been written, which, if my reading of some new evidence is correct, removes all cause for suspicion and leaves little or nothing to explain. We have already seen that the movements of Steele and Addison about this time can to some extent be followed in the editorship of *The Guardian* and in what is known of Steele's new political activities. Thus, simultaneously with Steele's active incursion into politics, Addison took over the conduct of the paper from July 1 to August 3, during which period every number is marked as his. From August 4 to 13, Steele resumed control, as is evidenced by his paper on Dunkirk (August 7) and Pope's letter to him (August 12) and the usual miscellaneous contributions of other people Then, commencing on August 14, another run of Addison's signatures, together with our knowledge of Steele's journey to Stockbridge on August 15 on election business (where he probably remained until he won the seat on August 25), shows that his friend was again in temporary charge of *The Guardian* at this critical period in Steele's career. On this evidence, therefore, I would suggest that the most natural (and quite unexciting) explanation of this much discussed letter is, that Addison, who had undertaken to look after his friend's paper during the stress of his political engagements, was suddenly called away at the beginning of August by some unforeseen emergency important enough to compel him to interrupt Steele's electioneering for some days; that Steele, summoned back to town, arrived just in time for a brief conversation with his friend, who, hurriedly departing, left on his hands *The Guardian* and the inevitable half-dozen last-minute commissions, one of which concerned the new pamphlet on Dennis, still damp from the press ('You might let him know somehow, Dick, that I had nothing to do with it, and say ...'); and that, during the next day or two, when Steele had a moment to spare, he remembered about the Dennis business, but, possibly not knowing his address at the moment, wrote to his publisher instead: 'August 4, 1713. Mr. Lintot, —Mr. Addison desired me to tell you ...'—as we have seen. Such an incident must have happened in effect a thousand times between friends in the management of joint concerns. How much or little Addison knew about the pamphlet beforehand—whether he had read the manuscript, had guessed or heard that Pope was its author, or not—we do not know. He has nevertheless been accused of bad faith in the matter, the charge being that knowing of the pamphlet beforehand and making no attempt to stop its publication, he therefore permitted it, and, having permitted it, caused this letter to be written. But the truth is, there is no evidence available to show, either that he made no attempt to stop it, or had the necessary authority to do so.

The Critical Specimen, 1711 (*continued*).

WITH the authorship of *The Narrative of Dr. Robert Norris* presumptively established and lacking only, it may seem, Pope's actual signature, we can also conclude our discussion of the earlier attack on Dennis. Both *The Critical Specimen* and *The Narrative* have been shown to have many connexions with Pope; it remains now to examine the reasons for thinking the two pamphlets the work of one hand. The evidence for this consists chiefly in the frequent use of the same material and, to some extent, of the same phraseology in both. We should, however, first note that while, on the one hand, Pope had no scruple about adapting, and even readapting, phrases and ideas from his earlier work (which, as I have shown elsewhere, is one of the most striking characteristics of his versification, and will in these pages become as apparent in his prose), or any hesitation at times about adapting to his use lines or phrases from the older writers, on the other hand it must be granted that similar pilferings from writers of his own day were comparatively rare, for obvious reasons; and he has never been known to borrow so much matter from any work of a contemporary, as *The Narrative* appears to derive from *The Critical Specimen*.

A reading of both pamphlets will make this duplication abundantly clear; and because we have in this case the two texts before us, it will be sufficient to note here the presence in both pieces of the following subjects: (*a*) the gibes at Dennis's fulminations against the Italian opera; (*b*) the ridicule of his unsuccessful works in general, and of certain plays and essays in particular; (*c*) the characteristic fun made of Lintot, first glimpsed in *The Critical Specimen* and developed in *The Narrative* (and, three years later, continued in the same vein in the pamphlets on Curll); (*d*) the teasing references to *The Spectator*, and (*e*) to Milton; (*f*) the descriptions of the effects of madness; (*g*) the absurd story of Dennis's fear of abduction and imprisonment in the Bastille by the French king (which I believe does not appear anywhere else in print before 1734); and, amongst several others, (*h*) Dennis's mannerisms—his staring and frowning, his ejaculatory 'O's,' his use of words like 'tremendous,' and oaths like 'S'Death.' It may be objected, with reason, that some of this material belongs naturally to the subject, and that two writers might independently make use of it. Nevertheless, so far as I have been able to ascertain, the greater part of it is peculiar to these two pamphlets and is not found in other attacks on Dennis before his death. Consequently its duplication here would seem to point to a common authorship of the *Specimen* and *Narrative*. This conclusion is corroborated by the frequent use in both of identical phraseology, of which the following examples may be cited:

(*a*) Of the Manner of Wearing his Breeches, with a short Essay to show that the most Natural Position of Rolls for Stockings is about one's Heels.

The Critical Specimen.

The Flap of his Breeches dangled between his Legs, and the Rolls of his Stockings fell down to his Ankles.

The Narrative.

(*b*) . . . whose turn'd Brains, or Pericranium crack'd or overladen with wild Ideas.

The Critical Specimen.

The Brain ferments till it be totally exhausted. We must eradicate these undigested Ideas out of the Perecranium.

The Narrative.

The explanation of Pope's repetition of so much matter

from an earlier work probably lies in the fact that *The Critical Specimen* was something of the nature of a misfire; it seems to have attracted no contemporary notice, and its extreme rarity to-day suggests that it had the smallest of sales. But apparently its jokes were (some of them) too good to be wasted, and the thrifty author served them up again with a more piquant sauce two years later.

The Critical Specimen concludes with a burlesque 'Advertisement' which calls for some discussion. It runs as follows:

There is in the Press and will speedily be publish'd Two Dissertations, The first by the Reverend Dr. *B——ly* proving from *Æsop's Fables* that the Author of them was not *Crooked* but *Strait*. The second by Mr. *Dennis* making it plain from the late *Essay* upon *Criticism* that the Author is by no means *Strait* but *Crooked*.

First, as regards the last nine words, the objection may possibly be made that Pope would have been unlikely to call attention to his physical disability in this manner; to which the answer would be that he was not calling attention to it, but laughing it off. For Dennis had already alluded to his deformity more than once in the course of his attack, one of his choicer similes for Pope being—

As there is no Creature in Nature so venomous, there is nothing so stupid and so impotent as a hunch-back'd Toad.

So that this burlesque advertisement, as well as the asterisked quotation of 'Hunch-back'd Toad' in the body of the pamphlet and the corresponding 'Remark' at the end, would, under the circumstances, appear to be a form of self-defence—an endeavour on Pope's part to show that he was untouched by Dennis's brutality.

The first allusion in the advertisement is obviously to Richard Bentley's *Dissertation upon the Epistles of Phalaris... And the Fables of Æsop*, 1697 (reprinted 1705), in which, treating of Æsop's physical appearance, after much argument he comes to the conclusion:''tis certain, he was no Deformed Person; and 'tis probable, he was very Handsom.' What there was about Bentley's argument that attracted Pope's attention, as it most certainly did, we cannot be sure; but psychologists would probably explain the fact by a sub-conscious desire on Pope's part (like the fox without a tail in Æsop's own fable) for companionship in deformity: if he could not be like other men, then other men (and great ones if possible) should be like him. And from that they would proceed to show that the bias of his mind against Bentley and his works, manifested from time to time throughout his life, might well have taken its initial tilt all unconsciously, when he first learnt that Bentley by straightening old Æsop's back would deprive him of a companion in misfortune, and so increase his sense of loneliness and singularity. However that may be, in the ninety-second number of *The Guardian* (June 26, 1713) Pope repeated the above gibe at Bentley's thesis, giving it as the opinion of 'Dick Distick' (a most amusing self-caricature, to which we shall return), as follows:

Dick Distick . . . is peremptorily of Opinion, against a great Reader, and all his Adherents, that *Æsop* was not a jot properer or handsomer than he is represented by the common Pictures. But the Soldier believes with the Learned Person above-mentioned; . . .

Nevertheless, for all Pope's sensitiveness—which there is no disputing—he was capable on occasion of jesting about his size and shape: 'It is likeness that begets affection, so my favourite dog is a little one, a lean one, and none of the finest shaped' (Letter to Cromwell, October 19, 1709). He could write: 'I . . . esteem myself the least thing like a man in England,' and go on to compare people of his proportions to 'frogs' (Letter to Cromwell, June 24, 1710); and could refer to himself as 'that little Alexander the women laugh at' (Letter to Caryll, January 25, 1711). And if those, and others of the sort, were private jokes to his friends, there was at least one occasion on which he made a public jest of his physical appearance. In the number of *The Guardian* above-mentioned, which together with the preceding number forms Pope's famous essay on 'The Club of Little Men,' besides making much delicious fun of the figures and foibles of little people (Pope himself is said to have been only about four feet six inches in height), he inserted the following sketch of himself.

The most eminent Persons of our Assembly are a little Poet, a little Lover, a little Politician, and a little Heroe. The first of these, *Dick Distick* by Name, we have elected President, not only as he is the shortest of us all, but because he has entertain'd so just a Sense of the Stature, as to go generally in Black that he may appear yet Less. Nay, to that Perfection is he arrived, that he *stoops* as he walks. The Figure of the Man is odd enough; he is a lively little Creature, with long Arms and Legs: A Spider is no ill Emblem of him. He has been taken at a Distance for a *small Windmill*. But indeed what principally moved us in his Favour was his Talent in Poetry, for he hath promised to undertake a long Work in *short Verse* to celebrate the Heroes of our Size. He has entertained so great a Respect for *Statius*, on the Score of that Line,

Major in exiguo regnabat corpore virtus,

that he once designed to translate the whole *Thebaid* for the sake of little *Tydeus*.

There can be no doubt that this description of Dick Distick was a whimsical caricature of Pope, and little doubt that it was recognized as such by all who knew him; and the hint about the translation of Statius—the first book of which had been published under his name scarce twelve months earlier—could hardly have been necessary at any time to verify the likeness. Here then we have an actual example of public self-ridicule in many respects comparable with the passage in the advertisement. If 'Dick Distick' hid Pope's real name from the multitude, so also did 'the Author of the Essay on Criticism'; for that poem, it must be remembered, was published anonymously, and, moreover, attracted so little public attention for some months and had so small a sale, that, although the first impression was only one thousand copies, Pope began to think the demand 'will hardly exceed the vent of that number'—which, in fact, it failed to do until the end of the following year when a second edition appeared. It would seem, therefore, that comparatively few people in those early months, during which *The Critical Specimen* was almost certainly published, were in a position

to know who 'the Author of the Essay on Criticism' was—
even fewer, probably, than later recognized him as the
'little Poet . . . Dick Distick.' And when the two jesting
allusions to Pope's physical appearance are compared, there
is really very little to choose between their apparent offen-
siveness (whether self-inflicted or not), between, on the one
hand, 'The second [Dissertation] by Mr. Dennis making it
plain from the late Essay upon Criticism that the Author is
by no means Strait but Crooked'; and on the other: 'The
Figure of the Man is odd enough; he is a lively little Creature, with long Arms and Legs: A Spider is no ill Emblem
of him.' From all of which it would appear that the 'Advertisement' not only does not lessen, but rather increases, the
credibility of Pope's authorship of *The Critical Specimen*.

Contributions to 'The Spectator,' 1711-1712.

IN THE concluding number of *The Spectator* (December 6,
1712) in which Steele acknowledged his debt to the various
contributors to the paper, he alluded first to Addison and
Budgell at some length, and then went on to say:

The other Assistances which I have had have been conveyed by
Letter . . . from unknown Hands. I have not been able to trace Favours of this kind, with any Certainty, but to the following Names,
which I place in the Order wherein I received the Obligation, tho'
the first I am going to Name can hardly be mentioned in a List wherein he would not deserve the Precedence. The Persons to whom I am
to make these Acknowledgements are Mr. *Henry Martyn*, Mr. *Pope*,
Mr. *Hughs*, Mr. *Carey* of *New-College* in *Oxford*, Mr. *Tickell* of
Queen's in the same University, Mr. *Parnelle*, and Mr. *Eusden* of
Trinity in *Cambridge*.

Exactly what 'the Order wherein I received the Obligation'
means is, however, not at all clear; for the sequence of
names is found to be based neither on a chronological ar-
rangement according to the dates on which the different
writers first appeared in the paper, nor on a quantitative
plan according to the number of contributions each had
made. Thus Eusden, for example, was a much earlier
contributor than Pope though the last to be named; and

d

Hughes, who has been credited with more than twenty papers and letters, is placed after Pope whose editors have never ascribed to him more than two—the poem, *Messiah*, and the 'Adrian' letter. But if Steele's words are doubtful, their intention is not; and if Martyn was named first as deserving precedence, then the second place which Pope fills must likewise have had some significance; consequently we may believe that those two contributions of Pope's do not represent all the 'Assistances' for which Steele so prominently thanked him. Moreover, as Pope himself, in the Preface to the *Works*, Vol. II, 1735, speaks of having written 'a few Spectators' (in addition to the *Messiah*), it is apparent that other pieces by his hand still await recognition or verification.

The Spectator, Nos. 406, 527, & 532.   On June 16, 1712, about a month after the anonymous *Messiah* had delighted the readers of *The Spectator*, there appeared in its 406th number an unsigned letter, which, although it has remained unidentified hitherto, has the unique interest of being the first indubitable piece of Pope's prose to be published. (The claims of four essays which preceded this letter will be considered later.) The letter, with some slight alterations, was included by Pope in both editions of his correspondence (1735 and 1737), where it purports to be a private letter to Steele, and is dated June 18, 1712. Originally, however, according to Steele's introductory remarks in *The Spectator*, it was addressed not to him, but to some unnamed friend. The truth would seem to be that it was written to no one in particular, but was simply a piece of literary composition cast in the popular epistolary form expressly for publication in *The Spectator*, and that Pope with his characteristic thriftiness and affection for his early work (which I have demonstrated elsewhere) re-used this old 'letter' to plump out his rather tenuous correspondence with Steele— who, Pope might characteristically have argued, as editor of the paper could colourably be said to be its initial recipient. Apart from the subsequent editions of *The Spectator*, the letter is here reprinted for the first time in its original form. In accordance with the general plan of the periodical it had no title; it was, however, indexed 'Letter about a city and country life'; I have therefore for convenience of reference entitled it, 'On a City and Country Life.'

The second piece of prose to be published, of which Pope's authorship is beyond question, appeared some five months later in *The Spectator*, No. 527 (November 4, 1712). This has also, I believe, escaped all his editors, biographers and bibliographers. It is an unsigned letter addressed to 'Mr. Spectator,' in which 'a languishing Lover' introduces and explains Pope's poem *On a Fan*. (In passing, it may be remarked of the poem, that this version shows two unrecorded variants when compared with that in the *Works* of 1717, where, in spite of the fact that some annotators of *The Spectator* have recognized Pope's hand in the poem, it is still generally supposed to have first appeared.) The letter itself has not previously been reprinted outside the pages of the periodical. Adopting the title Pope gave to the poem in 1717, I have called the whole piece 'On a Fan.'

'From Mr. Pope, on the verses spoken by the Emperor Adrian upon his death-bed;' thus is indexed the well-known *Spectator* letter—the last of the prose contributions incontestably Pope's. It was first printed in No. 532 (November 10, 1712) with some prefatory remarks by Steele, in which he revealed the writer's name, much to Pope's annoyance. Originally addressed to 'Mr. Spectator,' Pope included it later with some alterations in his published correspondence with Steele, where it is dated November 7, 1712. Taking a phrase from the letter itself, I have ventured to entitle it 'On the Last Words of Adrian.'

    The Spectator,   In addition to these, nine other papers
    Nos. 452 & 457.   may be ascribed to Pope's pen with much probability. They form two groups, one comprising seven pieces, the other two. Taking the latter first, these consist of two letters in Nos. 452 and 457, each containing burlesque proposals for newspapers, which Professor Sher-

burn in his recent work (*op. cit.*) has suggested were probably written by Pope, because the second of them outlines a projeĉt for a monthly periodical identical in effeĉt with his original idea of *Martinus Scriblerus.* One has only to compare the two projeĉts to see how convincing the likeness is. First in date, August 14, 1712, is the proposal as sketched in *The Speĉtator,* No. 457:

Having given you a Sketch of this Projeĉt, I shall, in the next place, suggest to you another for a Monthly Pamphlet, . . . I need not tell you, Sir, that there are several Authors in *France, Germany* and *Holland,* as well as in our own Country, that Publish every Month, what they call *An Account of the Works of the Learned,* . . . Now, Sir, it is my Design to Publish every Month *An Account of the Works of the Unlearned.* Several late Produĉtions of my own Country-men, who many of them make a very Eminent Figure in the Illiterate World, Encourage me in this Undertaking. . .

In a letter to Gay, dated Oĉtober 23 [1713?], Pope wrote:

Dr Swift much approves what I proposed, even to the very title, which I design shall be, The Works of the Unlearned, published monthly, in which whatever book appears that deserves praise, shall be depreciated ironically, and in the same manner that modern critics take to undervalue works of value, and to commend the high produĉtions of Grub-street.

Unfortunately there is some doubt about the date of this letter, the year having been omitted from it when it was printed in 1735. The Elwin-Courthope edition gives it as [1713]; but that year has recently been disputed by Professor Sherburn, who says, 'It should certainly be changed to [1712],' overlooking in his argument certain faĉts (summarized below)* which point to 1713 as the more probable year. But whether the close, or the closer, proximity in date of

* Only the more important can be cited here: (*a*) Pope's letter to Gay of November 13, 1712, in which he explains at length why he had not written to him for 'some months;' Pope would hardly have forgotten having written only three weeks earlier a letter of news and projeĉts like that of Oĉtober 23. (*b*) The friendly familiarity of the

these references to 'The Works of the Unlearned' is finally established matters little for our purpose. The repetition would seem unchallengeable, and there is moreover other evidence to confirm Pope's authorship of the *Spectator* letter for it contains two or three passages which in idea and phrase are paralleled in his avowed work of this period, the most interesting of them being related to the description of the virtuous old scandal-monger, Lady Blast, which follows:

> The Lady *Blast* . . . has such a particular Malignity in her Whisper, that it blights like an Easterly Wind, and withers every Reputation that it breaths upon . . . Her Whisper can make an innocent young Woman big with Child. . . In short, she can whisper Men Base or Foolish, Jealous or Ill-natured. . .

Pope was continually harping on this aspect of scandal in the same phraseology about this time. Thus in the first edition of *The Rape of the Lock* published three months earlier (May 20, 1712) we find two echoes:

> At ev'ry Word a Reputation dies. (i. 80).
> And all your Honour in a Whisper lost. (ii, 28).

Also in *The Temple of Fame*, which, although it was not published until 1715, Pope dated 1711, and which was actually read by Steele as early as November 12, 1712, are the lines:

> And at each Blast a Lady's Honour dies. (393).
> [Scandal] withers all before it as it flies. (341).

And curiously enough, Pope's private complaint of being himself slandered was couched in the same terms, when on December 21 of the same year, 1712, he wrote bitterly to Caryll: 'More men's reputations I believe are whispered

'October' letter when contrasted with the polite and complimentary tone of those of November 13 and December 24, 1712; the inference being that it was written later and not earlier than they. (c) The news in the 'October' letter about Parnell's contributions to 'Tonson's Miscellany' (*i.e.* Steele's *Poetical Miscellanies*, 1714, actually published December 29, 1713); it is extremely improbable that this collection either was being compiled, or had even been planned, as early as October, 1712.

away, than any otherways destroyed.' With the extreme probability of Pope's authorship of the letter in *The Spectator* No. 457 thus demonstrated, the earlier letter on newspapers in No. 452 becomes automatically attributable to his pen; for Addison's introduction to No. 457 says that it was 'written by the same Hand with that of last *Friday*,' which corroborates the opening sentence of the letter itself. On reading No. 452, any one familiar with Pope's correspondence of this period will remember having met in it several of the ideas about news and newspapers, in embryo or echo, which, though too lengthy or tenuous for quotation are in effect confirmatory of a common origin.

The Spectator, The problem is considerably more com-
The 'Z' papers. plicated as regards the larger group of seven papers, all of which are subscribed with the letter 'Z' in one or more of the first three editions of the periodical. When Steele explained in the last number of *The Spectator* that the letters C, L, I, O, were affixed to Addison's contributions, and X to Budgell's, he unfortunately left the other signature letters unidentified, and in some cases unidentifiable. To make matters worse, the same letter did not always signify the same writer, and the same writer might sometimes be given a letter and sometimes not. Witness, for instance, Steele's note appended to an unsigned paper, No. 537, as follows:

> I question not but my Reader will be very much pleased to hear, that the Gentleman who has obliged the World with the foregoing Letter, and who was the Author of the 210th Speculation on the Immortality of the Soul, the 375th on Virtue in Distress, the 525th on Conjugal Love, and two or three other very fine ones among those which are not lettered at the end, will soon publish a noble Poem, Intitled *An Ode to the Creator of the World,* occasioned by the Fragments of *Orpheus.*

The author thus indicated is, of course, John Hughes, to whom Steele ascribes two more unsigned papers in the introduction to No. 554, namely Nos. 541 and 554. But the point about Steele's identifications is that while the rest of

the papers given to Hughes were 'not lettered at the end,'
the first mentioned, No. 210, was, as we shall see, indiffer-
ently labelled T and Z in the earliest editions. And so we
arrive at another inconsistency which adds a further confusion to the mystery of the Z papers. Thus, of the ten
papers so signed in one or other of the first three editions
(*i.e.* i, the original sheets; ii, the first octavo edition; iii, the
first duodecimo edition), we find, in the third volume, No.
210 is lettered T in the first edition, Z in the second, and T
again in the third; No. 224 is lettered Z in the first, and has
no letter in the other two; and No. 232 is signed X in the
first, Z in the second, and is not signed in the third. The
fourth volume has three papers, namely Nos. 286, 292, and
316, signed Z in all three editions except that No. 292 has
no letter in the octavo edition. The sixth volume contains
the remaining four papers all uniformly signed Z in all editions. It is no wonder, then, that the latest editor of *The
Spectator* (1898) should write: 'There is great uncertainty
as to the authorship of the papers signed 'Z'; apparently
they are not all by the same writer.' Nevertheless, it seems
to me after a prolonged study of *The Spectator*, that, apart
from the five contributions previously considered, only the
Z papers—and not all of them—betray signs of Pope's
authorship. And I may perhaps add that my conclusions
were reached from an independent study of an early un-
annotated edition of the periodical, before I consulted such
annotated editions as have been landmarks in the study of
The Spectator, namely, the first, in 1789, edited by Bishop
Percy, Dr Calder, John Nichols and others; Bisset's edition (not so good) of 1793-4; Henry Morley's one-volume
edition [1868]; and the last two in 1897 and 1898 edited
by Gregory Smith and G. A. Aitken respectively; not omitting Nathan Drake's work on the contributors to the early
periodicals.

Before proceeding to discuss the papers piecemeal, a
word should be said regarding the earlier attributions of
them to Pope and other people. There are four papers bearing the signature Z in the sixth volume, namely, Nos. 404,

408, 425, and 467; and as early as the edition of 1789 the following note was appended to No. 408:

> As the same train of thought that runs through this Paper occurs not unfrequently in Pope's Works, and is illustrated very happily in his 'Essay on Man,' it is not unreasonable to suppose that Pope might be the writer of the Papers marked with the signature Z, of which there are four in this volume. See No. 404, No. 425, and No. 467.

Turning to No. 467 we find another note (evidently one of the less satisfactory results of multiple editorship which can be found elsewhere in that edition) to the following effect:

> It is suspected that this Paper, No. 467, was a tribute of gratitude and friendship from Mr John Hughes to his worthy patron Lord Cowper.

And a conflation of these two notes, giving the first three papers to Pope and the last to Hughes, seems to have been adopted by most of the later editors. Morley, however, substituted Budgell for Pope as the author of Nos. 404 and 425; G. Smith suggested that Hughes may have written all the Z papers, and G. A. Aitken offered Pope and Budgell as alternatives for Nos. 404, 408, 425, but favoured Hughes for No. 467. But none of the editors have adduced the least scrap of evidence—except what is found in the above notes, if that is evidence—for any of the varying ascriptions of the Z papers; and, so far as No. 467 is concerned, have been content unanimously to repeat in effect the 1789 footnote giving it to Hughes—in which they have the support both of Nathan Drake and the *Dictionary of National Biography* in its article on Earl Cowper. Whether the earliest ascription of this paper to Hughes was based on the supposed likeness between the character of Manilius in the essay and Hughes's 'worthy patron Lord Cowper,' or whether a chance ascription to Hughes suggested the likeness, I have been unable to discover; but the fact is that the two men were not known to each other in 1712 when this hypothetical tribute to the earl's kind patronage was written, or for several years later. Hughes's brother-in-law, William Duncombe, who in 1735 collected and published the poet's works in two volumes prefaced with a 'Life,' says explicitly:

> In the Year 1717, the Lord-Chancellor *Cowper* (to whom Mr.
> *Hughes* was then but lately known) was pleas'd, of his own Accord,
> and without any previous Solicitation, to make him his Secretary for
> the Commissions of the Peace, and to distinguish him with singular
> Marks of his Favour and Affection.

Nor is there anything, so far as I can ascertain, in either Lord or Lady Mary Cowper's 'Diaries,' or papers, to suggest an earlier acquaintance; neither is there any mention of Lord Cowper in Hughes's 'Letters' prior to the Cowper-Hughes correspondence which commences on September 27, 1717 and runs to within a month of the poet's death on February 17, 1720. Thus, seeing that Manilius is an intimate character study drawn apparently from close personal observation and acquaintance, it is obvious that either the writer, or the subject, has been mistaken by the old annotators, and, because of their interdependence, not improbably both. Moreover, this piece was not claimed for Hughes by his brother-in-law (who had access to the poet's papers) when he identified some twenty other contributions to *The Spectator* as Hughes's work, among which the only Z paper is the No. 210 earlier given to him by Steele, as we have seen. As a consequence of all the foregoing discussion it would appear that the previous attributions of the Z papers can in no way be regarded as sacrosanct, and that we are entitled to consider the possibility of Pope's authorship of any of them with an open mind.

If in default of other witness to his hand, we are obliged to rely on internal evidence to distinguish his pieces—that may be unfortunate, but it is no reason for refusing to examine such facts of the kind as are available. Thus, with an author like Pope, who both in verse and prose was perhaps unique in the extent to which he repeated himself, who used and re-used old material without compunction, who would serve up the same idea, differently dressed or not, on four or five different occasions, and whose favourite phrases seemed to run off his pen involuntarily, the presence within one

piece of two or three characteristic ideas or phrases which
appear elsewhere in his works, is sufficient to establish at
least the probability of his authorship—which probability
by cumulative effect approaches the nearer to certainty as
the number of these doubles increases. This method of identification by internal evidence alone cannot be better illus-
trated, and (I may perhaps add) justified, than by submit-
ting to this process the whole contents of No. 406 of *The
Spectator*, which consists of an introductory paragraph and
two anonymous letters, the author, or authors, of which no
editor of the periodical has yet identified. As the letter T,
affixed to this number, is one of the signatures Steele habitually used alike for the papers he wrote and those he merely
edited, and as the introduction takes a form frequently employed by him both in this periodical and *The Guardian*, the
first inference is that he either wrote or edited the whole
number. The former alternative, however, is immediately
discounted, because, although he gives no hint of the
authorship of the two letters which follow, he definitely implies that they came to him through different channels and
were written by different hands; after which he goes on to
say: 'I publish them together, that the Young and Old may
find something in the same Paper which may be suitable to
their respective Taste in Solitude.' Proceeding now to the
examination of the first letter, it is found to yield two or
three parallels to Pope's acknowledged work, as follows:

(*a*) The Consideration of this would make me very well contented
   with the Possession only of that Quiet which *Cowley* calls the
   Companion of Obscurity; but whoever has the Muses too for his
   Companions, can never be idle enough to be uneasy.

                                        Spectator, No. 406.

   The Muses, if you take them as companions, like all the rest,
are very pleasant and agreeable; but whoever should be forced to
live or depend upon them, would find himself in a very bad condition. That quiet, which Cowley calls the companion of obscurity, was not wanting to me...

                               Letter to Cromwell, Oct. 19, 1709.

(*b*) *Plutarch* just now told me, that 'tis in humane Life as in a Game at Tables...

Spectator, No. 406.

Human life, as Plutarch just now told me, is like a game at tables...

Letter to Cromwell, March 18, 1708.

(*c*) But there is another sort of People who seem design'd for Solitude, those I mean who have more to hide than to shew.

Spectator, No. 406.

There are some *solitary Wretches* who seem to have left the rest of Mankind, only as *Eve* left *Adam*, to meet the Devil in private.

Thoughts on Various Subjects.

To these doubles could be added two or three confirmatory mannerisms which though in themselves trifling are rarely absent from Pope's prose writings. The second letter presents a marked contrast in every way, for not only does it not read like Pope as a whole, but I cannot find even two consecutive words which are in the least reminiscent of him. On this evidence alone, it seems to me, we should be justified in saying of the two letters, that the extreme probability of Pope's authorship of the first approximated to certainty, and that he had nothing whatever to do with the second. The facts are that the first letter (as I mentioned early in this section) was reprinted and acknowledged by Pope in later life; and that the author of the second letter still remains unknown. But before leaving this illuminating testimony of Pope's characteristic methods of composition (which obviously has its bearing not only on his contributions to *The Spectator*, but also on all the other pieces which are included in the present volume on similar evidence) it is worth noting, that, in the first parallel (*a*) although the two passages contain similar phrases, the arguments contradict each other; and that in (*c*) while the root idea in both is recognizably the same, they have scarce two words in common.

The Spectator,   It will be convenient to begin our exami-
No. 404.   nation of the Z papers with No. 404, an
essay on 'Affectation, the misfortune of it' (to quote the
Index), published on June 13, 1712, two days before the
appearance of Pope's letter 'On a City and Country Life.'
Upwards of a dozen correspondences between this essay
and Pope's works could be cited, and it is notable that most
of them are found in pieces which he wrote in the preceding
or the following year. Five examples will perhaps suffice:

(*a*) Most of the Absurdity and Ridicule we meet with in the World,
is generally owing to the impertinent Affectation of excelling in
Characters Men are not fit for.

   No Man is Ridiculous for being what he is, but only in the
Affectation of being something more.

Guardian, No. 91. (1713.)

(*b*) [Nature] has sometimes made a Fool, but a Coxcomb is of a Man's
own making.

   And some made *Coxcombs* Nature meant but *Fools.*

Essay on Criticism, 27. (1711.)

(*c*) in the production of Vegetables; by the Assistance of Art and an
hot Bed, we may possibly extort an unwilling Plant, or an untimely Sallad; but how weak, how tasteless and insipid? Just as insipid
as the Poetry of *Valerio.*

   my green essays . . . first shoots of a tree which he has raised
himself . . . esteemed . . . as we value fruits for being early,
which nevertheless are the most insipid, and the worst of the
year.

Letter to Wycherley, March 25, 1705.

(*d*) the civil Oeconomy is formed in a Chain as well as the natural;
and in either Case the Breach but of one Link puts the Whole in
some Disorder.

   From Nature's Chain whatever Link you strike,
   Tenth, or ten thousandth, breaks the chain alike.

Essay on Man, i. 245–6.

(*e*) Men despise what they may be Masters of, and affect what they
are not fit for; they reckon themselves already possess'd of what

their Genius inclined them to, and so bend all their Ambition to
excell in what is out of their Reach . . .

> Like Kings we lose the Conquests gain'd before,
> By vain Ambition still t'extend them more:
> Each might his *sev'ral Province* well command;
> Wou'd all but *stoop* to what they *understand*.
> *Essay on Criticism*, 64–67.

Indeed, as a reading of the two pieces will make manifest,
not a little of this essay may be said to furnish prose illus-
trations and more or less close paraphrases of parts of the
Essay on Criticism, and especially of those passages of which
the key note is 'Follow Nature.' But there is, in addition,
another train of thought started, which, reappearing in the
next essay to be considered, leads us directly thither.

The Spectator, Only five days after the publication of the
No. 408. above paper it was followed by another
with the same signature Z—No. 408, 'On Reason and
Passion'—which it is difficult not to believe was the work
of the same hand, particularly as No. 404 shares with it in
some measure a matter of profound interest to students of
the poet. The parallel passage (*d*) above quoted, together
with the whole trend of this essay on reason and passion,
would seem to show that as early as 1712 Pope (if it was
Pope) was already beginning to work out for himself the
philosophical ideas 'Of the Nature and State of Man, with
respect to the Universe,' to which he was to give a lasting
expression in verse twenty years later. As previously stated,
the old annotators of *The Spectator* had cursorily noted the
resemblance between No. 408 and the *Essay on Man* and
other of Pope's works. And in truth, similarities and iden-
tities of idea, illustration and phrase abound; but as the
reader will have no difficulty in recognizing for himself
these early anticipations, the following three or four examples will be enough in this place:

(*a*) Humane Nature I always thought the most useful Object of
    humane Reason.

The proper study of Mankind is Man.

Essay on Man (2nd Ed.), ii, 2.

(*b*) One good Effect that will immediately arise from a near Observation of humane Nature, is that we shall cease to wonder at those Actions which Men are used to reckon wholly unaccountable.

Nature well known, no Miracles remain,
Comets are regular, and *Clodio* plain.

Moral Essays, i, 208–9.

(*c*) We shall no more admire at the Proceedings of *Cataline* or *Tiberius*, when we know the one was actuated by a cruel Jealousy, the other by a furious Ambition.

When *Cataline* by rapine swell'd his store,
When *Cæsar* made a noble Dame a whore,
In this the Lust, in that the Avarice
Were means, not ends; Ambition was the Vice.

Moral Essays, i, 212–15.

(*d*) As Nature has framed the several Species of Beings as it were in a Chain, so Man seems to be placed as the middle Link between Angels and Brutes.

Above, how high progressive life may go?
Around how wide? how deep extend below?
Vast Chain of Being! which from God began,
Ethereal Essence, Spirit, Substance, Man,
Beast, Bird, Fish, Insect! . . .

Essay on Man, i, 235–9.

Plac'd on this Isthmus of a Middle State, . . .
He hangs between; in doubt to act, or rest,
To deem himself a Part of God, or Beast.

Essay on Man, ii, 3–8.

The Spectator, No. 292.   Pope's hand may seem to be revealed yet more clearly perhaps in No. 292, which had appeared earlier in the year (February 4) with the same signature Z, and which, adapting a phrase from the essay itself, I have called 'The Additional Graces.' For in this essay is repeated an expression of Pope's own coining, which had appeared in print for the first time less than nine

months previously. In the *Essay on Criticism* (published
May 15, 1711) he had written:

> . . . in each
> Are *nameless Graces* which no Methods teach.

(ll. 143–4.)

And here within so short a time we find: 'The one is full
of numberless nameless Graces.' Other examples of the
phrase 'nameless graces' are extremely rare in the Eighteenth Century, the poet Thomson being said to be the
first after Pope to use it. Another repetition from the same
poem is found in:

> I shall here translate, because Action will best appear in its first
> Dress of Thought.

> Expression is the *Dress of Thought* . . .

Essay on Criticism, 318.

Though Pope did not originate the phrase 'dress of
thought' (for Boyle in the previous century had written,
'Eloquence, the dress of our thoughts'), it was still unusual
enough at this time to suggest the same hand in both passages. There are several other doubles of varying degrees
of approximation to Pope's work; and, in addition, a number of close parallels (later to be considered) to other papers
of the same Z signature, which, while not pointing to Pope
immediately, yet do so at one remove.

The Spectator,   A month later, on March 3, *The Spectator*
No. 316.   printed another Z paper, No. 316, to
which I have given the title, 'On Idleness,' in accordance
with the index reference. Its connexions with Pope appear
to be many and various. Indeed, the whole tone of the essay
is at one with the spirit that finds repeated expression in his
early correspondence, so that it is hardly an exaggeration to
say that much of the essay could be paraphrased by the
descriptions in his letters of his recurrent phases of lethargy.
For example:

(*a*) The regaining of my Liberty from a long State of Indolence
and Inactivity . . .

I believe no mortal ever lived in such indolence and inactivity of body.

Letter to Caryll, Jun., Dec. 5, 1712.

(*b*) Nothing lies upon our Hands with such Uneasiness [as Time], nor has there been so many Devices for any one thing, as to make it slide away imperceptibly and to no Purpose.

I am satisfied to trifle away my time any way ... as shopkeepers are glad to be rid of those goods at any rate, which would otherwise be always lying upon their hands.

Letter to Cromwell, March 18, 1708.

We have previously seen that Pope drew on this letter to Cromwell for material which he incorporated in No. 406 of *The Spectator*, and shall see further use of it.

I do not think it has been remarked before how fond Pope was of stream similes; they are to be found in many of his prose pieces as well as his verse, and not infrequently are repeated in different contexts. This essay contains two examples which reappear, one in the same year and one in the year following, in his acknowledged work, thus:

(*c*) But Indolence is a Stream which flows slowly on, but yet undermines the Foundation of every Virtue.

'Tis like a Stream that nourishes a Plant upon its Bank ... but at the same time is undermining it at the Root in secret.

Guardian, No. 132.

(*d*) like Water ... unless it be put into some Channel it has no Current, but becomes a Deluge without either Use or Motion.

in [Solitude] Men generally grow useless by too much Rest ... as Waters lying still, putrify and are good for nothing.

Spectator, No. 406.

And lastly, it would appear an incredible coincidence if an author other than Pope should, in addition to perpetrating all these parallels to Pope's work, also have been possessed of Pope's humanitarianism in which he was so much in advance of his day and generation. For Pope's dislike of hunting in particular and of what he called 'Sanguinary Sports' in general, of which we catch frequent glimpses in his letters, and to which he gave public expression in the following

year in his well-known *Guardian* essay, No. 61, seems also
to find an echo in this paper, in his raillery of fox-hunters,
and his pitiful glance at the 'poor animal.'

The Spectator,   The next Z essay to be considered is No.
No. 425.   425 (published July 8) which, following
the Index, I have entitled 'A Dream of the Seasons.' As it
appeared within less than a month of two other Z papers,
Nos. 404 and 408, the same author would seem to be indicated; and as there are grounds for supposing those to be
by Pope, this is probably his also. It is, however, impossible
to demonstrate his authorship of it very convincingly, the
reason being that because of its unusual subject it contains fewer parallels to his known works. Indeed, its most
striking correspondence is with a paper in *The Guardian* of
the following year, almost certainly by the same hand, but
not hitherto associated with Pope's name. Nevertheless the
Guardian essay has so much in common with his acknowledged work that his authorship of it is extremely probable.
(As the plan of the present work precludes an earlier discussion of the *Guardian* paper, No. 169, the reader is referred to page lxviii for the evidence.) The following parallel
may therefore be cited in this place, the first passage is, as
usual, from the essay under consideration.

> I reflected then upon the sweet Vicissitudes of Night and Day, on
> the charming Disposition of the Seasons, and their Return again in a
> perpetual Circle...

> When a Man has seen the Vicissitudes of Night and Day, Winter
> and Summer, Spring and Autumn, the returning Faces of the several
> Parts of Nature...
>
> *Guardian,* No. 169.

Affinities are however not entirely lacking between this
essay and Pope's authentic work; for the rather unusual
description, 'a Robe of Azure beset with Drops of Gold,'
recalls the line in *Windsor Forest,* 'The yellow Carp, in
Scales bedrop'd with Gold.' Moreover, Pope was exceedingly fond of the word 'imaginable' following a superlative
at the close of a sentence, a usage which, though possibly

e

not uncommon at that time, I do not remember meeting in the work of his contemporaries. But however that may be, between 1709 and 1717 this locution was repeated by him some score times, being found not only in his intimate letters, but in his formal prose pieces such as the Prefaces to the *Works* and the *Iliad* (where it appears three times), the *Discourse on Pastoral Poetry*, the Dedication of *The Rape of the Lock*, and elsewhere—*e.g.* 'the pleasantest journey imaginable,' 'the most pathetic imaginable,' 'the best-condition'd creatures imaginable,' etc.—and in this essay it turns up once again: 'the greatest gayety imaginable.' And we might also remark the curious concatenation of ideas— moonlight in garden or park, beauties of nature, thoughts of the hereafter—occurring in our essay and in a letter of the following year:

> The Moon shone bright, . . . The Reflection of it in the Water, the Fanning of the Wind rustling on the Leaves, the Singing of the Thrush and Nightingale, and the Coolness of the Walks, all conspired to make me lay aside all displeasing Thoughts, and brought me into such a Tranquility of Mind, as is I believe the next Happiness to that of hereafter.

> I have just been taking a solitary walk by moonshine in St. James's Park, full of the reflections of the transitory nature of all human delights, and giving my thoughts a loose into the contemplation of those sensations of satisfaction which probably we may taste in the more exalted company of separate spirits.
>
> *Pope to Caryll*, Sept. 20, 1713.

And so we come to the poet's life-long love of gardens and of garden-planning, in which art, according to Horace Walpole, he brought about reforms and helped to institute new fashions. If, as Professor Sherburn seems to think, Pope's famous essay on gardens in *The Guardian* (September 29, 1713) ridiculing 'the modern Practice of Gardening' with its craze for topiary work, was influenced by 'the amiable Simplicity' of the garden at Binfield where he had lived for the preceding twelve or more years; it might well be, that, in the admirably planned garden so exquisitely sketched in this essay, he was describing the ideal which by the nice management of his 'three rules' (embodying contrast, surprise, and concealment of the bounds) he subsequently sought to achieve both in the restricted grounds of his own house at Twickenham, and in the more lordly domains of a number of his titled friends. Thus all, or nearly all, of the favourite contrasts and surprises found in his later planning are displayed in this dream garden: grass plot and amphitheatre, parterre and wilderness, alleys and arbours, avenue, orangery, statues, and even the 'long Canals,' which are so tantalizingly glimpsed in *The Rape of the Lock,* but which at Twickenham were rendered superfluous with the Thames at the foot of his grass plot; and so far from seeing 'the marks of the scissars upon every plant and bush' in the contemporary taste, there is, consonant with his teaching in the following year, not so much as one effigy in evergreen in the whole picture. There are at least three other papers on gardens in *The Spectator,* two by Addison (Nos. 414 and 477) and one by Steele (No. 455), but they contain only vague and generalized descriptions, with nothing of the clearly conceived design and detail which in this essay would seem to reveal Pope's master-hand.

The Spectator, No. 224. The essay, No. 224, which, again adapting the index reference, I have entitled 'On the Desire of Distinction,' was published on November 16, 1711, with the signature Z. In addition to a number of repetitions which appear to point to our author, it contains—as we shall see later—several passages which have duplicates in other of the Z papers. For the moment three of the Pope parallels must suffice.

(*a*) The Desire of Distinction was doubtless implanted in our Natures as an additional Incentive to exert our selves in virtuous Excellence.

That Desire of Fame which is the Incentive to generous Actions.

Guardian, No. 4.

(*b*) It has . . . been frequently resented as a very great Slight, to leave any Gentleman out of a Lampoon or Satyr, . . . because it supposes the Person not eminent enough to be taken notice of.

We have no ladies [at Bath] who have the face, though some of them may have the impudence, to expeÆ a lampoon.

Letter to Martha Blount, OÆ. 6, [1714].

(c)   the disorderly Ferments of youthful Blood.

. . . while Youth ferments your Blood.

Windsor Forest, 93.

The SpeÆator,   The last of the Z papers to be considered
No. 467.   is No. 467, 'On the Love of Praise' (the title is once more derived from the Index), published on August 26, 1712. ConneÆed, as it seems, by a number of parallels both with Pope's known work and the other Z papers, its chief interest will be found to centre in the identity of the charaÆer of *Manilius*, which takes up so large a part of the essay, and which we have seen can no longer be labelled 'A Portrait of Earl Cowper by John Hughes.' On the assumption of Pope's authorship, I would suggest the probability of this being a sketch of his old friend, Sir William Trumbull, late Secretary of State, whom Pope from youth up had intimately known, but known only as an old statesman retired from public life and living as his near neighbour in the seclusion of Windsor Forest ('I shall now only draw him in his retirement . . .'). For though we may not know enough about Trumbull to be able to verify the truth of all the intimate touches in the portrait, its broad outlines agree with Pope's allusions to him in the poems with such remarkable completeness as would seem to identify at once the painter and the subjeÆ. The *Epitaph* on Trumbull, the invocation of the first pastoral, *Spring*, the lines in *Windsor Forest* (ll. 237–58), and especially the *Imitation of Martial* which Pope sent to Trumbull, probably because the lines were appropriate to the circumstances of the old man's past life and present retirement—if these and the few surviving letters of the Pope-Trumbull correspondence are compared with the charaÆer sketch in our essay, there will be little doubt, I imagine,

that Trumbull not only could have been, but probably was, the original of the portrait. (That is not, however, to deny the possibility of a trait or two being drawn from Pope's other worthy old friend, John Caryll.) But while there is this general but complete congruity between Z's character of *Manilius* and Pope's sketches of Trumbull, particular passages in parallel are not easy to demonstrate; nevertheless the following may be found to contain sufficient likeness in thought and feeling to point the argument.

(*a*) I shall now only draw him in his Retirement, and pass over . . . the Honours he has enjoy'd, and which now give a Dignity and Veneration to the Ease he does enjoy. 'Tis here that he looks back with Pleasure on the Waves and Billows thro' which he has steered to so fair an Haven; he is now intent upon the Practice of every Virtue. . . . Thus in his private domestick Employments he is no less glorious than in his publick.

> In prudent ease; still chearful, still resign'd; . . .
> He sees past days safe out of fortune's pow'r, . . .
> Reviews his life, and in the strict survey,
> Finds not one moment he cou'd wish away,
> Pleas'd with the series of each happy day.
> Such, such a man extends his life's short space,
> And from the goal again renews the race;
> For he lives twice, who can at once employ
> The present well, and ev'n the past enjoy.
>   *Imitation of Martial*, 3, 5, 7–13.

> *You*, that too Wise for Pride, too Good for Pow'r,
> Enjoy the Glory to be Great no more.
>   *Spring* (Invocation to Trumbull), 7–8.

It is also worth remarking that just as *Manilius* is compared to Atticus in the essay, so Trumbull is compared to him in *Windsor Forest* (l. 258):

> Thus *Atticus*, and *Trumbal* thus retir'd.

Apart from this apparent Trumbull connexion, other passages suggestive of Pope's authorship of the essay are fairly abundant, and though, when considered individually, not very striking perhaps, yet collectively they are difficult to account for on any other hypothesis. Most of these, as the following specimens show, are repetitions of ideas and points of view rather than of actual phraseology, though several examples of the last, and of Pope's mannerisms, could likewise be quoted.

(*b*) Others have sacrific'd themselves for a Name which was not to begin till they were dead.

> How vain the second Life in others Breath,
> Th'Estate which Wits inherit after Death!
> Ease, Health, and Life, for this we must resign . . .
> *Temple of Fame*, 505–7.
>
> . . . like fame, not to be had till after death.
> *Letter to Caryll*, July 13, 1714.

(*c*) His Liberality in another might almost bear the Name of Profusion; he seems to think it laudable even in the Excess, like that River which most enriches when it overflows.

> *Homer* scatters with a generous Profusion . . . *Homer* like the *Nile*, pours out his Riches with a boundless overflow.
> *Preface to the Iliad.*

(*d*) His Merit fares like the Pictures of *Raphael*, which are either seen with Admiration by all, or at least no one dare own he has no Taste for a Composition which has received so universal an Applause.

> All the world speaks well of you, and I should be under a necessity of doing the same, whether I cared for you or not.
> *Letter to Addison*, Oct. 10, 1714.

There are three other numbers of *The Spectator* signed Z in one or more of the first three editions; but as I cannot find the least suggestion of Pope's hand in them, and as, on evidence previously adduced, there is reason for thinking this signature was appended to the contributions of more than one person, they find no place in the present volume. Thus of the ten Z papers, only those we have discussed, namely, the second and the last six, can with any probability be ascribed to Pope. This discrimination is further confirmed by affinities of thought and expression which are found only between the seven essays, and which, by testifying to a common authorship of them, strengthens each separate attribution. A few examples of the parallelism of these particular Z papers may well conclude the discussion of Pope's contributions to *The Spectator*.

(*a*) if human Life be not a little moved with the gentle Gales of Hopes and Fears, there may be some Danger of its stagnating.

No. 224.

The Understanding . . . should be put in Motion by the gentle Gales of the Passions, which may preserve it from stagnating.

No. 408.

(*b*) It is the Business of Religion and Philosophy not so much to extinguish our Passions, as to regulate and direct them.

No. 224.

We must therefore be very cautious, least while we think to regulate the Passions, we should quite extinguish them.

No. 408.

(*c*) . . . done with a good Grace, and shine in the strongest Point of Light.

No. 292.

. . . as if there were some Point of Light which shone stronger upon him.

No. 467.

(*d*) Cloaths . . . by which, tho' her intrinsick Worth be not augmented, yet will it receive both Ornament and Lustre.

No. 292.

he gives a Lustre to the plainest Dress, whilst 'tis impossible the richest should communicate any to him.

No. 467.

(*e*) . . . if we want the Vigour and Resolution necessary for the exerting them.

No. 316.

. . . yet never failing to exert himself with Vigour and Resolution.

No. 467.

(*f*) The civil Oeconomy is formed in a Chain as well as the natural.

No. 404.

Nature has framed the several Species of Beings as it were in a Chain.

No. 408.

Contributions to 'The Guardian,' 1713.

THE last number of *The Spectator* was issued on December 6, 1712; but for some weeks previously Steele had been busy with plans for its successor, *The Guardian*. On November 12 he had written to Pope:

I have a design which I shall open a month or two hence, with the assistance of the few like yourself. If your thoughts are unengaged, I shall explain myself further.

Pope replied on November 16:

I shall be very ready and glad to contribute to any design that tends to the advantage of mankind, which, I am sure, all yours do. I wish I had but as much capacity as leisure, for I am perfectly idle.

How 'ready' Pope was may be judged from the fact that three days later (November 19) he was writing to Caryll asking for the return of all the letters his friend had ever received from him, saying in explanation:

I never kept any copies of such stuff as I write, but there are several thoughts which I throw out that way . . . that may be of use to me in a design I am lately engaged in, which will require so constant a flux of thought and invention that I can never supply it without some assistance, and it is not impossible but so many notions, written at different times, may save me a good deal of trouble. Pray forgive this, and keep my secret, which is of consequence.

He acknowledged the receipt of the letters on December 5, but, after some talk about them, came to the conclusion that 'they will not be of any great service to the design I mentioned to you.' We hear no more of Pope's share in this project until the following February, when he writes to Caryll from London (where he had gone to stay 'till Easter') as follows:

I have ten different employments at once that distract me every hour . . . my own poem [*Windsor Forest*, then in the press] to correct too, besides an affair with Mr. Steele, that takes up much consultation daily.

There can be no doubt whatever that all these mysterious hints and preparations had to do with Steele's forthcoming periodical, *The Guardian*, which began to appear next month; the secrecy surrounding it being conditioned by the plan of the paper in which the contributors were—as was customary—to be anonymous.

The first number of *The Guardian* was issued on March 12, 1713, and Pope's first contribution, the well-known essay on Dedications, appeared in the fourth number on March 16. The other papers, which, in the prefatory pages of the first edition of *The Guardian* in volume form, Steele ascribed to Pope, are Nos. 61 (Against Barbarity to Animals), 78 (Receit to make an Epick Poem), 91–92 (The Club of Little Men), and 173 (On Gardens), the last of which appeared only two days before the periodical ceased publication with its 175th number on October 1, 1713. So far it is all plain sailing, but after specifically naming these six 'papers' as Pope's, Steele concluded the list with the words 'and some others'—with which the troubles of an editor begin! To these six must of course be added No. 40, the famous ironical essay in praise of Philip's Pastorals, which Steele, not improbably at Pope's request, or because of the ill-feeling it had occasioned, refrained from ascribing to him; but which many years later Pope included with the other six in his *Works*.

In addition to these known contributions to *The Guardian*, there is a letter by Pope in No. 132 (August 12, 1713), which has not hitherto been identified. It is introduced, presumably by Steele, but not impossibly by Pope himself, with these words:

Mr. IRONSIDE,

The following Letter was really written by a young Gentleman in a languishing Illness, which both himself, and those who attended him, thought it impossible for him to outlive. If you think such an Image of the State of a Man's Mind in that Circumstance be worth Publishing, it is at your Service, and take it as follows.

Pope reprinted the letter with some slight revision in his published correspondence (1735 and 1737) as a private letter to Steele, dated July 15, 1712; but like his first letter in

The Spectator discussed above, it was probably written for publication. Our text follows the original version which has not hitherto been reprinted outside the pages of *The Guardian*, where it is indexed 'Sickness, its Effect on the Mind,' which for want of a title I have abbreviated to 'On Sickness.'

Nevertheless, even when these two are counted as Pope's, eight contributions spread over a period of seven months scarcely explain that active participation in *The Guardian* which would 'require so constant a flux of thought and invention' that Pope had to call in his letters for material; and still less would they seem to necessitate 'much consultation daily' with Steele. Mention too might be made of the testimony of *Addisoniana* (vol. ii, page 15) which in a note on *The Guardian* explicitly states: 'The principal aid in the first volume was derived from Pope; in the second, from Addison.' On the other hand, after it became known that Pope was contributing to this Whig periodical, and when his Tory friends began to express their disapproval of his collaboration with Steele, he always spoke of his *Guardians* as a 'few.' But 'fewness' is relative, and Pope was habitually equivocal on challenge; and had he written twice as many papers as he owned, they could still be legitimately called a few, in comparison with the hundred and seventy-five numbers issued. Wherefore it would seem that all Pope's preparations and consultations together with Steele's testimony to his further co-operation demand an inquiry into these unidentified 'papers.'

A glance at the dates of Pope's contributions to *The Guardian* at once suggests the early period of the paper as a promising field for search, and their occurrence becomes especially significant on a closer examination. We know that Steele is said not to have been aware of Pope's authorship of No. 40, 'On Pastorals' (indeed, Warburton says he refused at first to publish it because it seemed to compliment Philips at Pope's expense), and also that, as the essay itself was evoked by the neglect of Pope in the preceding series of papers on pastoral poetry, it was almost certainly written in the latter part of April. We are thus obliged to put No. 40 on one side for the moment, simply because it could not have been previously planned—or even thought of—by Pope and Steele in their preliminary consultations. Consequently we are faced with the remarkable fact that all Pope's enthusiastic preparations for work in *The Guardian* and all the later daily discussions with Steele apparently resulted in only one contribution from his pen during the first two months and more of publication, namely the essay 'On Dedications' in No. 4 (March 16). Such a mountain and such a mouse seem a little disproportionate.

The Guardian,   A careful reading of the early *Guardians*
No. 11.   reveals at least three papers in this period which appear to betray Pope's hand in the same manner as the 'Z' *Spectators* previously considered. The first of them is No. 11, 'The Grand Elixir,' which, in the acknowledgments prefixed to the reprint of the periodical in volume form, Steele expressly stated was written by Gay. Steele's ascription is not lightly to be set aside, nevertheless there is much reason to doubt it. Bishop Warburton, Pope's literary executor and confidant, included the piece as Pope's in the great edition of his *Works*—in which attribution he has been followed by subsequent editors down to, and including, Elwin and Courthope. And indeed, as will immediately be perceived, the essay is much more in the manner of Pope's lighter pieces than of Gay's one other humorous paper in *The Guardian;* besides which it is found to contain a number of parallels to passages in Pope's known works and letters. Gay may have been responsible for the original idea, and even perhaps for the first draught; but Pope would appear to have worked over the whole thing and so (at least for our purposes) made it his own. A few of the duplications of thought or phrase suggestive of Pope's authorship follow.

(*a*) Nothing is more necessary to Mankind in general than this pleasing Delirium [caused by flattery], which renders every one satisfied with himself.

Yet, after all, a man is certainly obliged to any one who can make him vain of himself, since at the same time he makes him satisfied with himself.

Letter to Caryll, Jan. 25, 1711.

(*b*) Upon a right Application of Praise of her Virtue, I threw the Lady into an agreeable waking Dream.

. . . or, like a weak woman, praised into an opinion of his own virtue.

Letter to Caryll, March 20, 1716.

(*c*) [The quack doctor's advice:] Let a Person be never so far gone, I advise him not to despair.

If you will needs be compared to a quack, you are like him that puts into his bills, 'Let no man be discouraged, for this doctor is one that delighteth much in matters of difficulty.'

Letter to Caryll, Jan. 25, 1711.

(*d*) Beware of Counterfeits, for such are abroad.

Counterfeits . . . begin with warning us of others' cheats, in order to make the more way for their own.

Letter to Steele, Dec. 30, 1711.

Quacks and Imposters are still cautioning us to beware of Counterfeits, and decry others cheats only to make more way for their own.   *Thoughts on Various Subjects.*

It is worth noting that the doubles (*a*) and (*c*) are both found in the same letter to Caryll—one of those which had recently been returned to Pope for the purposes of his *Guardian* essays. Furthermore, we know from *The Narrative of Dr. Robert Norris* what play Pope could make of a subject like a 'Mad Doctor'; here again, in this letter to *The Guardian* which antedates *The Narrative* by only four months, the methods of another 'Mad Doctor' are similarly satirized, and it is contrived that both quacks write in the first person and make use of like phrases. And lastly we may just remark that *Gnatho*'s 'universal restorative,' the *Obsequium Catholicon*, is not without its double in *A Key to the Lock* (written in the following year, though not published until 1715) where Barnivelt speaks of 'an universal medicine, or *Catholicon*.'

The Guardian,   The next two *Guardians* to claim our at-
No. 12.   tention, No. 12 'On False Criticks' and
No. 15 'On Easy Writing,' are stated in the latter to be the
work of one hand—which hand there is much reason to
believe was Pope's, because they so frequently duplicate
his ideas and expressions. This duplication is especially
noticeable in No. 12, in which the *Essay on Criticism* is paraphrased in not a few passages and inextricably pervades
much of the rest. Indeed one cannot help associating this
censure of false critics with Dennis's bitter denunciation of
the *Essay on Criticism* and its author nearly two years earlier,
both because it seems—while keeping strictly impersonal
—to combat some of the critic's indictments of the poet,
particularly the reiterated charge of excessive borrowing
from the ancients; and because Pope, as we know, never
could forget Dennis's attack on him. Curiously enough,
however, little more than three months before No. 12 was
published, and at the moment when Pope was searching
through his returned letters for subjects for his *Guardian*
essays, the same old charge seems to have been revived in
other quarters, for he wrote to Caryll (December 5, 1712)
complaining that whispers were going round that he was
'a great borrower.' It is therefore not at all improbable that
Dennis's earlier indictment and the new 'calumny' became
merged together in his resentment and so formed the occasion of this essay. Of the above-mentioned parallels a dozen
and more could be quoted, but we have space only for the
following examples:

(*a*) [Speaking of different styles] But Nature and Reason appoint
different Garbs for different Things.

> For diff'rent *Styles* with diff'rent *Subjects* sort,
> As several Garbs with Country, Town, and Court.
> *Essay on Criticism,* 322–3.

(*b*) In like manner an Imitation of the Air of *Homer* and *Virgil*
raises the Dignity of Modern Poetry, and makes it appear stately
and venerable.

> You may in the same manner give the venerable Air of Anti-

lxii   Prose Works *of* Alexander Pope

quity to your Piece, by darkening it up and down with *Old English*.

Guardian, No. 78.

(*c*) I will add further, that sometimes gentle Deviations, sometimes bold and even abrupt Digressions, . . . are Proofs of a noble
Genius.

> Thus *Pegasus*, a nearer way to take,
> May boldly deviate from the common Track . . .
> From *vulgar Bounds* with *brave Disorder* part,
> And *snatch* a *Grace* beyond the Reach of Art.
>
> *Essay on Criticism*, 150–5.

Pope's authorship of the paper is also the most probable
explanation of what appears to be a faint echo of a passage
in Addison's commendation of the *Essay on Criticism* (*Spectator*, No. 253). The young poet was very pleased with the
great man's praise, and must (one thinks) have read the
gratifying tribute more than once. Thus when, years later,
in the Preface to *The Works*, 1717, he had occasion to speak
of imitating the ancients, an idea or two from Addison's
encomium of the manner in which he had so beautifully
borrowed from them got entangled in his pen. For example,
Addison, summing up the inevitability of borrowing,
wrote: 'We have little else left us, but to represent the
common Sense of Mankind in more strong, more beautiful,
or more uncommon Lights'; and Pope, arguing the same
case, wrote: 'All that is left us is to recommend our productions by the imitation of the Ancients. . . . For to say truth,
whatever is very good sense must have been common sense
in all times.' Similarly, in the essay under discussion we
find that these same ideas (which Addison had derived
from Boileau) have also influenced the anonymous author's
pen.

Now Nature being still the same, it is impossible for any Modern
Writer to paint her otherwise than the Ancients have done. . . . All
that the most exquisite Judgment can perform is, out of that great
Variety of Circumstances, wherein natural Objects may be considered, to select the most beautiful; and to place Images in such View
and Lights, as will affect the Fancy after the most delightful manner.

The Guardian, No. 12.

Wit and fine Writing doth not consist so much in advancing things that are new, as in giving things that are known an agreeable Turn. It is impossible, for us who live in the later Ages of the World, to make Observations in Criticism, Morality, or in any Art or Science, which have not been touched upon by others. We have little else left us, but to represent the common Sense of Mankind in more strong, more beautiful, or more uncommon Lights.

Addison, in The Spectator, No. 253.

The possibility that Addison, Pope, and the author of the essay were each independently indebted to Boileau must be admitted, but it can have little weight in view of the fact that Pope had, on an unforgettable occasion, read and re-read Addison's summary of the French critic's remarks before he wrote on the same subject. When, therefore, in this essay, written as little as fifteen months after Addison's praise of Pope, we find the ideas expressed on that occasion reappearing on this, hard upon a renewal of the charge against Pope of borrowing; and when, in addition, they are accompanied by numerous other indications of Pope's hand, it is difficult to escape the conclusion that this is one of his 'other' papers, which Steele mentioned but unfortunately omitted to specify.

The Guardian, The essay 'On Easy Writing' (No. 15) No. 15. states that it was written by the author of No. 12; and as it continues the last subject discussed therein, and likewise contains repetitions of passages in Pope's acknowledged work, not to mention parallels to No. 12 itself, this dual corroboration strengthens the probability of their common origin. We need therefore instance no more than the following duplication of ideas.

(*a*) The Figures of Stile added to them serve only to hide a Beauty, however gracefully they are put on, and are thrown away like Paint upon a fine Complexion.

   Conceit is to nature what paint is to beauty; it is not only needless, but impairs what it would improve.

Letter to Walsh, July 2, 1706.

(*b*) So true it is, that Simplicity of all things is the hardest to be copied, and Ease to be acquired with the greatest Labour.

> True ease in writing comes from art, not chance,
> As those move easiest who have learn'd to dance.
>
> *Essay on Criticism*, 362–3.

(*c*) The selecting proper Circumstances, and placing them in agreeable Lights, are the finest Secrets of all Poetry.

> Out of that great Variety of Circumstances . . . to select the most beautiful; and to place Images in such View and Lights, as will affect the Fancy after the most delightful manner.
>
> *Guardian*, No. 12.

One point may seem to call for comment. In the second number of *The Guardian*, Steele began an account of the characters of the fictitious family of the 'Lizards,' whose chronicles are intermittently continued throughout the periodical by more than one hand. The convention seems to have been, that, whoever wrote about the Lizards, automatically assumed the rôle of 'Mr. Ironside,' the friend of the family and the supposed founder of *The Guardian*, although 'Mr. Ironside' was normally Steele's pseudonym. In all probability, therefore, the introduction of any member of the Lizard family in essays other than Steele's would mean that the writer had had some preliminary consultation with his or her original creator. Pope and Steele were in frequent consultation as we know, and thus we may account for the appearance of 'one of Lady Lizard's Daughters' in Pope's first contribution (No. 4) 'On Dedications,' and also, it would seem, for 'Mrs. Cornelia' and 'Mrs. Jane' in the essay under discussion. But even if consultation developed into collaboration on the latter occasion (which is not impossible), and Steele could be shown to be responsible for the irruption of the Lizards at the beginning and end of the paper (as well as for the concluding announcement of some future paper, or papers, on Pastoral Poetry, which is almost certainly an editorial addition), that would not lessen the probability of Pope's authorship of the body of the essay, 'On Easy Writing,' which properly commences with the second paragraph and begins by claiming a common origin with the foregoing paper 'On False Criticks'; for the evidence of his hand still stands, and he was, on occasion, not at all averse to collaboration.

The Guardian, During the first of the two periods of
   No. 106.   Addison's conduct of *The Guardian* previously mentioned (p. xx), he included a letter in No. 106 (Monday, July 13, 1713) with the following introductory remarks:

As I was making up my *Monday's* Provision for the Publick, I received the following Letter, which being a better Entertainment than any I can furnish out my self, I shall set it before the Reader, and desire him to fall on without further Ceremony.

It would appear, then, that although this number of *The Guardian* has Addison's symbol appended to it, we are justified in assuming that the letter thus introduced, which takes up the rest of the number and is signed 'Peter Puzzle,' was a contribution by another hand. Any one at all familiar with *The Rape of the Lock* must be struck by the extraordinary resemblances between that poem and the dream recounted in this letter—not in the 'story,' of course, but in the individual ideas, imagery and vocabulary. Almost every line of the dream finds an echo somewhere in the poem; and the significant fact about this parallelism is that it is found chiefly in those parts of *The Rape* which had not yet been printed, and on which Pope was from time to time during this year unquestionably at work; for it was not until December 8, 1713, that he wrote to Swift, 'I have finished the Rape of the Lock.' (It will be remembered that the short first version of the poem in two cantos was published anonymously on May 20, 1712, in the first edition of a poetical collection generally known as 'Lintot's Miscellany,' which I have shown elsewhere* to have been edited by Pope himself; and that the familiar complete ver-

---

*See 'Pope and the Miscellanies,' *The Nineteenth Century and After,* cxvi, pp. 566–80.

f

sion, expanded to five cantos, did not appear until March 2,
1714.) It is impossible here to note all the correspondences
between the two pieces, the cumulative effect of which
points very convincingly to a common origin; but a few
may be cited.

(*a*) I was placed by her in the Posture of *Milton*'s *Adam*. . . . As I
cast my Eye upon her Bosom, it appeared to be all of Chrystal, . . .
I saw every Thought in her Heart.

> . . . in her Breast reclin'd,
> He watch'd th' Ideas rising in her Mind.
> > *The Rape*, iii, 141–2.

Expos'd thro' Crystal to the gazing Eyes.

> *Ibid*, iv, 114.

(*b*) and many other Gewgaws, which lay so thick together, that
the whole Heart was nothing else but a Toy-shop.

> With varying Vanities, from ev'ry Part,
> They shift the moving Toyshop of their Heart.
> > *The Rape*, i, 99–100.

In like manner, 'a Hand of Cards in which I could see distinctly three Mattadors' recalls the famous game of Ombre,
when Belinda held in her hand three 'sable Matadores,'
Spadillio, Manillio, and Basto. In other duplications, an
idea taking up three or four lines of the dream is condensed
into as many words in the poem. Such, for example, is the
passage about the three successive lovers of Aurelia which
ends with 'For we justled one another out [of her heart] by
Turns, and disputed the Post for a great while'; the same
situation being thus summarized in the poem, 'their Heart
. . . where . . . Beaux banish Beaux'; similarly 'and Coaches
Coaches drive' is more lengthily (and perhaps more clearly)
expressed in 'a long Train of Coaches . . . that ran through
the Heart one after another in a very great hurry for above
half an Hour together,'—a conception sufficiently bizarre,
one would think, alone to establish Pope's identity. Moreover there is in the essay the ridiculous sequence: 'These
were driven off at last by a Lap-dog, who was succeeded by

a *Guiney* Pig, a Squirril and a Monky. I my self to my no
small Joy, brought up the Rear of these worthy Favourites'; which, with its satirical glance at humanity, puts one
in mind of the similarly incongruous list in the poem: 'Men,
Monkies, Lap-dogs, Parrots, perish all.' Further examples
of the resemblances between these two pieces need not be
quoted; but, just noting in passing that 'Aurelia' was the
name of the lady addressed in several love poems, which, as
I have shown in *Pope's Own Miscellany*, there is much evidence to believe were written by Pope in his youth, we may
conclude by mentioning one of the several parallels between our essay and other works of his. This is the story of
Momus which forms the basis of the whole dream, and of
which Pope made use on several other occasions.

Momus is said to have found Fault with the Make of a Man, because he had not a Window in his Breast.

If Momus's projeƈt had taken, of having windows in our breasts...
Letter to Lady M. W. Montagu, Aug. 18, 1716.

The old projeƈt of a window in the bosom, to render the soul of
man visible...
Letter to Jervas, Dec. 12, 1718.

And we find it yet once again, in a later number of *The
Guardian*, which (as we shall presently see) there is much
reason to attribute to Pope, in the following guise:

The Philosopher who wish'd he had a Window to his Breast, to
lay open his Heart to all the World....
Guardian, No. 172.

It would seem, then, that the only alternatives to Pope's
authorship are, first, that all these grotesque ideas found in
both essay and poem occurred independently to two people
at approximately the same date; and, secondly, that Pope
deliberately set himself to incorporate piecemeal in *The
Rape of the Lock*, and elsewhere, praƈtically all the ideas in
this particular number of *The Guardian*—either alternative
being considerably less probable than that the dream was
written by Pope, more or less at the same time as the additions to *The Rape* with which it has so much in common.

The Guardian,   Pope's new-found letter to *The Guardian,*
No. 169.   'On Sickness,' previously discussed, was
published on August 12, 1713, in No. 132, and was followed a few weeks later by an even graver essay 'On Nature
and Death' on September 24 in No. 169, which is probably
his work also. It not only abounds with ideas to which Pope
gave utterance elsewhere; but, in subject and manner, forms
so striking a pendant to the letter, that in all likelihood it
owes its inspiration to the same occasion. Such at least
might seem to be suggested by a passage in a private letter
to Gay, dated October 23:

> I have been perpetually troubled with sickness of late, which has
> made me so melancholy that the immortality of the soul has been my
> constant speculation, as the mortality of my body my constant plague.
> In good earnest, Seneca is nothing to a fit of illness.

We have already seen, that, when dating this letter, Pope
unfortunately omitted to add the year, and that although
1712 has recently been suggested, the balance of probabili-
ties seems rather to show that it was written in 1713. Thus
the melancholy tone of the *Guardian* essay 'On Nature and
Death,' would appear to reflect Pope's own turn of mind
consequent on a recent period of sickness. But the date of
that occasion, whether 1712 or 1713, does not really affect
the question of his authorship, simply because he had a
habit of keeping pieces by him for months, and sometimes
years, before publishing them. Thus, as we know from
other sources that he was grievously ill in 1712, and as, on
reprinting the letter, 'On Sickness,' in 1735, he dated it
July 15, 1712 (the dates of his printed letters are, however,
frequently unreliable!), it could well be that both the letter
and the essay were written that year, although not published until 1713.

The internal evidence pointing to Pope's authorship of
No. 169, consists for the most part in the presence of ideas
and points of view which he is known to have entertained
from time to time. But as the whole effect of them is not so
much a mosaic as a compound solution, such parallelism is

correspondingly difficult to demonstrate in the space at our disposal, though everywhere prevalent and by reason of that very prevalence convincing. A few of the more separable doubles, however, may be quoted.

(*a*) View him [*i.e.* Man] in that Part of Life when the natural Decay of his Faculties concurs with the Frequency of the same Objects to make him weary of this World.

> The same thing that makes old men willing to leave this world, ... long habit and weariness of the same track.
>
> *Letter to Caryll*, July 13, 1714.

(*b*) The Spectacle indeed is glorious, and may bear viewing several times. But in a very few Scenes of revolving Years, we feel a Satiety of the same Images, the Mind grows impatient to see the Curtain drawn and behold new Scenes disclosed.

> Though life for the most part, like an old play, be still the same, yet now and then a new scene may make it more entertaining.
>
> *Letter to Cromwell*, Aug. 29, 1709.

(*c*) To enjoy it [the World] as a Rational Being is to know it, to be sensible of its Greatness and Beauty, to be delighted with its Harmony, and by these Reflections to obtain just Sentiments of the Almighty Mind that framed it.

> But looks thro' *Nature* up to *Nature*'s GOD.
>
> *Essay on Man*, iv, 332.
>
> And last, to Nature's Cause thro' Nature led.
>
> *Dunciad*, iv, 468.

Here again in (*c*) we find the same anticipation of the philosophical ideas of Pope's later life which we noted in the discussion of No. 408 of *The Spectator*, where it has been thought by previous scholars to indicate his authorship. But there are further connexions with that essay, and with other of the 'Z' papers, which testify very strongly to the common origin of all these pieces ascribed to Pope. We need only instance the parallel before referred to:

(*d*) When a Man has seen the Vicissitudes of Night and Day, Winter and Summer, Spring and Autumn, the returning Faces of the several Parts of Nature ...

> I reflected then upon the sweet Vicissitudes of Night and Day,

on the charming Disposition of the Seasons, and their Return
again in a perpetual Circle . . .

Spectator, No. 425.

And we may end with the bare mention of such rather unusual phrases, at that time, as, 'the various Livery of the
Earth,' 'the Sable Hemisphere studded with Spangles,'
and 'frequent Returns of the same Things,' which can be
paralleled in the known work of Pope—and, most probably, in no other one writer of the same period.

The Guardian,   The last of the *Guardian* pieces to be con-
    No. 172.   sidered is the letter in No. 172 (published
September 28, 1713) which, adopting a phrase in it, I have
entitled 'On the Origin of Letters.' In addition to the internal evidence of Pope's hand in this piece, his authorship is
also suggested by evidence from other sources. First and
foremost of these is the translation of an epigram by Brébeuf
which in *Pope's Own Miscellany* I have shown reason for
believing was written by Pope. As first printed in 1717, it
ran as follows:

> Upon the PHENICIANS *Inventors of Letters.*
> From BREBÆUF.
>
> Those happy arts from their invention rise,
> Of painting speech, and speaking to the eyes;
> They first by various lines in figures wrought,
> Gave soul to words, and body to a thought.

We know from Pope's correspondence that he was well
acquainted with the works of Brébeuf as early as 1710, and
as most of his own contributions to the miscellany were
youthful work, it is very probable that the underlying idea
of this essay had been familiar to him—if indeed he had not
already translated the epigram—some two or three years
before *The Guardian* was thought of. There can be no question, I think, that the writer of the essay knew the epigram
either in the original French version or in Pope's translation, there being too much consonance of thought and expression between them to be otherwise explained; but, as

other evidence of Pope's hand is present in the essay, the possibility of any other person being concerned in it is exceedingly remote. As the reader may easily compare for himself Pope's quatrain above with the essay on page 141, we may at once pass on to note a few of the doubles existing in his acknowledged work, as follows:

(*a*) Who first made his Ideas set to his Pencil, and drew to his Eye the Picture of his Mind.

> So when the faithful *Pencil* has design'd
> Some *fair Idea* of the Master's Mind.
> *Essay on Criticism*, 484–5.

(*b*) By it [the invention of letters] ... what is spoken and thought at one Pole, may be heard and understood at the other.

> [Letters] Speed the soft intercourse from soul to soul,
> And waft a sigh from *Indus* to the *Pole*.
> *Eloisa to Abelard*, 57–8.

(*c*) I know not whether we ought not to attribute the Invention of them [Letters] to the Assistance of a Power more than Human.

> Heav'n first taught letters for some wretches aid.
> *Eloisa to Abelard*, 51.

(*d*) The Philosopher who wish'd he had a Window to his Breast, to lay open his Heart to all the World, ...

> Momus's project . . . of having windows in our breasts . . . while a man showed his heart to all the world . . .
> *Letter to Lady M. W. Montagu*, Aug. 18, 1716.

Other examples of parallel (*d*), having been cited earlier (p. lxvii), need not here be repeated. One last point of interest is that, many years later, Pope again referred to the subject of the essay and the epigram, when in *The Dunciad*, iii, 96, he wrote: 'The soil that arts and infant letters bore,' and explained the line in a footnote: 'Phoenicia, Syria, &c. where Letters are said to have been invented.'

The five foregoing *Guardians* are, to judge by internal evidence, the only prose pieces in the periodical to betray Pope's hand (apart, of course, from the eight which he at one time or another owned, and 'The Grand Elixir' given to him by Warburton). That there should be so few among the hundred and more unsigned papers shows that this kind of evidence is really selective in its effect and not comprehensive, and that Pope's parallels tended to be his individual expressions rather than common form—which would appear to add yet further to the probability that these essays are those 'others' which (according to Steele's testimony) 'have Mr. Pope for their Author.'

The Dedication of 'The Rape of the Lock.'

IN ITS original form of two cantos, *The Rape of the Lock* was first printed anonymously and without any dedication in *Miscellaneous Poems and Translations. By Several Hands*, 1712 (published May 20), a poetical collection generally spoken of as 'Lintot's Miscellany' after the publisher's name, but, as already mentioned, actually edited by Pope himself. Although in that version there was nothing to reveal Belinda's real name, it was not long before Miss Arabella Fermor began to be known as the heroine of the poem, and a certain amount of quite unwarrantable scandal began to be whispered about to her disparagement. And it was this untoward circumstance which eventually gave rise to the Dedication—so at least we gather from Pope's letters. To illustrate this the briefest of quotations will suffice. Pope wrote to Caryll Junior (November 8, 1712):

> Sir Plume [Sir George Brown] blusters, I hear; nay, the celebrated lady herself is offended, and, which is stranger, not at herself, but me. . . . Is not this enough to make a man for the future neither presume to blame injustice or pity innocence? . . . as in Belinda's [case]; to act with more reserve and write with less?

Indeed, the poet himself seems to have been threatened with personal castigation, according to his remarks in a subsequent letter to the same friend (December 5): 'If Sir Plume should take pains to dress me. . . .' Nevertheless, during the ensuing twelvemonth Pope was not to be deterred from endeavouring to make the poem the perfect thing we know; thus on December 15, 1713, he could write to Caryll:

I have been employed, since my being here in the country, in finishing the additions to the Rape of the Lock, a part of which I remember I showed you. I have some thoughts of dedicating that poem to Mrs. Fermor by name, as a piece of justice in return to the wrong interpretations she has suffered under on the score of that piece.

And on January 9, 1714, he reports again to Caryll:

As to the Rape of the Lock, I believe I have managed the dedication so nicely that it can neither hurt the lady nor the author. I writ it very lately, and upon great deliberation. The young lady approves of it, and the best advice in the kingdom, of the men of sense, has been made use of in it, even to the Treasurer's [the Earl of Oxford]. A preface which salved the lady's honour, without affixing her name, was also prepared, but by herself superseded in favour of the dedication. Not but that, after all, fools will talk, and fools will hear them.

The superseded 'preface,' which Pope seems to have printed three years later, has after two centuries of anonymity been recently identified with reasonable certainty and reprinted by the present writer.* The approved Dedication duly appeared in the first enlarged edition of *The Rape of the Lock* on March 2, 1714. It is a very characteristic piece of writing, and is now for the first time included on its own merits in Pope's collected prose works.

A Key to the Lock, 1715.

OF THE authorship of the pseudonymous pamphlet *A Key to the Lock . . . By Esdras Barnivelt, Apoth.* 1715, there is of course no doubt. Pope showed it to various friends the year before it was printed; within a few days of its publication he received £10 15s. from Lintot for it; and he included it in the second volume of his Prose Works in 1741. Every student of Pope knows it and has always known it. Nevertheless, a few interesting points about it—some of which do not seem to have been recorded hitherto—are perhaps worth noting in this place. We first hear of it, I believe, in a letter from Arbuthnot to Pope dated September 7, 1714, where he speaks of some author who might 'have allegor-

* See *Pope's Own Miscellany*, Norman Ault, 1935 (pp. lxxi-lxxvii, 107).

ised all his adventures into a plot, and found out mysteries somewhat like the Key to the Lock'; and when Swift first read the pamphlet in print (June 27, 1715), he wrote that Pope had 'changed it a good deal' since he saw it in manuscript—which two letters amply confirm 'Barnivelt's' statement in the 'Epistle Dedicatory' that 'It was indeed written some Months since.' The exact date of its publication is a little uncertain; advertisements in several newspapers show that it was not later than April 28, and in *The Flying Post* for April 21–23 it was announced to be published on April 25. However that may be, barely a month passed before the second edition was advertised in *The Post-Man* for May 28–31: 'This Day is published the 2d Edition of, A Key to the Lock . . .', and subsequent advertisements mention that 'some Congratulatory Poems' were included in it. These 'Congratulatory Poems' do not appear in the first edition; for which reason, and because they are themselves very interesting (though not so much perhaps as poetry), I have ventured to reprint this pamphlet from the second edition instead of the first. Pope himself, when he included the *Key* in the 'Second Volume' of the *Miscellanies*, 1727, and again in the second volume of his Prose Works, 1741, omitted the poems; and as, together with the 'Epistle Dedicatory,' they have been similarly excluded from all subsequent collected editions of his works, these four poems of Pope's indubitable authorship are now reprinted for the first time, I believe, for some two hundred years. Their comparative inaccessibility, therefore, may possibly explain why all Pope's editors and biographers hitherto seem to have overlooked the poems, and thus have missed—amongst other things in them—his first public allusion to Tickell's rival translation of the *Iliad*, Book I, in which Addison was so deeply implicated. It appears in the poem which purports to have emanated from *The Grumbler*, and is an obvious gibe at the machinations by which Tickell and his supporters sought to synchronize the publication of his translation with that of the first volume of Pope's *Iliad*.

A Papist wear the Laurel! is it fit?
O *Button!* summon all thy Sons of Wit!
Join in the common Cause e'er 'tis too late;
Rack your Inventions some, and some *in time* translate.

It is worth remarking, perhaps, that this appeared in print on May 31, some days *before* either translation was published. The 'Congratulatory Poems' also throw some fresh light on the guerilla warfare waged against Pope by Philip Horneck and Thomas Burnet, to whose attacks he has generally been supposed to have made no reply (to save repetition, however, the discussion of these feuds is postponed to the following section). And lastly, it is not without interest to note that with *A Key to the Lock* Pope seems to have set a new fashion in writing, if we may believe an amusing reference to it in the course of an attack on Addison's *Freeholders* in *Weekly Remarks* for February 18, 1716:

I believe, tho' *Esdras Barnivelt* by the Arch Mysteries which he singularly found out in the Rape of the Lock might have first given rise to the Freeholders way of writing, that he would, notwithstanding, tell this modern Author, that he had not perfectly understood his new Scheme, and that he talks Policy like an Apothecary . . .

The Dignity, Use, and Abuse of Glass-Bottles, 1715.

Among the odd assortment of papers—envelopes, letters, drafts and notes of all kinds—which were preserved from destruction two centuries ago, simply because 'paper-sparing Pope' had chanced to scribble some lines of his translation of the *Iliad* on the backs of them, and which are now treasured as the 'Homer MSS.' in the British Museum, is a letter from his friend, Charles Jervas the painter, containing the only known allusion to what has long been regarded as a 'lost' work by Pope. The letter is dated 'June ye 12*th* 1715,' and runs:

Dr Mr P.—
I had your Last in due time.
Shall I send you the £100 in Bills or Cash. and when?
Gay had a Copy of the Farewell [*i.e.* Pope's poem, 'A Farewell to London In the Year 1715'] with yr Injunctions. No other extant.

Ld Harvey had the Homer & Letter, & bids me thank the Author.

I hear nothing of the Sermon—The Generality will take it for the Deanes and that will hurt neither you nor him.

Gay will be with you on Saturday next. he also works hard. . . .

More of the letter need not be quoted. It was printed in full in Pope's correspondence by Elwin and Courthope, who added the following footnote: 'The sermon was not published by Pope in his works, and has never been identified.'

For the Sermon to have escaped detection for two centuries, when so many other of Pope's surreptitiously published works have been identified, obviously implies that he must have taken unusual pains to conceal his connexion with it; and the more careful concealment in turn implies some special need for secrecy, some danger attendant on an exposure of his authorship, which even Pope, who was far from timid in such matters, dared not risk, and at which Jervas himself hints in his use of the word 'hurt.' The letter shows, moreover, that Swift rather than Pope would be taken to be the author, which looks as though Pope, on this occasion, was so little content with mere anonymity for the safeguarding of his secret, that for additional security he had somehow implicated Swift in the business. Judging from Jervas's letter, therefore, any dissertation which is put forward as this unknown work of Pope's must, at the very outset, satisfy at least four different and distinct conditions: (*a*) it must be of such a nature as to be described, literally or metaphorically, by the term 'sermon'; (*b*) it must have some ostensible connexion with Swift, and none with Pope; (*c*) it should contain matter of a highly explosive character; and (*d*) it must have been published before June 12, 1715, but so shortly before as to be still a matter for comment and concern.

An intensive search for a work which should fulfil these rather remarkable conditions, at length brought to light an advertisement of a publication in *The Post-Man* for May 21-24, 1715 (apparently the only announcement to be inserted in the newspapers), as follows:

This Day is published,
The Dignity, Use and Abuse of Glass-Bottles, set forth in a Sermon preach'd to an Illustrious Assembly, and now published for the
use of the Inferiour Clergy. By the Author of the Tale of a Tub.
Sold by S. Keimer at the Printing Press in Paternoster Row.

And when a copy of the work itself was finally discovered,
a brief examination was sufficient to show that it ideally
satisfies the aforesaid conditions: (*a*) it is specifically called
a Sermon; (*b*) it purports to have been written by Swift; (*c*)
its writing is by turns so libellous, indecent and profane
that Pope would never have dared to set his name to it; and
(*d*) it was published, as the above advertisement shows, less
than three weeks before Jervas wrote his letter. There can
be little doubt therefore that this is the pamphlet of which
Jervas was speaking; for the existence of another pamphlet
likewise fulfilling all these conditions would be a coincidence of such complexity as to be scarcely thinkable.
Nevertheless to eliminate as far as is humanly possible that
barest of chances, I have examined every sermon I could
trace dated 1715, which could be suspected however remotely of being a rival claimant, as well as every book advertisement in all the periodicals issued during the first six
months of that year, that have survived in the great col-
lections of the Bodleian and the British Museum, and have
found no alternative.

Presumptive proof that this is 'the Sermon' about which
Jervas wrote to Pope having been thus established, the
question of authorship must next be discussed; but first,
because of the attribution on the title-page, and because the
four known copies of the pamphlet are each ascribed to
Swift in the various catalogues ('The Generality will take it
for the Deanes'!), it would be as well, perhaps, to clear
away any suspicion of his complicity in its production, before proceeding to discuss its apparent connexions with
Pope. During the whole of 1715—and indeed for eleven
subsequent years—Swift was resident in Ireland, whither
he had gone in August of the preceding year 'without,' as

he foreboded, 'a probability of returning'; and his letter to
Pope of June 28, 1715, written with all the despondency of
an exile, proves itself to have been his first communication
with him since leaving England ten months earlier. The
Sermon, therefore, could not have been written by Swift in
collaboration with Pope. Moreover, as the pamphlet alludes to a recent event in the London literary world—the
publication of a 'Print' of the 'German Doctor'—and, as
we shall see, apparently quotes from an attack on Pope published in *The Grumbler* little more than a fortnight previously, it is just as impossible to believe that Swift was the
sole author of the Sermon. One has only to think of the pos-
tal facilities of the period, when the packet-boats left Holy-
head for Dublin twice a week only, and news from Dublin
normally took from seven to nine days to reach the London
papers, to realize the extreme improbability that Swift
could have received in Dublin a newspaper published in
London on May 6, written the pamphlet, posted it to
London, and have it set up, printed and published by May
24. And thus, quite apart from the unlikelihood of his
acknowledging, or even anonymously perpetrating, a blas-
phemous burlesque sermon, apart from the dissimilarity of
his prose style and the lack of motive, Swift may be acquit-
ted not only of any participation in, but even any knowledge
of, the production of this pamphlet.

The evidence for Pope's authorship of the Sermon is
both abundant and varied. For the majority of people, perhaps, the most authentic witness may seem to be Jervas's
letter, simply because the long-recognized interpretation of
his allusion to 'the Sermon,' as meaning 'your Sermon,' is
the most reasonable one, if we may judge from the context.
Jervas, writing from London, was obviously telling Pope
(who had left town a fortnight or so previously) the latest
news about his various works: 'Gay had a Copy of the Farewell . . . Ld Harvey had the Homer & Letter . . . I hear
nothing of the Sermon . . .' 'The Farewell,' 'The Homer,'
'the Sermon'—as all three are mentioned in sequence, without a break and without the slightest distinction made be-

tween them; as Pope was the author of the first two; and as no other book is mentioned until the end of the letter when something is said about 'Tickell's Homer,' common sense would immediately suggest that the third was likewise written by Pope. This conclusion is upheld by corroborative evidence of two kinds: first, the internal witness of his hand in idea and expression, and secondly, the testimony of occasion.

At this stage of the Introduction it should not be necessary to draw attention yet once again to the extent, unique among his peers, to which Pope consciously or unconsciously repeated himself in his works. At so early a date he can have had few or no imitators, at least of his prose; consequently, as the Sermon abounds in echoes of Pope and (except for scriptural quotations) of Pope only, each of these numerous parallels adds its share, little or much, in confirmation of his authorship. The more important are as follows:

(*a*) But narrow-soul'd Men, like narrow-neck'd Bottles, hold much but give little, nay, and that little too with much Difficulty and murmuring; . . . the less they bestow, the more Noise they make about it.

It is with narrow-soul'd People as with narrow-neck'd Bottles: The less they have in them, the more noise they make in pouring it out.

Thoughts on Various Subjects.

Although these *Thoughts* of Pope's were not published as a collection until 1727, and therefore find no place in the present volume, the importance of the above parallel compels me to anticipate a few observations on them. The collection consists of nearly a hundred separate and unrelated aphorisms, one-half of which, at the moment of writing, I have discovered to be also embedded in his various works. Many of these can be dated before 1717, in fact two of them were used by him elsewhere within two months of the publication of the Sermon, and another within four months; and more than twenty of them appear in his works within

lxxx   Prose Works *of* Alexander Pope

two years of that date, some indeed several times over. On the other hand, I have not encountered any of them in the works of other writers before 1727; and, putting aside the two which Pope himself distinguished by the initials 'T. K.' and 'D. A.' (the first of which he also acknowledges in a letter to Swift as the saying of 'a friend of mine'), there are, so far as I know, not the slightest grounds in reason or probability for supposing they are not what he claims them to be—his own original ideas. Pope was obviously rather proud of his *Thoughts on Various Subjects*, for he placed them first of all his miscellaneous writings when reprinting them in the second volume of his collected prose pieces. Moreover, although a 'borrowed' thought may be incorporated in a long work with some chance of being overlooked, or, even if recognized, pardoned (few are the writers who do not owe something to somebody!), yet that is a very different method of adoption from that of including a 'borrowed' aphorism as a separate entity, standing alone and numbered, in a collection of one's own witty sayings; and whatever else we may think of Pope, we cannot imagine him simple enough to have courted exposure in so futile a manner. Again, the suggestion, at first sight plausible enough, that the 1727 'Thought' may have been derived from his subconscious memory of the anonymous 1715 Sermon, besides leaving unexplained all the other Pope parallels in the latter (not to mention the rest of the evidence pointing to his authorship), is also discounted by the presence of the very distinctive epithet 'narrow-soul'd,' which, though it probably originated with Milton, was still so rare in this period that it seems not to have been used by any of Pope's contemporaries on the one hand, while on the other it happened to be something of a favourite with Pope at this very time, for it is also found in two of his letters of the previous year, 1714, 'the narrow-souled people,' and yet once again in *The Critical Specimen*, 1711, 'the Narrow-Souled Principles.' From all of which it is clear that the onus of proof must lie with those who would deny that the 'Thought' in the foregoing parallel was originally Pope's.

(*b*) There are ... Properties common to both Bottles and Women
   ... neither of 'em will be quiet or silent, but in a continual Motion
   and Ferment, unless they be extremely well stopt.

> And Maids turn'd Bottels, call aloud for Corks.
>
> *Rape of the Lock* (1714), iv, 54.

being ... confin'd, and well stopt, nothing grows so frothy, pert
and bouncing.   *Art of Sinking.*

Remembering that the *Art of Sinking* dates, at least in part,
from the previous year, 1714, and was possibly of multiple
authorship, it is nevertheless noticeable that, about this
time, Pope had frequently in mind the idea of fermentation,
not only as an image of physical energy, as in the foregoing
passages and in the line from *Windsor Forest*: 'Ye vig'rous
Swains! while Youth ferments your Blood' (previously
cited with yet another 'ferment' passage, on page lii), but
also as a symbol of political unrest, as is shown both in the
Sermon and in the second edition of the *Key to the Lock*
published only a week later, as follows:

(*c*) As for Politicians, how can they better set before us the Submission we owe to Government, than by the Example of good and
   sound Bottles which remain peaceable and quiet under the Limitation of such Corks as are establish'd and set over them, while
   those who fly out into rebellious Workings ... lose their Liquor.

> Ripe Politicks the Nation's Barrel fill,
> None can like thee its Fermentation still.
> Ingenious Writer, lest thy Barrel split ...
>
> *Key to the Lock.*

Even more significant, because the imagery is more unusual, is the repetition of the subject of glass manufacture
in the Sermon and the Preface to *The Iliad*, which were published within a fortnight of each other, both in allusions to
the properties of glass itself, and also to the actual process of
glass-blowing. The latter runs thus:

(*d*) So you (O ye Bottles) were at first vile Ashes; but, no sooner
   was the informing Breath blown into you, but your loose Atoms
   assum'd a Shape ...

g

> Like Glass in the Furnace which grows to a greater Magni-
> tude . . . only as the Breath within is more powerful . . .
> *Preface to The Iliad.*

There is, moreover, a culinary parallel which would be
difficult, if not impossible, to match in the work of his contemporaries, but which is peculiarly characteristic of Pope
who—'valetudinaire' though he might be—always took a
very human interest in the kitchen. This can be seen in not
a few passages in his letters earlier and later, and at greater
length in his famous *Receit to make an Epick Poem*, in which,
less than two years previously, the vocabulary of the cook is
most expertly employed with a similarly satirical effect; and
other instances occur elsewhere. Here in the Sermon is a
passage which immediately recalls another of the kind in
one of Pope's letters; the anonymous author is attacking
the 'German Doctor' who, says he, would continue to be
worthless even—

(*e*) were he slash'd, season'd, and serv'd up in a Ragoo.

> When a stale cold fool is well heated, and hashed by a satirical
> cook, he may be tossed up into a kickshaw not disagreeable.
> *Letter to Caryll, Jun.* (Dec. 5, 1712).

Several other examples similarly duplicating Pope's ideas
and distinctive points of view at this period could be quoted
from the Sermon, as well as phrases which he frequently
used; but space allows only two of the latter to be quoted:

(*f*) I will therefore now give the finishing Stroke.

> . . . to help to give him the finishing stroke.
> *Letter to Wycherley* (June 23, 1705), and
> *Letter to Caryll* (July 31, 1710).

the Author gives the finishing Stroke.
> *Clue to Non-Juror*, 1718.

I hope to put a finishing stroke
> *Letter to Broome* (April 6, 1723).

(*g*) the most beautiful Flowers of their Pulpit-Rhetorick.

Flowers of Rhetoric in Sermons and serious Discourses
> *Thoughts on Various Subjects.*

without collecting all the Flowers of Rhetorick.

Key to the Lock.

Where we strow flowers of rhetoric.

Letter to Lady M. W. Wortley (Aug. 20, 1716).

Not to the long arm of coincidence can we credibly ascribe all the numerous repetitions of Pope's thought and expression from which the foregoing few parallels are chosen—coincidence would need to be Briareus for that!—nor can they all be reasonably explained by the prevailing literary usage of the period, simply because so many of them were personal and not general; and since neither coincidence nor usage can be made to account for all the other evidence pointing to Pope, his authorship of the Sermon remains the only hypothesis which covers all the facts thus far considered.

The Sermon was obviously written in a holiday mood, a temporary freedom from inhibitions, which, as so often with Pope, meant a total disregard of all the proprieties except one—namely, that of literary form. Thus while the fiction of the sermon is carefully sustained throughout, from the opening invocation to the closing prayer, he contrives to display in 'Pulpit-Rhetorick' almost every aspect of his many-sided sense of humour. The burlesque pedantry of *Martinus Scriblerus* (which dates in part from the previous year or two) is here in full measure, and the vein of profane parody which in the following year was to produce his *Version of the First Psalm*; here too, are the wit and foolery, the whimsical parenthesis and apt classical quotation, characteristic of his more irresponsible prose, not to mention (were it but possible!) his neo-Rabelaisianism—jokes about excreta, and so forth—which, as the present volume testifies, pervades his pasquinades, and is not absent from such pieces as *The Dunciad*; and all together they appear to stamp the pamphlet as authentic Pope. His own attitude to the Sermon is probably indicated in one of the stanzas of *A Farewell to London In the Year* 1715. There is much evidence to believe that this poem, which, it will be remembered, was also alluded to by Jervas in the above-mentioned letter and like the Sermon was never acknowledged by Pope, was written during the last week of May, within a few days, that is, of the publication of the Sermon. And as it is unquestionably autobiographical in content, with specific mention of circumstances and occasions, one must suppose that the following lines—amongst those in which Pope is reviewing his various recent activities in Town—were not written without meaning:

> Still idle, with a busy air,
> > Deep whimsies to contrive;
> The gayest valetudinaire,
> > Most thinking rake alive.

And since no published 'whimsies' by Pope can be traced to this period except the *Key to the Lock* (which, having been written for the most part in the previous year, possibly should not be counted) and *The Dignity, Use, and Abuse of Glass-Bottles*, it is probable that these lines both constitute Pope's sole existing reference to the Sermon, and show us in what light he regarded it. It was a whimsy.

Nevertheless it can be predicted that students of the period will find in 'The Preface' matter of more engrossing interest; for it is there that the point of the pamphlet is couched. The author (whoever he was), while ostensibly writing in defence of the Sermon, quotes and explodes a number of ridiculous objections to it supposedly raised by various critics; but the matter is so contrived that the actual result is a ruthless counter-attack on the more malevolent of Pope's enemies.

To at least one student of Pope it had long been a subject for wonder that the poet, who rarely forgave and never forgot an injury, and who, both earlier and later, had no compunction about repaying his detractors in their own coin with increment from his nimbler wit, should not have answered more promptly and vigorously than he is said to have done the unprovoked and apparently organized attacks made by the 'Buttonians' and others on his physical disad-

vantages, religion, and poetical reputation, during the critical six months preceding the publication of the first volume
of *The Iliad* on June 4, 1715. Moreover, these attacks on
him were both more numerous and persistent than have
hitherto been supposed. As early as December 10, 1714,
for instance, a large part of that day's issue of a periodical
entitled *The High-German Doctor* was taken up by an account of a fictitious dialogue between 'Parnassus Bernard
of Fleet Street' (*i.e.* Lintot, the prospective publisher of *The
Iliad*) and 'Mezereon' (*i.e.* Philip Horneck, the author of
The High-German Doctor) in which Pope's great undertaking is unmercifully ridiculed, and the poet and publisher
alike bantered on that and other counts. And Horneck followed this up with other attacks in the issues of his paper
dated March 15 and April 23. Similarly, Thomas Burnet,
from March to the end of May, was making himself very
unpleasant to Pope in various numbers of his paper *The
Grumbler*; and, in his burlesque *Homerides* (written in collaboration with Duckett and published on March 7), he
endeavoured to prejudice the public against Pope's forthcoming *Iliad*. And there were others.

It was a curious feature of Pope's mentality, that, with
all his skill in dissimulation and love of intrigue, at any hint
of exposure he almost invariably betrayed his hand by pro-
testing too much. So many instances could be cited that it
is hardly an exaggeration to say that the more loudly he
denied a thing the more deeply is he found to be involved
in it. Thus, with regard to his enemies during the early
part of his career, he repeatedly said that he never deigned
to reply to their attacks; for instance: 'I . . . insulted no adversary with ill language, or when I could not attack a
Rival's works, encourag'd reports against his Morals' (Preface to *The Works*, 1717); 'whatever they [his detractors,
known and unknown] writ or said I never retaliated' (Letter to Swift, 1723); and in the prefatory matter to *The Dunciad* and in the notes, he continually stated that in spite of
provocation he had withheld the lash hitherto. The contents
of the present volume disclose a different picture! Never-

theless, there is this to be said on Pope's behalf about his counter-attacks, that, compared with the innumerable provocations he received, they are extraordinarily few down to 1727—possibly because, being anonymous, they have not even yet all been identified.

Much the same tale of Pope's disregard of his traducers is told by those of his biographers who have chronicled in any detail the troubled months which preceded the publication of *The Iliad*. They have all overlooked the fact that Pope retaliated upon his more troublesome assailants in the second edition of *A Key to the Lock* (published May 31), where he satirically caricatures Burnet and Horneck, both in the manner and matter of their contributions to their respective periodicals, *The Grumbler* and *The High-German Doctor*. Pope wickedly wrote under their pseudonyms two 'Congratulatory Poems' addressed to Esdras Barnivelt (who was, of course, Pope himself) on his exposure of the supposed Jacobite and Romish propaganda concealed by Pope in *The Rape of the Lock*,—a little involved, perhaps, but very good fun nevertheless. (The hitherto unrecorded gibe at Tickell and Addison for their complicity in the rival translation of the *Iliad* has already been mentioned.) And it now appears that to these counter-attacks of Pope we must add the Preface to the Sermon.

With the discovery of this pamphlet, the 'battle of the Iliad,' 1715, assumes an aspect differing still more widely from that formerly presented to us. No longer either aloof from the strife or merely bantering the foe, Pope would now seem to have been engaged in the thick of the struggle; and if, in the pamphlet, he is found to be fighting (to quote one of his enemies) 'like little Teucer' behind the shield of 'the Author of the Tale of a Tub,' his shafts fly none the less unerringly to their mark. His most irritating and persistent enemy had been Burnet, one of Addison's 'little Senate,' yet, nevertheless, a man whose reputation was at that time most unsavoury (though, later, he reformed to such effect as to attain both judgeship and knighthood before his death). Pope's reply to this man contains amongst

other things a particular charge which throws a lurid light
on a passage in *The Dunciad* (iii, 179–184) and the poet's
subsequent note on it; for Pope was still incensed enough
after thirteen years to repeat the charge (in which Duckett
was now included) in the first edition of that work, though
in later editions he relented enough to make some excision
and explain away the rest of the passage by saying in a footnote that he did not mean what it meant. In the poem, Pope
provided some clues to the names of his victims; in the
pamphlet, however, Burnet's name is entirely suppressed;
but to any one at all conversant with the period there can
be little doubt of the person indicted. And as Burnet's name
was in everybody's mouth during the three or four months
previous to the appearance of the Sermon (by reason of his
pamphlet, *The Necessity of Impeaching the Late Ministry*,
published February 8, 1715, which contributed in no small
measure to precipitate a political crisis of the first importance), and as he seems to have been the only prominent
person at that particular time whose private character was
being so widely impugned on that particular count, it is obvious that his contemporaries would have no difficulty at
all in identifying him with the person attacked in the Preface to the Sermon, even were other allusions to him lacking. In the 'Epistle' prefixed to *A Key to the Lock* (published
about April 25), Pope, speaking as Barnivelt, had inserted
a little advertisement (deleted in 1727) of *The Rape of the
Lock* while ostensibly disparaging it, thus:

The uncommon Sale of this Book (for above 6000 of 'em have
been already vended) was also a farther Reason ... to put a stop to its
further Progress.

Eleven days later, Burnet's paper, *The Grumbler* for May 6,
contained a long animadversion on Pope's 'Pranks,' from
which we may quote the following:

Another obliges the World with a *Key* to his own *Lock*, in which
the *Wards* are all false: Under the borrowed Shape of an Apothecary,
he modestly takes an opportunity to commend the Smoothness of his
own Verses, and to publish a Sale of Six Thousand of his Books. The
same Arch Wag, a little before this, gave us ...

Less than three weeks later our pamphlet appeared, in which the anonymous author, taking to himself the appellation, 'Arch Wag,' just bestowed on Pope, and speaking in the character of the supposedly clerical author of the Sermon, translates the *Grumbler*'s accusation against Pope into ecclesiastical terms, and answers it thus:

> Methinks I hear some fleering Puppies say, 'however our Clergy dress up their Modulations the grand Topick they all go upon is Preferment.' And are our Author's deviatory Measures, Means to mend his Fortune? Why not? Mayn't an Arch-Wagg expect...

And though I cannot pretend to have tracked down all the topical and probably personal allusions scattered through the Preface, there can, I think, be little doubt that the 'Sour Fellow' of its opening words was also intended for *The Grumbler*, Burnet, especially as he had painted himself in that character in several numbers of his paper: in the issue of April 7, for example, he confessed that he was 'not Sour or Splenetick out of Choice, but of Necessity'; and on April 19 declared that his kindred were recognizable by 'the Sourness of their Countenances.' Horneck, however, is immediately identifiable 'under the title of the *German Doctor*' whose general worthlessness is ridiculed, and whose lucubrations could only be accounted for by the bottle. And in this accusation of drunkenness Burnet is also included later —two bottles, we learn, being enough at any time to make a *Doctor*, and three whatever Burnet was. Thus once more, in this singling out for reprisal the two men, Horneck and Burnet, who of all Pope's antagonists had been the most assiduous in abuse during the previous three months or so, who had nothing in common, I believe, except their enmity to him, and who were actually caricatured by him a week later in the *Key to the Lock*, we appear to find yet another reason for ascribing the pamphlet, which opens with this counter-attack, to Pope's retaliatory pen.

The only serious objection—and even this on examination would seem to be more apparent than real—which can, I think, be brought against Pope's authorship of the

Sermon, is that on the title-page it is attributed to 'the Author of the Tale of a Tub.' In other words, Would Pope have played this rather dubious trick on his friend Swift? Any answer to that must obviously be a matter of opinion, which, though it may be based on an estimate of Pope's character arrived at after a study of all the known facts of his life, remains still an opinion. On the view of his character which has been held with general uniformity by students of Pope from his own day until quite recent times, no one, I believe, would have thought his performance of such a trick at all improbable. And although there can be little doubt that the less-pleasing traits of his personality have been over-emphasized in the past (as Professor Sherburn has been at some pains to point out), no amount of special pleading can acquit Pope of habitual double-dealing and oblique procedure in literary affairs, of deceit and equivocal practices in transactions with his friends from time to time, or even, on occasion, of acts of treachery to them. And it is doubtful whether any one at all familiar with the details of Pope's life would, even to-day, be prepared to deny the possibility of his having indirectly fathered this pamphlet on Swift.

Bearing in mind that the eighteenth-century ethic—or, at least, conduct—differed not a little from ours on many points, let us look at the actual facts.

(i) Three, if not four, publications, not all by the same hand and none of them by Swift, had previously appeared in London with the ascription 'By the Author of the Tale of a Tub' on their title-pages, one of them as recently as the preceding year (namely, *Essays Divine, Moral, and Political ... By the Author of the Tale of a Tub,* 1714). It was therefore no unheard of trick which the writer of the Sermon perpetrated; indeed, in view of all the other pieces that previously had been even more directly attributed to Swift, one more false ascription could hardly have caused him any disquiet —one would think—even supposing he ever heard of it; while, as regards the public, his name had been so frequently used as a stalking horse for the anonymous, that the attribution to him of such a pamphlet as ours at this time must in the nature of things have been largely discredited at sight.

(ii) A burlesque Sermon was published on May 24, 1715, which, whether by Pope or not, purported to have been written by Swift. Was it, or was it not, the 'Sermon' alluded to by Jervas? We must either suppose that there were two pamphlets published at approximately the same date, both of them implicating the dean at a time when, resident in Ireland, he was no longer in the public eye, both of them having some interest for, or connexion with, Pope, and furthermore, that one of them has vanished so completely as to leave no trace or record to tell it ever existed— all of which is incredible; or we must believe our Sermon to be the one referred to by Jervas.

(iii) Within three weeks of the publication of the Sermon Jervas wrote to Pope: 'I hear nothing of the Sermon—The Generality will take it for the Deanes and that will hurt neither you nor him.' Did it, or did it not, do Swift any harm? One thing is certain, namely, that Jervas, who appears to have been a friend of Swift as well as of Pope, and who lived in London and probably had a more extensive acquaintance there than either of them, was in a better position than anyone to-day can possibly be to judge what would be the effect on Swift's reputation of the Sermon being ascribed to him; and was confident it would not hurt him. Moreover, his judgment is confirmed in so far that no contemporary comment on, or reference to, the Sermon or its effects, either by Swift or any one else, has yet come to light. Nor should it be forgotten that *The Tale of a Tub* was itself an anonymous publication; that Swift never publicly acknowledged it; and therefore that there must always have been some uncertainty about his authorship—to which, later, no less a person than Dr Johnson attested, when he said: 'I doubt if the Tale of a Tub was his . . .' There is thus no warrant whatever for any one at this day either to picture in his indignant mind the awful result of the publication of this Sermon on Swift's contemporary (and none too fair) reputation, or to think that Pope had ever contemplated its doing his friend any harm.

(iv) There is the undeniable witness of Jervas's letter that Pope was somehow concerned in, or about, the Sermon; (v) there are parallels in the Sermon which unquestionably point to Pope as its author; and (vi) there are, on the one hand, both place and occasion in the literary warfare of 1715 into which—if Pope wrote it—the Sermon completely fits; and, on the other hand, no known place, or occasion, or author for it, if Pope did not write it.

In conclusion, to accept Pope's authorship of the Sermon is not necessarily (having regard to the man and the times) to accuse him of any unbelievable, or even unforgivable, degree of temerity or turpitude. He almost certainly regarded the thing as a 'whimsy,' and its ascription to 'the Author of the Tale of a Tub' as nothing more than a practical joke, which was all the better for being old, because it would be so much the more baffling as a screen for himself, and so much the less likely to be thought to indicate an authentic work—in which view Jervas would seem to have shared, for his letter was obviously written in reply to one from Pope. About the end of May, after probably the busiest and most trying five months of his life, Pope had returned from town to the peace of Windsor Forest, where, on June 3, he wrote to Miss Blount that he was already at work on the next year's instalment of *The Iliad*. But he had left so many irons in the fire at London, it is no wonder that he was soon writing Jervas a letter, the main trend of which, although it has not survived, is deducible in part from his friend's reply. It was evidently a letter clamorous for news of his various enterprises, and full of instructions and commissions about such matters as the belated subscriptions for *The Iliad*, his 'old sword,' Tickell's rival translation, Gay's prospective visit, and so forth; and amongst them and not the least urgent of them would seem to have been a request to be told what the town was saying about his sermon on *The Dignity, Use, and Abuse of Glass-Bottles*, published only a week or so previously. What Jervas replied on this point we saw at the beginning of this section, but only now at the end are we in a position to interpret it. Thus Jervas says, or seems to say, 'No one in town is talking about your Sermon yet; but only the Generality will be taken in by the ascription and think it Swift's. The people who really matter—friends, critics, persons of place and position—will not be deceived for a moment, either by the old trick of the title-page or by the style, and, consequently, it cannot do him any real harm; and you have covered up your tracks too completely to be suspected by any one.' And, curiously enough, Jervas seems to have been right in every respect.*

The Preface to 'The Iliad,' 1715.

THE full story of Pope's great undertaking and its repercussions in the contemporary literary world has yet to be told; but unfortunately this is not the place to tell it. In the previous section and elsewhere we have, however, caught incidental glimpses of the animosities and jealousies which even the preliminary announcements of the work could arouse, as well as something of the poet's attitude towards his detractors. That Pope was apprehensive of such treatment almost from the beginning is revealed in his letters; for example, nearly a year before the first volume of *The Iliad* was issued, he wrote to Caryll (July 25, 1714) saying:

I must expect an hundred attacks upon the publication of my Homer . . . and be prepared to suffer all sorts of public persecution. It is certainly to be lamented that if any man does but endeavour to distinguish himself, or gratify others by his studies, he is immediately treated as a common enemy . . . and assaulted as generally as if his whole design were to prejudice the state and ruin the public.

Nevertheless, however he expressed his resentment in other places, little of it is betrayed in his admirable Preface, where, if anywhere, one might have expected to find it, and

---

* The main purport of this section appeared as an article entitled 'Pope's Lost Sermon on Glass-Bottles' in *The Times Literary Supplement* for June 6, 1935. It has, however, been largely rewritten and expanded with fresh matter to deal with the more relevant criticism put forward in the ensuing correspondence, June 13–July 11.

only in one paragraph towards the close is it perceptible in any degree of warmth:

What I have done is submitted to the Publick, from whose Opinions I am prepared to learn; tho' I fear no Judges so little as our best Poets, . . . As for the worst, whatever they shall please to say, they may give me some Concern as they are unhappy Men, but none as they are malignant Writers. I was guided in this Translation by Judgments very different from theirs, and by Persons for whom they can have no Kindness, if an old Observation be true, that the strongest Antipathy in the World is that of Fools to Men of Wit.

The Preface has always been regarded as one of the major prose works of Pope, and yet, during the last fifty years or so, it has probably been less read than any of them. The chief reason for this neglect is, doubtless, that it has rarely been printed apart from the poem (even Elwin and Courthope, who included the preface to Shakespeare in their edition of Pope's works, refused it a place); thus when the poem itself most undeservedly fell out of favour, this admirable piece of prose became inextricably involved in the same fate. The Preface of course appeared in the first of the six volumes of *The Iliad*—unlike the Dedication which rather surprisingly is found in the last—and the present reprint follows the text of the first edition of Volume I, which was published, like Tickell's rival translation of the first book, in the early part of June 1715. The exact date of publication thus becomes unusually important; and as it seems hitherto to have been mistakenly ascribed to June 6, a last word may be added on that point. It will be remembered that the first issue of *The Iliad* was subscribed for, and that the preliminary announcements in the newspapers stated that 'on Monday the 6th Day of June' copies would be delivered to the subscribers. At the last moment, however, Lintot seems to have changed his mind (Pope being then at Binfield), and produced it two days earlier, possibly with the idea of outwitting the promoters of the rival venture who apparently were plotting for a simultaneous publication of the two translations. For, despite the fact that *The Post Boy* of June 4 repeated its preliminary advertisement of June 2, giving 'Notice to the Subscribers . . . that the first Vol. . . . will be ready to be deliver'd to them' on June 6, Lintot appears to have rushed an amended advertisement that same day into another, and presumably later, paper, *The Evening Post* (June 4), in which he announced:

This Day the first Vol. of Mr. Pope's Translation of Homer will be deliver'd in Quires to the Subscribers upon giving up their Receipts or paying their Subscription Money, to Bernard Lintott between the Temple Gates in Fleetstreet.

The Three Lampoons against Curll.

No one at this time of day is likely to question Pope's responsibility for the three anonymous lampoons against Edmund Curll, the bookseller, included in the present volume. Nevertheless the facts are that Pope never explicitly owned them, that the evidence for his authorship of the first is either purely circumstantial or of the nature of contemporary gossip, and that little or no attempt has yet been made either to establish his connexion with the other two, or to discover why they came to be written and when they were published. They have simply been taken for granted. Much of interest to students of Pope attaches to these lampoons, however, and the many fresh facts concerning them and their author that have come to light since they were last discussed, may therefore be incorporated in a brief summary of the causes and (so far as this volume is concerned) the effects of Pope's quarrel with Curll, of which they were the outcome. For this reason the three lampoons (the first two of which, it may be noted, have never before been reprinted from the original pamphlets) are now to be considered separately and in their chronological order.

I. *A Full and True Account,* 1716.

This pamphlet, the title of which runs: *A Full and True Account of a Horrid and Barbarous Revenge by Poison on the Body of Mr. Edmund Curll, Bookseller, With a Faithful Copy of his Last Will and Testament,* tells its own tale pretty completely; and if Pope's revenge, first in the administration of

the emetic, and next in this 'Account' of it, seems disproportionate to the alleged offence, it should be borne in mind
that Pope had previously suffered from Curll's malpractices
which, amongst other things, included the piratical publication of one or two of his less presentable poems. Pope's
resentment had thus been accumulating for at least two
years, when, two days after the appearance of the second
volume of *The Iliad* on March 24, 1716, matters were
brought to a head by the publication of *Court Poems*, 1716
(misprinted 1706), in which Curll was the prime mover,
though other booksellers were also concerned. This production is a slender pamphlet containing three poems,
namely, *The Basset-Table*, *The Drawing-Room* and *The Toilet*, with a title-page saying that the poems 'were found in a
Pocket-Book taken up in Westminster-Hall,' and an 'Advertisement,' or preface, which, after suggesting their author might be 'a Lady of Quality' (Lady Mary Wortley
Montagu), or 'Mr. Gay,' or 'the Judicious Translator of
Homer,' concludes with these words: 'Thus having im-
partially given the Sentiment of the Town ... every Body
is at Liberty to bestow the Laurel as they please'—which
liberty, it is no exaggeration to say, has ever since been duly
exercised by everybody, including all the editors of the
three poets alluded to, with the most conflicting results.

Admittedly, the problem of the authorship of *Court
Poems* is baffling, and cannot even now be regarded as
settled. For instance, to note only three points, any of which
by itself would have carried conviction: (*a*) These poems
are three of a set of six *Town Eclogues*, written at or about
the same time, all categorically claimed by Lady Mary in
an existing autograph manuscript in the possession of Lord
Harrowby; (*b*) Gay asserted his authorship of *The Toilet* by
including it in his *Poems*, 1720; (*c*) Warburton, Pope's
confidant and literary executor, declared that *The Basset-
Table* was written by Pope, and included it in his works in
1751. After a study of the various claims, ascriptions, and
repudiations, and of the poems themselves, the most probable solution, it seems to me, is that Lady Mary was pri-

marily responsible for the whole set, having no doubt derived the idea from Gay's *Araminta. A Town Eclogue* (the first English poem in this genre), which had appeared in Steele's *Poetical Miscellanies*, 1714; that by some unexplained co-operation Gay had a part—possibly even the major part—in the 1716 version of *The Toilet* (his 1720 version, besides containing many variants, is thirty lines longer than this, which may explain its inclusion among his own poems); and that *The Basset-Table* had been 'corrected' by Pope in the rather drastic manner usual with him.

But whatever may be the ultimate solution of the problem (if ever it is solved), there can be little doubt of Curll's intention to implicate Lady Mary in the matter; and as Pope had become deeply attached to her since their first acquaintance in the previous year, he must have been more than a little perturbed at Curll's allusion to her; for the poems were satires on several persons of importance at court. It seems probable, then, that Professor Sherburn—whose recent account of the whole affair is the most illuminating we have—is right in thinking that the decisive factor which moved Pope for once to take the matter into his own hands and punish an offence in person, can be traced to his relations with Lady Mary. The further suggestion that 'her anger was the moving force' (for which there is no evidence) is, however, less convincing. Rather would it seem, both from Pope's unquestioned regard for her and from the long footnote in the *Dunciad* (ii, 58), that his personal encounter with Curll was due to a chivalrous desire to protect the lady. Thus the champion entered the lists with an emetic in his hands—for us, laughter and tears press close on that moment, when, his pigmy stature and feeble doctor-ridden frame making corporal castigation of any antagonist impossible, he chose his weapon from the only armoury with which he was at all familiar, the medicine chest (possibly with Arbuthnot's assistance)—and thus the enemy was laid low and the victor returned to his tent well pleased. But the most grotesque thing about the whole grotesque affair is, that Pope, having acted in this unwonted manner, should have sat down immediately and recounted the episode at length without the least reserve of his name and part in it, except of course as the author of the *Account*.

If the suppression of Lady Mary's connexion with the poems had been Pope's aim, as well as the punishment of Curll, he was for the moment completely successful; for Curll at once concentrated all his attention on him, and from April 5 onwards widely advertised the offending pamphlet as 'Mr. Pope's Court Poems.' But that was not Curll's only rejoinder to Pope's lampoon; he promptly had recourse to the newspapers, and with malicious cunning threatened Pope with the publication of a book, which, though it never materialized, must have caused many of Pope's subscribers and the poet himself some uncomfortable moments. (To anticipate a little, I may mention that this trick was repeated by Curll after each of the other two lampoons Pope subsequently wrote against him, and helps to determine the dates newly attributed to them.) Thus, after first preparing the way on April 7 by a burlesque advertisement in *The Flying-Post* of 'The Second Part of Mr. Pope's *Popish* Translation of Homer,' and a notification of a forthcoming ballad called *The Catholick Poet*, he published in the same paper three days later the following announcement:

To prevent any farther Imposition on the Publick, there is now preparing for the Press by several Hands,

HOMER defended: Being a Detection of the many Errors committed by Mr. *Pope*, in his pretended Translation of *Homer*, wherein is fully prov'd that he neither understands the Original, nor the Author's Meaning, and that in several Places he has falsified it on Purpose. To which is added, a Specimen of a Translation of the first Book of the *Odysses*, which has lain printed by Mr. Lintott for some Time, and which he intends to publish, in Order to prejudice Mr. *Tickell*'s excellent Version. Any Gentlemen who have made Observations upon Mr. *Pope*'s

b

Homer, and will be pleas'd to send them to Mr. Curl, at
the Dial and Bible against St. Dunstan's Church in Fleetstreet, shall have them faithfully inserted in this Work.

The chronology of the various events which began the
life-long quarrel between Pope and Curll is worth noting.
Court Poems was published (according to the *Account*) on
Monday, March 26, two days after the second volume of
The Iliad had been issued to the subscribers; the emetic
was administered on Wednesday, March 28; and almost
certainly by Saturday, March 31, Pope's lampoon had been
written, printed and published, because on Tuesday, April
3, *The Flying-Post* printed an advertisement by John Oldmixon denying the charges Pope had made against him in
the pamphlet. Thereafter followed Curll's newspaper attacks, of which the one above quoted may be said to end (at
least as far as we are concerned) the first chapter of the
Pope–Curll quarrel.

II. *A Further Account*, 1716.

UNFORTUNATELY no announcement has been found in the
newspapers of the publication of any of Pope's three lampoons against Curll. And though a closely approximate
date for the first has been derived from other sources, similar information has not hitherto been forthcoming for the
other two, with the result that widely differing dates have
been suggested for them, varying from April to June, 1716,
for *A Further Account*, and for *A Strange but True Relation*
(which is undated) almost any year from 1717 to 1732. It
may therefore be worth while to inquire whether or not
their dates of publication can be more precisely determined.

Presumably because of its title, *A Further Account Of the
most Deplorable Condition of Mr. Edmund Curll, Bookseller.
Since his being Poison'd on the 28th of March*, Pope's second
pamphlet has always been supposed to have followed hard
on the first; but that is a pure conjecture unsupported by
any known fact. On the other hand, an examination of the
text reveals—in addition to several allusions to Curll's
various machinations subsequent to the appearance of the

'emetic' pamphlet—two definite references which cannot reasonably be explained unless the date of publication was much later than what has been generally supposed. The first is, that in the list of the (mostly fanciful) humiliations which, in the narrative, Curll confesses to have suffered, Pope makes him refer to the various punishments—the tossing in a blanket, the caning and kicks—inflicted on him by the boys at Westminster School on August 2 of this same year, as reported in the newspapers. That Pope knew of this incident is shown in his letter to Teresa Blount of August 7, 1716: 'Mr. Edmund Curll has been exercised in a blanket, and whipped at Westminster school by the boys, whereof the common prints have given some account;' (and a ballad on the subject also appeared, to which we shall return later). Ordinary retribution like canings and kicks can have little significance for our purpose; but what of 'twice was I toss'd in a Blanket'? Another allusion to that form of punishment, unconnected with the Westminster episode, *might* possibly be found in the literary output of 1716—I do not know, but think it extremely improbable; but an attempt to explain its presence in the *Account* by a kind of second sight that enabled Pope to speak of it in connexion with Curll before it happened to Curll, would appear to be hopeless in view of the existence of other evidence that the pamphlet was published after, and not before, the Westminster affair. The second reference points to an even later date. It appears in the narrative at the point where Curll is summoning his authors to a council, among whom is 'the young Man who is writing my new *Pastorals.*' This can be none other than Thomas Purney, an obscure author whose works have been recently reprinted by Mr H. O. White, to whom I am indebted for various particulars about his life. Purney was twenty-one on August 1 of this year, and his first volume of poems, entitled, *Pastorals. After the simple Manner of Theocritus*, was published on November 16, 1716, though post-dated on the title-page 1717. It is therefore hardly credible that Pope should have been aware, in the early part of this year, of this wholly unknown young man's contract with Curll, even supposing it existed at that time. Much more likely is it that Purney, only recently graduated at Cambridge, came to town with his *Pastorals* in his pocket, and was somehow picked up by Curll who had a way of getting hold of young writers just down from the universities; and that, if Pope had heard of him before the *Pastorals* was published, it was from some chance coffee-house or printing-house gossip when the book was in the press. Indeed, seeing that Pope had some grievance, real or fancied, against every one of Curll's 'authors' who can be identified, it is difficult to understand why Pope should have alluded to Purney at all, unless he had first read the preface (called 'Advertisement') to his *Pastorals*. Here evidently lies the explanation of the puzzle; for in his discussion of the English writers of pastorals Purney not only omits to mention Pope's work in the kind, but, like many other people, was deceived by the irony of Pope's *Guardian* essay, No. 40, 'On Pastorals' (which, incidentally, he ascribes to Addison) and praises 'the incomparable *Pastorals* of Mr. *Phillips*.' It is practically certain, therefore, that Pope's allusion to Purney in *A Further Account* was due to this provocation, and, consequently, that this paragraph, at least, was not written before November 16, and most probably some days later; in which case the publication of Pope's second lampoon against Curll is pushed still nearer to December. This conclusion seems to be confirmed by a passage in a letter from Pope to Jervas in Ireland, dated November 14, 1716, which runs: 'Gay . . . has broke forth in a courageous couplet or two upon Sir Richard Blackmore. He has printed it with his name to it, and bravely assigns no other reason, than that the said Sir Richard has abused Dr. Swift. I have also suffered in the like cause, and shall suffer more.' As Blackmore's abuse of Swift appeared in the first volume of his *Essays*, published March 7, 1716, the last sentence of the excerpt apparently explains why Pope made fun of him three weeks later in his first lampoon against Curll; though what Pope had 'suffered' on that score at the date of his letter remains unknown. More to our purpose, however, is his anticipation of further trouble; for it could, and probably does, mean that he was then writing, or had just written, something else against Blackmore which would have that result. There is no known work of Pope's to which such words could refer at that time except *A Further Account*, in which the ridicule of Blackmore might almost be said to have been developed into one of its major themes.

With the late date of Pope's second lampoon against Curll presumptively proved, it is necessary further to inquire how it came to be written at that particular time, and what effect, if any, it had on Curll. In other words, we must find a gap in the Pope–Curll story towards the end of the year into which *A Further Account* will fit, although hitherto it has had no definite place assigned to it, but has been left floating vaguely round the 'emetic' episode. First, then, as regards the occasion; it is becoming increasingly certain in the light of recent work on Pope (and to some extent, perhaps, in the foregoing pages) that the old conception of his character, as a kind of literary assassin who delighted in making indiscriminate and unprovoked attacks on more or less innocent people, has no foundation in fact. On the other hand, few people of his attainments were quicker than he to resent and revenge any injury or insult. It is probable, therefore, that these separate attacks on Curll had each its own special provocation, and were not merely further efforts to wipe off the old score. Now Curll, as might have been expected after the emetic, had continued his attentions to Pope throughout the summer of 1716: he had surreptitiously obtained and published his notorious poems *The Worms* (May 1) and the *Version of the First Psalm* (June 30); he had fostered and published vitriolic attacks on him, like *The Catholick Poet* and *A True Character of Mr. Pope* (May 31), and had continued the vendetta in the newspapers. And yet, except for Pope's equivocal disavowal of the *First Psalm* (July 31), we do not know that he made any public reply to Curll's continued transgressions against him alone. On August 1, however, Lady Mary left

England for Constantinople at the height of Pope's passionate devotion to her, and was followed across Europe by the most fervent of letters. Then on September 15, the following advertisement (in which Curll was unquestionably concerned) appeared in *The Evening Post:*

This Day is publish'd,

More Court Poems. Part 2d. Containing, 1. The Dream, or, Melesinda's Lamentation on the Burning of her Smock. 2. The Hyde-Park Ramble. With some other Pieces, Written by a Lady of Quality. To which are added, The Worms, a Satire. Also a Version of the first Psalm, for the Use of a young Lady. Printed for J. Roberts near the Oxford Arms in Warwick-lane, price 1s. where may be had, the first Part of Court Poems, viz. The Basset-Table, the Drawing-Room, the Toilet, pr. 6d.

But that was not all, in the book itself (which is post-dated 1717) there is a footnote to *The Ramble*, which reads:

This POEM was compos'd to please some Satyrical *Court-Ladies*. The *Story* is too well known among the *Beau Monde* to want a Key. The best Lines in it are taken from FONTAINE, and a fam'd Female *Wit* assisted in the Translation.

Some of the pieces in *Court Poems, Part II*, had previously been printed in another collection called *State Poems*, published by Curll on May 19, and amongst them was *The Ramble* with its footnote. But as there was nothing in the advertisements of the book, or on its title-page, even remotely implicating Lady Mary, Pope seems to have made no move, and Curll apparently grew bolder. Now, however, for the first time since *Court Poems* was published in March, Lady Mary and Pope are again associated in a Curll publication which by its very title, *Court Poems, Part II*, was obviously intended to recall the former scandal and suggest it was the work of the same author or authors. How soon Pope and Lady Mary were thought to have written *The Ramble* between them is not known; but Curll reprinted *Court Poems, Part II*, in the following year (August 6) with a new title, *Pope's Miscellany. The Second Part*, and inserted her name in the footnote to the poem so that it ended thus: 'And a fam'd Female *Wit*, (the Lady *W—y M—gue*,) assisted in the Translation.' It is extremely prob-able, therefore, that this is the poem referred to in *Pope Alexander's Supremacy* (1729) where Pope is accused of having written 'a second Lampoon, wherein he spared not the most exalted Characters, though under feigned Names; and . . . threw the scandalous Imputation of having wrote this Libel, on a Lady of Quality, whose Wit is equal to her Beauty, and whose Character might have suffer'd by this impudent Forgery of his.' However that may have been, we know that Pope was in town (or, possibly, Chiswick) about the time of Curll's announcement of *More Court Poems* on September 15; and it is very probable that his immediate reaction to it—like causes producing like effects —was a repetition of the hot indignation evoked by the earlier *Court Poems*, and that, a second emetic being im-practicable, he sketched out a sequel to the story of the original potion, and called it *A Further Account*. But the long vacation was no time for publishing (except for the re-stricted output of a few booksellers like Curll, who needed 'daily books' for 'daily bread'); and Pope had perforce to delay his vengeance. He left London in the meantime, and made journeys to York and Bath with Lord Burlington in October. Back again in town early in November, he pub-lished on the seventh of the month his single-sheet squib, *God's Revenge against Punning* (assuming that he wrote it); and then, a fortnight or three weeks later, followed it with this belated second attack on Curll. (Another reason which may just possibly have influenced Pope in his decision to publish *A Further Account* at that moment, namely, the ap-pearance on November 22 of *A Letter from Sir J— B— to Mr. P—*, is discussed below in the section on *God's Revenge against Punning*.)

What seems to have been Curll's reply to this second lampoon has not hitherto been identified or reprinted; it will therefore be of interest to students of Pope, especially as it helps to determine the approximate date of *A Further Account*, and, like his earlier rejoinder, threatens Pope with

the publication of another book that never appeared. But
before quoting it, a word or two should be said of the devices Curll frequently employed in his literary skirmishes.
It is noteworthy, for instance, that he was curiously like
Pope in his readiness to meet attack, and in favouring the
method of counter-attack rather than of defence; the result
being that, in the Pope–Curll quarrel, attack and counter-
attack (after the lapse of two centuries) often seem at first
sight to have no relation to one another. To make matters
worse, both combatants generally fought in disguise. Thus,
while Pope normally preferred anonymity for this warfare,
Curll as often as not went to work pseudonymously, using
the names of certain other booksellers whom he persuaded
from time to time to co-operate with him in his dubious
projects. At this particular period his most usual partners,
or screens, were J. Roberts (in whose name, for instance,
both the volumes of *Court Poems* had been issued); R. Burleigh (a woman, who amongst other things sponsored
Curll's unauthorized publication of Pope's disreputable
Version of the First Psalm), and Sarah Poping. Of the last
named it should be noted that, earlier in the year, she had
actually been taken into custody on account of one of
Curll's publications which bore her imprint, only to be released a few days later when Curll himself was apprehended
and imprisoned as the real offender.* And it is this same
woman in whose name Curll's counterblast to *A Further
Account* appeared in *The St. James's Post* for December 7–
10, 1716, in the manner following.

There is preparing for the *Press*,
A Satyr, entitled, *Pope* on the Stool of
Repentance: Or, the Purge given to *Sir Alexander Knaw-post*,
to prepare his Body for the New Madhouse, erected for the
cure of Atheists, Blasphemers, Libertines, Punsters, Jaco-
bites, and other prophane Lunaticks: To which is added,
a *Challenge* to this Rhiming Knight upon several nice and
curious Points in *Philosophy, Poetry, and Conversation,* which
if he refuses to Answer, he'll be posted for a B———d. The

* See *The Unspeakable Curll*, R. Straus, 1927, p. 65 ff.

Purge and Challenge prescrib'd upon Reading a *Dogrel Poem* of
Sir *Alexander*'s (called *Neck or Nothing* or a consolatory
Letter from Mr. *Dunton* to Mr. *Curll*, upon his being toss'd
in a Blanket) and Dedicated to those *Noble and Illustrious Patriots* that *POPE* basely (and undeservedly) slander'd in his
late Infamous Libel, entitled, *God's Revenge against Punning*.
The whole *Satyr* written by Dr. *Dunton*, Physician to the
New Madhouse, and explain'd by a *Copper Plate*, representing
(at one View) Sir *Alexander's prophane Life and Writings*,
which are all Inserted and Answered in this *Purge*.

> *Deaf to all Means which might most proper seem*
> *Towards their Cure, they run stark Mad in Rhime.*
>   Oldham.

Note, That Dr. *Dunton*'s *Purge* may want no Ingredient
that is necessary to bring this Patient (Sir *Alexander*) to his
right Senses, it will be compleated in a Book of 1s. price, or
else will be inserted in his Weekly Paper entitled, *Dunton*'s
Madhouse, till the whole is compleated, but neither this
Purge nor *Madhouse* will be publish'd, till *Pope* has been lasht
(both in Prose and Verse) by those First-rate Wits that are
to prove him a fit Patient for *Dunton*'s *Madhouse*. *DUNTON*'s
PURGE when ready for publication, will be sold by *S. Poping*
in *Pater-noster-row*; where is now to be had, The 7th Edition of *Dunton's Recantation* . . . Also the 5th Edition of . . . . . .

This advertisement raises many interesting points, but
we have space only to note those bearing on our argument.
First, then, although this reply of Curll's makes no mention of *A Further Account* (just as his earlier reply had not
mentioned *A Full and True Account*), the fact that it is set
in the same key obviously betrays the connexion between
them. Compelled to descend to particulars, it is noticeable
that the 'close-stool' motif, which may almost be said to
dominate Pope's second piece (as the 'vomit' dominated
the first), is echoed in Curll's reiteration of 'purge' throughout the advertisement, not to mention his opening pun on
'stool'; similarly the sustained insinuation that Curll is
going mad is countered by the assertion that Pope is already a fit subject for the 'New Madhouse.' Secondly, it is
difficult to see why Curll chose this particular moment to

issue a highly opprobrious advertisement, if it was not in
retaliation for Pope's recently published lampoon, for it has
all the appearance of having been written in the first heat
of resentment. The real provocation, therefore, can hardly
have been the 'Dogrel Poem' on the Westminster episode;
for that seems to have been published soon after the event,
and it would have been unlike Curll to have waited four
months before retorting.(Few people can have known that
the author of the ballad was Samuel Wesley, then an usher
at the school; thus Curll may possibly have thought it
Pope's, and, when *A Further Account* touched again on the
sore spot, responded accordingly.)Nor can the real provocation have been *God's Revenge against Punning*, for that has
nothing whatever to do with Curll, directly or indirectly,
and is in itself quite inoffensive. Further, it may be remarked of the genuine John Dunton, who had actually written a pamphlet called *Neck or Nothing* in 1713, and some of
whose works were in fact published by Sarah Poping, that
he had nothing to do with either Wesley's ballad or Curll's
announcement; for although the latter concludes with advertisements of two or three of his authentic books, they
seem to have been appended chiefly to add verisimilitude
to the phantom projects of the wholly fictitious 'Dr. Dunton' of Curll's invention. It would appear, therefore, that
the real provocation which impelled Curll to the frenzied
retort of December 10, must be sought in some offence
against him recently committed by Pope. But no such attack at this period has yet been identified by Pope scholars.
Here then is a definite gap in the Pope–Curll story into
which *A Further Account* fits completely and satisfactorily.
And as all the available evidence points to the same conclusion, I would suggest that Pope's second lampoon against
Curll was published about the last week of November or
the first two or three days of December 1716. And thus, as
far as Pope's prose works are concerned, ends the second
chapter of the Pope–Curll quarrel.

III. *A Strange but True Relation.*

Pope's third lampoon against Curll, *A Strange but True Relation how Edmund Curll, of Fleetstreet, Stationer, . . . was converted from the Christian Religion by . . . Jews: And how he was circumcis'd . . .*, has apparently survived only in *Miscellanies. The Third Volume*, 1732; for which reason it has often been supposed never to have been published in pamphlet form. I have found evidence, however, which not only proves that it had an earlier existence (presumably as a separate pamphlet, like the previous lampoons), but also helps to fix an approximate date for its publication. This evidence consists of an advertisement (to which we shall return later) issued on April 12, 1720, in which the lampoon is alluded to in the following words: 'A Relation of Mr. Curll's Conversion to Judaism, and of his Circumcision.' With the latest possible date of publication thus established, the next clue is supplied by the text itself which mentions 'the late Mr. Addison,' and as he died on June 17, 1719, the earliest possible date is similarly fixed. From this it follows, that, as the fictitious operation is stated in the text to have been performed 'on the 17th of March,' the year 1720 was implied (as is usual with references within the current year), and, consequently, that the pamphlet was published between March 17 and April 12. Abundant corroboration is found in the repeated allusions in the narrative to stock-jobbing and 'bubbles,' because we know that the gambling mania in South Sea stock, which seems to have started in February, reached unprecedented heights of frenzy during March. Innumerable contemporary references in the newspapers and elsewhere testify to the prevalent excitement at this date. For example, on March 25 a book was published 'very necessary for these Times,' entitled: *The Anatomy of Exchange-Alley; or, A System of Stock-Jobbing. Proving that Scandalous Trade, as it is now carried on, to be Knavish in its Private Practice, and Treason in its Publick*'; and ballads on this unscrupulous traffic were sold in the streets, and even appeared in the journals.

But although it is clear that Pope makes use of the contemporary financial situation in lampooning Curll, the question remains, what new offence had Curll committed that Pope should attack him at this particular time? The only answer available, and I believe the true one, is to be found in the first item of the following announcement which appeared in *The Post Boy* for March 19–22, 1720:

> This Day is publish'd the Two following Poems,
> 1. The Second Eve; a Poem on the Lady Mary Wortley Mountague. By Mr. Pope.
> 2. Scating: A Poem. By Mr. Addison. With a Preface concerning it. Price 6d.
> Printed for T. Bickerton ... W. Meadows ... E. Curll ... W. Lewis ... J. Graves ... and T. Griffith ...

Noting in passing that of all these booksellers' names only Curll's appears in the imprint of this piratical publication of a poem generally believed to be Pope's, it should be remembered that, in spite of Curll's persistent and offensive activities against Pope, the only two occasions on record before 1720 when Pope had attacked him were—according to the evidence available—those on which the bookseller's invidious attentions had previously been directed against Lady Mary (or, it may be, Lady Mary and Pope in conjunction) in 1716. It is difficult, therefore, not to believe that it was Curll's publication of this poem on March 22, 1720, again associating their names, which was the provocation of Pope's third lampoon, published, as we now know, between March 17 and April 12. Indeed, there are not wanting indications (such as they are) which suggest that the lampoon was actually written and published early in April and therefore after *The Second Eve* had appeared. We might note, for instance, that in the *Relation* some days are supposed to have elapsed between the 'operation' (March 17) and the writing of the whole story; and that, whereas in the first lampoon, which was written late in March 1716, Pope refers to a recent date as 'Monday the 26th inst' omitting to name the current month; in this lampoon he tells us that the operation was performed 'on the 17th of March' which apparently indicates that the narrative was not written in March but in some subsequent month; seeing however that it was published before April 12, some day in the first week of April would appear, from all the foregoing evidence, to be the most probable date we can assign to the publication of *A Strange but True Relation*.

With the sequence of these events reasonably assured, it is not surprising to find Curll once again repeating his old tactics, and, in return for the lampoon, threatening Pope with yet another phantom publication. The preliminary advertisement of this 'book' has already been alluded to, and a passage from it quoted; but the whole thing is extremely interesting, and, as it has never been reprinted, will perhaps be welcomed by students of Pope. It appeared in *The Daily Post* for April 12, 1720, as follows:

Next Week will be publish'd, adorn'd with the Effigies of Mr. Pope, curiously engraven,
The POPE-ish Controversy compleat, viz.

I. An Account of the poysoning of Mr. Curll the Bookseller in Fleetstreet; with a true Copy of his Last Will and Testament. II. The humble Petition of Barnaby Bernard Lintot to the Town. III. The Catholick Poet; a Ballad. IV. The Westminster Expedition successfully perform'd by Mr. Curll. V. A Relation of Mr. Curll's Conversion to Judaism, and of his Circumcision. VI. Proper Notes and various Readings to the whole. Dedicated to Mr. Pope; wherein are recited the surprizing Adventures of his Bookseller, who, in one Campaign, ventur'd Drowning, Hanging, and Starving; with the Secret History of the Translation of Homer by Mr. Pope, and his Assistants. Written by Mr. Curll. *Nemo me impune Lacessit.* Printed for the Author.

With this retort of Curll's to Pope's third lampoon, we, too, have 'the Pope-ish controversy compleat,' at least as regards the present volume. And indeed, although their quarrel continued beyond our immediate purview, as Pope changed his method of counter-attack, *A Strange but True Relation* is actually the last of the pamphlets he wrote against Edmund Curll, bookseller.

God's Revenge against Punning, 1716.

As originally issued, *God's Revenge against Punning* was printed on both sides of a single sheet (mistakenly called a broadside), which was published on November 7, 1716, according to an advertisement in *The St. James's Post* of that date. Properly, therefore, it should have been discussed between the first and second of the lampoons against Curll which for convenience sake have been considered together. The piece was included, with some excision, by Pope in the *Miscellanies* (as we shall see), and is now reprinted for the first time in its entirety from the original sheet, copies of which are extremely scarce, only five having as yet been recorded. Disregarded by former editors of Pope, possibly because it was known only in the abbreviated version of 1732, *God's Revenge against Punning* has of late years been thought to be his by several people, but with insufficient or no reason offered in support of the attribution. Professor Sherburn in his recent biography opines that it is 'very likely either by Pope or Arbuthnot,' but while advancing no evidence for the latter alternative, for the former cites only a letter to Teresa Blount—to which we shall return. The evidence on which the skit is included in the present volume is drawn from a number of sources, with such cumulative effect that, in the absence of anything in the least contradictory, it will be found to amount (I believe) to presumptive proof of Pope's authorship.

In the first place, Pope included *God's Revenge against Punning* in the group of pieces at the beginning of *Miscellanies. The Third Volume*, 1732, which comprises Dr. Norris's *Narrative* and the three pamphlets on Curll, *God's Revenge* being placed fifth. Moreover, in that collection the piece has been revised by the excision of references to religion and the Deity, and of other passages, exactly as have the accompanying reprints of pamphlets which we know to be Pope's.

Secondly, there is the above-mentioned letter to Miss Blount, dated August 7 (that is, three months before this piece was produced), in which Pope, retailing what he calls 'news,' states, amongst other items: 'Mr. Gay has had a fall from his horse, and broken his fine snuff-box.' The last paragraph of *God's Revenge*—which curiously enough was deleted in the 1732 reprint—runs: 'A *Devonshire* Man of Wit, for only saying, in a jesting manner, *I get Up*—*Pun a Horse*, instantly fell down, and broke his Snuff-box and Neck, and lost the Horse.' It is perhaps needless to say either that Gay was a Devonshire man, or that his accident, or at least the breaking of the snuff-box, was a piece of information unlikely to be known outside the immediate circle of his friends, of whom Pope was perhaps the most intimate.

Thirdly, there is the pretence in the original version that the piece was written by 'J. Baker, Knight' (his signature and his concluding pious ejaculation being among the deletions of the 1732 version); and this ascription and its peculiar phrasing become not a little significant in view of the fact that Pope had played this same trick in the same manner only the year before, when (as we know) he fathered one of his own poems on 'James Baker, Knight' in *A Key to the Lock*.

Fourthly, there was published on November 22 (according to *The St. James's Post* of November 23, 1716) a reply to *God's Revenge*, which seems to have been overlooked by all students of Pope hitherto. It was issued in the same form as the skit itself (namely, a single sheet printed on both sides), with the title: *A Letter from Sir J— B— to Mr. P—, upon Publishing of a Paper, intituled, God's Revenge against Punning . . . By J. Baker Kt.*; and its contents leaves no doubt of the identity of 'Mr. P—.' It begins thus:

REPTILE,

Although thou hast long been undermining my Reputation by thy customary Arts of Calumny and Detraction, thou hast never thought of any Means so effectual for this End, as that of ascribing any of thy own Works to me.

The writer goes on to instance other reprehensible 'practices' of Pope, with much outrageous abuse of his person intermingled. Thus he had 'father'd a bawdy Psalm on King *David*,' he was 'one of those Practitioners who give Men involuntary Vomits,' and so on; not the least of which misdeeds being that he should publish 'that idle Lampoon,' *God's Revenge*, 'under my Name,' and thus 'wound the Order of Knighthood through my sides;' for which sins 'we who heretofore . . . used to extol thee to the skies, shall continue so to do, but——in a Blanket.' To judge from the whole tone of the *Letter* and these various allusions, and especially from the prominence given to the unfortunate 'emetic' episode, it is possible that Curll had something to do with this attack on Pope; for although his name does not appear in the imprint, 'Printed for J. Baker and T. Warner,' it is recorded by Mr Straus (*op. cit.*) that he had business dealings with both of those booksellers within six months of the publication of the *Letter*. And if Pope had suspected Curll's hand in this attack, that might help to explain the appearance of his second lampoon against him, *A Further Account*, which, as we have seen above, must have been published only a week or two later.

Fifthly, in the attack on Pope which was disguised as an advertisement in *The St. James's Post* for December 7–10, 1716 (quoted at length in a preceding section), there occurs the following allusion: '. . . those *Noble and Illustrious Patriots* that *POPE* basely (and undeservedly) slander'd in his late Infamous Libel, entitled, *God's Revenge against Punning*.' And though too much reliance, of course, cannot normally be placed on Curll's statements, the important fact about this is that he was in the position to know the truth; for *God's Revenge* was published by J. Roberts, with whom, as we have seen, Curll was in close contact at this period, and who was actually one of his most frequent 'screens.'

Sixthly, twenty days after the publication of *God's Revenge against Punning*, there appeared (November 27) an anonymous ballad in pamphlet form, entitled, *An Heroi-Comical Epistle From a certain Doctor To a certain Gentle-*

Woman, In Defence of the most Ancient Art of Punning, which was written (not improbably by Arbuthnot) in answer to the mock strictures on the pun in *God's Revenge*. Thus it sets out to flout 'James Baker' and 'all his Arguments . . . brought from the *Devil*, or the *Pope*'; and after quoting Scripture and citing the practice of the church in support of punning, concludes thus:

> But, dearest NANN, I smell the bottom
> Of all our Anti-punsters (rott 'em;)
> It is a *Popish-Jesuit* Plot,
> By *Tore Jacobites* begot; . . .
> And tho' our *Words* may squint awry
> Yet they shall know that we can spy
> Their *Popish Plot* with *Half an Eye*.

That 'the Pope' and 'Popish' are the usual play on our author's name is obvious and once again connects him with *God's Revenge*.

Lastly, there was published, apparently some time in December (the actual day has eluded my search), a pamphlet entitled: *Mr. Joanidian Fielding His True and Faithful Account Of the . . . Comet Which was Seen . . . at Constantinople . . . By E. Parker, Philomath*, which is dated 1716 and contains humorous prognostications for the ensuing twelvemonth. And here, after references to Curll (mentioning the emetic, blanketing, etc.), Sir J— Baker, and Moor (the worm-powder quack, celebrated by Pope), occurs the following paragraph:

> If the Pope be not Eat up by Pun-aises, for Anathema's that he never denounc'd, he shall at least be Tickled to Death, or receive a Phillip from St. *Ambrose*.

Again, if any explanation of 'the Pope' were needed, the sly allusions to Tickell's rival translation of the *Iliad*, and to the quarrel between Ambrose Philips and Pope would be more than sufficient to establish his identity.

The total result of all these various testimonies to Pope's authorship of the piece, together with the complete lack of evidence suggestive of any other author, would appear to

i

justify at least the temporary inclusion of *God's Revenge against Punning* in the Pope canon.

Prose Pieces from 'The Works,' 1717.

RARELY can the first collected 'Works' of a young poet (for at this date Pope was only just turned twenty-nine) have been offered to the world in such magnificence of dress and such a choice of styles, as was the book advertised by Lintot in *The Daily Courant* for June 3, 1717, in the following words:

This Day is Published,

The whole Works of Mr. Pope, containing all his genuine Pieces, both those which have been already printed, and those design'd for the Press, in one Volume 4to and Folio, large and small Paper, with several Ornaments in Copper, engrav'd by Mr. Gribelin.

And in truth they are handsome volumes, and so imposing in size (even the quartos measure eleven inches or more in height) that a young poet might well express a whimsical uncertainty of their ultimate function, whether as monument or as tombstone. It is no wonder, then, that Pope endeavoured to rise to the occasion in the Preface, in which he set out to make 'a general confession of all my thoughts of my own poetry, resolving with the same freedom to expose myself, as it is in the power of any other to expose them'; or that, so doing, he was at pains to work into this glittering mosaic so many of the thoughts which he had thrown off from time to time in his letters to his friends. For, whether he had retained them in that amazing memory of his, or had kept notes of them, the fact remains that the Preface is exceptional even among his works for its number of self-echoes. Nor can one be surprised if, following his usual practice with his more important pieces, prose and verse, he should have submitted it in manuscript to his friends for criticism and advice. Among those who thus read it was Atterbury, whose opinion of it has survived in a letter published by Pope in his correspondence in 1737, where we learn that its 'modesty and good sense' were what most impressed the bishop. Other criticisms which Pope may have received in that way do not seem to have been thought worth printing—perhaps they were given by word of mouth; not improbably, however, they are reflected in the differences existing between the manuscript version and that of the first edition of 1717, the text of which is followed in the present reprint. The Preface is deservedly one of the best known of Pope's prose works; and, while it has been praised by various people for qualities not always compatible, at least one critic of note (Joseph Warton) esteemed it 'one of the best pieces of prose in our language.'

In its original form *A Discourse on Pastoral Poetry* is unquestionably the earliest surviving prose work written by Pope with a view to publication. The first version of it, entitled 'An Essay on Pastoral,' still exists, together with the four *Pastorals*, in his autograph; but the manuscript of the 'Essay' unfortunately lacks at least one leaf at the end—a mutilation of long standing seeing that it was remarked by Wakefield nearly one hundred and fifty years ago.* In a 'Mem.' written by Pope on the blank page facing the beginning of the Essay, and obviously dating some years later than the rest of the manuscript, he names twelve people through whose hands 'This Copy' had passed; after which he goes on to say: 'Only ye 3rd Eclog was written since some of these saw ye other 3. wch were written as they here stand wth ye Essay, anno 1704.—Ætat meæ, 16.'—a statement which might mean several things, at least as regards the Essay. But whatever he meant by it, from 1717 onwards he always asserted that both the *Discourse* and the *Pastorals* were 'Written in the Year 1704.' This date, however, while not inherently impossible, cannot be verified on the evidence at present available, and has frequently been questioned by scholars; for it is undeniable that Pope was all his life rather proud of his poetic precocity and tended to exaggerate the youthfulness of his juvenile works. The earliest

* This manuscript, probably Pope's first 'clean copy,' was sold at Messrs Sotheby's in 1922, and is now, I believe, in America.

unimpugnable reference to the existence of the Pastorals,
or rather, 'a Pastoral,' is Tonson's letter to Pope (still extant
among the Homer MSS.) dated April 20, 1706, as follows:

Sr I have lately seen a pastoral of yours in Mr. Walshs & Mr.
Congreves hands which is extremely ffine & is generally approv'd off
by the best Judges in poetry. . . . If you design your Poem for the
Press no person shall be more Carefull in the printing of it, nor no one
can give a greater Incouragem^t to it; than Sr Yr [&c.]

Jacob Tonson.

This looks as though Tonson, and, by inference, Walsh
and Congreve also, did not know at that date of the existence of the other three Pastorals, which, seeing that Walsh
and Congreve are supposed to be amongst the earliest of
Pope's London friends, and also that Pope himself says the
poems were not all written at one time, in turn suggests that
the other three poems either were not yet written, or were
so far from being finished that Pope could not even mention them to his friends. But the Essay, in a passage excised
in 1717, confesses itself to have been written after the com-
pletion of the four Pastorals; and on this view it is possible
that it dates as late as 1706 or even 1707.

This deleted passage is especially interesting both as
being the longest bit of Pope's early prose to survive untouched by later revision, and as showing that Pope's
sprightliness of wit was native and irrepressible, and would
bubble up even when for the first time, so far as we know,
he set himself to write a formal prose treatise and (to use
his own expression) studied to be dull. He had been speaking of *The Shepherd's Calendar*, and the deleted passage
(according to Wakefield's transcript) runs thus:

'Twas from hence I took my first design of the following eclogues.
For looking upon Spenser as the father of English Pastoral, I thought
myself unworthy to be esteemed even the meanest of his sons, unless
I bore some resemblance of him. But as it happens with degenerate
offspring, not only to recede from the virtues, but to dwindle from the
bulk of their ancestors: so I have copied Spenser in miniature, and reduced his twelve months into four seasons.

To resume—the four Pastorals were placed in Tonson's

hands in 1708; they were published, without the Essay, in his *Poetical Miscellanies: The Sixth Part*, probably on May 2, 1709 (casual mention is made of 'Mr. Tonson's new Miscellany' in *The Tatler* of May 7), and were again printed without it in 1716. And it was not until the Pastorals came to be included in Pope's *Works* in 1717 that they were accompanied by the Essay according to his original intention. It should therefore be remembered that although this piece first appeared in print in 1717, and although it was subjected to much correction, including the addition and deletion of whole passages, and was even rechristened for the occasion, *A Discourse on Pastoral Poetry* nevertheless remains essentially the same treatise as when Pope wrote it in his youth.

A Clue to ... the Non-Juror, 1718.

POPE's quarrel with Colley Cibber, like his endless feuds with Dennis and Curll which have occupied so many of the previous pages, is obscure in its origin. If, in lack of other evidence, we had to accept Cibber's own account of it in *A Letter from Mr. Cibber to Mr. Pope*, 1742, it would seem to have begun in Pope's resentment at a short speech interpolated by Cibber in a performance of *The Rehearsal*. As is well known, both Pope and Arbuthnot were concerned with Gay in the writing of the ill-fated comedy, *Three Hours after Marriage*, in which a farcical contrivance introducing two lovers, one disguised as a mummy and one as a crocodile, met with much ridicule on its production on January 16, 1717. During its brief run Cibber had taken the part of Plotwell (one of the lovers), and, shortly after the piece had been withdrawn, he had followed it on February 7 with a revival of *The Rehearsal* with himself in the role of Bays, to which character (as he carefully explains in the *Letter*) 'there had always been allow'd such ludicrous Liberties of Observation, upon any thing new, or remarkable, in the state of the Stage, as Mr. Bays might think proper to make.' With this explanation he proceeds with his narrative of the incident as follows:

I, Mr. *Bays*, when the two Kings of *Brentford* came from the Clouds into the Throne again, instead of what my Part directed me to say, made use of these Words, viz. "Now, Sir, this Revolution, I had some Thoughts of introducing, by a quite different Contrivance; but my Design taking air, some of your sharp Wits, I found, had made use of it before me; otherwise I intended to have stolen one of them in, in the Shape of a *Mummy*, and t'other, in that of a *Crocodile*."

It was this interpolation, Cibber goes on to say, which was taken by Pope as a personal insult, and so led to a stormy interview between them behind the scenes—an interview which, according to other accounts, was followed the next night by 'an unmannerly battle of fisticuffs' (to use Pope's phrase on another occasion) between Gay and Cibber. Nevertheless, the actor stuck to his text—or, rather, his gag—throughout the rest of the brief run of the piece; and he says it was his insistence on repeating the gibe that constituted the offence which Pope never forgot or forgave. However that may be, indications are not wanting to suggest that even before this episode little love was lost between Cibber and Pope (if we can omit the other two collaborators in the comedy); for instance, in the character of Plotwell, Cibber was given a speech reflecting on himself as a dramatist only too willing to father the work of other writers; but which of the three was responsible for this stroke, and others, is not known. Nor is it quite clear, amidst the general criticism and derision of the play and its three authors, why Pope in particular should have been so incensed at Cibber's mockery in particular; for although Pope certainly came in for his share of the common ridicule, Gay's name alone had appeared, in advertisement and title-page, as the author of the play, and he had acknowledged only anonymous help in the preface; and further, his letter to Pope, apparently written soon after the performance, shows that it was against Pope's advice that the crocodile had been introduced. It would therefore appear that the origin of the Pope–Cibber quarrel lay still further back, and, possibly, may never be discovered.

Our concern, however, is not so much with the cause of

the quarrel as with the tangible effect of it among the early
prose works of Pope, where it seems to have taken the form
of an anonymous pamphlet which appeared some twelve
months after the above-mentioned events. Cibber had produced in the meantime (on December 6, 1717, to be precise) his Whiggish adaptation of Molière's *Le Tartuffe*,
called *The Non-Juror*, which play, though successful in the
theatre, was much attacked both in newspapers and pamphlets because of its political bias. In Cibber's *Letter* of
1742, mentioned above, he expressly charges Pope with
(amongst other things) the authorship of one of these
'libels.' Thus, speaking of *The Non-Juror*, he says:

> There is another whimsical Fact relating to this Play ... At this
> time there came out a Pamphlet (the Title I have forgot) but the
> given Name of the Author was *Barnevelt*, which every body believed
> to be fictitious. The Purport of this odd Piece of Wit was to prove,
> that *the Non-Juror* in its Design, its Characters, and almost every
> Scene of it, was a closely couched Jacobite Libel against the Govern-
> ment: And, in troth, the Charge in some places was so shrewdly
> maintained, that I almost liked the Jest myself; at least, it was so
> much above the Spirit, and Invention of the Daily-Paper Satyrists,
> that all the sensible Readers I met with, without Hesitation gave it to
> Mr. *Pope*. And what afterwards left me no doubt of it was, that he
> published the same Charge against his own *Rape of the Lock*, proving
> even the Design of that too, by the same sort of merry Innuendos, to
> have been as audacious a Libel, as the other Pamphlet had made *The
> Non-Juror*. In a word, there is so much Similitude of Stile, and
> Thought, in these two Pieces, that it is scarce possible to give them to
> different Authors.

Former editors of Pope have conjectured that this unnamed pamphlet may have been *A Compleat Key to the Non-
Juror ... By Mr. Joseph Gay*, 1718; but that idea has been
effectually exploded by Professor Sherburn,* whose arguments need not here be repeated. Further, he suggested
that Cibber was alluding to an anonymous skit called *The
Plot Discover'd; or, a Clue to the Comedy of the Non-Juror*,
1718—with which identification I am in agreement, being

* See *Manly Anniversary Studies*, 1923, pp. 176–9.

able to supplement his evidence with much new matter and some correction of detail. I propose therefore to restate the case for Pope's authorship of the *Clue* as I now see it.

Although *The Non-Juror* was produced on December 6, 1717, the play does not seem to have been published until January 2, 1718. About six weeks later, that is, on Saturday, February 15, an advertisement in *The Post Boy* announced:

> This Day is publish'd,
> A CLUE to the Comedy of the NON-JUROR; with some Hints of Consequence relating to that Play: In a Letter to N. Rowe, Esq; Poet Laureat to his Majesty. To which are subjoin'd, Some Verses written by Mr. Rowe. *Quo Musa tendis? define pervicax Referre Sermones Deorum.* Hor. Printed for E. Curll...

Except for punctuation and the sentence 'To which . . . Mr. Rowe,' this advertisement will be seen to agree with the title-page of the first edition reproduced in facsimile on page 303. By what by-paths of intrigue this unsponsored pamphlet was placed in Curll's hands for publication will probably never be known. But Curll was a man whom few people could out-manœuvre. Within three days he appears to have discovered the author of this little plot for anonymous publication; and, only too glad to kill two birds with one stone—at once to annoy Pope, and obtain the advertisement value of his name—he promptly issued another announcement of the pamphlet, which, with a most ingenious ambiguity pointing both to his discovery of its author as well as to its theme, he rechristened (for advertising purposes only, as yet) *The Plot Discover'd*. When we remember that it was an old trick of the booksellers to advertise a book on successive days as 'This day is published . . .' (thereby adding to the troubles of modern bibliographers), we shall not be surprised that Curll employs the same wile in this second advertisement which he inserted in *The Evening Post* for February 15–18, 1718:

> This Day is publish'd the two following Books,
> I. The PLOT DISCOVER'D; or, a Clue to the Comedy of the

Non-Juror. With some Hints of Consequence relating to that Play. In a Letter to N. Rowe, Esq; Poet Laureat to his Majesty . . . To which is subjoin'd some Verses written by Mr. Rowe, pr. 6d. [The Manuscript of this Pamphlet was sent to me on Tuesday last, and I was this Morning given to understand, that this signal Favour was conferr'd on me by Mr. Pope, for which I hereby return my most grateful Acknowledgment for the same. E. Curll.] II. The Verses . . .

Pope made no reply to this; and subsequent advertisements (*e.g.* March 4 and 8) spoke of the pamphlet even more directly, and still without contradiction, as: 'Mr. Pope's Clue to the Non-Juror: Or, the Plot discover'd.' Then, in *The Post Boy* of March 18–20, was announced:

This Day is publish'd, the second Edition of
A CLUE to the NON-JUROR: Or, The Plot Discovered, with some Hints of Consequence relating to that Play. In a Letter to N. Rowe Esq;

> Be gen'rous Pope, nor strive to be conceal'd,
> Since your own CLUE its Author has reveal'd;
> Go on, the Frauds of Cibber to explain,
> And prove him, what he is, a —— in Grain.

Of the second edition it should be remarked that Curll has now incorporated his equivocal advertisement-title in the title-page, which reads: *The Plot Discover'd: Or, A Clue to the Comedy of the Non-Juror . . . The Second Edition*, 1718; other points to be noted being that it is not a mere reissue of the sheets of the first edition with a new title-page, for alterations have been made in sheets A, B, and C, and a different half-title has been provided, on the verso of which now appears the above quatrain, urging Pope to own the book. Moreover, subsequent advertisements of the second edition (March 25, and April 15 and 24) continue to attribute it to Pope—and still he makes no disavowal.

While there is unfortunately nothing in Pope's surviving correspondence which throws any light on the *Clue* itself, one or two letters about this time contain ironical references to *The Non-Juror*, which were quoted by Cibber in 1742 (from the published correspondence) to prove Pope's early animosity to him. Mention might also be made of a suggestive allusion in a letter to Digby (March 31, 1718), where, speaking of Lady Scudamore's rustication, Pope says that although she 'has not seen Cibber's play of the Nonjuror. I rejoiced the other day to see a libel on her toilet;' for it might be surmised that this juxtaposition of 'Nonjuror' and 'libel' is not without significance, and Pope's joy at recognizing the 'libel' points to its being the *Clue*. In this connexion it may be just worth noting that only two days earlier he had written to Caryll that Martha Blount 'is picking up a large collection of libels to send to you.' Lastly, there is the casual remark in a previous letter to the same, dated February 4 (at which time he was probably writing the *Clue*), that one of his immediate occupations is 'play hunting'—a curious expression which he leaves unexplained.

Pope's obvious interest in Cibber's play, running concurrently with his silent acquiescence in Curll's repeated affirmation of his authorship of *A Clue to . . . the Non-Juror*, adds something to the credibility of Curll's ascription. For though it is customary to suspect Curll's probity in such matters, this long series of advertisements cannot be shrugged away, especially when we remember, that, with the exception of the equivocally ascribed *Court Poems* and its disguised reprints, every single work he had published and specifically attributed to Pope, had up to this point been Pope's indisputable—if disreputable—progeny. But we have, happily, not to rely only on Curll's ascription; for the *Clue* agrees, as no other pamphlet of the period does, with Cibber's description of Pope's attack on *The Non-Juror*, in spite of the fact that, the lapse of four and twenty years not having improved Cibber's memory for detail, inconsistencies occur. Regarding these, it may be noted that they are exactly the mistakes of dates, titles, etc. such as an incensed old man, confident of his main fact and too hot for patient verification of minor points, would be likely to make when writing from memory. A comparison of the *Clue* with the passage from the *Letter* above cited can leave little doubt, I imagine, either that Cibber is referring to the *Clue* or that he is convinced of Pope's responsibility for it. The *Letter* is dated at the end, July 7, 1742; and not long after there appeared an anonymous answer to it, entitled, *A Blast upon Bays; Or, A New Lick at the Laureat*, with the appended date, July 29, 1742, which modern scholarship has attributed to Pope. This pamphlet will be included in due course in the subsequent volume of Pope's Prose Works, 1721–1744, with the evidence for its attribution to him; but a quotation of the passage in which he appears tacitly to acknowledge his authorship of *A Clue to . . . the Non-Juror* may perhaps be permitted here. After rebutting some of Cibber's charges, he goes on to say:

> The other Part of the Story, concerning the Pamphlet without a Title, under the fictitious Name of *Barnevelt*, is much more probable; because a Piece of so much Wit and Humour, as you represent it, could not but sell, and be lucrative to the Author; especially if he was then, as he is said to have been since, his own Book-Seller.
>
> The Purport of this Pamphlet, you tell us, "was to prove that *the Nonjuror . . . was a closely couch'd Jacobite Libel against the Government . . .*" But how it should come into your Head, that he had farther Views in this Frolick than to exercise the Wantonness of his Fancy, when you confess that he afterwards publish'd the same Charge against his own *Rape of the Lock*, is what no body can account for but yourself.

Evidently Cibber did not keep copies, as Pope did, of the attacks made against him; it is therefore understandable that, after twenty-four years, he should have forgotten which of the two kindred pieces, the *Clue*, or the *Key to the Lock*, was signed 'Barnevelt,' and thus provided Pope with matter for his ambiguous reply. So, too, with the mistake about priority of publication; though here Cibber possibly had in mind the third edition of the *Key*, published in 1718, in which he may have read the piece for the first time. Notwithstanding, as regards the 'Purport' of the two tracts, and their 'Similitude of Stile and Thought,' Cibber cannot be gainsaid, and he has probably said enough to establish in all reasonable minds the identity of the unnamed pam-

phlet. Further corroboration—if any one should still think
it necessary—could be found in the like methods of argument and the dozen or so repetitions of phraseology in the
two pieces, not to mention the parallels between the *Clue*
and other works of Pope, which together might perhaps
seem (in a favourite phrase of our author appearing here
yet once again) to 'give the finishing stroke.'

The Dedication of 'The Iliad,' 1720.

No piece of Pope's prose could more admirably conclude
the present volume than the brief Dedication with which
our author brought to a close his long labours on *The Iliad*.
Unassumingly printed at the very end of the notes to the
sixth and last volume, it is, in the grave dignity of its utterance and the cadence of its rhythms, probably as fine a piece
of prose writing as the eighteenth century can show.

For the student of Pope, however, who is seeking to know
the man behind his work and understand something of his
strangely compounded character, not the least interesting
thing about this noble Dedication is that it was apparently
written at about the same time as the most unpleasant of
all his lampoons, *A Strange but True Relation*; for the Dedication, though not published until May 12, was actually
dated at the end 'March 25, 1720,' and it was during that
last week of March, or the first few days of April, that we
have reason to believe the lampoon was written and rushed
into print. Such amazing contrasts of style and matter as
these two pieces reveal could hardly be matched in two
simultaneous works of any other author of Pope's standing;
nevertheless this coincidence of opposites is only an extreme example of his not infrequent practice: another instance of the kind in this volume would seem to be the writing of the ribald skit, *God's Revenge against Punning*, published November 7, 1716, and of the great Preface to *The
Works* dated only three days later. Indeed, it would appear
that the tone of many of his less decorous pieces (which were
of course always anonymous) was a not unnatural—if de-

plorable—reaction to the prolonged strain and labour entailed by his major works. Thus, if the partial view of Pope's character and genius which had so long overstressed his less reputable works and the less appealing traits of his character is now held to be false, it is not more false than that which would seek to gloze them over or entirely suppress them. And if the new pieces which the foregoing pages have shown reason to lay at his door may not all be thought to 'add new glories to his name,' yet on the assumption that they are his, they are as essential to a right understanding of the man, the artist, and his period, as is the lofty tribute to friendship which at once crowns and closes this collection of the earlier prose works of Alexander Pope.

A Note on the Texts

THE title-pages of those works which were first published separately in pamphlet form, have been reproduced in facsimile from the originals for use in this volume, with two exceptions, namely, that of *A Full and True Account*, which has necessarily been reduced from its larger page measuring 12 ins. × 7½ ins.; and that of *A Strange but True Relation*, of which no copy seems to have survived.

The texts of the present reprints follow the first editions of all the various pieces except *A Key to the Lock*, which has been set up from the enlarged second edition, and *A Strange but True Relation*, which perforce reproduces the version of 1732, for the reason above mentioned. Two divergencies from the typographical usages of the originals are also to be noted in the substitution of s for f throughout, and in the restriction of inverted commas to the beginning and end of the passages thus distinguished. Apart from these modifications and the few textual corrections recorded below, Pope's prose works, authentic and putative, are now for the first time reprinted as he gave them to the world, with the added convenience, however, that as far as possible the names of persons and places, which in the old texts were disguised by dashes and dots, are completed within square brackets, thus, W[indso]r F[ores]t. Square brackets are also used to enclose the few corrections incorporated in the texts, except those of obvious misprints such as inverted or dropped letters; but all corrections alike are recorded in the subjoined list, together with the original readings and the authority (if any) for the change.

Page 3, line 7. [made]. Omitted in 1711.

13, Chapter 14. First. Frst (in 1711).

21, line 5. remarkable. remarkabe (in folio).

21, l. 8. [ingenuous]. ingenious (in folio); ingenuous (in 1st 8vo).

34, l. 7. [tost]. lost (in folio); tost (in 1st 8vo).

42, l. 22. *Tam. Tum* (in folio and later edns.); *Tam* (Pope, 1737).

54, l. 29. of Merriment. of of Merriment (in folio).

91, l. 24. [to Nature]. Omitted in folio, restored in 1st 8vo (compare p. 94, l. 1).

97, l. 10. before they are. before they they are (in folio).

112, l. 15. *dolisque. dobisque* (in folio); *dolisque* (in later edns. and in Ovid Met. xv, 120).

145, l. 24. [that]. Omitted in folio, supplied in later edns. Pope in 1741 corrected it thus—Descriptions extant of them.

146, l. 12. excellent. excel- (in folio, at the end of a line).

159, l. 6. *Criticism. Criticisms* (in 1713); *Criticism* (in 1732).

163, l. 23. This line was enclosed in square brackets in 1713; round brackets are substituted to avoid confusion with corrections.

176, l. 13. omit. emit (in 2nd edn); omit (in 1st edn).

176, l. 17. [an]. Omitted in 2nd edn, present in 1st edn.

206, l. 18. And. and (in 1715).

210-12. The original printer got confused when numbering the sub-divisions of Part I, as will be apparent from the cross headings of 1715 which read as follows:

p. 210. 2. *From your Manner of being made.*

p. 211. Part III. *The FORM.*

p. 212. Fourthly, *From the End for which they were made.*

211, l. 22. Figure. Eigure (in 1715).

213, l. 4. Place. Piace (in 1715).

214, Quotation. (From *Ars Poetica*, 434–5). *mero* was misprinted *mora* in 1715.

214, l. 22. Οἴνω Ἀ'λήθεια. Οἴνω Ἀ'ληθεῖα (in 1715).

216, Cross heading: *A dreadful . . . Bottles.* Period omitted after *Bottles* in 1715.

217, ll. 19–20. Original text reads: '. . . Stone speak, much a Bottle; which had this, more for the Horrour of . . .' an evident displacement of 'more' by the printer.

218, l. 15. and. aud (in 1715.)

218, Quotation. (From Ovid Met. i, 758). Badly misprinted in 1715 thus: *Pudæt hæc opprobria nobis eu diu potuisse,* etc.

226, l. 9. his Characters. this Characters (in 1715).

241, l. 31. raise. praise (in 1715).

243, l. 31. with. wih (in 1715).

264, l. 11. will otherwise. will, otherwise (in 1716); will otherwise (in 1732).

273, Title-page. Owing to an accident the comma after *CURLL* does not exactly reproduce the original.

281, l. 9. there. their (in 1716); there (in 1732).

308, l. 23. *Principles.* Period after *Principles* was misplaced after 'distilled' in 1st and 2nd edns.

311, l. 6. time. Full stop omitted after 'time' in 1st edn; restored in 2nd edn.

311, l. 28. seems. seem (in 1st edn); seems (in 2nd edn).

313, l. 15. of 'em. of e'm (in 1st and 2nd edns).

317, Title. Christian. Christiau (in 1732).

321, l. 3. unknown. unkown (in 1732).

THE
CRITICAL
SPECIMEN.

Ipsa ingens Arbos, faciemque simillima lauro;
Et si non Alium late jactaret odorem,
Laurus erat. ——— ——— ——— Virg.

LONDON:

Printed in the Year, 1711.

A

SPECIMEN

OF THE

PREFACE

WHEN I first resolv'd to write the Life of the *Renown'd* Rinaldo Furioso, Critick *of the Woful Countenance, my Inclinations naturally led me to* Blank Verse, *and to lay a Scheme for a Poem of the* Epick *kind; but I was soon brought off from such an Undertaking when I consider'd, that the* Critick's *Life was [made] up of such a Medly of Adventures, that though some of them might appear very Noble in the true* Sublime, *yet others were so indifferent that they would have made but a very odd Figure in that Dress: Another prevailing Argument against an* Epick *Poem was, that the* Criticks Extravagancies *could be reduc'd into no manner of Time, for his Whimsical Notions began from his Cradle, and have continued with him ever since.*

There are several Similies, *that are in great Reputation at this present, which are attributed to the Productions of his Youth; by which, it was conjectur'd by his Nurse, and some others of as sound Judgment, that, with his Years, he would arrive to be a famous Poet. 'Tis reported, that he was the first that compared the* Moon *to a* Green Cheese, *an* Ugly Fellow *to an* Owl

in an Ivy-Bush, *and introduced that general* Simile
now so much in Vogue amongst the Beau Monde, *as like,
as* any thing, *with several others that are now Exstant
in Conversation.*

Another Reason against the Epick Poem, *was, that
the* Critick's *Actions did not tend towards bringing
about one great Design; for it is manifest by several of
his Pranks, that he aimed at being both a* Critick *and a*
Poet; *and besides, I could not have raised him to any
Degree of Eminency in Either, without deviating from
the Truth.*

*I must confess, I should have been at very little Loss
for the Machinary of the Poem, and that Angels and
Devils might have been introduced with very little trouble: I had a Design to have made the Devil make his
first Appearance at the* Critick's *reading* Milton *back-
wards, which I concluded would have been a very natural Incident, and not have hauled him in by Head and
Shoulders. Upon my communicating this thought to a
Friend, I was easily persuaded that a Repetition of
some of his own Lines would have raised him altogether
as properly; upon which, I immediately made choice of
some for that purpose.*

I only mention this, to satisfie the Reader *that I had
some Thoughts of writing an* Epick Poem *upon this Subject: But I hope my Reasons against it, have fully convinced him that my digesting the* Critick's *Life in the
following manner, as is to be seen in the Contents of the
Chapters, will be most Advantagious for the* Critick,
and for the Diversion of all my Candid Readers.

*Before I alter'd my first Design, I had made two
Descriptions of the Morning, one of the Evening, ano-*

ther of Midnight; with a Simile, *and some other Sketches
which I resolv'd to* Embellish *when I finish'd the* Epick
Poem *I have been before speaking off. I hope the* Reader
will pardon my inserting the Simile, *being very loath to
lose so beautiful a* Fragment: *I would have introduc'd
it just before the* Critick *utter'd the ever Memorable
Sentence as is now related in the* 17th Chapter: *Having first describ'd him frowning and swelling with Anger and Resentment, as ready to burst with Passion. I
would have proceeded thus,*

> So on *Mæotis'* Marsh, (where Reeds and Rushes
> Hide the deceitful Ground, whose waving Heads
> Oft' bend to *Auster*'s blasts, or *Boreas'* Rage,
> The Haunt of the voracious *Stork* or *Bittern*,
> Where, or the *Crane*, Foe to *Pygmæan* Race,
> Or Ravenous *Corm'rants* shake their flabby Wings,
> And from soak'd Plumes disperse a briny Show'r,
> Or spread their feather'd Sails against the Beams,
> Or, of the Rising or *Meridian* Sun)
> *A baneful *Hunch-back'd Toad*, with look Maligne,
> Glares on some Traveller's unwary steps,
> Whether by Chance, or by Misfortune led
> To tread those dark unwholsome, misty Fens,
> Rage strait Collects his Venom all at once,
> And swells his bloated Corps to largest size.

I shall trouble the Reader *no farther with an Account of my first Design, but say something of my present Undertaking.*

*I am not without some Apprehensions of having this
Work taken out of my Hands, since a false* Cervantes,
and Counterfeit Bickerstaffs *have already endeavoured*

*to impose upon Mankind. But how far the True ones surpass the Impostors, I shall not insist upon; least some envious Critick should from thence infer that I by in*nuendo *was Haranguing in praise of my own Productions. I shall say only this, That if such Upstarts should arise, take the Advice of Dr.* Case, *which you will find at every Corner throughout the City*; READ, TRY, JUDGE, AND SPEAK AS YOU FIND.

Before I proceed farther, it is necessary that I say something of the different Kinds of Criticks, *range them in their several Orders, and speak to them seperately,* &c.

A

SPECIMEN

OF

A Treatise in *Folio*, to be printed by Subscription,

ENTITULED,

The Mirror of Criticisme:

OR,

The History of the Renown'd *Rinaldo Furioso*, Critick of the Woful Countenance.

With a further Comparison of the Renown'd *Rinaldo Furioso*, Critick of the Woful Countenance, and the valiant Restorer of Chivalry Don *Quixote de la Mancha*.

THIS Work containing *several New Discoveries, never made before*; and being of a very curious and uncommon Nature, will ('tis hop'd) deserve a particular encouragement from the Critical Part of the Town. It will be publish'd either by single Chapters, or in the whole, as the Majority of Subscribers shall please to Appoint; who are desir'd to pay half a Guinea down, and the other half when the Book is delivered. The Author gives Notice, that when his Subscriptions are full, he will (like most of his Contemporaries) begin the Work, or *at least Print a fair List of the Subscribers Names, Titles,* *and* Places *of* Abode, so curiously, and in so fair a Letter, that *no Reasonable Man shall grudge his Money for it.* He will in a short time give Information by an Advertisement in the *Spectator* where Subscriptions are to be taken in, being at present much divided in his Opinion, whether to prefer the every way excellent Mr. *Jacob Tonson,* Junior, or Mr. *Bernard Lintot* to be his Bookseller, for the latter of whom he has had a particular consideration since he received from his Honoured Friend *Isaac Bickerstaff,* Esq; the *Eulogium* of —* That Eminent and Worthy Citizen Mr. *Bernard Lintot.*

CHAPTER, 4th.

Of the Critick's *first Extravagance, How he took a* Hobby-Horse *for* Pegasus, *with some other Conceits, not unworthy* Attention, *being the shortest Chapter in the whole* Book.

Cervantes has been very Particular in the Description of Don *Quixote*'s Horse, 1. though I find, by his own Confession, that he has omitted several passages relating to the Adventures of that serviceable Creature, which *Cid Hamet Benengeli* thought very material to the better illustrating his History.

The *Don* was so cursedly pester'd with Enchanters, that he very often by the height of Imagination, or rather by the delusion of some envious Necromancers, mistook Appearances, so that, to his Sight, *Windmills* appeared *Briareuses,* and *Puppets* real Kings and Queens; but by all the Accounts I can

* *Vid.* Tatler, 160.

meet with, *Rosinante* seems to be a real Horse of Flesh and Bones, and not a wooden Machine endow'd with any hidden Magical Power. In this respect, I mean in the difference of their Horses, the *Critick*'s Extravagance, goes beyond the *Don*'s; for 'tis credibly Attested, that one Day, collecting all his Courage, He, his adventrous Leg with bold Essay, rais'd from the ground, and (Oh presumptuous Deed!) an *Hobby-Horse* bestrode, while the *Great Youth*, that rein'd *Bellerophon*, proud chaumping Steed, prompted Ambition, and his Breast inspir'd with Emulating Ardor; so have I often seen in *Bethlem College* a poor unhappy Mortal, whose turn'd Brains, or Pericranium crack'd or overladen with wild Ideas, which confus'dly jumble and shatter his disappointed Judgment, Uniting all his Force at once, with Looks that show high thoughts and daring Enterprise, bound o'er some slender Chip, or straw Minute. *The Mirror of Criticisme* being thus mounted without a Saddle, (for he scorn'd to make use of one of his Father's making) 2. thrice scamper'd o'er the Floor, whilst, as he scowr'd along, the Stick with sinuous Trace pursu'd, though ne'er to overtake his wandring steps. He fancy'd that he was now mounted on *Pegasus*, and that he had travelled several Leagues through the Air towards Mount *Parnassus*; during his Imaginary Flight, he was heard to repeat with great vehemence the following Rhapsody.

☞ *Fly* Pegasæan *Steed, thy Rider bear,*
To breath the Sweets of pure Parnassian *Air,*
Aloft I'm swiftly born, methinks I rise,

3. *And with my Head* Sublime *can reach the Sky.*
   Large Gulps of Aganippe'*s streams I'll draw,*
   And give to Modern Writers Classic *Law*;
   In Grecian Buskins *Tragedy shall Mourn,*
   And to its Ancient *Mirth the* Comic Sock *return.*

After he had utter'd the Preceeding Lines several
times with a thund'ring Voice, he put himself into
distorted Figures, and screw'd his Visage into New
Grimaces, crying aloud, *s'Death,* I'm 4 *Roscius,* I'm
Roscius, I'm *Roscius.* He travels at least once a Week
in this manner to make a Visit to the Muses. It happen'd, as he was one Day bestriding his Hobby-
Horse, to come into his Head that he had never read
in *Milton,* or any of *the Ancients,* that *Pegasus* wore
Bells; upon which, he in a very great rage tore the
Bells from his Hobby-Horse, wisely imagining *Pegasus* to be like a Millers Horse, that while he listned
to their gingling he slacken'd his Pace, and he has
rid him without *Bells* ever since.

Here it will be necessary to inform the Reader of
the *Criticks* Chimærical Notions of the *Muses.* He
always maintain'd that the *Muses* were a Company
of Book learn'd Country Wenches, that liv'd upon a
High Hill that reach'd above the Clouds, not unlike
the Peak of *Tenariff*; that they had very Hoarse
Voices, and had an utter Aversion to all kinds of Musick, that their Mien was Stiff, without the least mixture of the Stately or Janty, that though most of
them were lame, yet they always Scamper'd the
Plains like Rural Hoydens who on rustick Heel and
with uneven Hobling, frisk and bound o'er the Cham-

paign. He held further, that their Faces were home-
ly and without Ornament, that they were of a Braw-
ny Strong Complexion, that they understood the Art
of Flying, which they had communicated to himself
Milton, 5. and two or three others: that they were the
Inventers of the Dumb Bell, which is put in Motion
with much Labour, but makes no manner of *Musick*:
That they had great Skill in Opticks, and had instructed him to see faults in others, and Beautys in
himself that could be discover'd by no body else,
with some other Notable Inventions which will more
naturally imbellish some of the Following Chapters.

The Contents of the Chapters.

Chapter 1.

OF the Criticks Nativity, and how he was oblig'd to the Stars, not for the good fortune or
sense they gave him, but for the many *Sublime Similes* they supply'd him with.

Chapter 2.

Of his Education, Person, Parts, and *other inconsiderable Matters*; with some Reflections *very Critical
and Satyrical, but nothing to the Purpose.*

Chapter 3.

How after leaving the College, he generously de-
spis'd the *Narrow Soul'd Principles*, taught there, and
fell in with the *Modern, free and daring Principles* of
the Town, as favouring much more of *Publick Spirit*,
together with his *Private Reasons* for so doing.

Chapter 4.

Of the Criticks first Extravagance, How he took a *Hobby-Horse* for *Pegasus*, with some other conceits not unworthy Attention, being the shortest Chapter in the whole Book.

Chapter 5.

How the *Critick* was dub'd a Poet by a conceited frolicksome Country Lass call'd *Moria* which he fancy'd to be one of the *Muses*, with a dissertation upon the *Laurel*, the *Ivy* and *Bays*, and some other Matters very surprizing.

Chapter 6.

How the *Critick* read *Milton* Backward.

Chapter 7.

How he found out that a Minister's Cassock might make two pair of Breeches, and of his Printing a *Probation Sermon*, to make it Manifest that he was *out of* Holy Orders.

Chapter 8.

Of the *Criticks* excellent expedient not to be seen in Dirty Shoos, which was to be carried in a Chair.

Chapter 9.

How when some People were displeas'd at the shortness of his Coat, he made an ample satisfaction with the length of his Sword.

Chapter 10.

How he wrote a Dialogue, which he fancy'd to be a Comedy.

Chapter 1 1.

Of the Bombarding of *Gibraltar*, and how several of the Cheifs engaged in this dreadful enterprise were contrary to the Law of Arms, almost pelted to Death with *Apples* and *Orange-Peel*.

Chapter 1 2.

Of the *Criticks* mortal aversion to the *Catt-call*.

Chapter 1 3.

How the *Critick* was taken up for a *Plotter*, and his being discharg'd as not Guilty, upon a diligent search amongst all his Papers.

Chapter 1 4.

How he took it in his Head that he had made something like a Tragedy, and how C[*ibbe*]r the *Pantomine* read the First Page *all over*. Of the *Blind Critick who* judg'd at sight.

Chapter 1 5.

How C[*hristophe*]r R[*i*]ch, Esq; having perus'd the whole, intreated the Author with great Civility to acquaint him *whether it were one of your Tragedys or your Comedys?* and likewise by what Argument he induced C[*hristophe*]r R[*i*]ch, Esq; to believe it really was a Tragedy.

Chapter 1 6.

How by the *Wonderful force of Magick* he prevail'd with *one* Mr. W[*il*]ks to believe he might pass for an Honourable *Roman Senator*, and with one Mr. B[*oo*]th that he represented a *Roman Tyrant*, and possess'd several others with the like imaginations.

Chapter 17.

Of the Heinous and Unparalell'd Affront offer'd to the most perfect Tragedy since *Euripides*, and how, to the great dishonour of the Stage, and without the least regard to their illustrious Characters the aforesaid *Roman Tyrant* and others of very little inferior Dignity were surpris'd in a Brandy Shop, which occasioned that ever Memorable Sentence of the *Criticks. Immortal Gods, how can it be, that those who are Brandy Drinkers in the Morning, should become Noble Romans at Night!*

Chapter 18.

Of the Success of the *What d'ye call 'um* and the *Criticks Third Night.*

Chapter 19.

The Manner of his buying a pair of Breeches, and what they Cost him *besides Coach Hire*, with other particulars worthy Remark.

Chapter 20.

Of the Manner of Wearing his Breeches, with a short Essay to show that the most Natural Position of *Rolls for Stockings* is about ones Heels.

Chapter 21.

Of the Duel design'd to be fought on Horseback between the *Critick* and a certain *Colonel*, and how it was deferr'd by reason the *Critick* was not vers'd in the *Manage*, and could not procure a War Horse.

Chapter 22.

How the *Critick* fell into a swoon at hearing an

Opera and what he said at his Recovery. An Extract of his Dissertation against *Operas.*

Chapter 23.

A Discourse of the *Critick* concerning the exact *Contraction* and *Extension* of the *Muscles* of a True *Hypercritical* Countenance, the most learned manner of *Frowning,* as it were with judgment; together with the *whole Art of Staring.*

Chapter 24.

Of the Difficulties he found in attaining to a *C[la]p,* his Discourse with *Hippocrates,* and how at last he was enabled to get one.

Chapter 25.

How *Hippocrates* generously refus'd to take any Fees for the said *C[la]p.*

Chapter 26.

How he writ upon occasion (*vide Spect.* 47.) two good Lines, being the most wonderful and surprizing Adventure in the whole Book.

Chapter 27.

How the *Critick* ingeniously drew *Three Cherubims,* and several *Myriads* of *Subaltern Spirits* out of *Paradise,* which since enter'd into the service of my *L[or]d M[arlbr]o,* and how some of Satan's Angels deserted to the Duke of *Bavaria.*

Chapter 28.

Of the most *amazing Discovery* the *Critick* ever made, showing how and in what manner the *Soul* of a *Late King* was chang'd into a *Seraphim.**

* *See the Battle of* Ramellies, *or the* Power *of* Union, *a Poem.*

Chapter 29.

Of his Invention of a wonderful *Mustard Bowl* of a prodigious Size for the Players to make *Thunder* with, and the *Tremendous Effects* it had on the *Child* of an Eminent *Citizen.*

Chapter 30.

Of the near Resemblance of Mr. *D*[*ur*]*fy* and the *Critick,* both in their Persons and Writings, so that they were often taken one for the other.

Chapter 31.

How the *Critick* had Fourscore Guineas from a certain Nobleman for a Dedication; and how he made a Lady Miscarry at one of his Things that he call'd Tragedy's; with a Discourse upon *Æschylus,* or the *Power of Fustian.*

Chapter 32.

How the *Critick* was invited aboard a Ship at the *Buoy* and *Oar* by an *Officer of the Custom-House,* and how notwithstanding all his *Specious Complements,* he discovered that there was a Design to *Trapan him into* France.

Chapter 33.

The *Critick*'s Reasons for his Suspicion, showing the Extream desire of the *French King* to have him in the *Bastile,* because the sharpness of his *Satyr* (next to Dr. *Partridge*'s) had most provok'd that Monarch, and impair'd his Health more than all the Ill Success of his Armies.

Chapter 34.

A Contention in Civility and good Breeding be-

tween the Critick and a little Gentleman of *W*[*indso*]*r*
F[*ore*]*st*, in which the little Gentleman had some Advantage.

Chapter 35.

How, and what Year, Month, and Day, the Critick
is to dye, what Will he is to Make, and what dying
Words he shall utter, where, and by whom he is to
be buried, and what Funeral Orations and Elegies
will be made upon him, with his Epitaph a Prophecy, by the *True Individual* Isaac Bickerstaff, *Esq*;

N.B. *For the greater Beauty and Variety of the Impression, the Subscribers are desired to take Notice that the Vertues of the* Critick *are to
be printed in a very small neat* Elzevir *Character, and his Extravagancies in a Noble large Letter, on Royal Paper.*

To the Reader from the Bookseller.

B*Y* the Author's Leave *least I should give the Renown'd* Rinaldo
Furioso the Fatigue *of Playing the* Critick *upon this single Chapter,* I have employ'd *one of my Authors to make the following short Remarks.*

Remarks on the Foregoing Chapter.

* T HE Author has been very just in the Application of this
Simile, though he has not dealt so ingeniously with Mankind
as to own that he took the Hint from Mr. *Dennis*'s Critical and
Satyrical Reflections. *vid.* Crit. and Sat. Reflections. 1 *vide* Don
Quixote. 2 *Numero Deus impare gaudet* vid. Virg. 3 *Sublimi feriam
Sydera Vertice.* vid. Hor. ☞ The Author has made the *Critick*
Speak his *Rhapsody* in Rhime, which seems to deviate from his Character, but this, in my Opinion, wants no Excuse, since it was before
he had taken the Bells off his *Hobby-Horse.* 4 *Roscius* was a *Roman*
Player, *vid. Hor.* 5 Several Judicious *Criticks* of my Acquaintance
seem here to doubt the Matter of Fact, since it cannot be sufficiently
prov'd from any of his Writings, that he ever allow'd any Proficient
in this Art of Flying Except himself and *Milton.*

C

ADVERTISEMENT

THere is in the Press and will speedily be publish'd Two Disser-
tations, The first by the Reverend Dr. *B[ent]ly* proving from
Æsop's Fables that the Author of them was not *Crooked* but *Strait*,
The second by Mr. *Dennis* making it plain from the late *Essay* upon
Criticisme that the Author is by no means *Strait* but *Crooked*.

Price of this *Specimen* to all but Subscribers Two Pence. And for
the Encouragement of such well dispos'd Persons as will give it about
in Charity 20 *s. per* Hundred.

Contributions
to *The Spectator*
1711-1712

[*On the* DESIRE *of* DISTINCTION]

—— *Fulgente trahit constrictos Gloria curru*
Non minus ignotos generosis ——   Hor. Sat. 6.

IF we look abroad upon the great Multitude of
Mankind, and endeavour to trace out the Principles of Action in every Individual, it will, I
think, seem highly probable that Ambition runs
through the whole Species, and that every Man in
Proportion to the Vigour of his Complection is more
or less actuated by it. It is indeed no uncommon thing
to meet with Men, who, by the natural Bent of their
Inclinations, and without the Discipline of Philosophy, aspire not to the Heights of Power and Grandeur; who never set their Hearts upon a numerous
Train of Clients and Dependancies, nor other gay
Appendages of Greatness; who are contented with a
Competency, and will not molest their Tranquility
to gain an Abundance: But it is not therefore to be
concluded that such a Man is not ambitious; his Desires may have cut out another Channel, and determin'd him to other Pursuits; the Motive however may
be still the same; and in these Cases likewise the Man
may be equally pushed on with the Desire of Distinction.

Though the pure Consciousness of worthy Actions, abstracted from the Views of popular Applause,
be to a generous Mind an ample Reward, yet the Desire of Distinction was doubtless implanted in our
Natures as an additional Incentive to exert our selves
in virtuous Excellence.

This Passion indeed, like all others, is frequently perverted to evil and ignoble Purposes; so that we may account for many of the Excellencies and Follies of Life upon the same innate Principle, to wit, the Desire of being remarkable: For this as it has been differently cultivated by Education, Study, and Converse, will bring forth suitable Effects as it falls in with an[ingenuous]Disposition or a corrupt Mind; it does accordingly express it self in Acts of Magnanimity or selfish Cunning, as it meets with a good or a weak Understanding. As it has been employed in embellishing the Mind or adorning the Outside; it renders the Man eminently Praise-worthy or ridiculous. Ambition therefore is not to be confined only to one Passion or Pursuit; for as the same Humours in Constitutions otherwise different affect the Body after different Manners, so the same aspiring Principle within us sometimes breaks forth upon one Object, sometimes upon another.

It cannot be doubted but that there is as great a Desire of Glory in a Ring of Wrestlers or Cudgel-Players, as in any other more refined Competition for Superiority. No Man that could avoid it, would ever suffer his Head to be broken but out of a Principle of Honour; this is the secret Spring that pushes them forward, and the Superiority which they gain above the undistinguished Many, does more than repair those Wounds they have received in the Combat. 'Tis Mr. *Waller*'s Opinion, that *Julius Cæsar*, had he not been Master of the *Roman* Empire, would in all Probability have made an excellent Wrestler.

Great Julius *on the Mountains bred,*
A Flock perhaps or Herd had led;
He that the World subdued, had been
But the best Wrestler on the Green.

That he subdued the World, was owing to the Accidents of Art and Knowledge; had he not met with those Advantages, the same Sparks of Emulation would have kindled within him, and prompted him to distinguish himself in some Enterprize of a lower Nature. Since therefore no Man's Lot is so unalterably fixed in this Life, but that a thousand Accidents may either forward or disappoint his Advancement, it is, methinks, a pleasant and inoffensive Speculation, to consider a great Man as divested of all the adventitious Circumstances of Fortune, and to bring him down in one's Imagination to that low Station of Life, the Nature of which bears some distant Resemblance to that high one he is at present possessed of. Thus one may view him exercising in Miniature those Talents of Nature, which being drawn out by Education to their full Length, enable him for the Discharge of some important Employment. On the other Hand, one may raise uneducated Merit to such a Pitch of Greatness, as may seem equal to the possible Extent of his improved Capacity.

Thus Nature furnishes a Man with a general Appetite of Glory, Education determines it to this or that particular Object. The Desire of Distinction is not, I think, in any Instance more observable than in the Variety of Out-sides and new Appearances, which the Modish part of the World are oblig'd to provide, in order to make themselves remarkable; for any thing glaring and particular, either in Behaviour or Apparel, is known to have this good Effect, that it catches the Eye, and will not suffer you to pass over the Person so adorn'd without due notice and Observation. It has likewise, upon this Account, been frequently resented as a very great Slight, to leave any Gentleman out of a Lampoon or Satyr, who has as much right to be there as his Neighbour, because it supposes the Person not eminent enough to be taken notice of. To this passionate fondness for Distinction are owing various frolicksome and irregular Practices, as sallying out into Nocturnal Exploits, breaking of Windows, singing of Catches, beating the Watch, getting Drunk twice a Day, killing a great Number of Horses; with many other Enterprizes of the like fiery Nature: For certainly many a Man is more Rakish and Extravagant than he would willingly be, were there not others to look on and give their Approbation.

One very common, and at the same time the most absurd Ambition that ever shew'd it self in Humane Nature, is that which comes upon a Man with Experience and old Age, the Season when it might be expected he should be wisest; and therefore it cannot receive any of those lessening Circumstances which do, in some measure, excuse the disorderly Ferments of youthful Blood: I mean the passion for getting Money, exclusive of the Character of the Provident Father, the Affectionate Husband, or the Generous Friend. It may be remarked, for the Comfort of honest Poverty, that this Desire reigns most in those who

have but few good Qualities to recommend 'em. This
is a Weed that will grow in a barren Soil. Humanity,
Good Nature, and the Advantages of a Liberal Education, are incompatible with Avarice. 'Tis strange
to see how suddenly this abject Passion kills all the
noble Sentiments and generous Ambitions that adorn
Humane Nature; it renders the Man who is over-run
with it a peevish and cruel Master, a severe Parent,
an unsociable Husband, a distant and mistrustful
Friend. But it is more to the present Purpose to consider it as an absurd Passion of the Heart, rather than
as a vicious Affection of the Mind. As there are frequent Instances to be met with of a proud Humility,
so this Passion, contrary to most others affects Applause, by avoiding all Shew and Appearance; for this
reason it will not sometimes endure even the common
Decencies of Apparel. *A covetous Man will call himself poor, that you may sooth his Vanity by contradicting
him.* Love, and the Desire of Glory, as they are the
most natural, so they are capable of being refined into the most delicate and rational Passions. 'Tis true,
the wise Man who strikes out of the secret Paths of a
private Life for Honour and Dignity, allured by the
Splendor of a Court, and the unfelt Weight of publick Employment, whether he succeeds in his Attempts or no, usually comes near enough to this
painted Greatness to discern the Dawbing; he is then
desirous of extricating himself out of the Hurry of
Life, that he may pass away the Remainder of his
Days in Tranquility and Retirement.

It may be thought then but common Prudence in
a Man not to change a better State for a worse, nor

ever to quit that which he knows he shall take up
again with Pleasure; and yet if human Life be not a
little moved with the gentle Gales of Hopes and
Fears, there may be some Danger of its stagnating in
an unmanly Indolence and Security. It is a known
Story of *Domitian*, that after he had possessed himself of the *Roman* Empire his Desires turn'd upon
catching Flies. Active and Masculine Spirits in the
Vigour of Youth neither can nor ought to remain at
Rest: If they debar themselves from aiming at a noble Object, their Desires will move downwards, and
they will feel themselves actuated by some low and
abject Passion. Thus if you cut off the top Branches
of a Tree, and will not suffer it to grow any higher,
it will not therefore cease to grow, but will quickly
shoot out at the Bottom. The Man indeed who goes
into the World only with the narrow Views of Self-
Interest, who catches at the Applause of an idle Multitude, as he can find no solid Contentment at the
End of his Journey, so he deserves to meet with Dis-
appointments in his Way: But he who is actuated by
a nobler Principle, whose Mind is so far enlarged as
to take in the Prospect of his Country's Good, who
is enamour'd with that Praise which is one of the
fair Attendants of Virtue, and values not those Ac-
clamations which are not seconded by the impartial
Testimony of his own Mind; who repines not at the
low Station which Providence has at present allotted
him, but yet would willingly advance himself by justifiable Means to a more rising and advantageous
Ground; such a Man is warmed with a generous
Emulation; it is a virtuous Movement in him to wish

and to endeavour that his Power of doing Good may be equal to his Will.

The Man who is fitted out by Nature, and sent into the World with great Abilities, is capable of doing great Good or Mischief in it. It ought therefore to be the Care of Education to infuse into the untainted Youth early Notices of Justice and Honour, that so the possible Advantages of good Parts may not take an evil Turn, nor be perverted to base and unworthy Purposes. It is the Business of Religion and Philosophy not so much to extinguish our Passions, as to regulate and direct them to valuable well-chosen Objects: When these have pointed out to us which Course we may lawfully steer, 'tis no Harm to set out all our Sail; if the Storms and Tempests of Adversity should rise upon us, and not suffer us to make the Haven where we would be, it will however prove no small Consolation to us in these Circumstances, that we have neither mistaken our Course, nor fallen into Calamities of our own procuring.

Religion therefore (were we to consider it no further than as it interposes in the Affairs of this Life) is highly valuable, and worthy of great Veneration; as it settles the various Pretensions, and otherwise interfering Interests of mortal Men, and thereby consults the Harmony and Order of the great Community; as it gives a Man room to play his Part, and exert his Abilities; as it animates to Actions truly laudable in themselves, in their Effects beneficial to Society; as it inspires rational Ambitions, correct Love, and elegant Desires.

The Spectator, No. 224. Friday, November 16, 1711.

[*The* ADDITIONAL GRACES]

Illam, quicquid agit, quoquo Vestigia flectit,
Componit furtim, subsequiturque decor.

Tibull. L. 4.

AS no one can be said to enjoy Health, who is only not sick, without he feel within himself a lightsome and invigorating Principle, which will not suffer him to remain idle, but still spurs him on to Action; so in the Practice of every Virtue, there is some additional Grace required, to give a Claim of excelling in this or that particular Action. A Diamond may want polishing, though the Value be still intrinsically the same; and the same Good may be done with different Degrees of Lustre. No Man should be contented with himself that he barely does well, but he should perform every thing in the best and most becoming Manner that he is able.

Tully tells us, he wrote his Book of *Offices*, because there was no Time of Life in which some correspondent Duty might not be practis'd; nor is there a Duty without a certain Decency accompanying it, by which every Virtue 'tis joined to will seem to be doubled. Another may do the same thing, and yet the Action want that Air and Beauty which distinguish it from others; like that inimitable Sun-shine *Titian* is said to have diffus'd over his Landschapes; which denotes them his, and has been always unequall'd by any other Person.

There is no one Action in which this Quality I am speaking of will be more sensibly perceived, than in granting a Request, or doing an Office of Kindness. *Mummius*, by his Way of consenting to a Benefaction, shall make it lose its Name; while *Carus* doubles the Kindness and the Obligation: From the first the desir'd Request drops indeed at last, but from so doubtful a Brow, that the obliged has almost as much reason to resent the Manner of bestowing it, as to be thankful for the Favour it self. *Carus* invites with a pleasing Air, to give him an Opportunity of doing an Act of Humanity, meets the Petition half Way, and consents to a Request with a Countenance which proclaims the Satisfaction of his Mind in assisting the Distressed.

The Decency then that is to be observed in Liberality, seems to consist in its being performed with such Cheerfulness, as may express the godlike Pleasure is to be met with in obliging one's Fellow-Creatures; that may shew good Nature and Benevolence overflow'd, and do not, as in some Men, run upon the Tilt, and Taste of the Sediments of a grutching uncommunicative Disposition.

Since I have intimated that the greatest Decorum is to be preserved in the bestowing our good Offices, I will illustrate it a little by an Example drawn from private Life, which carries with it such a Profusion of Liberality, that it can be exceeded by nothing but the Humanity and good Nature which accompanies it. It is a Letter of *Pliny*'s, which I shall here translate, because the Action will best appear in its first Dress of Thought, without any foreign or ambitious Ornaments.

PLINY to *QUINTILIAN*.

'Tho' I am fully acquainted with the Contentment

and just Moderation of your Mind, and the Confor-
mity the Education you have given your Daughter
bears to your own Character; yet since she is suddenly to be married to a Person of Distinction, whose
Figure in the World makes it necessary for her to be
at a more than ordinary Expence in Cloaths and
Equipage suitable to her Husband's Quality; by
which, tho' her intrinsick Worth be not augmented,
yet will it receive both Ornament and Lustre: And
knowing your Estate to be as moderate as the Riches
of your Mind are abundant, I must challenge to my
self some Part of the Burthen; and as a Parent of your
Child, I present her with Twelve hundred and fifty
Crowns towards these Expences; which Sum had
been much larger, had I not feared the Smallness of
it would be the greatest Inducement with you to accept of it. Farewell.'

Thus should a Benefaction be done with a good
Grace, and shine in the strongest Point of Light; it
should not only answer all the Hopes and Exigen-
cies of the Receiver, but even out-run his Wishes:
'Tis this happy manner of Behaviour which adds
new Charms to it, and softens those Gifts of Art and
Nature, which otherwise would be rather distasteful
than agreeable. Without it Valour would degenerate
into Brutality, Learning into Pedantry, and the gen-
teelest Demeanour into Affectation. Even Religion
its self, unless Decency be the Handmaid which waits
upon her, is apt to make People appear guilty of
Sourness and ill Humour: But this shews Virtue in
her first original Form, adds a Comeliness to Reli-

gion, and gives its Professors the justest Title to the Beauty of Holiness. A Man fully instructed in this Art, may assume a thousand Shapes, and please in all: He may do a thousand Actions shall become none other but himself; not that the things themselves are different, but the manner of doing them.

If you examine each Feature by its self, *Aglaura* and *Calliclea* are equally handsome; but take them in the Whole, and you cannot suffer the Comparison: The one is full of numberless nameless Graces, the other of as many nameless Faults.

The Comeliness of Person and Decency of Behaviour, add infinite Weight to what is pronounc'd by any one. 'Tis the want of this that often makes the Rebukes and Advice of old rigid Persons of no Effect, and leave a Displeasure in the Minds of those they are directed to: But Youth and Beauty, if accompanied with a graceful and becoming Severity, is of mighty Force to raise, even in the most Profligate, a Sense of Shame. In *Milton* the Devil is never describ'd asham'd but once, and that at the Rebuke of a beauteous Angel.

> *So spake the Cherub, and his grave Rebuke*
> *Severe in youthful Beauty, added Grace*
> *Invincible: Abash'd the Devil stood,*
> *And felt how awful Goodness is, and saw*
> *Virtue in her own Shape how lovely! saw, and pin'd*
> *His Loss.*

The Care of doing nothing unbecoming has accompanied the greatest Minds to their last Moments: They avoided even an indecent Posture in the very

Article of Death. Thus *Cæsar* gather'd his Robe about him, that he might not fall in a Manner unbecoming of himself; and the greatest Concern that appeared in the Behaviour of *Lucretia*, when she stabb'd her self, was, that her Body should lie in an Attitude worthy the Mind which had inhabited it.

> ————*Ne non procumbat honeste*
> *Extrema hæc etiam cura, cadentis erat.*

> '*Twas her last Thought, How decently to fall.*

The Spectator, No. 292. Monday, February 4, 1712.

[*On* IDLENESS]

Libertas; quæ sera tamen respexit Inertem.

Virg. Ecl. 1.

Mr. SPECTATOR,

IF you ever read a Letter which is sent with the
more Pleasure for the Reality of its Complaints,
this may have Reason to hope for a favourable
Acceptance; and if Time be the most irretreivable
Loss, the Regrets which follow will be thought, I
hope, the most justifiable. The regaining of my Liberty from a long State of Indolence and Inactivity,
and the Desire of resisting the farther Encroachments
of Idleness, make me apply to you; and the Uneasiness with which I recollect the past Years, and the
Apprehensions with which I expect the Future, soon
determin'd me to it.

Idleness is so general a Distemper, that I cannot
but imagine a Speculation on this Subject will be of
universal use. There is hardly any one Person without some Allay of it; and thousands besides my self
spend more Time in an idle Uncertainty which to
begin first of two Affairs, than wou'd have been sufficient to have ended them both. The Occasion of
this seems to be the Want of some necessary Employment, to put the Spirits in Motion, and awaken them
out of their Lethargy. If I had less Leisure, I should
have more; for I should then find my Time distinguish'd into Portions, some for Business, and others
for the indulging of Pleasures: But now one Face of
Indolence over-spreads the whole, and I have no
Land-mark to direct my self by. Were one's Time a

little straitned by Business, like Water inclos'd in its Banks, it would have some determin'd Course; but unless it be put into some Channel it has no Current, but becomes a Deluge without either Use or Motion.

When *Scanderbeg* Prince of *Epirus* was dead, the *Turks*, who had but too often felt the Force of his Arm in the Battles he had won from them, imagin'd that by wearing a Piece of his Bones near their Heart, they shou'd be animated with a Vigour and Force like to that which inspir'd him when living. As I am like to be but of little use whilst I live, I am resolv'd to do what Good I can after my Decease; and have accordingly order'd my Bones to be dispos'd of in this Manner for the Good of my Countrymen, who are troubled with too exorbitant a Degree of Fire. All Fox-hunters upon wearing me, would in a short Time be brought to endure their Beds in a Morning, and perhaps even quit them with Regret at Ten: Instead of hurrying away to teaze a poor Animal, and run away from their own Thoughts, a Chair or a Chariot would be thought the most desirable Means of performing a Remove from one Place to another. I should be a Cure for the unnatural Desire of *John Trott* for Dancing, and a Specifick to lessen the Inclination Mrs. *Fidget* has to Motion, and cause her always to give her Approbation to the present Place she is in. In fine, no *Egyptian* Mummy was ever half so useful in Physick, as I should be to these feaverish Constitutions, to repress the violent Sallies of Youth, and give each Action its proper Weight and Repose.

I can stifle any violent Inclination, and oppose a

d

Torrent of Anger, or the Sollicitations of Revenge, with Success. But Indolence is a Stream which flows slowly on, but yet undermines the Foundation of every Virtue. A Vice of a more lively Nature were a more desirable Tyrant than this Rust of the Mind, which gives a Tincture of its Nature to every Action of ones Life. It were as little Hazard to be [tost] in a Storm, as to lay thus perpetually becalm'd: And it is to no Purpose to have within one the Seeds of a thousand good Qualities, if we want the Vigour and Resolution necessary for the exerting them. Death brings all Persons back to an Equality; and this Image of it, this Slumber of the Mind, leaves no Difference between the greatest Genius and the meanest Understanding: A Faculty of doing things remarkably praise-worthy thus conceal'd, is of no more use to the Owner, than a Heap of Gold to the Man who dares not use it.

To-Morrow is still the fatal Time when all is to be rectified: To-Morrow comes, it goes, and still I please my self with the Shadow, whilst I lose the Reality; unmindful that the present Time alone is ours, the future is yet unborn, and the past is dead, and can only live (as Parents in their Children) in the Actions it has produced.

The Time we live ought not to be computed by the Number of Years, but by the Use has been made of it; thus 'tis not the Extent of Ground, but the yearly Rent which gives the Value to the Estate. Wretched and thoughtless Creatures, in the only Place where Covetousness were a Virtue we turn Prodigals! Nothing lies upon our Hands with such

Uneasiness, nor has there been so many Devices for any one thing, as to make it slide away imperceptibly and to no Purpose. A Shilling shall be hoarded up with Care, whilst that which is above the Price of an Estate, is flung away with Disregard and Contempt. There is nothing now-a-days so much avoided, as a sollicitous Improvement of every Part of Time; 'tis a Report must be shun'd as one tenders the Name of a Wit and a fine Genius, and as one fears the dreadful Character of a laborious Plodder: But notwithstanding this, the greatest Wits any Age has produced thought far otherwise; for who can think either *Socrates* or *Demosthenes* lost any Reputation, by their continual Pains both in overcoming the Defects and improving the Gifts of Nature. All are acquainted with the Labour and Assiduity with which *Tully* acquired his Eloquence. *Seneca* in his Letters to *Lucelius* assures him, there was not a Day in which he did not either write something, or read and epitomize some good Author; and I remember *Pliny* in one of his Letters, where he gives an Account of the various Methods he used to fill up every Vacancy of Time, after several Imployments, which he enumerates; Sometimes, says he, I hunt; but even then I carry with me a Pocket-Book, that whilst my Servants are busied in disposing of the Nets and other Matters, I may be employed in something that may be useful to me in my Studies; and that if I miss of my Game, I may at least bring home some of my own Thoughts with me, and not have the Mortification of having caught nothing all Day.

Thus, Sir, you see how many Examples I recall to

Mind, and what Arguments I use with my self to regain my Liberty: But as I am afraid 'tis no ordinary Perswasion that will be of Service, I shall expect your Thoughts on this Subject with the greatest Impatience, especially since the Good will not be confined to me alone, but will be of universal Use. For there is no Hopes of Amendment where Men are pleased with their Ruin, and whilst they think Laziness is a desirable Character: Whether it be that they like the State it self, or that they think it gives them a new Lustre when they do exert themselves, seemingly to be able to do that without Labour and Application, which others attain to but with the greatest Diligence. I am,

SIR,

Your most obliged humble Servant,

Samuel Slack.

The Spectator. No. 316.   Monday, March 3, 1712.

[*On* AFFECTATION]

Continuo has leges æternaque fœdera certis
Imposuit natura locis.   Virg.

NATURE does nothing in vain; the Creator of the Universe has appointed every thing to a certain Use and Purpose, and determined it to a settled Course and Sphere of Action, from which, if it in the least deviates, it becomes unfit to answer those Ends for which it was designed. In like Manner is it in the Dispositions of Society, the civil Oeconomy is formed in a Chain as well as the natural; and in either Case the Breach but of one Link puts the Whole into some Disorder. It is, I think, pretty plain, that most of the Absurdity and Redicule we meet with in the World, is generally owing to the impertinent Affectation of excelling in Characters Men are not fit for, and for which Nature never designed them.

Every Man has one or more Qualities which may make him useful both to himself and others: Nature never fails of pointing them out, and while the Infant continues under her Guardianship, she brings him on in his Way, and then offers herself for a Guide in what remains of the Journey; if he proceeds in that Course, he can hardly miscarry: Nature makes good her Engagements; for as she never promises what she is not able to perform, so she never fails of performing what she promises. But the Misfortune is, Men despise what they may be Masters of, and affect what they are not fit for; they reckon themselves already

possess'd of what their Genius inclined them to, and
so bend all their Ambition to excell in what is out of
their Reach: Thus they destroy the Use of their natural Talents, in the same Manner as covetous Men
do their Quiet and Repose; they can enjoy no Satisfaction in what they have, because of the absurd Inclination they are possessed with for what they have
not.

Cleanthes had good Sense, a great Memory, and a
Constitution capable of the closest Application: In a
Word, there was no Profession in which *Cleanthes*
might not have made a very good Figure; but this
wont satisfy him, he takes up an unaccountable
Fondness for the Character of a fine Gentleman; all
his Thoughts are bent upon this, instead of attending
a Dissection, frequenting the Courts of Justice, or
studying the Fathers. *Cleanthes* reads Plays, dances,
dresses, and spends his Time in Drawing-rooms, instead of being a good Lawyer, Divine, or Physician;
Cleanthes is a downright Coxcomb, and will remain
to all that knew him a contemptible Example of Talents misapplied. It is to this Affectation the World
owes its whole Race of Coxcombs: Nature in her
whole Drama never drew such a Part; she has sometimes made a Fool, but a Coxcomb is always of a Man's
own making, by applying his Talents otherwise than
Nature designed, who ever bears an high Resentment
for being put out of her Course, and never fails of
taking her Revenge on those that do so. Opposing
her Tendency in the Application of a Man's Parts,
has the same Success as declining from her Course in
the Production of Vegetables; by the Assistance of

Art and an hot Bed, we may possibly extort an unwilling Plant, or an untimely Sallad; but how weak,
how tasteless and insipid? Just as insipid as the Poetry
of *Valerio*: *Valerio* had an universal Character, was
genteel, had Learning, thought justly, spoke correctly; 'twas believed there was nothing in which
Valerio did not excell; and 'twas so far true, that
there was but one; *Valerio* had no Genius for Poetry,
yet he's resolved to be a Poet; he writes Verses, and
takes great Pains to convince the Town, that *Valerio*
is not that extraordinary Person he was taken for.

If Men would be content to graft upon Nature,
and assist her Operations, what mighty Effects might
we expect? *Tully* would not stand so much alone in
Oratory, *Virgil* in Poetry, or *Cæsar* in War. To build
upon Nature, is laying the Foundation upon a Rock;
every thing disposes its self into Order as it were of
Course, and the whole Work is half done as soon as
undertaken. *Cicero*'s Genius inclined him to Oratory, *Virgil*'s to follow the Train of the Muses; they
piously obeyed the Admonition, and were rewarded.
Had *Virgil* attended the Bar, his modest and ingenuous Virtue would surely have made but a very indifferent Figure; and *Tully*'s declamatory Inclination
would have been as useless in Poetry. Nature, if left
to her self, leads us on in the best Course, but will do
nothing by Compulsion and Constraint; and if we
are not satisfied to go her Way, we are always the
greatest Sufferers by it.

Wherever Nature designs a Production, she always disposes Seeds proper for it, which are as absolutely necessary to the Formation of any moral or

intellectual Excellence, as they are to the Being and
Growth of Plants; and I know not by what Fate and
Folly it is, that Men are taught not to reckon him
equally absurd that will write Verses in Spite of Nature, with that Gardiner that should undertake to
raise a Junquil or Tulip without the Help of their
respective Seeds.

As there is no good or bad Quality that does not
affect both Sexes, so it is not to be imagined but the
fair Sex must have suffered by an Affectation of this
Nature, at least as much as the other. The ill Effect
of it is in none so conspicuous as in the two opposite
Characters of *Cælia* and *Iras*; *Cælia* has all the
Charms of Person, together with an abundant Sweetness of Nature, but wants Wit, and has a very ill
Voice; *Iras* is ugly and ungenteel, but has Wit and
good Sense: If *Cælia* would be silent, her Beholders
would adore her; if *Iras* would talk, her Hearers
would admire her; but *Cælia*'s Tongue runs inces-
santly, while *Iras* gives herself silent Airs and soft
Languors; so that 'tis difficult to perswade ones self
that *Cælia* has Beauty, and *Iras* Wit: Each neglects
her own Excellence, and is ambitious of the other's
Character; *Iras* would be thought to have as much
Beauty as *Cælia*, and *Cælia* as much Wit as *Iras*.

The great Misfortune of this Affectation is, that
Men not only lose a good Quality, but also contract
a bad one: They not only are unfit for what they
were designed, but they assign themselves to what
they are not fit for; and instead of making a very
good Figure one Way, make a very ridiculous one
another. If *Semanthe* would have been satisfied with

her natural Complexion, she might still have been celebrated by the Name of the Olive Beauty; but *Semanthe* has taken up an Affectation to White and Red, and is now distinguish'd by the Character of the Lady that paints so well. In a Word, could the World be reform'd to the Obedience of that fam'd Dictate, *Follow Nature*, which the Oracle of *Delphos* pronounc'd to *Cicero* when he consulted what Course of Studies he should pursue, we should see almost every Man as eminent in his proper Sphere as *Tully* was in his, and should in a very short Time find Impertinence and Affectation banish'd from among the Women, and Coxcombs and false Characters from among the Men. For my Part, I could never consider this preposterous Repugnancy to Nature any otherwise, than not only as the greatest Folly, but also one of the most heinous Crimes, since it is a direct Opposition to the Disposition of Providence, and, (as *Tully* expresses it) like the Sin of the Giants, an actual Rebellion against Heaven.

The Spectator. No. 404.   Friday, June 13, 1712.

[*On a* CITY *and* COUNTRY LIFE]

Dear Sir,

YOU have obliged me with a very kind Letter; by which I find you shift the Scene of your Life from the Town to the Country, and enjoy that mixt State which wise Men both delight in, and are qualified for. Methinks most of the Philosophers and Moralists have run too much into Extremes in praising entirely either Solitude or publick Life; in the former Men generally grow useless by too much Rest, and in the latter are destroy'd by too much Precipitation: as Waters lying still, putrify and are good for nothing; and running violently on, do but the more Mischief in their Passage to others, and are swallow'd up and lost the sooner themselves. Those who, like you, can make themselves useful to all States, should be like gentle Streams, that not only glide through lonely Vales and Forests amidst the Flocks and Shepherds, but visit populous Towns in their Course, and are at once of Ornament and Service to them. But there is another sort of People who seem design'd for Solitude, those I mean who have more to hide than to shew: As for my own Part, I am one of those of whom *Seneca* says, *Tam Umbratiles sunt, ut putent in turbido esse quicquid in luce est.* Some Men, like Pictures, are fitter for a Corner than a full Light; and I believe such as have a natural Bent to Solitude, are like Waters which may be forc'd into Fountains, and exalted to a great Height, may make a much nobler Figure and a much louder Noise, but after all run more smoothly, equally, and plentifully, in their own natural Course upon the Ground. The Consideration of this would make me very well contented with the Possession only of that Quiet which *Cowley* calls the Companion of Obscurity; but whoever has the Muses too for his Companions, can never be idle enough to be uneasy. Thus, Sir, you see I would flatter my self into a good Opinion of my own Way of living: *Plutarch* just now told me, that 'tis in humane Life as in a Game at Tables, one may wish he had the highest Cast, but if his Chance be otherwise, he is e'en to play it as well as he can, and make the best of it.

I am,

SIR,

Your most obliged,

and most humble Servant.

The Spectator. No. 406.   Monday, June 16, 1712.

[*On* REASON *and* PASSION]

*Decet affeɛus animi neque se nimium erigere, nec sub-
jacere serviliter.*   Tull. de Finibus.

Mr. SPECTATOR,

I HAVE always been a very great Lover of your
Speculations, as well in Regard to the Subjeɛt,
as to your Manner of treating it. Humane Nature I always thought the most useful Objeɛt of humane Reason, and to make the Consideration of it
pleasant and entertaining, I always thought the best
Employment of humane Wit: Other Parts of Philosophy may perhaps make us wiser, but this not only
answers that End, but makes us better too. Hence it
was that the Oracle pronounced *Socrates* the wisest of
all Men living, because he judiciously made Choice
of humane Nature for the Objeɛt of his Thoughts;
an Enquiry into which as much exceeds all other
Learning, as it is of more Consequence to adjust the
true Nature and Measures of Right and Wrong, than
to settle the Distance of the Planets, and compute the
Times of their Circumvolutions.

One good Effeɛt that will immediately arise from
a near Observation of humane Nature, is, that we
shall cease to wonder at those Aɛtions which Men
are used to reckon wholly unaccountable; for as nothing is produced without a Cause, so by observing
the Nature and Course of the Passions, we shall be
able to trace every Aɛtion from its first Conception
to its Death: We shall no more admire at the Proceedings of *Catiline* or *Tiberius,* when we know the

one was actuated by a cruel Jealousy, the other by a furious Ambition; for the Actions of Men follow their Passions as naturally as Light does Heat, or as any other Effect flows from its Cause; Reason must be employed in adjusting the Passions, but they must ever remain the Principles of Action.

The strange and absurd Variety that is so apparent in Mens Actions, shews plainly they can never proceed immediately from Reason; so pure a Fountain emits no such troubled Waters: They must necessarily arise from the Passions, which are to the Mind as the Winds to a Ship, they only can move it, and they too often destroy it; if fair and gentle they guide it into the Harbour; if contrary and furious they overset it in the Waves: In the same Manner is the Mind assisted or endangered by the Passions; Reason must then take the Place of Pilot, and can never fail of securing her Charge if she be not wanting to her self: The Strength of the Passions will never be accepted as an Excuse for complying with them; they were designed for Subjection, and if a Man suffers them to get the upper Hand, he then betrays the Liberty of his own Soul.

As Nature has framed the several Species of Beings as it were in a Chain, so Man seems to be placed as the middle Link between Angels and Brutes: Hence he participates both of Flesh and Spirit by an admirable Tie, which in him occasions perpetual War of Passions; and as a Man inclines to the angelick or brute Part of his Constitution, he is then denominated good or bad, virtuous or wicked; if Love, Mercy, and good Nature prevail, they speak him of the

Angel; if Hatred, Cruelty, and Envy predominate, they declare his Kindred to the Brute. Hence it was that some of the Ancients imagined, that as Men in this Life inclined more to the Angel or the Brute, so after their Death they should transmigrate into the one or the other; and it would be no unpleasant Notion to consider the several Species of Brutes, into which we may imagine that Tyrants, Misers, the Proud, Malicious, and Ill-natured might be changed.

As a Consequence of this Original, all Passions are in all Men, but all appear not in all; Constitution, Education, Custom of the Country, Reason, and the like Causes, may improve or abate the Strength of them, but still the Seeds remain, which are ever ready to sprout forth upon the least Encouragement. I have heard a Story of a good religious Man, who, having been bred with the Milk of a Goat, was very modest in Publick by a careful Reflection he made on his Actions, but he frequently had an Hour in Secret, wherein he had his Frisks and Capers; and if we had an Opportunity of examining the Retirement of the strictest Philosophers, no Doubt but we should find perpetual Returns of those Passions they so artfully conceal from the Publick. I remember *Matchiavel* observes, that every State should entertain a perpetual Jealousy of its Neighbours, that so it should never be unprovided when an Emergency happens; in like Manner should the Reason be perpetually on its Guard against the Passions, and never suffer them to carry on any Design that may be destructive of its Security; yet at the same Time it must be careful, that it don't so far break their Strength as to render

them contemptible, and consequently it self unguarded.

The Understanding being of its self too slow and
lazy to exert it self into Action, it's necessary it should
be put in Motion by the gentle Gales of the Passions,
which may preserve it from stagnating and Corruption; for they are as necessary to the Health of the
Mind, as the Circulation of the animal Spirits is to
the Health of the Body; they keep it in Life, and
Strength, and Vigour; nor is it possible for the Mind
to perform its Offices without their Assistance: These
Motions are given us with our being, they are little
Spirits that are born and dye with us; to some they
are mild, easy, and gentle, to others wayward and
unruly, yet never too strong for the Reins of Reason
and the Guidance of Judgment.

We may generally observe a pretty nice Proportion between the Strength of Reason and Passion;
the greatest Genius's have commonly the strongest
Affections, as on the other Hand, the weaker Under-
standings have generally the weaker Passions; and 'tis
fit the Fury of the Coursers should not be too great
for the Strength of the Charioteer. Young Men
whose Passions are not a little unruly, give small
Hopes of their ever being considerable; the Fire of
Youth will of Course abate, and is a Fault, if it be a
Fault, that mends every Day; but surely unless a
Man has Fire in Youth, he can hardly have Warmth
in Old age. We must therefore be very cautious, least
while we think to regulate the Passions, we should
quite extinguish them, which is putting out the Light
of the Soul; for to be without Passion, or to be hur-

ried away with it, makes a Man equally blind. The extraordinary Severity used in most of our Schools has this fatal Effect, it breaks the Spring of the Mind, and most certainly destroys more good Genius's than it can possibly improve. And surely 'tis a mighty Mistake that the Passions should be so intirely subdued; for little Irregularities are sometimes not only to be born with, but to be cultivated too, since they are frequently attended with the greatest Perfections. All great Genius's have Faults mixed with their Virtues, and resemble the flaming Bush which has Thorns among Lights.

Since therefore the Passions are the Principles of humane Actions, we must endeavour to manage them so as to retain their Vigour, yet keep them under strict Command; we must govern them rather like free Subjects than Slaves, least while we intend to make them obedient, they become abject, and unfit for those great Purposes to which they were designed. For my Part I must confess, I could never have any Regard to that Sect of Philosophers, who so much insisted upon an absolute Indifference and Vacancy from all Passion; for it seems to me a thing very inconsistent for a Man to divest himself of Humanity, in order to acquire Tranquility of Mind, and to eradicate the very Principles of Action, because it's possible they may produce ill Effects.

I am,
SIR,
Your affectionate Admirer,
T. B.

The Spectator. No. 408. Wednesday, June 18, 1712.

[*A* DREAM *of the* SEASONS]

Frigora mitescunt Zephyris, Ver proterit Æstas
Interitura, simul
Pomifer Autumnus fruges effuderit, & mox
Bruma recurrit iners.   Hor.

Mr. SPECTATOR,

THERE is hardly any thing gives me a more
sensible Delight, than the Enjoyment of a
cool still Evening after the Uneasiness of a
hot sultry Day. Such a one I pass'd not long ago,
which made me rejoyce when the Hour was come
for the Sun to set, that I might enjoy the Freshness
of the Evening in my Garden, which then affords
me the pleasantest Hours I pass in the whole Four
and twenty. I immediately rose from my Couch, and
went down into it. You descend at first by twelve
Stone Steps into a large Square divided into four
Grass-plots, in each of which is a Statue of white
Marble. This is separated from a large Parterre by a
low Wall, and from thence, thro' a Pair of Iron Gates,
you are led into a long broad Walk of the finest
Turf, set on each Side with tall Yews, and on either
Hand border'd by a Canal, which on the Right di-
vides the Walk from a Wilderness parted into Variety
of Allies and Arbours, and on the Left from a kind
of Amphitheatre, which is the Receptacle of a great
Number of Oranges and Myrtles. The Moon shone
bright, and seem'd then most agreeably to supply the
Place of the Sun, obliging me with as much Light as
was necessary to discover a thousand pleasing Objects, and at the same Time divested of all Power of

e

Heat. The Reflection of it in the Water, the Fanning
of the Wind rustling on the Leaves, the Singing of
the Thrush and Nightingale, and the Coolness of the
Walks, all conspired to make me lay aside all displeasing Thoughts, and brought me into such a Tranquility of Mind, as is I believe the next Happiness to
that of hereafter. In this sweet Retirement I naturally fell into the Repetition of some Lines out of a
Poem of *Milton*'s, which he entitles *Il Penseroso*, the
Ideas of which were exquisitely suited to my present
Wandrings of Thought.

> *Sweet Bird! that shun'st the Noise of Folly,*
> *Most musical! most melancholly!*
> *Thee Chauntress, oft the Woods among,*
> *I wooe to hear thy Evening Song;*
> *And missing thee, I walk unseen*
> *On the dry, smooth-shaven Green,*
> *To behold the wandring Moon,*
> *Riding near her highest Noon,*
> *Like one that hath been led astray,*
> *Thro' the Heav'ns wide pathless Way,*
> *And oft, as if her Head she bow'd,*
> *Stooping thro' a fleecy Cloud.*
>
> *Then let some strange mysterious Dream,*
> *Wave with his Wings in airy Stream,*
> *Of lively Portraiture display'd,*
> *Softly on my Eyelids laid;*
> *And as I wake, sweet Musick breathe*
> *Above, about, or underneath;*
> *Sent by Spirits to Mortals Good,*
> *Or th' unseen Genius of the Wood.*

I reflected then upon the sweet Vicissitudes of
Night and Day, on the charming Disposition of the
Seasons, and their Return again in a perpetual Circle; and oh! said I, that I could from these my declining Years, return again to my first Spring of
Youth and Vigour; but that alas! is impossible: All
that remains within my Power, is to soften the Inconveniencies I feel, with an easy contented Mind,
and the Enjoyment of such Delights as this Solitude
affords me. In this Thought I sate me down on a
Bank of Flowers and dropt into a Slumber, which
whether it were the Effect of Fumes and Vapours, or
my present Thoughts, I know not; but methought
the Genius of the Garden stood before me, and introduc'd into the Walk where I lay this Drama and
different Scenes of the Revolution of the Year, which
whilst I then saw, even in my Dream, I resolv'd to
write down, and send to the SPECTATOR.

The first Person whom I saw advancing towards
me, was a Youth of a most beautiful Air and Shape,
tho' he seem'd not yet arriv'd at that exact Proportion and Symmetry of Parts which a little more Time
wou'd have given him; but however, there was such
a Bloom in his Countenance, such Satisfaction and
Joy, that I thought it the most desirable Form that I
had ever seen. He was cloath'd in a flowing Mantle
of green Silk, interwoven with Flowers: He had a
Chaplet of Roses on his Head, and a *Narcissus* in his
Hand; Primroses and Violets sprang up under his
Feet, and all Nature was cheer'd at his Approach.
Flora was on one Hand and *Vertumnus* on the other
in a Robe of changeable Silk. After this I was sur-

priz'd to see the Moon-beams reflected with a sudden glare from Armour, and to see a Man compleatly arm'd advancing with his Sword drawn. I was soon inform'd by the Genius it was *Mars*, who had long usurp'd a Place among the Attendants of the *Spring*. He made Way for a softer Appearance, it was *Venus*, without any Ornament but her own Beauties, not so much as her own Cestus, with which she had incompass'd a Globe, which she held in her right Hand, and in her left she had a Sceptre of Gold. After her followed the Graces with their Arms intwined within one another, their Girdles were loosed, and they moved on to the Sound of soft Musick, striking the Ground alternately with their Feet: Then came up the three Months which belong to this Season. As *March* advanced towards me, there was methought in his Look a louring Roughness, which ill befitted a Month which was rank'd in so soft a Season; but as he came forwards his Features became insensibly more mild and gentle: He smooth'd his Brow and look'd with so sweet a Countenance that I could not but lament his Departure, though he made way for *April*. He appear'd in the greatest Gayety imaginable, and had a thousand Pleasures to attend him: His Look was frequently clouded, but immediately return'd to its first Composure, and remain'd fix'd in a Smile. Then came *May* attended by *Cupid*, with his Bow strung, and in a Posture to let fly an Arrow: As he pass'd by methought I heard a confused Noise of soft Complaints, gentle Extasies, and tender Sighs of Lovers; Vows of Constancy, and as many Complainings of Perfidiousness; all which the Winds wafted away assoon as they had reached my Hearing. After these I saw a Man advance in the full Prime and Vigor of his Age, his Complexion was sanguine and ruddy, his Hair black, and fell down in beautiful Ringlets not beneath his Shoulders, a Mantle of hair-colour'd Silk hung loosely upon him: He advanc'd with a hasty Step after the *Spring*, and sought out the Shade and cool Fountains which plaid in the Garden. He was particularly well pleas'd when a Troop of *Zephyrs* fann'd him with their Wings: He had two Companions who walk'd on each Side, that made him appear the most agreeable, the one was *Aurora* with Fingers of Roses, and her Feet dewy, attir'd in grey: The other was *Vesper* in a Robe of Azure beset with Drops of Gold, whose Breath he caught whilst it pass'd over a Bundle of Honey-Suckles and Tube-roses which he held in his Hand. *Pan* and *Ceres* followed them with four Reapers, who danced a Mor-rice to the Sound of Oaten Pipes and Cymbals. Then came the attendant Months, *June* retain'd still some small Likeness of the *Spring*; but the other two seem'd to step with a less vigorous Tread, especially *August*, who seem'd almost to faint whilst for half the Steps he took the Dog-Star levell'd his Rays full at his Head: They pass'd on and made Way for a Person that seemed to bend a little under the Weight of Years; his Beard and Hair, which were full grown, were compos'd of an equal Number of black and grey; he wore a Robe which he had girt round him of a yellowish Cast, not unlike the Colour of fallen Leaves, which he walk'd upon. I thought he hardly made Amends for expelling the foregoing Scene by the large Quantity of Fruits which he bore in his Hands. *Plenty* walk'd by his Side with an healthy fresh Countenance, pouring out from an Horn all the various Product of the Year. *Pomona* followed with a Glass of Cyder in her Hand, with *Bacchus* in a Chariot drawn by Tygres, accompanied by a whole Troop of Satyrs, Fauns, and Sylvans. *September*, who came next, seemed in his Looks to promise a new *Spring*, and wore the Livery of those Months. The succeeding Month was all soil'd with the Juice of Grapes, as if he had just come from the Wine-Press. *November*, though he was in this Division, yet by the many Stops he made seem'd rather inclin'd to the *Winter*, which follow'd close at his Heels: He advanced in the Shape of an old Man in the Extremity of Age: The Hair he had was so very white it seem'd a real Snow; his Eyes were red and piercing, and his Beard hung with a great Quantity of Icicles: He was wrap'd up in Furrs, but yet so pinch'd with excess of Cold, that his Limbs were all contracted and his Body bent to the Ground, so that he could not have supported himself had it not been for *Comus* the God of Revels, and *Necessity* the Mother of Fate, who sustain'd him on each Side. The Shape and Mantle of *Comus* was one of the things that most surpriz'd me; as he advanc'd towards me his Countenance seem'd the most desirable I had ever seen: On the fore Part of his Mantle was pictur'd Joy, Delight, and Satisfaction, with a thousand Emblems of Merriment, and Jests with Faces looking two Ways at once; but as he pass'd from me I was amaz'd at a Shape so little correspondent to his Face: His Head was bald, and all the rest of his Limbs appear'd old and deformed. On the hinder Part of his Mantle was represented Murder, with dishevel'd Hair and a Dagger all bloody, Anger in a Robe of Scarlet, and Suspicion squinting with both Eyes; but above all the most conspicuous was the Battle of the *Lapithæ* and the *Centaurs*. I detested so hideous a Shape and turned my Eyes upon *Saturn*, who was stealing away behind him with a Scythe in one Hand and an Hour-Glass in t'other unobserv'd. Behind *Necessity* was *Vesta* the Goddess of Fire, with a Lamp which was perpetually supply'd with Oyl, and whose Flame was eternal. She cheer'd the rugged brow of *Necessity*, and warm'd her so far as almost to make her assume the Features and Likeness of *Choice*. *December, January* and *February*, pass'd on after the rest all in Furrs; there was little Distinction to be made amongst them, and they were only more or less displeasing as they discover'd more or less Haste towards the grateful Return of *Spring*.

The Spectator, No. 425.   Tuesday, July 8, 1712.

[PROPOSALS *for* NEWS PAPERS]

I.

Mr. SPECTATOR,

YOU must have observed, that Men who frequent Coffee-houses, and delight in News, are
pleased with every thing that is Matter of Fact,
so it be what they have not heard before. A Victory,
or a Defeat, are equally agreeable to them. The shut-
ting of a Cardinal's Mouth pleases them one Post,
and the opening of it another. They are glad to hear
the *French* Court is removed to *Marli*, and are afterwards as much delighted with its Return to *Versailles*.
They read the Advertisements with the same Curiosity as the Articles of Publick News; and are as pleased to hear of a Pye-bald Horse that is stray'd out of a
Field near *Islington*, as of a whole Troop that has
been engaged in any Foreign Adventure. In short,
they have a Relish for every thing that is News, let
the matter of it be what it will; or to speak more
properly, they are Men of a Voracious Appetite, but
no Taste. Now, Sir, since the great Fountain of
News, I mean the War, is very near being dried up;
and since these Gentlemen have contracted such an
inextinguishable Thirst after it; I have taken their
Case and my own into Consideration, and have
thought of a Project which may turn to the Advantage of us both. I have Thoughts of Publishing a
daily Paper, which shall comprehend in it all the
most remarkable Occurrences that pass in every little
Town, Village and Hamlet, that lie within ten Miles
of *London*, or in other Words, within the Verge of the

Penny-Post. I have pitched upon this Scene of Intelligence for two Reasons; first, because the Carriage of Letters will be very cheap; and secondly, because I may receive them every Day. By this means my Readers will have their News fresh and fresh, and many worthy Citizens, who cannot Sleep with any Satisfaction at present, for want of being informed how the World goes, may go to Bed contentedly, it being my Design to put out my Paper every Night at nine a Clock precisely. I have already established Correspondencies in these several Places, and received very good Intelligence.

By my last Advices from *Knights-bridge* I hear that a Horse was clapped into the Pound on the third Instant, and that he was not released when the Letters came away.

We are inform'd from *Pankridge*, that a dozen Weddings were lately celebrated in the Mother Church of that Place, but are referred to their next Letters for the Names of the Parties concerned.

Letters from *Brompton* advise, That the Widow *Blight* had received several Visits from *John Milldew* which affords great matter of Speculation in those Parts.

By a Fisherman which lately touched at *Hammersmith*, there is Advice from *Putney*, that a certain Person well known in that Place, is like to lose his Election for Church-warden; but this being Boat News, we cannot give entire Credit to it.

Letters from *Paddington* bring little more, than that *William Squeak*, the Sow-gelder, passed through that Place the 5th Instant.

They advise from *Fulham*, that things remained there in the same State they were. They had Intelligence, just as the Letters came away, of a Tub of excellent Ale just set abroach at *Parsons Green*; but this wanted Confirmation.

I have here, Sir, given you a Specimen of the News with which I intend to entertain the Town, and which, when drawn up regularly in the form of a News Paper, will, I doubt not, be very acceptable to many of those Publick-Spirited Readers, who take more delight in acquainting themselves with other Peoples Business than their own. I hope a Paper of this kind, which lets us know what is done near home, may be more useful to us, than those which are filled with Advices from *Zug* and *Bender*, and make some Amends for that Dearth of Intelligence, which we may justly apprehend from times of Peace. If I find that you receive this Project favourably, I will shortly trouble you with one or two more; and in the mean time am, most worthy Sir, with all due Respect,

Your most obedient,

and most humble Servant.

The Spectator, No. 452.   Friday, August 8, 1712.

II

SIR,

THE kind Reception you gave my last *Friday*'s Letter, in which I broached my Project of a News Paper, encourages me to lay before you two or three more; for, you must know, Sir, that we look upon you to be the *Lowndes* of the learned World, and cannot think any Scheme practicable or rational before you have approved of it, tho' all the Mony we raise by it is on our own Funds, and for our private Use.

I have often thought that a *News-Letter of Whispers*, written every Post, and sent about the Kingdom, after the same manner as that of Mr. *Dyer*, Mr. *Dawkes*, or any other Epistolary Historian, might be highly gratifying to the Publick, as well as beneficial to the Author. By Whispers I mean those Pieces of News which are communicated as Secrets, and which bring a double Pleasure to the Hearer; first, as they are private History, and in the next place, as they have always in them a Dash of Scandal. These are the two chief Qualifications in an Article of News, that recommend it, in a more than ordinary manner, to the Ears of the Curious. Sickness of Persons in high Posts, Twilight Visits paid and received by Ministers of State, Clandestine Courtships and Marriages, Secret Amours, Losses at Play, Applications for Places, with their respective Successes or Repulses, are the Materials in which I chiefly intend to deal.

I have two Persons, that are each of them the Representative of a Species, who are to furnish me with those Whispers which I intend to convey to my Correspondents. The first of these is *Peter Hush*, descended from the Ancient Family of the *Hushes*. The other is the old Lady *Blast*, who has a very numerous Tribe of Daughters in the two great Cities of *London* and *Westminster*. *Peter Hush* has a whispering Hole in most of the great Coffee-houses about Town. If you are alone with him in a wide Room, he carries you up into a Corner of it, and speaks in your Ear. I have seen *Peter* seat himself in a Company of seven or eight Persons, whom he never saw before in his Life; and after having looked about to see there was no one that over-heard him, has communicated to them in a low Voice, and under the Seal of Secrecy, the Death of a great Man in the Country, who was perhaps a Fox-hunting the very moment this Account was giving of him. If upon your entring into a Coffee-house you see a Circle of Heads bending over the Table, and lying close by one another, it is ten to one but my Friend *Peter* is among them. I have known *Peter* publishing the Whisper of the Day by eight a Clock in the Morning at *Garraway*'s, by twelve at *Will*'s, and before two at the *Smyrna*. When *Peter* had thus effectually launched a Secret, I have been very well pleased to hear People whispering it to one another at second Hand, and spreading it about as their own; for you must know, Sir, the great Incentive to Whispering is the Ambition which every one has of being thought in the Secret, and being looked upon as a Man who has Access to greater People than one would imagine. After having given you this Account of *Peter Hush*, I proceed to that vertuous Lady, the old Lady *Blast*, who is to communicate to me the private Transactions of the Crimp Table, with all the *Arcana* of the fair Sex. The Lady *Blast*, you must understand, has such a particular Malignity in her Whisper, that it blights like an Easterly Wind, and withers every Reputation that it breaths upon. She has a particular knack at making private Weddings, and last Winter married above five Women of Quality to their Footmen. Her Whisper can make an innocent young Woman big with Child, or fill an healthful young Fellow with Distempers that are not to be named. She can turn a Visit into an Intrigue, and a distant Salute into an Assignation. She can beggar the Wealthy, and degrade the Noble. In short, she can whisper Men Base or Foolish, Jealous or Ill-natured, or, if occasion requires, can tell you the Slips of their Great Grandmothers, and traduce the Memory of honest Coachmen that have been in their Graves above these hundred Years. By these, and the like helps, I question not but I shall furnish out a very handsom News Letter. If you approve my Project, I shall begin to Whisper by the very next Post, and question not but every one of my Customers will be very well pleased with me, when he considers that every Piece of News I send him is a Word in his Ear, and lets him into a Secret.

Having given you a Sketch of this Project, I shall, in the next place, suggest to you another for a Monthly Pamphlet, which I shall likewise submit to your Spectatorial Wisdom. I need not tell you, Sir, that there are several Authors in *France*, *Germany* and *Holland*, as well as in our own Country, that Publish every Month, what they call *An Account of the Works of the Learned*, in which they give us an Abstract of all such Books as are Printed in any Part of *Europe*. Now, Sir, it is my Design to Publish every Month, *An Account of the Works of the Unlearned*. Several late Productions of my own Country-men, who many of them make a very Eminent Figure in the Illiterate World, Encourage me in this Undertaking. I may, in this Work, possibly make a Review of several Pieces which have appeared in the Foreign *Accounts* above-mentioned, tho' they ought not to have been taken Notice of in Works which bear such a Title. I may, likewise, take into Consideration such Pieces as appear, from time to time, under the Names of those Gentlemen who Compliment one another, in Publick Assemblies, by the Title of the *Learned Gentlemen*. Our Party-Authors will also afford me a great Variety of Subjects, not to mention Editors, Commentators, and others, who are often Men of no Learning, or what is as bad, of no Knowledge. I shall not enlarge upon this Hint; but if you think any thing can be made of it, I shall set about it with all the Pains and Application that so useful a Work deserves.

I am ever,

Most Worthy Sir, &c.

The Spectator, No. 457. Thursday, August 14, 1712.

[*On the* LOVE *of* PRAISE]

—— *Quodcunque meæ poterunt Audere Camænæ*
Seu Tibi par poterunt, seu, quod spes abnuit ultra;
Sive minus; certeque canent minus; omne vovemus
Hoc tibi; ne tanto careat mihi nomine Charta.

Tibull. ad Messalam.

THE Love of Praise is a Passion deeply fix'd in the Mind of every extraordinary Person, and those who are most affected with it, seem most to partake of that Particle of the Divinity which distinguishes Mankind from the inferior Creation. The supreme Being it self is most pleased with Praise and Thanksgiving; the other Part of our Duty is but an Acknowledgment of our Faults, whilst this is the immediate Adoration of his Perfections. 'Twas an excellent Observation, That we then only despise Commendation when we cease to deserve it; and we have still extant two Orations of *Tully* and *Pliny*, spoken to the greatest and best Princes of all the *Roman* Emperors, who, no Doubt, heard with the greatest Satisfaction, what even the most disinterested Persons, and at so large a Distance of Time, cannot read without Admiration. *Cæsar* thought his life consisted in the Breath of Praise, when he profess'd he had liv'd long enough for himself when he had for his Glory; others have sacrific'd themselves for a Name which was not to begin till they were dead, giving away themselves to purchase a Sound which was not to commence till they were out of hearing: But by Merit and superior Excellencies not only to gain, but, whilst living, to enjoy a great and universal Reputation, is the last Degree of Happiness which we can hope for here. Bad Characters are dispers'd abroad with Profusion, I hope for Example Sake, and (as Punishments are design'd by the Civil Power) more for the deterring the Innocent, than the chastising the Guilty. The Good are less frequent, whether it be that there are indeed fewer Originals of this Kind to copy after, or that, thro' the Malignity of our Nature, we rather delight in the Ridicule than the Virtues we find in others. However, it is but just, as well as pleasing, even for Variety, sometimes to give the World a Representation of the bright Side of humane Nature, as well as the dark and gloomy! The Desire of Imitation may, perhaps, be a greater Incentive to the Practice of what is good, than the Aversion we may conceive at what is blameable; the one immediately directs you what you shou'd do, whilst the other only shews you what you shou'd avoid: And I cannot at present do this with more Satisfaction, than by endeavouring to do some Justice to the Character of *Manilius*.

It wou'd far exceed my present Design, to give a particular Description of *Manilius* thro' all the Parts of his excellent Life: I shall now only draw him in his Retirement, and pass over in Silence the various Arts, the courtly Manners, and the undesigning Honesty by which he attained the Honours he has enjoy'd, and which now give a Dignity and Veneration to the Ease he does enjoy. 'Tis here that he looks back with Pleasure on the Waves and Billows thro' which he has steered to so fair an Haven; he is now intent upon the Practice of every Virtue, which a great Knowledge and Use of Mankind has discovered to be the most useful to them. Thus in his private domestick Employments he is no less glorious than in his publick; for 'tis in Reality a more difficult Task to be conspicuous in a sedentary inactive Life, than in one that is spent in Hurry and Business; Persons engag'd in the latter, like Bodies violently agitated, from the Swiftness of their Motion have a Brightness added to them, which often vanishes when they are at Rest; but if it then still remain, it must be the Seeds of intrinsick Worth that thus shine out without any foreign Aid or Assistance.

His Liberality in another might almost bear the Name of Profusion; he seems to think it laudable even in the Excess, like that River which most enriches when it overflows: But *Manilius* has too perfect a Taste of the Pleasure of doing good, ever to let it be out of his Power; and for that Reason he will have a just Oeconomy, and a splendid Frugality at home, the Fountain from whence those Streams should flow which he disperses abroad. He looks with Disdain on those who propose their Death as the Time when they are to begin their Munificence; he will both see and enjoy (which he then does in the highest Degree) what he bestows himself; he will be the living Executor of his own Bounty, whilst they who have the Happiness to be within his Care and Patronage at once, pray for the continuation of his Life, and their own good Fortune. No one is out of the reach of his Obligations; he knows how, by proper and becoming Methods, to raise himself to a

f

Level with those of the highest Rank; and his good
Nature is a sufficient Warrant against the want of
those who are so unhappy as to be in the very lowest.
One may say of him, as *Pindar* bids his Muse say of
Theron.

> *Swear, that* Theron *sure has sworn,*
> *No one near him shou'd be Poor.*
> *Swear that none e'er had such a gracefulArt,*
> *Fortune's Free-Gifts as freely to impart,*
> *With an unenvious Hand, and an unbounded*
>   *Heart.*

Never did *Atticus* succeed better in gaining the
universal Love and Esteem of all Men, nor steer with
more Success betwixt the Extreams of two contending Parties. 'Tis his peculiar Happiness, that while he
espouses neither with an intemperate Zeal, he is not
only admir'd, but, what is a more rare and unusual
Felicity, he is belov'd and caress'd by both; and I
never yet saw any Person, of whatsoever Age or Sex,
but was immediately struck with the Merit of *Manilius.* There are many who are acceptable to some particular Persons, whilst the rest of Mankind look upon
them with Coldness and Indifference; but he is the
first whose entire good Fortune it is ever to please
and to be pleased, where-ever he comes to be admir'd, and where-ever he is absent to be lamented.
His Merit fares like the Pictures of *Raphael,* which
are either seen with Admiration by all, or at least no
one dare own he has no Taste for a Composition
which has received so universal an Applause. Envy
and Malice find it against their Interest to indulge

Slander and Obloquy. 'Tis as hard for an Enemy to
detract from, as for a Friend to add to his Praise. An
Attempt upon his Reputation is a sure lessening of
one's own; and there is but one Way to injure him,
which is to refuse him his just Commendations, and
be obstinately silent.

It is below him to catch the Sight with any Care of
Dress; his outward Garb is but the Emblem of his
Mind, it is genteel, plain, and unaffected; he knows
that Gold and Embroidery can add nothing to the
Opinion which all have of his Merit, and that he
gives a Lustre to the plainest Dress, whilst 'tis impossible the richest should communicate any to him. He
is still the principal Figure in the Room: He first en-
gages your Eye, as if there were some Point of Light
which shone stronger upon him than on any other
Person.

He puts me in mind of a Story of the famous *Bussy
d'Amboise*, who at an Assembly at Court, where every
one appear'd with the utmost Magnificence, relying
upon his own superior Behaviour, instead of adorning himself like the rest, put on that Day a plain Suit
of Cloaths, and dress'd all his Servants in the most
costly gay Habits he could procure: The Event was,
that the Eyes of the whole Court were fix'd upon
him, all the rest look'd like his Attendants, whilst he
alone had the Air of a Person of Quality and Distinction.

Like *Aristippus*, whatever Shape or Condition he
appears in, it still sits free and easy upon him; but in
some Part of his Character, 'tis true, he differs from
him; for as he is altogether equal to the Largeness of

his present Circumstances, the Rectitude of his Judgment has so far corrected the Inclinations of his Ambition, that he will not trouble himself with either the Desires or Pursuits of any thing beyond his present Enjoyments.

A thousand obliging Things flow from him upon every Occasion, and they are always so just and natural, that it is impossible to think he was at the least Pains to look for them. One would think it were the Dæmon of good Thoughts that discovered to him those Treasures, which he must have blinded others from seeing, they lay so directly in their Way. Nothing can equal the Pleasure is taken in hearing him speak, but the Satisfaction one receives in the Civility and Attention he pays to the Discourse of others. His Looks are a silent Commendation of what is good and praise-worthy, and a secret Reproof to what is licentious and extravagant. He knows how to appear free and open without Danger of Intrusion, and to be cautious without seeming reserved. The Gravity of his Conversation is always enlivened with his Wit and Humour, and the Gayety of it is temper'd with something that is instructive, as well as barely agreeable. Thus with him you are sure not to be merry at the Expence of your Reason, nor serious with the Loss of your good Humour; but, by a happy Mixture in his Temper, they either go together, or perpetually succeed each other. In fine, his whole Behaviour is equally distant from Constraint and Negligence, and he commands your Respect, whilst he gains your Heart.

There is in his whole Carriage such an engaging

Softness, that one cannot perswade one's self he is ever actuated by those rougher Passions, which, wherever they find Place, seldom fail of shewing themselves in the outward Demeanour of the Persons they belong to: But his Constitution is a just Temperature between Indolence on one Hand and Violence on the other. He is mild and gentle, whereever his Affairs will give him Leave to follow his own Inclinations; but yet never failing to exert himself with Vigour and Resolution in the Service of his Prince, his Country, or his Friend.

The Spectator, No. 467. Tuesday, August 26, 1712.

[*On a* FAN]

Mr. SPECTATOR,

YOU will oblige a languishing Lover if you will please to print the enclosed Verses in your next Paper. If you remember the *Metamorphosis*, you know *Procris*, the fond Wife of *Cephalus*, is said to have made her Husband, who delighted in the Sports of the Wood, a Present of an unerring Javelin. In Process of Time he was so much in the Forest, that his Lady suspected he was pursuing some Nymph, under the Pretence of following a Chace more innocent. Under this Suspicion she hid herself among the Trees to observe his Motions. While she lay concealed, her Husband, tired with the Labour of Hunting, came within her Hearing. As he was fainting with Heat, he cry'd out, *Aura veni*; *Oh charming Air approach.*

The unfortunate Wife taking the word *Air* to be the Name of a Woman, began to move among the Bushes, and the Husband believing it a Deer, threw his Javelin and kill'd her. This History painted on a Fan, which I presented to a Lady, gave Occasion to my growing poetical.

> *Come gentle Air! th' Eolian Shepherd said,*
> *While* Procris *panted in the secret Shade;*
> *Come gentle Air! the fairer* Delia *cries,*
> *While at her Feet her Swain expiring lies.*
> *Lo the glad Gales o'er all her Beauties stray,*
> *Breathe on her Lips, and in her Bosom play.*

On a Fan

In Delia'*s Hand this Toy is fatal found,*
Nor did that fabled Dart more surely wound.
Both Gifts destructive to the Givers prove,
Alike both Lovers fall by those they love:
Yet guiltless too this bright Destroyer lives,
At Random wounds, nor knows the Wounds she gives:
She views the Story with attentive Eyes,
And pities Procris *while her Lover dies.*

The Spectator, No. 527.

Tuesday, November 4, 1712.

[*On the* LAST WORDS *of* ADRIAN]

Mr. SPECTATOR,

I WAS the other Day in Company with five or six Men of some Learning; where chancing to mention the famous Verses which the Emperor *Adrian* spoke on his Death-bed, they were all agreed that 'twas a Piece of Gayety unworthy that Prince in those Circumstances. I could not but dissent from this Opinion: Methinks it was by no Means a gay, but a very serious Soliloquy to his Soul at the Point of his Departure; in which Sense I naturally took the Verses at my first reading them when I was very young, and before I knew what Interpretation the World generally put upon them.

Animula vagula, blandula,
Hospes Comesque corporis,
Quæ nunc abibis in loca?
Pallidula, rigida, nudula,
Nec (ut soles) dabis Joca!

Alas, my Soul! thou pleasing Companion of this Body, thou fleeting Thing that art now deserting it! whither art thou flying? to what unknown Region? Thou art all trembling, fearful, and pensive. Now what is become of thy former Wit and Humour? thou shalt jest and be gay no more! I confess I cannot apprehend where lies the Trifling in all this; 'tis the most natural and obvious Reflection imaginable to a dying Man; and if we consider the Emperor was a Heathen, that Doubt concerning the future Fate of his Soul will seem so

far from being the Effect of want of Thought, that
'twas scarce reasonable he should think otherwise;
not to mention that here is a plain Confession included of his Belief in its Immortality. The diminutive
Epithets of *Vagula*, *Blandula*, and the rest, appear
not to me as Expressions of Levity, but rather of En-
dearment and Concern; such as we find in *Catullus*,
and the Authors of *Hendeca-syllabi* after him, where
they are used to express the utmost Love and Tenderness for their Mistresses——If you think me right
in my Notion of the last Words of *Adrian*, be pleased
to insert this in the *Spectator*; if not, to suppress it.

I am, &c.

The Spectator, No. 532.

Monday, November 10, 1712.

Contributions to
The Guardian
1713

[*On* DEDICATIONS]

It matters not how false or forc't,
So the best things be said o' th' worst;
It goes for nothing when 'tis said,
Only the Arrow's drawn to th' head,
Whether it be a Swan or Goose
They level at: So Shepherds use
To set the same Mark on the Hip
Both of their sound and rotten Sheep.

Hudibras.

THOUGH most Things which are wrong in their own Nature are at once confessed and absolv'd in that single Word the *Custom*; yet there are some, which as they have a dangerous Tendency, a thinking Man will the less excuse on that very Account. Among these I cannot but reckon the common Practise of *Dedications*, which is of so much the worse Consequence, as 'tis generally used by People of Politeness, and whom a Learned Education for the most part ought to have inspired with nobler and juster Sentiments. This Prostitution of Praise is not only a Deceit upon the Gross of Mankind, who take their Notion of Characters from the Learned; but also the better Sort must by this means lose some part at least of that Desire of Fame which is the Incentive to generous Actions, when they find it promiscuously bestowed on the Meritorious and Undeserving: Nay, the Author himself, let him be supposed to have ever so true a Value for the Patron, can find no Terms to express it, but what have been already used, and rendered suspected by Flatterers. Even Truth itself in a Dedication is like an Honest Man in a Disguise or Vizor-Masque, and will appear a Cheat by being drest so like one. Tho' the Merit of the Person is beyond Dispute, I see no reason that because one Man is eminent, therefore another has a right to be impertinent, and throw Praises in his Face. 'Tis just the Reverse of the Practise of the Ancient *Romans*, when a Person was advanced to Triumph for his Services: As they hired People to rail at him in that Circumstance, to make him as humble as they could, we have Fellows to flatter him, and make him as Proud as they can. Supposing the Writer not to be Mercenary, yet the great Man is no more in Reason obliged to thank him for his Picture in a Dedication, than to thank the Painter for that on a Sign-Post; except it be a less Injury to touch the most Sacred Part of him, his Character, than to make free with his Countenance only. I shou'd think nothing justified me in this Point, but the Patron's Permission before-hand, that I shou'd draw him as like as I cou'd; whereas most Authors proceed in this Affair just as a Dawber I have heard of, who not being able to draw Portraits after the Life, was used to paint Faces at Random, and look out afterwards for People whom he might persuade to be like them. To express my Notion of the Thing in a Word: To say more to a Man than one thinks, with a Prospect of Interest, is dishonest; and without it, foolish. And whoever has had Success in such an Undertaking, must of necessity at once, think himself in his Heart a Knave for having done it, and his Patron a Fool for having believed it.

I have sometimes been entertained with considering Dedications in no very common Light. By observing what Qualities our Writers think it will be most pleasing to others to compliment them with, one may form some Judgment which are most so to themselves; and, in consequence, what sort of People they are. Without this View one can read very few Dedications but will give us cause to wonder, either how such things came to be said at all, or how they were said to such Persons? I have known an Hero complimented upon the decent Majesty and State he assumed after Victory; and a Nobleman of a different Character applauded for his Condescension to Inferiors. This would have seemed very strange to me, but that I happened to know the Authors. He who made the first Compliment was a lofty Gentleman, whose Air and Gait discovered when he had published a new Book; and the other tippled every Night with the Fellows who laboured at the Press while his own Writings were working off. 'Tis observable of the Female Poets and Ladies Dedicatory, that here (as elsewhere) they far exceed us in any Strain or Rant. As Beauty is the thing that Sex are piqu'd upon, they speak of it generally in a more elevated Style than is used by the Men. They adore in the same manner as they would be adored. So when the Authoress of a famous Modern Romance begs a young Nobleman's Permission to pay him her *Kneeling Adorations*, I am far from censuring the Expression, as some Criticks would do, as deficient in Gram-

mar or Sence; but I reflect, that Adorations paid in
that Posture are what a Lady might expect herself,
and my Wonder immediately ceases. These, when
they flatter most, do but as they would be done unto;
for as none are so much concerned at being injured
by Calumnies, as they who are readiest to cast them
upon their Neighbours; so 'tis certain none are so
guilty of Flattery to others, as those who most ardent-
ly desire it themselves.

What led me into these Thoughts, was a Dedication I happened upon this Morning. The Reader
must understand that I treat the least Instances or
Remains of Ingenuity, with respect in what Places
soever found, or under whatever Circumstances of
Disadvantage. From this Love to Letters I have been
so happy in my Searches after Knowledge, that I
have found unvalued Repositories of Learning in the
Lining of Bandboxes. I look upon these Pasteboard
Edifices, adorned with the Fragments of the Ingenious, with the same Veneration as Antiquaries upon
ruined Buildings, whose Walls preserve divers In-
scriptions and Names, which are no where else to be
found in the World. This Morning, when one of
Lady *Lizard*'s Daughters was looking over some
Hoods and Ribbands, brought by her Tirewoman,
with great Care and Diligence, I employed no less in
examining the Box which contained them; it was
lined with certain Scenes of a Tragedy, written (as
appeared by a part of the Title there extant) by one
of the Fair Sex. What was most legible was the Dedication; which, by reason of the Largeness of the
Characters, was least defaced by those *Gothick* Orna-

ments of Flourishes and Foliage, wherewith the Compilers of these sort of Structures do often industriously obscure the Works of the Learned. As much of it as I could read with any Ease, I shall communicate to the Reader, as follows.

'**** Though it is a kind of *Prophanation* to approach your Grace with so poor an *Offering*, yet when I reflect how acceptable a *Sacrifice* of First-Fruits was to *Heaven*, in the earliest and *purest Ages of Religion*, that they were honour'd with *solemn Feasts*, and *consecrated to Altars* by a *Divine Command*, **** upon that Consideration, as an Argument of particular *Zeal*, I dedicate. *** 'Tis impossible to behold you without *Adoring*; yet dazled and aw'd by the *Glory* that surrounds you, Men feel a *sacred Power*, that refines their Flames, and renders them pure as those we ought to offer to the Deity. ***** The *Shrine* is worthy the *Divinity* that inhabits it. In your Grace we see what Woman was before she fell, how nearly allied to the *Purity* and *Perfection* of *Angels*. And WE ADORE AND BLESS THE GLORIOUS WORK!'

Undoubtedly these, and other Periods of this most Pious Dedication, could not but convince the Dutchess of what the Eloquent Authoress assures her at the End, that she was her Servant *with most ardent Devotion*. I think this a Pattern of a new Sort of Stile, not yet taken Notice of by the Criticks, which is above the Sublime, and may be called *the Celestial*; that is, when the most sacred Phrases appropriated to the Honour of the Deity, are applied to a Mortal of good Quality. As I am naturally emulous, I cannot but endeavour, in Imitation of this Lady, to be the Inventor, or, at least, the first Producer of a new kind of Dedication, very different from hers and most others, since it has not a Word but what the Author religiously thinks in it. It may serve for almost any Book, either Prose or Verse, that has, is, or shall be published, and might run in this manner.

The AUTHOR to HIMSELF.

Most Honoured Sir,

THESE Labours, upon many Considerations, so properly belong to none as to you: First, as it was your most earnest Desire alone that could prevail upon me to make them publick: Then, as I am secure (from that constant Indulgence you have ever shown to all which is mine) that no Man will so readily take them into Protection, or so zealously defend them. Moreover, there's none can so soon discover the Beauties; and there are some Parts, which 'tis possible few besides your self are capable of understanding. Sir, the Honour, Affection and Value I have for you are beyond Expression; as great, I am sure, or greater, than any Man else can bear you. As for any Defects which others may pretend to discover in you, I do faithfully declare I was never able to perceive them; and doubt not but those Persons are actuated purely by a Spirit of Malice or Envy, the inseparable Attendants on shining Merit and Parts, such as I have always esteemed yours to be. It may perhaps be looked upon as a kind of Violence to Modesty, to say this to you in Publick; but you may believe me, 'tis

g

no more than I have a thousand times thought of you in Private. Might I follow the Impulse of my Soul, there is no Subject I could launch into with more Pleasure than your Panegyrick. But since something is due to Modesty, let me conclude by telling you, that there's nothing so much I desire as to know you more thoroughly than I have yet the Happiness of doing. I may then hope to be capable to do you some real Service; but 'till then can only assure you, that I shall continue to be, as I am more than any Man alive,

Dearest Sir,

Your Affectionate Friend, and

The greatest of your Admirers.

The Guardian, No. 4.   Monday, March 16, 1713.

[*The* GRAND ELIXIR]

To the GUARDIAN.

SIR,

AS you profess to encourage all those who any way contribute to the Publick Good, I flatter my self I may claim your Countenance and Protection. I am by Profession a Mad Doctor, but of a peculiar Kind; not of those whose Aim it is to remove Phrenzies, but one who makes it my Business to confer an agreeable Madness on my Fellow-Creatures, for their mutual Delight and Benefit. Since it is agreed by the Philosophers, that Happiness and Misery consist chiefly in the Imagination, nothing is more necessary to Mankind in general than this pleasing Delirium, which renders every one satisfied with himself, and persuades him that all others are equally so.

I have for several Years, both at home and abroad, made this Science my particular Study, which I may venture to say I have improved in almost all the Courts of *Europe*; and have reduced it into so safe and easie a Method, as to practise it on both Sexes, of what Disposition, Age or Quality soever, with Success. What enables me to perform this great Work, is the Use of my *Obsequium Catholicon*, or the *Grand Elixir*, to support the Spirits of Human Nature. This Remedy is of the most grateful Flavour in the World, and agrees with all Tastes whatever. 'Tis delicate to the Senses, delightful in the Operation, may be taken at all Hours without Confinement, and is as

properly given at a Ball or Play-house as in a private
Chamber. It restores and vivifies the most dejected
Minds, corrects and extracts all that is painful in the
Knowledge of a Man's Self. One Dose of it will instantly disperse it self through the whole Animal
System, dissipate the first Motions of Distrust so as
never to return, and so exhilerate the Brain, and
rarifie the Gloom of Reflection, as to give the Patients a new Flow of Spirits, a Vivacity of Behaviour,
and a pleasing Dependance upon their own Capacities.

Let a Person be never so far gone, I advise him not
to despair; even though he has been troubled many
Years with restless Reflections, which by long Neglect have hardened into settled Consideration.
Those that have been stung with Satyr may here
find a certain Antidote, which infallibly disperses all
Remains of the Poison that has been left in the Understanding by bad Cures. It fortifies the Heart
against the Rancour of Pamphlets, the Inveteracy of
Epigrams, and the Mortification of Lampoons; as
has been often experienced by several Persons of
both Sexes, during the Seasons of *Tunbridge* and the
Bath.

I could, as farther Instances of my Success, produce Certificates and Testimonials from the Favourites and Ghostly Fathers of the most eminent Princes
of *Europe*, but shall content my self with the Mention of a few Cures, which I have performed by this
my *Grand Universal Restorative*, during the Practice
of one Month only since I came to this City.

Cures in the Month of February, 1713.

George Spondee, Esq; Poet, and Inmate of the Parish of St. *Paul's Covent-Garden,* fell into violent Fits of the Spleen upon a thin Third Night. He had been frighted into a Vertigo by the Sound of Catcalls on the First Day; and the frequent Hissings on the Second made him unable to endure the bare Pronunciation of the Letter *S.* I searched into the Causes of his Distemper; and by the Prescription of a Dose of my *Obsequium,* prepared *secundum Artem,* recovered him to his Natural State of Madness. I cast in at proper Intervals the Words, *Ill Taste of the Town, Envy of Criticks, bad Performance of the Actors,* and the like. He is so perfectly cured, that he has promised to bring another Play upon the Stage next Winter.

A Lady of professed Virtue, of the Parish of St. *James's Westminster,* who hath desired her Name may be concealed, having taken Offence at a Phrase of double Meaning in Conversation, undiscovered by any other in the Company, suddenly fell into a cold Fit of Modesty. Upon a right Application of Praise of her Virtue, I threw the Lady into an agreeable waking Dream, settled the Fermentation of her Blood into a warm Charity, so as to make her look with Patience on the very Gentleman that offended.

Hilaria, of the Parish of St. *Giles's in the Fields,* a Coquet of long Practice, was by the Reprimand of an old Maiden reduced to look grave in Company, and deny her self the Play of the Fan. In short, she was brought to such melancholy Circumstances, that she would sometimes unawares fall into Devotion at Church. I advised her to take a few *innocent Freedoms with occasional Kisses*, prescribed her the *Exercise of the Eyes*, and immediately raised her to her former State of Life. She on a sudden recovered her Dimples, furled her Fan, threw round her Glances, and for these two *Sundays* last past has not once been seen in an attentive Posture. This the Church-Wardens are ready to attest upon Oath.

Andrew Terror, of the *Middle-Temple*, *Mohock*, was almost induced by an aged Bencher of the same House to leave off bright Conversation, and pore over *Cook upon Littleton*. He was so ill that his Hat began to flap, and he was seen one Day in the last Term at *Westminster Hall*. This Patient had quite lost his Spirit of Contradiction; I, by the Distillation of a few of my vivifying Drops in his Ear, drew him from his Lethargy, and restored him to his usual vivacious Misunderstanding. He is at present very easie in his Condition.

I will not dwell upon the Recital of the innumerable Cures I have performed within twenty Days last past; but rather proceed to exhort all Persons, of whatever Age, Complexion or Quality, to take as soon as possible of this my intellectual Oyl; which applied at the Ear seizes all the Senses with a most agreeable Transport, and discovers its Effects, not only to the Satisfaction of the Patient, but all who converse with, attend upon, or any way relate to him or her that receives the kindly Infection. It is often administred by Chamber-maids, Valets, or any the most ignorant Domestick; it being one peculiar Excellence of this my Oyl, that 'tis most prevalent, the more unskilful the Person is or appears who applies it. It is absolutely necessary for Ladies to take a Dose of just before they take Coach to go a visiting.

But I offend the Publick, as *Horace* said, when I trespass on any of your Time. Give me Leave then, Mr. *Ironside*, to make you a Present of a Drachm or two of my Oyl; though I have Cause to fear my Prescriptions will not have the Effect upon you I could wish: Therefore I do not endeavour to bribe you in my Favour by the Present of my Oyl, but wholly depend upon your Publick Spirit and Generosity; which, I hope, will recommend to the World the useful Endeavours of,

SIR,

Your most Obedient,
most Faithful, most Devoted,
most Humble Servant
and Admirer,

GNATHO.

† Beware of Counterfeits, for such are abroad.

N.B. I teach the *Arcana* of my Art at reasonable Rates to Gentlemen of the Universities, who desire to be qualified for writing Dedications; and to young Lovers and Fortune-hunters, to be paid at the Day of Marriage. I instruct Persons of bright Capacities to flatter others, and those of the meanest to flatter themselves.

I was the first Inventor of Pocket Looking-Glasses.

The Guardian, No. 11. Tuesday, March 24, 1713.

[*On* FALSE CRITICKS]

Vel quia nil rectum, nisi quod placuit sibi, ducunt:
Vel quia turpe putant parere minoribus—— Hor.

WHEN a Poem makes its first Appearance in the World, I have always observed, that it gives Employment to a greater number of Criticks, than any other kind of Writing. Whether it be that most Men, at some time of their Lives, have try'd their Talent that way, and thereby think they have a right to judge; or whether they imagine, that their making shrewd Observations upon the Polite Arts, gives them a pretty figure; or whether there may not be some Jealousie and Caution in bestowing Applause upon those who write chiefly for Fame. Whatever the Reasons be, we find few discouraged by the Delicacy and Danger of such an Undertaking.

I think it certain, that most Men are naturally not only capable of being pleased with that which raises agreeable Pictures in the Fancy, but willing also to own it. But then there are many, who, by false Applications of some Rules ill understood, or out of Deference to Men whose Opinions they value, have formed to themselves certain Schemes and Systems of Satisfaction, and will not be pleased out of their own way. These are not Criticks themselves, but Readers of Criticks, who, without the Labour of perusing Authors, are able to give their Characters in general; and know just as much of the several Species of Poetry, as those who read Books of Geography do of the Genius of this or that People or Nation. These Gentlemen deliver their Opinions sententiously, and in general Terms; to which it being impossible readily to frame compleat Answers, they have often the Satisfaction of leaving the Board in Triumph. As young Persons, and particularly the Ladies, are liable to be led aside by these Tyrants in Wit, I shall examine two or three of the many Stratagems they use, and subjoin such Precautions as may hinder candid Readers from being deceived thereby.

The first I shall take Notice of is an Objection commonly offered, *viz. That such a Poem hath indeed some good Lines in it, but it is not a regular Piece.* This for the most part is urged by those whose Knowledge is drawn from some famous *French* Criticks, who have written upon the Epic Poem, the Drama, and the great kinds of Poetry, which cannot subsist without great Regularity; but ought by no means to be required in Odes, Epistles, Panegyricks, and the like, which naturally admit of greater Liberties. The Enthusiasm in Odes and the Freedom of Epistles is rarely disputed; But I have often heard the Poems upon Publick Occasions written in Heroic Verse, which I chuse to call Panegyricks, severely censured upon this Account; the Reason whereof I cannot guess, unless it be, that because they are written in the same kind of Numbers and Spirit as an Epic Poem, they ought therefore to have the same Regularity. Now an Epic Poem, consisting chiefly in Narration, it is necessary that the Incidents should be related in the same Order that they are supposed to have been transacted. But in Works of the abovementioned kind, there is no more reason that such Order should be observed, than that an Oration should be as methodical as an History. I think it sufficient that the great Hints, suggested from the Subject, be so disposed, that the first may naturally prepare the Reader for what follows, and so on; and that their Places cannot be changed without Disadvantage to the whole. I will add further, that sometimes gentle Deviations, sometimes bold and even abrupt Digressions, where the Dignity of the Subject seems to give the Impulse, are Proofs of a noble Genius; as winding about, and returning artfully to the main Design, are Marks of Address and Dexterity.

Another Artifice made use of by Pretenders to Criticism, is an Insinuation, *That all that is good is borrowed from the Ancients.* This is very common in the Mouths of Pedants, and perhaps in their Hearts too; but is often urged by Men of no great Learning, for Reasons very obvious. Now Nature being still the same, it is impossible for any Modern Writer to paint her otherwise than the Ancients have done. If, for Example, I were to describe the General's Horse at the Battel of *Blenheim*, as my Fancy represented such a noble Beast, and that Description should resemble what *Virgil* hath drawn for the Horse of his Hero, it would be almost as ill-natured to urge that I had stolen my Description from *Virgil*, as to reproach the Duke of *Marlborough* for fighting only like *Æneas.* All that the most exquisite Judgment can perform is, out of that great Variety of Circumstances, wherein natural Objects may be considered, to select the most beautiful; and to place Images in such Views and Lights, as will affect the Fancy after the most delightful manner. But over and above a

just Painting of Nature, a learned Reader will find a
new Beauty superadded in a happy Imitation of some
famous Ancient, as it revives in his Mind the Pleasure he took in his first reading such an Author. Such
Copyings as these give that kind of double Delight
which we perceive when we look upon the Children
of a beautiful Couple; where the Eye is not more
charm'd with the Symmetry of the Parts, than the
Mind by observing the Resemblance transmitted
from Parents to their Offspring, and the mingled
Features of the Father and the Mother. The Phrases
of Holy Writ, and Allusions to several Passages in
the Inspired Writings, (though not produced as
Proofs of Doctrine) add Majesty and Authority to
the noblest Discourses of the Pulpit: In like manner
an Imitation of the Air of *Homer* and *Virgil* raises the
Dignity of modern Poetry, and makes it appear
stately and venerable.

The last Observation I shall make at present is
upon the Disgust taken by those Criticks, who put on
their Cloaths prettily, and dislike every thing that is
not written *with Ease.* I hereby therefore give the
genteel part of the learned World to understand, that
every Thought which is agreeable [to Nature], and
exprest in Language suitable to it, is written with
Ease. There are some Things which must be written
with Strength, which nevertheless are easie. The
Statue of the *Gladiator*, though represented in such a
Posture as strains every Muscle, is as easie as that of
Venus; because the one expresses Strength and Fury
as naturally as the other doth Beauty and Softness.
The Passions are sometimes to be rouzed, as well as

the Fancy to be entertained; and the Soul to be exalted and enlarged, as well as soothed. This often requires a raised and figurative Stile; which Readers of
low Apprehensions, or soft and languid Dispositions
(having heard of the Words *Fustian* and *Bombast*) are
apt to reject as stiff and affected Language. But Nature and Reason appoint different Garbs for different Things; and since I write this to the Men of
Dress, I will ask them if a Soldier, who is to mount a
Breach, should be adorned like a Beau, who is
spruced up for a Ball?

The Guardian, No. 12. Wednesday, March 25, 1713.

[*On* EASY WRITING]

—— *sibi quivis*
Speret idem, sudet multum, frustraque laboret,
Ausus idem ——   Hor.

I CAME yesterday into the Parlour, where I
found Mrs. *Cornelia*, my Lady's third Daughter, all alone, reading a Paper, which, as I afterwards found, contained a Copy of Verses upon Love
and Friendship. She, I believe, apprehended that I
had glanced my Eye upon the Paper, and by the
Order and Disposition of the Lines might distinguish that they were Poetry; and therefore, with an
innocent Confusion in her Face, she told me I might
read them if I pleased, and so withdrew. By the
Hand, at first sight, I could not guess whether they
came from a Beau or a Lady; but having put on my
Spectacles, and perused them carefully, I found by
some peculiar Modes in Spelling, and a certain Negligence in Grammar, that it was a Female Sonnet. I
have since learned, that she hath a Correspondent in
the Country who is as bookish as herself; that they
write to one another by the Names of *Astrea* and
Dorinda, and are mightily admired for their easie
Lines. As I should be loath to have a Poetess in our
Family, and yet am unwilling harshly to cross the
Bent of a young Lady's Genius, I chose rather to
throw together some Thoughts upon that kind of
Poetry which is distinguished by the Name of *Easie*,
than to risque the Fame of Mrs. *Cornelia*'s Friend, by
exposing her Work to publick View.

I have said, in a foregoing Paper, that every

Thought which is agreeable to Nature, and expressed in a Language suitable to it, is written with Ease; which I offered in answer to those who ask for Ease in all Kinds of Poetry; and it is so far true, as it states the Notion of easie Writing in general, as that is opposed to what is forced or affected. But as there is an easie Mein, an easie Dress, peculiarly so called; so there is an easie sort of Poetry. In order to write easily, it is necessary, in the first place, to think easily. Now, according to different Subjects, Men think differently; Anger, Fury, and the rough Passions, awaken strong Thoughts: Glory, Grandeur, Power, raise great Thoughts: Love, Melancholy, Solitude, and whatever gently touches the Soul, inspires easie Thoughts.

Of the Thoughts suggested by these gentle Subjects, there are some which may be set off by Style and Ornament: Others there are, which the more simply they are conceived, and the more clearly they are expressed, give the Soul proportionably the more pleasing Emotions. The Figures of Stile added to them serve only to hide a Beauty, however gracefully they are put on, and are thrown away like Paint upon a fine Complexion. But here not only Liveliness of Fancy is requisite to exhibit a great variety of Images; but also of Niceness of Judgment to cull out those, which, without the Advantage of Foreign Art, will shine by their own intrinsick Beauty. By these means, whatsoever seems to demand Labour being rejected, that only which appears to be easie and natural will come in; and so Art will be hid by Art, which is the Perfection of easie Writing.

I will suppose an Author to be really possessed with the Passion which he writes upon, and then we shall see how he would acquit himself. This I take to be the safest way to form a Judgment of him; since if he be not truely moved, he must at least work up his Imagination as near as possible to resemble Reality. I choose to instance in Love, which is observed to have produced the most finished Performances in this Kind. A Lover will be full of Sincerity, that he may be believed by his Mistress; he will therefore think simply, he will express himself perspicuously, that he may not perplex her; he will therefore write unaffectedly. Deep Reflections are made by an Head undisturbed; and Points of Wit and Fancy are the Work of an Heart at Ease: These two Dangers then, into which Poets are apt to run, are effectually removed out of the Lover's way. The selecting proper Circumstances, and placing them in agreeable Lights, are the finest Secrets of all Poetry; but the Recollection of little Circumstances is the Lover's sole Meditation, and relating them pleasingly the Business of his Life. Accordingly we find that the most celebrated Authors of this Rank excel in Love-Verses. Out of ten thousand Instances I shall name one, which I think the most delicate and tender I ever saw.

To my self I sigh often, without knowing why;
And when absent from Phyllis, *methinks I could die.*

A Man who hath ever been in Love will be touched at the reading of these Lines; and every one, who now feels that Passion, actually feels that they are true.

From what I have advanced it appears, how difficult it is to write easily. But when easie Writings fall into the Hands of an ordinary Reader, they appear to him so natural and unlaboured, that he immediately resolves to write, and fancies that all he hath to do is to take no Pains. Thus he thinks indeed simply, but the Thoughts, not being chosen with Judgment, are not beautiful; he, it is true, expresses himself plainly, but flatly withal. Again, if a Man of Vivacity takes it in his Head to write in this Way, what Self-denial must he undergo, when bright Points of Wit occur to his Fancy? How difficult will he find it to reject florid Phrases, and pretty Embellishments of Style? So true it is, that Simplicity of all things is the hardest to be copied, and Ease to be acquired with the greatest Labour. Our Family knows very well how ill Lady *Flame* looked, when she imitated Mrs. *Jane* in a plain Black Suit. And, I remember, when *Frank Courtly* was saying the other Day, that any Man might write easie, I only ask'd him, If he thought it possible that Squire *Hawthorn* should ever come into a Room as he did? He made me a very handsome Bow, and answered with a Smile, *Mr.* IRONSIDE, *you have convinced me.*

I shall conclude this Paper, by observing that *Pastoral* Poetry, which is the most considerable Kind of easie Writing, hath the oftenest been attempted with ill Success of any sort whatsoever. I shall therefore, in a little time, communicate my Thoughts upon that Subject to the Publick.

The Guardian, No. 15.   Saturday, March 28, 1713.

[On PASTORALS]

Compulerantque Greges Corydon & Thyrsis in unum.
Ex illo Corydon, Corydon est tempore nobis.

I DESIGNED to have troubled the Reader with no farther Discourses of *Pastorals*, but being informed that I am taxed of Partiality in not mentioning an Author, whose Eclogues are published in the same Volume with Mr. *Philips's*; I shall employ this Paper in Observations upon him, written in the free Spirit of Criticism, and without Apprehension of offending that Gentleman, whose Character it is, that he takes the greatest Care of his Works before they are published, and has the least Concern for them afterwards.

I have laid it down as the first Rule of Pastoral, that its Idea should be taken from the Manners of the *Golden Age*, and the Moral form'd upon the Representation of Innocence; 'tis therefore plain that any Deviations from that Design degrade a Poem from being true Pastoral. In this view it will appear that *Virgil* can only have two of his Eclogues allowed to be such: His First and Ninth must be rejected, because they describe the Ravages of Armies, and Oppressions of the Innocent; *Corydon's* criminal Passion for *Alexis* throws out the Second; the Calumny and Railing in the Third are not proper to that State of Concord; the Eighth represents unlawful Ways of procuring Love by Inchantments, and introduces a Shepherd whom an inviting Precipice tempts to Self-Murder. As to the Fourth, Sixth, and Tenth,

h

See Rapin   they are given up by * *Heinsius, Salmasius,*
de Carm.   *Rapin,* and the Criticks in general. They
Past. *pars* 3.   likewise observe that but eleven of all the
Idyllia of *Theocritus* are to be admitted as Pastorals;
and even out of that Number the greater Part will be
excluded for one or other of the Reasons abovementioned. So that when I remark'd in a former Paper,
that *Virgil's* Eclogues, taken all together, are rather
Select Poems than *Pastorals*; I might have said the
same thing, with no less Truth, of *Theocritus.* The
Reason of this I take to be yet unobserved by the
Criticks, *viz. They never meant them all for Pastorals.*
Which it is plain *Philips* hath done, and in that Particular excelled both *Theocritus* and *Virgil.*

As Simplicity is the distinguishing Characteristick
of Pastoral, *Virgil* hath been thought guilty of too
Courtly a Stile; his Language is perfectly pure, and
he often forgets he is among Peasants. I have frequently wonder'd that since he was so conversant in
the Writings of *Ennius*, he had not imitated the Rusticity of the *Doric*, as well, by the help of the old obsolete *Roman* Language, as *Philips* hath by the anti-
quated *English:* For Example, might he not have
said *Quoi* instead of *Cui*; *Quoijum* for *Cujum*; *volt* for
vult, &c. as well as our Modern hath *Welladay* for
Alas, Whilome for *of Old, make mock* for *deride,* and
witless Younglings for *simple Lambs,* &c. by which
Means he had attained as much of the Air of *Theocritus,* as *Philips* hath of *Spencer.*

Mr. *Pope* hath fallen into the same Error with *Virgil.* His Clowns do not converse in all the Simplicity
proper to the Country: His Names are borrow'd

from *Theocritus* and *Virgil*, which are improper to the Scene of his Pastorals. He introduces *Daphnis*, *Alexis* and *Thyrsis* on *British* Plains, as *Virgil* had done before him on the *Mantuan*; whereas *Philips*, who hath the strictest Regard to Propriety, makes choice of Names peculiar to the Country, and more agreeable to a Reader of Delicacy; such as *Hobbinol*, *Lobbin*, *Cuddy*, and *Colin Clout*.

So easie as Pastoral Writing may seem, (in the Simplicity we have described it) yet it requires *great Reading*, both of the *Ancients* and *Moderns*, to be a Master of it. *Philips* hath given us manifest Proofs of his Knowledge of Books; it must be confessed his Competitor hath imitated some single Thoughts of the Ancients well enough, if we consider he had not the Happiness of an University Education; but he hath dispersed them, here and there, without that Order and Method which Mr. *Philips* observes, whose whole third Pastoral is an Instance how well he hath studied the fifth of *Virgil*, and how judiciously reduced *Virgil*'s Thoughts to the Standard of Pastoral; as his Contention of *Colin Clout* and the *Nightingale* shows with what Exactness he hath imitated *Strada*.

When I remarked it as a principal Fault to introduce Fruits and Flowers of a Foreign Growth, in Descriptions where the Scene lies in our Country, I did not design that Observation should extend also to Animals, or the Sensitive Life; for *Philips* hath with great Judgement described *Wolves* in *England* in his first Pastoral. Nor would I have a Poet slavishly confine himself (as Mr. *Pope* hath done) to one particular Season of the Year, one certain time of the

Day, and one unbroken Scene in each Eclogue. 'Tis plain *Spencer* neglected this Pedantry, who in his Pastoral of *November* mentions the mournful Song of the Nightingale:

Sad Philomel *her Song in Tears doth steep.*

And Mr. *Philips*, by a Poetical Creation, hath raised up finer Beds of Flowers than the most industrious Gardiner; his Roses, Lillies and Daffadils blow in the same Season.

But the better to discover the Merits of our two Contemporary Pastoral Writers, I shall endeavour to draw a Parallel of them, by setting several of their particular Thoughts in the same light, whereby it will be obvious how much *Philips* hath the Advantage. With what Simplicity he introduces two Shepherds singing alternately.

Hobb. *Come,* Rosalind, *O come, for without thee*
What Pleasure can the Country have for me:
Come, Rosalind, *O come; my brinded Kine,*
My snowy Sheep, my Farm, and all is thine.

Lanq. *Come* Rosalind, *O come; here shady Bowers*
Here are cool Fountains, and here springing
Flow'rs.
Come, Rosalind; *Here ever let us stay,*
And sweetly wast our live-long Time away.

Our other Pastoral Writer, in expressing the same Thought, deviates into downright Poetry.

Streph. *In Spring the Fields, in Autumn Hills I love,*
At Morn the Plains, at Noon the shady Grove,

But Delia *always; forc'd from* Delia'*s Sight,*
Nor Plains at Morn, nor Groves at Noon de-
    light.

Daph.   Sylvia'*s like Autumn ripe, yet mild as* May,
    More bright than Noon, yet fresh as early Day;
    Ev'n Spring displeases, when she shines not here.
    But blest with her, 'tis Spring throughout the
    Year.

In the first of these Authors, two Shepherds thus in-
nocently describe the Behaviour of their Mistresses.

Hobb.   *As* Marian *bath'd, by chance I passed by,*
    She blush'd, and at me cast a side-long Eye:
    Then swift beneath the Crystal Wave she try'd
    Her beauteous Form, but all in vain, to hide.

Lanq.   *As I to cool me bath'd one sultry Day,*
    Fond Lydia *lurking in the Sedges lay.*
    The Wanton laugh'd, and seem'd in Haste to fly;
    Yet often stopp'd, and often turn'd her Eye.

The other Modern (who it must be confessed hath a
knack of Versifying) hath it as follows.

Streph.   *Me gentle* Delia *beckons from the Plain,*
    Then, hid in Shades, eludes her eager Swain;
    But feigns a Laugh, to see me search around,
    And by that Laugh the willing Fair is found.

Daph.   *The sprightly* Sylvia *trips along the Green,*
    She runs, but hopes she does not run unseen;
    While a kind Glance at her Pursuer flyes,
    How much at Variance are her Feet and Eyes!

There is nothing the Writers of this kind of Poetry

are fonder of, than Descriptions of Pastoral Presents.
Philips says thus of a Sheephook.

> *Of Season'd Elm; where Studs of Brass appear,*
> *To speak the Giver's Name, the Month and Year.*
> *The Hook of polish'd Steel, the Handle turn'd,*
> *And richly by the Graver's Skill adorn'd.*

The other of a Bowl embossed with Figures.

> *———— where wanton Ivy twines,*
> *And swelling Clusters bend the curling Vines;*
> *Four Figures rising from the Work appear,*
> *The various Seasons of the rolling Year;*
> *And what is That which binds the radiant Sky,*
> *Where twelve bright Signs in beauteous Order lie.*

The Simplicity of the Swain in this Place, who forgets the Name of the *Zodiack*, is no ill Imitation of
Virgil; but how much more plainly and unaffectedly
would *Philips* have dressed this Thought in his *Doric*?

> *And what That hight, which girds the Welkin sheen,*
> *Where twelve gay Signs in meet array are seen.*

If the Reader would indulge his Curiosity any farther in the Comparison of Particulars, he may read
the first Pastoral of *Philips* with the second of his
Contemporary, and the fourth and sixth of the former, with the fourth and first of the latter; where
several Parallel Places will occur to every one.

Having now shown some Parts, in which these
two Writers may be compared, it is a Justice I owe to
Mr. *Philips*, to discover those in which no Man can

compare with him. First, That *beautiful Rusticity*, of
which I shall only produce two Instances, out of a
hundred not yet quoted.

> *O woful Day! O Day of Woe, quoth he,*
> *And woful I, who live the Day to see!*

That Simplicity of Diction, the Melancholy Flowing
of the Numbers, the Solemnity of the Sound, and
the easie Turn of the Words, in this *Dirge* (to make
use of our Author's Expression) are extreamly Elegant.

In another of his Pastorals, a Shepherd utters a
Dirge not much inferior to the former, in the following Lines.

> *Ah me the while! ah me! the luckless Day,*
> *Ah luckless Lad! the rather might I say;*
> *Ah silly I! more silly than my Sheep,*
> *Which on the flowry Plains I once did keep.*

How he still Charms the Ear with these artful Repetitions of the Epithets; and how significant is the last
Verse! I defy the most common Reader to repeat
them, without feeling some Motions of Compassion.

In the next Place I shall rank his *Proverbs*, in
which I formerly observed he excells: For Example,

> *A rolling Stone is ever bare of Moss;*
> *And, to their Cost, green Years old Proverbs cross.*
> —— *He that late lyes down, as late will rise,*
> *And, Sluggard-like, till Noon-day snoaring lyes.*
> *Against Ill-Luck all cunning Fore-sight fails;*
> *Whether we sleep or wake it nought avails.*
> —— *Nor fear, from upright Sentence, Wrong.*

Lastly, His *Elegant Dialect*, which alone might prove him the eldest Born of *Spencer*, and our only true *Arcadian*; I should think it proper for the several Writers of Pastoral, to confine themselves to their several *Counties*. *Spencer* seems to have been of this Opinion: for he hath laid the Scene of one of his Pastorals in *Wales*, where with all the Simplicity natural to that Part of our Island, one Shepherd bids the other *Goodmorrow* in an unusual and elegant Manner.

> Diggon Davy, *I bid hur God-day:*
> Or Diggon *hur is, or I mis-say.*

Diggon answers,

> *Hur was hur while it was Day-light;*
> *But now hur is a most wretched Wight*, &c.

But the most beautiful Example of this kind that I ever met with, is in a very valuable Piece, which I chanced to find among some old Manuscripts, entituled, *A Pastoral Ballad*; which I think, for its Nature and Simplicity, may (notwithstanding the Modesty of the Title) be allowed a Perfect Pastoral: It is composed in the *Somersetshire* Dialect, and the Names such as are proper to the Country People. It may be observed, as a further Beauty of this Pastoral, the Words *Nymph, Dryad, Naiad, Fawn, Cupid,* or *Satyr*, are not once mentioned through the whole. I shall make no Apology for inserting some few Lines of this excellent Piece. *Cicily* breaks thus into the Subject, as she is going a Milking;

> Cicily. Rager *go vetch tha* * *Kee, or else tha Zun,*
> *Will quite be go, be vore c'have half a don.*

*That is the *Kine* or *Cows*.

Roger. *Thou shouldst not ax ma tweece, but I've a be*
To dreave our Bull to Bull tha Parson's Kee.

It is to be observed, that this whole Dialogue is formed upon the Passion of Jealousie; and his mentioning
the Parson's Kine naturally revives the Jealousie of
the Shepherdess *Cicily,* which she expresses as follows:

Cicily. *Ah* Rager, Rager, *chez was zore avraid*
Ween in yond Vield you kiss'd tha Parsons
Maid:
Is this the Love that once to me you zed,
When from tha Wake thou brought'st me Gin-
gerbread?
Roger. Cicily *thou charg'st me false,—I'll zwear to*
thee,
Tha Parson's Maid is still a Maid for me.

In which Answer of his are express'd at once that
Spirit of Religion, and that *Innocence of the Golden*
Age, so necessary to be observed by all Writers of
Pastoral.

At the Conclusion of this Piece, the Author recon-
ciles the Lovers, and ends the Eclogue the most Simply in the World.

So Rager *parted vor to vetch tha Kee,*
And vor her Bucket in went Cicily.

I am loath to show my Fondness for Antiquity so far
as to prefer this Ancient *British* Author to our present *English* Writers of Pastoral; but I cannot avoid
making this obvious Remark, that both *Spencer* and

Philips have hit into the same Road with this old *West Country* Bard of ours.

After all that hath been said, I hope none can think it any Injustice to Mr. *Pope*, that I forbore to mention him as a Pastoral Writer; since upon the whole, he is of the same Class with *Moschus* and *Bion*, whom we have excluded that Rank; and of whose Eclogues, as well as some of *Virgil*'s, it may be said, that according to the Description we have given of this sort of Poetry, they are by no means *Pastorals*, but *something Better*.

The Guardian, No. 40.   Monday, April 27, 1713.

[*Against* BARBARITY *to* ANIMALS]

——— *Primoque a cæde ferarum*
Incaluisse putem maculatum sanguine ferrum.

Ovid.

I CANNOT think it extravagant to imagine, that Mankind are no less, in Proportion, accountable for the ill Use of their Dominion over Creatures of the lower Rank of Beings, than for the Exercise of Tyranny over their own Species. The more entirely the Inferior Creation is submitted to our Power, the more answerable we should seem for our Mismanagement of it; and the rather, as the very Condition of Nature renders these Creatures incapable of receiving any Recompence in another Life for their ill Treatment in this.

'Tis observable of those noxious Animals, which have Qualities most powerful to injure us, that they naturally avoid Mankind, and never hurt us unless provoked, or necessitated by Hunger. Man, on the other Hand, seeks out and pursues even the most inoffensive Animals, on purpose to persecute and destroy them.

Montaigne thinks it some Reflection upon Human Nature it self, that few People take Delight in seeing Beasts caress or play together, but almost every one is pleased to see them lacerate and worry one another. I am sorry this Temper is become almost a distinguishing Character of our own Nation, from the Observation which is made by Foreigners of our beloved Pastimes, *Bear-baiting*, *Cock-fighting*, and the like. We should find it hard to vindicate the destroying of any thing that has Life, meerly out of Wantonness; yet in this Principle our Children are bred up, and one of the first Pleasures we allow them, is the Licence of inflicting Pain upon poor Animals: Almost as soon as we are sensible what Life is our selves, we make it our Sport to take it from other Creatures. I cannot but believe a very good Use might be made of the Fancy which Children have for Birds and Insects. Mr. *Lock* takes Notice of a Mother who permitted them to her Children, but rewarded or punished them as they treated them well or ill. This was no other than entring them betimes into a daily Exercise of Humanity, and improving their very Diversion to a Virtue.

I fancy too, some Advantage might be taken of the common Notion, that 'tis ominous or unlucky to destroy some sorts of Birds, as *Swallows* and *Martins*; this Opinion might possibly arise from the Confidence these Birds seem to put in us by building under our Roofs, so that it is a kind of Violation of the Laws of Hospitality to murder them. As for *Robin-red-breasts* in particular, 'tis not improbable they owe their Security to the old Ballad of *the Children in the Wood*. However it be, I don't know, I say, why this Prejudice, well improved and carried as far as it would go, might not be made to conduce to the Preservation of many innocent Creatures, which are now exposed to all the Wantonness of an ignorant Barbarity.

There are other Animals that have the Misfortune, for no manner of Reason, to be treated as common

Enemies where-ever found. The Conceit that a *Cat* has *nine Lives* has cost at least nine Lives in ten of the whole Race of 'em: Scarce a Boy in the Streets but has in this Point outdone *Hercules* himself, who was famous for killing a Monster that had but *Three Lives.* Whether the unaccountable Animosity against this useful Domestick may be any Cause of the general Persecution of *Owles,* (who are a sort of feathered Cats) or whether it be only an unreasonable Pique the Moderns have taken to a serious Countenance, I shall not determine. Tho' I am inclined to believe the former; since I observe the sole Reason alledged for the Destruction of *Frogs* is because they are like *Toads.* Yet amidst all the Misfortunes of these unfriended Creatures, 'tis some Happiness that we have not yet taken a Fancy to eat them: For should our Countrymen refine upon the *French* never so little, 'tis not to be conceived to what unheard of Torments *Owles, Cats,* and *Frogs* may be yet reserved.

When we grow up to Men, we have another Succession of Sanguinary Sports; in particular *Hunting.* I dare not attack a Diversion which has such Authority and Custom to support it, but must have leave to be of Opinion, that the Agitation of that Exercise, with the Example and Number of the Chasers, not a little contribute to resist those *Checks,* which Compassion would naturally suggest in behalf of the Animal pursued. Nor shall I say with Monsieur *Fleury,* that this Sport is *a Remain of the* Gothic *Barbarity*; but I must animadvert upon a certain Custom yet in Use with us, and barbarous enough to be derived from the *Goths,* or even the *Scythians*: I mean

that Savage Compliment our Huntsmen pass upon
Ladies of Quality, who are present at the Death of a
Stag, when they put the Knife in their Hands to cut
the Throat of a helpless, trembling and weeping
Creature.

—— *Questuque cruentus,*
Atque Imploranti similis. ——

But if our *Sports* are destructive, our *Glottony* is
more so, and in a more inhuman Manner. *Lobsters
roasted alive, Piggs whipp'd to Death, Fowls sowed up,*
are Testimonies of our outragious Luxury. Those,
who (as *Seneca* expresses it) divide their Lives betwixt an Anxious Conscience and a Nauseated Stomach, have a just Reward of their Gluttony in the
Diseases it brings with it: For Human Savages, like
other wild Beasts, find Snares and Poyson in the Pro-
visions of Life, and are allured by their Appetite to
their Destruction. I know nothing more shocking, or
horrid, than the Prospect of one of their Kitchins
cover'd with Blood, and filled with the Cries of Creatures expiring in Tortures. It gives one an Image of
a *Giant's Den* in a Romance, bestrow'd with the scattered Heads and mangled Limbs of those who were
slain by his Cruelty.

The excellent *Plutarch* (who has more Strokes of
Good-nature in his Writings than I remember in any
Author) cites a Saying of *Cato* to this effect, *That
'tis no easie Task to preach to the Belly which has no
Ears.* 'Yet if (says he) we are ashamed to be so out of
Fashion as not to Offend, let us at least Offend with
some Discretion and Measure. If we kill an Animal

for our Provision, let us do it with the Meltings of
Compassion, and without tormenting it. Let us consider, that 'tis in its own Nature Cruelty to put a living Creature to Death; we at least destroy a Soul that
has Sense and Perception'——In the Life of *Cato* the
Censor, he takes occasion from the severe Disposition of that Man to Discourse in this manner. 'It
ought to be esteemed a Happiness to Mankind, that
our Humanity has a wider Sphere to exert itself in,
than bare Justice. It is no more than the Obligation
of our very Birth to practise Equity to our own
kind, but Humanity may be extended thro' the
whole Order of Creatures, even to the meanest: Such
Actions of Charity are the Over-flowings of a mild
Good nature on all below us. It is certainly the part
of a well-natured Man to take care of his Horses and
Dogs, not only in expectation of their Labour while
they are Foals and Whelps, but even when their old
Age has made them incapable of Service.'

History tells us of a wise and polite Nation that rejected a Person of the first Quality, who stood for a
Judiciary Office, only because he had been observed
in his Youth, to take pleasure in tearing and murder-
ing of Birds. And of another that expelled a Man out
of the Senate for dashing a Bird against the Ground
which had taken shelter in his Bosom. Every one
knows how remarkable the *Turks* are for their Humanity in this kind: I remember an *Arabian* Author,
who has written a Treatise to show, how far a Man,
supposed to have subsisted in a Desart Island, without any Instruction, or so much as the sight of any
other Man, may, by the pure Light of Nature, attain

the Knowledge of Philosophy and Virtue. One of
the first things he makes him observe is, that Universal Benevolence of Nature in the Protection and Preservation of its Creatures. In Imitation of which, the
first Act of Virtue he thinks his Self-taught Philosopher would of Course fall into is, to Relieve and Assist all the Animals about him in their Wants and Dis-
tresses.

Ovid has some very tender and pathetick Lines
applicable to this Occasion.

> *Quid meruistis oves, placidum pecus, inque tegendos*
> *Natum homines, pleno quæ fertis in Ubere nectar?*
> *Mollia quæ nobis vestras velamina lanas*
> *Præbetis; vitaque magis quam morte juvatis.*
> *Quid meruere boves, animal sine fraude dolisque,*
> *Innocuum, simplex, natum tolerare labores?*
> *Immemor est demum, nec frugum munere dignus,*
> *Qui potuit, curvi dempto modo pondere aratri,*
> *Ruricolam mactare suum——*
> *Quam male consuevit, quam se parat ille cruori*
> *Impius humano, Vituli qui guttura cultro*
> *Rumpit, & immotas præbet mugitibus aures!*
> *Aut qui vagitus similes puerilibus hædum*
> *Edentem jugulare potest!——*

Perhaps that Voice or Cry so nearly resembling the
Human, with which Providence has endued so many
different Animals, might purposely be given them to
move our Pity, and prevent those Cruelties we are
too apt to inflict on our Fellow Creatures.

There is a Passage in the Book of *Jonas*, when God
declares his Unwillingness to destroy *Nineveh*, where
methinks that Compassion of the Creator, which ex-

tends to the meanest Rank of his Creatures, is expressed with wonderful Tenderness——*Should I not spare Nineveh the great City, wherein are more than six thousand Persons——And also much Cattel?* And we have in *Deuteronomy* a Precept of great Goodnature of this sort, with a Blessing in Form annexed to it in those Words. *If thou shalt find a Birds Nest in the way, thou shalt not take the Damm with the young: But thou shalt in any wise let the Damm go; that it may be well with thee, and that thou may'st prolong thy days.*

To conclude, there is certainly a Degree of Gratitude owing to those Animals that serve us; as for such as are Mortal or Noxious, we have a Right to destroy them; and for those that are neither of Advantage or Prejudice to us, the common Enjoyment of Life is what I cannot think we ought to deprive them of.

This whole Matter, with regard to each of these Considerations, is set in a very agreeable Light in one of the *Persian* Fables of *Pilpay*, with which I shall end this Paper.

A Traveller passing thro' a Thicket, and seeing a few Sparks of a Fire, which some Passengers had kindled as they went that way before, made up to it. On a sudden the Sparks caught hold of a Bush, in the midst of which lay an Adder, and set it in Flames. The Adder intreated the Traveller's Assistance, who tying a Bag to the end of his Staff, reached it, and drew him out: He then bid him go where he pleased, but never more be hurtful to Men, since he owed his Life to a Man's Compassion. The Adder, however, prepared to sting him, and when he expostulated how unjust it was to retaliate Good with Evil, I shall do no more (said the Adder) than what you Men

i

practise every Day, whose Custom it is to requite Benefits with Ingratitude. If you can deny this Truth, let us refer it to the first we meet. The Man consented, and seeing a Tree, put the Question to it in what manner a good Turn was to be recompenced? If you mean according to the Usage of Men (replied the Tree) by its contrary, I have been standing here these hundred Years to protect them from the scorching Sun, and in requital they have cut down my Branches, and are going to saw my Body into Planks. Upon this the Adder insulting the Man, he appealed to a second Evidence, which was granted, and immediately they met a Cow. The same Demand was made, and much the same Answer given, that among Men it was certainly so. I know it (said the Cow) by woful Experience; for I have served a Man this long time with Milk, Butter and Cheese, and brought him besides a Calf every Year: but now I am old, he turns me into this Pasture, with design to sell me to a Butcher, who will shortly make an end of me. The Traveller upon this stood confounded, but desired, of Courtesie, one Trial more, to be finally judged by the next Beast they should meet. This happened to be the Fox, who upon hearing the Story in all its Circumstances, could not be persuaded it was possible for the Adder to enter in so narrow a Bag. The Adder to convince him went in again; when the Fox told the Man he had now his Enemy in his Power, and with that he fastened the Bag, and crushed him to Pieces.

The Guardian, No. 61.   Thursday, May 21, 1713.

[*A* RECEIT *to make an* EPICK POEM]

————*Docebo*
Unde parentur opes, quid alat, formetque Poetam.

Hor.

IT is no small Pleasure to me, who am zealous in the Interests of Learning, to think I may have the Honour of leading the Town into a very new and uncommon Road of Criticism. As that kind of Literature is at present carried on, it consists only in a Knowledge of Mechanick Rules, which contribute to the Structure of different sorts of Poetry, as the Receits of good Houswives do to the making Puddings of Flower, Oranges, Plumbs, or any other Ingredients. It would, methinks, make these my Instructions more easily intelligible to ordinary Readers, if I discoursed of these Matters in the Stile in which Ladies Learned in Œconomicks dictate to their Pupils for the Improvement of the Kitchin and Larder.

I shall begin with Epick Poetry, because the Criticks agree it is the greatest Work Human Nature is capable of. I know the *French* have already laid down many Mechanical Rules for Compositions of this Sort, but at the same time they cut off almost all Undertakers from the Possibility of ever performing them; for the first Qualification they unanimously require in a Poet, is a *Genius*. I shall here endeavour (for the Benefit of my Countrymen) to make it manifest, that Epick Poems may be made *without a Genius*, nay without Learning or much Reading. This must necessarily be of great Use to all those Poets who confess they never Read, and of whom the World is convinced they never Learn. What *Moliere* observes of making a Dinner, that any Man can do it *with Mony*, and if a profest Cook cannot *without*, he has his Art for nothing; the same may be said of making a Poem, 'tis easily brought about by him that *has* a Genius, but the Skill lies in doing it without one. In pursuance of this End, I shall present the Reader with a plain and certain *Recipe*, by which even Sonneteers and Ladies may be qualified for this grand Performance.

I know it will be objected, that one of the chief Qualifications of an Epick Poet, is to be knowing in all Arts and Sciences. But this ought not to discourage those that have no Learning, as long as Indexes and Dictionaries may be had, which are the Compendium of all Knowledge. Besides, since it is an established Rule, that none of the Terms of those Arts and Sciences are to be made use of, one may venture to affirm, our Poet cannot impertinently offend in this Point. The Learning which will be more particularly necessary to him, is the ancient Geography of Towns, Mountains, and Rivers: For this let him take *Cluverius*, Value Four-pence.

Another Quality required is a compleat Skill in Languages. To this I answer, that it is notorious Persons of no Genius have been oftentimes great Linguists. To instance in the *Greek*, of which there are two Sorts; the Original *Greek*, and that from which our Modern Authors translate. I should be unwilling to promise Impossibilities, but modestly speaking, this may be learned in about an Hour's time with

Ease. I have known one, who became a sudden Professor of *Greek*, immediately upon Application of the
Left-hand Page of the *Cambridge Homer* to his Eye.
It is, in these Days, with Authors as with other Men,
the well bred are familiarly acquainted with them at
first Sight; and as it is sufficient for a good General to
have *survey'd* the Ground he is to conquer, so it is
enough for a good Poet to have *seen* the Author he is
to be Master of. But to proceed to the Purpose of
this Paper.

A Receit to make an *Epick* Poem.

For the *Fable*.

*Take out of any old Poem, History-books, Romance,
or Legend, (for instance* Geffry of Monmouth *or* Don
Belianis of Greece) *those Parts of Story which afford
most Scope for long Descriptions: Put these Pieces together, and throw all the Adventures you fancy into one
Tale. Then take a Hero, whom you may chuse for the
Sound of his Name, and put him into the midst of these
Adventures: There let him* work, *for twelve Books; at
the end of which you may take him out, ready prepared
to conquer or to marry; it being necessary that the Conclusion of an Epick Poem be fortunate.*

To make an Episode. *Take any remaining Adventure of your former Collection, in which you could no
way involve your Hero; or any unfortunate Accident
that was too good to be thrown away; and it will be of
Use, applyed to any other Person; who may be lost and
evaporate in the Course of the Work, without the least
Damage to the Composition.*

For the Moral and Allegory. *These you may Ex-*

*tract out of the Fable afterwards at your Leisure; Be
sure you strain them sufficiently.*

For the Manners.

For those of the Hero, take all the best Qualities you
*can find in all the best celebrated Heroes of Antiquity;
if they will not be reduced to a Consistency, lay 'em all
on a heap upon him. But be sure they are Qualities
which your* Patron *would be thought to have; and to
prevent any Mistake which the World may be subject to,
select from the Alphabet those Capital Letters that
compose his Name, and set them at the Head of a Dedication before your Poem. However, do not absolutely observe the exact Quantity of these Virtues, it not being
determined whether or no it be necessary for the Hero
of a Poem to be an honest Man——For the* Under-
Characters, *gather them from* Homer *and* Virgil, *and
Change the Names as Occasion serves.*

For the Machines.

*Take of Deities, Male and Female, as many as you
can use. Separate them into two equal parts, and keep*
Jupiter *in the middle. Let* Juno *put him in a Ferment,
and* Venus *mollifie him. Remember on all Occasions to
make use of Volatile* Mercury. *If you have need of Devils, draw them out of* Milton's Paradise, *and extract
your Spirits from* Tasso. *The Use of these Machines is
evident; for since no Epick Poem can possibly subsist
without them, the wisest way is to reserve them for your
greatest Necessities. When you cannot extricate your
Hero by any Human Means, or your self by your own
Wit, seek Relief from Heaven, and the Gods will do*

your Business very readily. This is according to the di-rect Prescription of Horace *in his Art of Poetry.*

Nec Deus intersit, nisi dignus vindice *Nodus*
Inciderit——

That is to say, a Poet should never call upon the Gods
for their Assistance, but when he is in great Per-
plexity.

For the Descriptions.

For a Tempest. *Take* Eurus, Zephyr, Auster *and*
Boreas, *and cast them together in one Verse. Add to
these of Rain, Lightning, and of Thunder (the loudest
you can)* quantum sufficit. *Mix your Clouds and Billows well together till they foam, and thicken your Description here and there with a Quicksand. Brew your
Tempest well in your Head, before you set it a blowing.*

For a Battel. *Pick a large quantity of Images and
Descriptions from* Homer's *Iliads, with a Spice or two
of* Virgil, *and if there remain any Overplus, you may
lay them by for a* Skirmish. *Season it well with* Similes,
and it will make an Excellent Battel.

For a Burning Town. *If such a Description be necessary, because it is certain there is one in* Virgil, *Old*
Troy *is ready burnt to your Hands. But if you fear
That would be thought* borrowed, *a Chapter or two of
the Theory of the* Conflagration, *well circumstanced,
and done into Verse, will be a good* Succedaneum.

As for Similes *and* Metaphors, *they may be found
all over the Creation, the most ignorant may gather
them, but the danger is in applying them. For this, advise with your Bookseller.*

For the Language.

(*I mean the* Diction.) *Here it will do well to be an Imitator of* Milton, *for you'll find it easier to imitate him in this than any thing else.* Hebraisms *and* Grecisms *are to be found in him, without the trouble of Learning the Languages. I knew a* Painter, *who* (*like our* Poet) *had no* Genius, *make his* Dawbings *be thought* Originals *by setting them in the* Smoak: *You may in the same manner give the venerable* Air *of* Antiquity *to your* Piece, *by darkening it up and down with* Old English. *With this you may be easily furnished upon any Occasion, by the* Dictionary *commonly* Printed *at the end of* Chaucer.

I must not conclude, without cautioning all Writers without Genius in one material Point; which is, never to be afraid of having *too much Fire* in their Works. I should advise rather to take their warmest Thoughts, and spread them abroad upon Paper; for they are observed to cool before they are read.

The Guardian, No. 78.   Wednesday, June 10, 1713.

[*The* CLUB *of* LITTLE MEN]

I.

To NESTOR IRONSIDE, *Esq*;

SIR,

I REMEMBER a Saying of yours concerning Persons in low Circumstances of Stature, that their Littleness would hardly be taken Notice of, if they did not manifest a Consciousness of it themselves in all their Behaviour. Indeed, the Observation that no Man is Ridiculous for being what he is, but only in the Affectation of being something more, is equally true in regard to the Mind and the Body.

I question not but it will be pleasing to you to hear, that a Sett of us have formed a Society, who are sworn to *Dare to be Short*, and boldly bear out the Dignity of Littleness under the Noses of those Enormous Engrossers of Manhood, those Hyperbolical Monsters of the Species, the tall Fellows that overlook us.

The Day of our Institution was the *Tenth* of *December*, being the *Shortest* of the Year, on which we are to hold an Annual Feast over a Dish of *Shrimps*.

The Place we have chosen for this Meeting is in the *Little Piazza*, not without an Eye to the Neighbourhood of Mr. *Powel*'s Opera, for the Performers of which we have, as becomes us, a Brotherly Affection.

At our first Resort hither an old Woman brought her Son to the Club Room, desiring he might be Educated in this School, because she saw here were finer Boys than ordinary. However, this Accident no way discouraged our Designs. We began with sending Invitations to those of a Stature not exceeding *five Foot*, to repair to our Assembly; but the greater part returned Excuses, or pretended they were not qualified.

One said he was indeed but five Foot at present, but represented that he should soon exceed that Proportion, his Perriwig-maker and Shoe-maker having lately promised him three Inches more betwixt them.

Another alledged he was so unfortunate as to have one Leg shorter than the other, and whoever had determined his Stature to *five Foot*, had taken him at a Disadvantage; for when he was mounted on the other Leg he was at least *five Foot two Inches and a half*.

There were some who questioned the exactness of our Measures, and others, instead of complying, returned us Informations of People yet shorter than themselves. In a Word, almost every one recommended some Neighbour or Acquaintance, whom he was willing we should look upon to be less than he. We were not a little ashamed that those, who are past the Years of Growth, and whose Beards pronounce them Men, should be guilty of as many unfair Tricks, in this Point, as the most aspiring *Children* when they are measured.

We therefore proceeded to fit up the Club-Room, and provide Conveniences for our Accommodation. In the first Place we caus'd a total Removal of all the *Chairs, Stools, and Tables*, which had served the *gross of Mankind* for many Years. The Disadvantages we had undergone, while we made use of these, were unspeakable. The President's whole Body was sunk in the Elbow-Chair, and when his Arms were spread over it, he appeared (to the great lessening of his Dignity) like a *Child* in a *Go-cart:* It was also so wide in the Seat, as to give a Wag Occasion of saying, that notwithstanding the President sate in it there was a *Sede Vacante.* The Table was so high that one, who came by chance to the Door, seeing our Chins just above the Pewter Dishes, took us for a Circle of Men that sate ready to be shaved, and sent in half a dozen Barbers. Another time one of the Club spoke contumeliously of the President, imagining he had been Absent, when he was only eclypsed by a *Flask* of *Florence* which stood on the Table in a Parallel Line before his Face. We therefore new furnished the Room in all Respects proportionably to us, and had the Door made lower, so as to admit no Man of above five Foot high, without brushing his Foretop, which whoever does is utterly unqualified to sit among us.

Some of the Statutes of the Club are as follow:

I. If it be proved upon any Member, tho' never so duly qualified, that he strives as much as possible to get above his Size, by Stretching, Cocking, or the like; or that he hath stood on Tiptoe in a Crowd, with design to be taken for as tall a Man as the rest; or hath privily conveyed any large Book, Cricket, or other Device under him, to exalt him on his Seat: Every such Offender shall be sentenced to Walk in Pumps for a whole Month.

II. If any Member shall take Advantage from the

Fulness or Length of his Wig, or any part of his Dress, or the immoderate Extent of his Hat, or otherwise, to seem larger or higher than he is; *it is Ordered*, he shall wear *Red Heels* to his Shoes, and a *Red Feather* in his Hat, which may apparently mark and set Bounds to the Extremities of his small Dimension, that all People may readily find him out between his Hat and his Shoes.

III. If any Member shall purchase a Horse for his own Riding, above fourteen Hands and a half in height, that Horse shall forthwith be Sold, a *Scotch Galloway* bought in its stead for him, and the Overplus of the Money shall treat the Club.

IV. If any Member, in direct Contradiction to the Fundamental Laws of the Society, shall wear the Heels of his Shoes exceeding one Inch and half, it shall be interpreted as an open Renunciation of Littleness, and the Criminal shall instantly be expell'd. *Note*. The Form to be used in expelling a Member shall be in these Words; *Go from among us, and be tall if you can!*

It is the unanimous Opinion of our whole Society, that since the Race of Mankind is granted to have decreas'd in Stature from the beginning to this present, it is the Intent of Nature it self, that Men should be little; and we believe, that all Human Kind shall at last *grow down* to *Perfection*, that is to say, be reduced to our own Measure.

I am, very Litterally,
Your Humble Servant,
Bob Short.

The Guardian, No. 91.   Thursday, June 25, 1713.

[*The* CLUB *of* LITTLE MEN]

II.

Homunculi quanti sunt, cum recogito! Plautus.

To NESTOR IRONSIDE, *Esq*;
SIR,

THE Club rising early this Evening, I have
time to finish my Account of it. You are already acquainted with the Nature and Design
of our Institution; the Characters of the Members,
and the Topicks of our Conversation, are what remain for the Subject of this Epistle.

The most eminent Persons of our Assembly are a
little Poet, a little Lover, a little Politician, and a
little Heroe. The first of these, *Dick Distick* by Name,
we have elected President, not only as he is the shortest of us all, but because he has entertain'd so just a
Sense of the Stature, as to go generally in Black that
he may appear yet Less. Nay, to that Perfection is he
arrived, that he *stoops* as he walks. The Figure of the
Man is odd enough; he is a lively little Creature, with
long Arms and Legs: A Spider is no ill Emblem of
him. He has been taken at a Distance for a *small
Windmill.* But indeed what principally moved us in
his Favour was his Talent in Poetry, for he hath promised to undertake a long Work in *short Verse* to
celebrate the Heroes of our Size. He has entertained
so great a Respect for *Statius*, on the Score of that
Line,

Major in exiguo regnabat corpore virtus,

that he once designed to translate the whole *Thebaid* for the sake of little *Tydeus*.

Tom. Tiptoe, a dapper black Fellow, is the most gallant Lover of the Age. He is particularly nice in his Habiliments; and to the end Justice may be done him that way, constantly employs the same Artist who makes Attire for the neighb'ring Princes and Ladies of Quality at Mr. *Powel*'s. The Vivacity of his Temper inclines him sometimes to boast of the Favours of the Fair. He was, 'tother Night, excusing his Absence from the Club on Account of an Assignation with a Lady, (and, as he had the Vanity to tell us, a Tall one too) who had consented to the full Accomplishment of his Desires that Evening. But one of the Company, who was his Confident, assured us she was a Woman of Humour, and made the Agreement on this Condition, That his Toe should be tied to hers.

Our *Politician* is a Person of *real Gravity*, and *professed Wisdom*. Gravity in a Man of this Size, compared with that of one of ordinary Bulk, appears like the Gravity of a Cat compared with that of a Lion. This Gentleman is accustomed to talk to himself, and was once over-heard to compare his own Person to a *little Cabinet*, wherein are locked up all the Secrets of State, and refined Schemes of Princes. His Face is pale and meager, which proceeds from much watching and studying for the Welfare of *Europe*, which is also thought to have stinted his Growth: For he hath destroyed his own Constitution with taking care of that of the Nation. He is what Mons. *Balzac* calls *a great Distiller of the Maxims of* Tacitus: When he

Speaks, it is slowly and Word by Word, as one that is loth to enrich you too fast with his Observations; like a Limbeck that gives you, Drop by Drop, an Extract of the Simples in it.

The last I shall mention is *Tim. Tuck*, the Hero. He is particularly remarkable for the length of his Sword, which intersects his Person in a cross Line, and makes him appear not unlike a Fly, that the Boys have run a Pin thro', and set a walking. He once challenged a tall Fellow for giving him a blow on the Pate with his Elbow as he pass'd along the Street. But what he especially values himself upon is, that in all the Campaigns he has made, he never once *Duck'd* at the whizz of a Cannon Ball. *Tim.* was full as large at fourteen Years old as he is now. This we are tender of mentioning, your little Heroes being generally Cholerick.

These are the Gentlemen that most enliven our Conversation: The Discourse generally turns upon such Accidents, whether Fortunate or Unfortunate, as are daily occasioned by our Size: These we faithfully communicate, either as Matter of Mirth, or of Consolation to each other. The President had lately an unlucky Fall, being unable to keep his Legs on a Stormy Day; whereupon he informed us it was no new Disaster, but the same a certain Ancient Poet had been subject to; who is recorded to have been so light, that he was obliged to poize himself against the Wind with Lead on one side, and his own Works on the other. The *Lover* confest the other Night that he had been cured of Love to a tall Woman, by reading over the Legend of *Ragotine* in *Scarron*, with his

Tea, three Mornings successively. Our Hero rarely acquaints us with any of his unsuccessful Adventures: And as for the *Politician*, he declares himself an utter Enemy to all kind of Burlesque, so will never discompose the Austerity of his Aspect by laughing at our Adventures, much less discover any of his own in this ludicrous Light. Whatever he tells of any Accidents that befal him is by way of Complaint, nor is he ever laughed at but in his Absence.

We are likewise particularly careful to communicate in the Club all such Passages of History, or Characters of Illustrious Personages, as any way reflect Honour on little Men. *Tim. Tuck* having but just Reading enough for a Military Man, perpetually entertains us with the same Stories, of little *David* that conquered the mighty *Goliah*, and little *Luxembourg* that made *Lewis* XIV. a *Grand Monarque*, never forgetting Little *Alexander the Great. Dick Distick* celebrates the exceeding Humanity of *Augustus*, who called *Horace, Lepidissimum Homunciolum*; and is wonderfully pleased with *Voiture* and *Scarron*, for having so well described their Diminutive Forms to all Posterity. He is peremptorily of Opinion, against a great Reader, and all his Adherents, that *Æsop* was not a jot properer or handsomer than he is represented by the common Pictures. But the Soldier believes with the Learned Person above-mentioned; for he thinks none but an impudent Tall Author could be guilty of such an unmannerly Piece of Satire on little Warriors, as his Battle of the *Mouse* and the *Frog*. The *Politician* is very proud of a certain King of *Egypt*, called *Bocchor*, who, as *Diodorus* as-

sures us, was a Person of very low Stature, but far
exceeded all that went before him *in Discretion and
Politicks.*

As I am Secretary to the Club, 'tis my Business
whenever we meet to take Minutes of the Transactions: This has enabled me to send you the foregoing
Particulars, as I may hereafter other Memoirs. We
have Spies appointed in every Quarter of the Town,
to give us Informations of the Misbehaviour of such
refractory Persons as refuse to be subject to our Statutes. Whatsoever aspiring Practices any of these our
People shall be guilty of in their Amours, single Com-
bats, or any indirect means to Manhood, we shall certainly be acquainted with, and publish to the World
for their Punishment and Reformation. For the President has granted me the sole Propriety of exposing
and showing to the Town all such intractable Dwarfs,
whose Circumstances exempt them from being carried about in Boxes: Reserving only to himself, as
the Right of a Poet, those *Smart Characters* that will
shine in *Epigrams.* Venerable *Nestor,* I salute you in
the Name of the Club.

BOB SHORT, *Secretar.*

The Guardian, No. 92.   Friday, June 26, 1713.

k

[*On a* DREAM *of a* WINDOW *in his* MISTRESS'S BREAST]

SIR,

YOUR two Kinsmen and Predecessors of Immortal Memory, were very famous for their Dreams and Visions, and contrary to all other Authors never pleased their Readers more than when they were Nodding. Now it is observed, that the *Second-sight* generally runs in the Blood; and, Sir, we are in hopes that you yourself, like the rest of your Family, may at length prove a Dreamer of Dreams, and a Seer of Visions. In the mean while I beg leave to make you a Present of a Dream, which may serve to lull your Readers till such time as you your self shall think fit to gratifie the Publick with any of your Nocturnal Discoveries.

You must understand, Sir, I had Yesterday been reading and ruminating upon that Passage where *Momus* is said to have found Fault with the Make of a Man, because he had not a Window in his Breast. The Moral of this Story is very obvious, and means no more than that the Heart of Man is so full of Wiles and Artifices, Treachery and Deceit, that there is no guessing at what he is from his Speeches and outward Appearance. I was immediately reflecting how happy each of the Sexes would be, if there was a Window in the Breast of every one that makes or receives Love. What Protestations and Perjuries would be saved on the one Side, what Hypocrisie and Dissimulation on the other? I am my self very far gone in this Passion for *Aurelia*, a Woman of an unsearchable Heart. I would give the World to know the Secrets of it, and particularly whether I am really in her good Graces, or if not, who is the happy Person.

I fell asleep in this agreeable Reverie, when on a sudden methought *Aurelia* lay by my Side. I was placed by her in the Posture of *Milton*'s *Adam*, and *with Looks of Cordial Love hung over her enamour'd*. As I cast my Eye upon her Bosom, it appeared to be all of Chrystal, and so wonderfully transparent, that I saw every Thought in her Heart. The first Images I discovered in it were Fans, Silks, Ribbonds, Laces, and many other Gewgaws, which lay so thick together, that the whole Heart was nothing else but a Toy-shop. These all faded away and vanished, when immediately I discerned a long Train of Coaches and six, Equipages and Liveries that ran through the Heart one after another in a very great hurry for above half an Hour together. After this, looking very attentively, I observed the whole space to be filled with a Hand of Cards, in which I could see distinctly three Mattadors. There then followed a quick Succession of different Scenes. A Play-house, a Church, a Court, a Poppet-show, rose up one after another, till at last they all of them gave Place to a Pair of new Shoes, which kept footing in the Heart for a whole Hour. These were driven off at last by a Lap-dog, who was succeeded by a *Guiney* Pig, a Squirril and a Monky. I my self, to my no small Joy, brought up the Rear of these worthy Favourites. I was rav-

ished at being so happily posted and in full Possession of the Heart: But as I saw the little Figure
of my self Simpering, and mightily pleased with its
Situation, on a sudden the Heart methought gave a
Sigh, in which, as I found afterwards, my little Representative vanished; for upon applying my Eye I
found my Place taken up by an ill-bred awkward
Puppy with a Mony-bag under each Arm. This
Gentleman, however, did not keep his Station long
before he yielded it up to a Wight as disagreeable as
himself, with a white Stick in his Hand. These three
last Figures represented to me in a lively manner the
Conflicts in *Aurelia*'s Heart between Love, Avarice
and Ambition. For we justled one another out by
Turns, and disputed the Post for a great while. But
at last, to my unspeakable Satisfaction, I saw my self
entirely settled in it. I was so transported with my
Success, that I could not forbear hugging my dear
Piece of Chrystal, when to my unspeakable Mortification I awaked, and found my Mistress metamorphosed into a Pillow.

This is not the first time I have been thus disappointed.

O Venerable NESTOR, if you have any Skill in
Dreams, let me know whether I have the same Place
in the real Heart, that I had in the Visionary one: To
tell you truly, I am perplexed to Death between
Hope and Fear. I was very Sanguine till 11 a-Clock
this Morning, when I over-heard an unlucky old
Woman telling her Neighbour that Dreams always
went by Contraries. I did not indeed before, much
like the Chrystal Heart, remembring that confound-

ed Simile in *Valentinian* of a Maid *as cold as Chrystal never to be Thaw'd.* Besides I verily believe if I had slept a little longer that awkward Whelp with his Mony Bags would certainly have made his second Entrance. If you can tell the fair one's Mind, it will be no small proof of your Art, for I dare say it is more than she her self can do. Every Sentence she speaks is a Riddle, all that I can be certain of is, that I am her and,

Your humble Servant,

Peter Puzzle.

The Guardian, No. 106.   Monday, July 13, 1713.

[*On* SICKNESS]

Dear Sir,

YOU formerly observed to me, that nothing made a more ridiculous Figure in a Man's Life, than the Disparity we often find in him Sick and Well. Thus one of an unfortunate Constitution is perpetually exhibiting a miserable Example of the Weakness of his Mind, or of his Body, in their Turns. I have had frequent Opportunities of late to consider my self in these different Views, and hope I have received some Advantage by it. If what Mr. *Waller* says be true, that

> *The Soul's dark Cottage, batter'd and decay'd,*
> *Lets in new Light thro' Chinks that Time has made:*

Then surely Sickness, contributing no less than old Age to the shaking down this Scaffolding of the Body, may discover the inclosed Structure more plainly. Sickness is a sort of early old Age; it teaches us a Diffidence in our Earthly State, and inspires us with the Thoughts of a future, better than a thousand Volumes of Philosophers and Divines. It gives so warning a Concussion to those Props of our Vanity, our Strength and Youth, that we think of fortifying our selves within, when there is so little dependance on our Outworks. Youth, at the very best, is but a Betrayer of Human Life in a gentler and smoother manner than Age: 'Tis like a Stream that nourishes a Plant upon its Bank, and causes it to flourish and blossom to the Sight, but at the same time is undermining it at the Root in secret. My Youth has dealt more fairly and openly with me; it has afforded several Prospects of my Danger, and given me an Advantage not very common to young Men, that the Attractions of the World have not dazzled me very much; and I began where most People end, with a full Conviction of the Emptiness of all sorts of Ambition, and the unsatisfactory Nature of all human Pleasures.

When a smart Fit of Sickness tells me this Scurvy Tenement of my Body will fall in a little time, I am e'en as unconcern'd as was that honest *Hibernian*, who (being in Bed in the great Storm some Years ago, and told the House would tumble over his Head) made Answer, *What care I for the House? I am only a Lodger.*

I fancy 'tis the best time to die when one is in the best Humour, and so excessively weak as I now am, I may say with Conscience, that I'm not at all uneasie at the Thought that many Men, whom I never had any Esteem for, are likely to enjoy this World after me. When I reflect what an inconsiderable little Atome every single Man is, with respect to the whole Creation, methinks 'tis a Shame to be concerned at the Removal of such a trivial Animal as I am. The Morning after my *Exit*, the Sun will rise as bright as ever, the Flowers smell as sweet, the Plants spring as green, the World will proceed in its old Course, People will laugh as heartily, and Marry as fast, as they were used to do. *The Memory of Man* (as it is elegantly exprest in the Wisdom of *Solomon*) *passeth away as the remembrance of a Guest that tarrieth but one Day.*

There are Reasons enough, in the fourth Chapter of the same Book, to make any young Man contented with the Prospect of Death. *For honourable Age is not that which standeth in length of Time, or is measured by number of Years. But Wisdom is the gray Hair to Men, and an unspotted Life is old Age.* He was taken away speedily, lest that *Wickedness should alter his Understanding, or Deceit beguile his Soul.*

I am,

Yours.

The Guardian, No. 132.

Wednesday, August 12, 1713.

[*On* NATURE *and* DEATH]

—— *Cælumque tueri*
Jussit ——   Ovid.

I N fair Weather, when my Heart is cheered, and
I feel that Exaltation of Spirits which results
from Light and Warmth, joined with a beautiful
Prospect of Nature, I regard my self as one placed
by the Hand of God in the midst of an ample Theatre,
in which the Sun, Moon and Stars, the Fruits also,
and Vegetables of the Earth, perpetually changing
their Positions, or their Aspects, exhibit an Elegant
Entertainment to the Understanding, as well as to
the Eye.

Thunder and Lightning, Rain and Hail, the painted
Bow, and the glaring Comets, are Decorations of
this mighty Theatre. And the Sable Hemisphere
studded with Spangles, the blue Vault at Noon, the
glorious Gildings and rich Colours in the Horizon, I
look on as so many successive Scenes.

When I consider things in this Light, methinks it
is a sort of Impiety to have no Attention to the
Course of Nature, and the Revolutions of the Heavenly Bodies. To be regardless of those *Phænomena*
that are placed within our View, on purpose to entertain our Faculties, and display the Wisdom and
Power of their Creator, is an Affront to Providence
of the same kind, (I hope it is not Impious to make
such a Simile) as it wou'd be to a good Poet, to sit out
his Play without minding the Plot or Beauties of it.

And yet how few are there who attend to the Drama of Nature, its Artificial Structure, and those admirable Machines, whereby the Passions of a Philosopher are gratefully agitated, and his Soul affected with the sweet Emotions of Joy and Surprize? How many Fox-hunters and Rural Squires are to be found in *Great Britain*, who are ignorant that they have all this while lived on a Planet, that the Sun is several thousand times bigger than the Earth; and that there are other Worlds within our View, greater and more glorious than our own. Ay, but, says some illiterate Fellow, I enjoy the World, and leave others to contemplate it. Yes, you Eat and Drink, and run about upon it, that is, you enjoy it as a Brute; but to enjoy it as a Rational Being is to know it, to be sensible of its Greatness and Beauty, to be delighted with its Harmony, and by these Reflections to obtain just Sentiments of the Almighty Mind that framed it.

The Man who, unembarrassed with vulgar Cares, leisurely attends to the flux of things in Heaven, and things on Earth, and observes the Laws by which they are governed, hath secured to himself an easie and convenient Seat, where he beholds with Pleasure all that passes on the Stage of Nature; while those about him are, some fast asleep, and others struggling for the highest Places, or turning their Eyes from the Entertainment prepared by Providence, to play at Push-pin with one another.

Within this ample Circumference of the World, the glorious Lights that are hung on high, the Meteors in the middle Region, the various Livery of the

Earth, and the Profusion of good things that distinguish the Seasons, yield a Prospect which annihilates
all Human Grandeur. But when we have seen frequent Returns of the same Things, when we have
often viewed the Heaven and the Earth in all their
various Array, our Attention flags and our Admiration ceases. All the Art and Magnificence in Nature,
could not make us pleased with the same Entertainment, presented a hundred Years successively to
our View.

I am led into this way of Thinking by a Question
started the other Night, *viz.* Whether it were possible that a Man should be weary of a fortunate and
healthy Course of Life? My Opinion was, that the
bare Repetition of the same Objects, abstracted from
all other Inconveniencies, were sufficient to create in
our Minds a distaste of the World; and that the Ab-
horrence old Men have of Death, proceeds rather
from a Distrust of what may follow, than from the
Prospect of losing any present Enjoyments. For (as
an ancient Author somewhere expresses it·) when a
Man has seen the Vicissitudes of Night and Day,
Winter and Summer, Spring and Autumn, the returning Faces of the several Parts of Nature, what is
there further to detain his Fancy here below?

The Spectacle indeed is glorious, and may bear
viewing several times. But in a very few Scenes of revolving Years, we feel a Satiety of the same Images,
the Mind grows impatient to see the Curtain drawn
and behold new Scenes disclosed, and the Imagination is in this Life filled with a confused Idea of the
next.

Death, considered in this Light, is no more than passing from one Entertainment to another. If the present Objects are grown tiresome and distasteful, it is in order to prepare our Minds for a more exquisite Relish of those which are fresh and new. If the good things we have hitherto enjoyed are transient, they will be succeeded by those which the inexhaustible Power of the Deity will supply to eternal Ages. If the Pleasures of our present State are blended with Pain and Uneasiness, our future will consist of sincere unmixed Delights. Blessed Hope! the Thought whereof turns the very Imperfections of our Nature into Occasions of Comfort and Joy.

But what Consolation is left to the Man who hath no Hope or Prospect of these things? View him in that Part of Life when the natural Decay of his Faculties concurs with the frequency of the same Objects to make him weary of this World, when, like a Man who hangs upon a Precipice, his present Situation is uneasie, and the Moment that he quits his Hold, he is sure of sinking into Hell or Annihilation.

There is not any Character so hateful as his who Invents Racks and Tortures for Mankind. The *Free-Thinkers* make it their Business to introduce Doubts, Perplexities and Despair into the Minds of Men, and, according to the Poet's Rule, are most justly punished by their own Schemes.

The Guardian, No. 169.
Thursday, September 24, 1713.

[*On the* ORIGIN *of* LETTERS]

——Vitam excoluere per Artes. Virg.

Mr. IRONSIDE,

I HAVE been a long time in Expectation of something from you on the Subject of Speech and Letters: I believe the World might be as agreeably entertain'd, on that Subject, as with any thing that ever came into the Lion's Mouth. For this End I send you the following Sketch. And am,

Yours,

Philogram.

Upon taking a View of the several Species of living Creatures our Earth is stocked with, we may easily observe, that the lower Orders of them, such as Insects and Fishes, are wholly without a Power of making known their Wants and Calamities: Others, which are conversant with Man, have some few ways of expressing the Pleasure and Pain they undergo by certain Sounds and Gestures; but Man has articulate Sounds whereby to make known his inward Sentiments and Affections, tho' his Organs of Speech are no other than what he has in common with many other less perfect Animals. But the use of Letters, as significative of these Sounds, is such an additional Improvement to them, that I know not whether we ought not to attribute the Invention of them to the Assistance of a Power more than Human.

There is this great Difficulty which could not but attend the first Invention of Letters, to wit, That all the World must conspire in affixing steadily the same Signs to their Sounds, which affixing was at first as arbitrary as possible; there being no more Connexion between the Letters, and the Sounds they are expressive of, than there is between those Sounds and the Ideas of the Mind they immediately stand for: Notwithstanding which Difficulty, and the Variety of Languages, the *Powers* of the Letters in each are very nearly the same, being in all Places about Twenty Four.

But be the Difficulty of the Invention as great as it will, the Use of it is manifest, particularly in the Advantage it has above the Method of conveying our Thoughts by Words or Sounds, because this way we are confined to narrow Limits of Place and Time; whereas we may have occasion to correspond with a Friend at a distance, or a desire, upon a particular Occasion, to take the Opinion of an Honest Gentleman, who has been dead this thousand Years. Both which Defects are supplied by the Noble Invention of Letters; by this means we materialize our Ideas, and make them as lasting as the Ink and Paper, their Vehicles. This making our Thoughts by *Art* visible to the Eye, which *Nature* had made intelligible only by the Ear, is next to the adding a sixth Sense, as it is a Supply in case of the Defect of one of the five *Nature* gave us, namely Hearing, by making the Voice become visible.

Have any of any School of Painters, gotten themselves an Immortal Name, by drawing a Face, or

Painting a Landskip, by laying down on a piece of
Canvas a Representation only of what Nature had
given them Originals? What Applauses will he merit,
who first made his Ideas set to his Pencil, and drew
to his Eye the Picture of his Mind! Painting represents the outward Man, or the Shell; but can't reach
the Inhabitant within, or the very Organ by which
the Inhabitant is revealed: This Art may reach to represent a Face, but can't paint a Voice. *Kneller* can
draw the Majesty of the Queen's Person; *Kneller*
can draw her Sublime Air, and paint her bestowing
Hand as fair as the Lilly; but the Historian must inform Posterity, that she has one peculiar Excellence
above all other Mortals, that her Ordinary Speech is
more charming than Song.

But to drop the Comparison of this Art with any
other, let us see the Benefit of it in itself. By it the
English Trader may hold Commerce with the In-
habitants of the *East* or *West Indies*, without the
Trouble of a Journey. Astronomers seated at the distance of the Earth's Diameter asunder, may confer;
what is spoken and thought at one Pole, may be
heard and understood at the other. The Philosopher
who wish'd he had a Window to his Breast, to lay
open his Heart to all the World, might as easily have
reveal'd the Secrets of it this way, and as easily left
them to the World, as wish'd it. This silent Art of
speaking by Letters, remedies the Inconvenience
arising from distance of Time, as well as Place, and
is much beyond that of the *Egyptians*, who cou'd
preserve their Mumies for ten Centuries. This preserves the Works of the Immortal part of Men, so as

to make the Dead still useful to the Living. To this we are beholden for the Works of *Demosthenes* and *Cicero*, of *Seneca* and *Plato*; without it the Iliad of *Homer*, and Ænead of *Virgil* had died with their Authors, but by this Art those excellent Men still speak to us.

I shall be glad if what I have said on this Art, give you any new Hints for the more useful or agreeable Application of it.

I am,

SIR, &c.

The Guardian, No. 172,

Monday, September 28, 1713.

[*On* GARDENS]

I LATELY took a particular Friend of mine to my House in the Country, not without some Apprehension that it could afford little Entertainment to a Man of his Polite Taste, particularly in Architecture and Gardening, who had so long been conversant with all that is beautiful and great in either. But it was a pleasant Surprize to me, to hear him often declare, he had found in my little Retirement that Beauty which he always thought wanting in the most celebrated Seats, or if you will Villa's, of the Nation. This he described to me in those Verses with which *Martial* begins one of his Epigrams:

Baiana nostri Villa, Basse, Faustini,
Non otiosis ordinata myrtetis,
Viduaque platano, tonsilique buxeto,
Ingrata lati spatia detinet campi,
Sed rure vero, barbaroque lætatur.

There is certainly something in the amiable Simplicity of unadorned Nature, that spreads over the Mind a more noble Sort of Tranquility, and a loftier Sensation of Pleasure, than can be raised from the nicer Scenes of Art.

This was the Taste of the Ancients in their Gardens, as we may discover from the Descriptions [that]

1

are extant of them. The two most celebrated Wits of
the World have each of them left us a particular Picture of a Garden; wherein those great Masters, being
wholly unconfined, and Painting at Pleasure, may be
thought to have given a full Idea of what they esteemed most excellent in this way. These (one may
observe) consist intirely of the useful Part of Horti-
culture, Fruit Trees, Herbs, Water, &c. The Pieces
I am speaking of are *Virgil*'s Account of the Garden
of the old *Corycian*, and *Homer*'s of that of *Alcinous*.
The first of these is already known to the *English*
Reader, by the excellent Versions of Mr. *Dryden* and
Mr. *Addison*. The other having never been attempted in our Language with any Elegance, and being
the most beautiful Plan of this sort that can be imagined, I shall here present the Reader with a Translation of it.

The Gardens of *Alcinous*, from *Homer*'s *Odyss.* 7.

> *Close to the Gates a spacious Garden lies,*
> *From Storms defended and inclement Skies:*
> *Four Acres was th' allotted Space of Ground,*
> *Fenc'd with a green Enclosure all around.*
> *Tall thriving Trees confest the fruitful Mold;*
> *The red'ning Apple ripens here to Gold,*
> *Here the blue Figg with luscious Juice o'erflows,*
> *With deeper Red the full Pomegranate glows,*
> *The Branch here bends beneath the weighty Pear,*
> *And verdant Olives flourish round the Year.*
> *The balmy Spirit of the Western Gale*
> *Eternal breathes on Fruits untaught to fail:*
> *Each dropping Pear a following Pear supplies,*

On Apples Apples, Figs on Figs arise:
The same mild Season gives the Blooms to blow,
The Buds to harden, and the Fruits to grow.
   Here order'd Vines in equal Ranks appear

With all th' United Labours of the Year,
Some to unload the fertile Branches run,
Some dry the black'ning Clusters in the Sun,
Others to tread the liquid Harvest join,
The groaning Presses foam with Floods of Wine.
Here are the Vines in early Flow'r descry'd,
Here Grapes discolour'd on the sunny Side,
And there in Autumn's *richest Purple dy'd.*

   Beds of all various Herbs, for ever green,
In beauteous Order terminate the Scene.

   Two plenteous Fountains the whole Prospect
     crown'd;
This thro' the Gardens leads its Streams around,
Visits each Plant, and waters all the Ground:
While that in Pipes beneath the Palace flows,
And thence its Current on the Town bestows;
To various Use their various Streams they bring,
The People one, and one supplies the King.

Sir *William Temple* has remark'd, that this Description contains all the justest Rules and Provi-
sions which can go toward composing the best Gardens. Its Extent was four *Acres*, which, in those times
of Simplicity, was look'd upon as a large one, even
for a Prince: It was inclos'd all round for Defence;
and for Conveniency join'd close to the Gates of the
Palace.

He mentions next the Trees, which were Standards, and suffered to grow to their full height. The fine Description of the Fruits that never failed, and the eternal Zephyrs, is only a more noble and poetical way of expressing the continual Succession of one Fruit after another throughout the Year.

The *Vineyard* seems to have been a Plantation distinct from the *Garden*; as also the *Beds of Greens* mentioned afterwards at the Extremity of the Inclosure, in the Nature and usual Place of our *Kitchen Gardens*.

The two Fountains are disposed very remarkably. They rose within the Inclosure, and were brought by Conduits or Ducts, one of them to water all Parts of the Gardens, and the other underneath the Palace into the Town, for the Service of the Publick.

How contrary to this Simplicity is the modern Practice of Gardening; we seem to make it our Study to recede from Nature, not only in the various Tonsure of Greens into the most regular and formal Shapes, but even in monstrous Attempts beyond the reach of the Art it self: We run into Sculpture, and are yet better pleas'd to have our Trees in the most awkward Figures of Men and Animals, than in the most regular of their own.

> *Hinc & nexilibus videas e frondibus hortos,*
> *Implexos late muros, & Mœnia circum*
> *Porrigere, & latas e ramis surgere turres;*
> *Deflexam & Myrtum in Puppes, atque ærea rostra:*
> *In buxisque undare fretum, atque e rore rudentes.*
> *Parte alia frondere suis tentoria Castris;*
> *Scutaque spiculaque & jaculantia citria Vallos.*

I believe it is no wrong Observation that Persons of Genius, and those who are most capable of Art, are always most fond of Nature, as such are chiefly sensible, that all Art consists in the Imitation and Study of Nature. On the contrary, People of the common Level of Understanding are principally delighted with the little Niceties and Fantastical Operations of Art, and constantly think that *finest* which is least Natural. A Citizen is no sooner Proprietor of a couple of Yews, but he entertains Thoughts of erecting them into Giants, like those of *Guild-hall*. I know an eminent Cook, who beautified his Country Seat with a Coronation Dinner in Greens, where you see the Champion flourishing on Horseback at one end of the Table, and the Queen in perpetual Youth at the other.

For the benefit of all my loving Countrymen of this curious Taste, I shall here publish a Catalogue of Greens to be disposed of by an eminent Town-Gardiner, who has lately applied to me upon this Head. He represents, that for the Advancement of a politer sort of Ornament in the Villa's and Gardens adjacent to this great City, and in order to distinguish those Places from the meer barbarous Countries of gross Nature, the World stands much in need of a Virtuoso Gardiner who has a Turn to Sculpture, and is thereby capable of improving upon the Ancients of his Profession in the Imagery of Evergreens. My Correspondent is arrived to such Perfection, that he cuts Family Pieces of Men, Women or Children. Any Ladies that please may have their own Effigies in Myrtle, or their Husbands in Hornbeam. He is a Puritan Wag, and never fails, when he shows his Garden, to repeat that Passage in the Psalms, *Thy Wife shall be as the fruitful Vine, and thy Children as Olive Branches round thy Table*. I shall proceed to his Catalogue, as he sent it for my Recommendation.

Adam and *Eve* in Yew; *Adam* a little shatter'd by the fall of the Tree of Knowledge in the great Storm; *Eve* and the Serpent very flourishing.

The Tower of *Babel*, not yet finished.

St. *George* in Box; his Arm scarce long enough, but will be in a Condition to stick the Dragon by next *April*.

A *green Dragon* of the same, with a Tail of Ground Ivy for the present.

N.B. *These two not to be Sold separately.*

Edward the *Black Prince* in Cypress.

A *Laurustine* Bear in Blossom, with a Juniper Hunter in Berries.

A Pair of Giants, *stunted*, to be sold cheap.

A Queen *Elizabeth* in Phylyræa, a little inclining to the Green Sickness, but of full growth.

Another Queen *Elizabeth* in Myrtle, which was very forward, but Miscarried by being too near a Savine.

An old Maid of Honour in Wormwood.

A topping *Ben Johnson* in Lawrel.

Divers eminent Modern Poets in Bays, somewhat blighted, to be disposed of a Pennyworth.

A Quick-set Hog shot up into a Porcupine, by its being forgot a Week in rainy Weather.

A Lavender Pigg with Sage growing in his Belly.

Noah's Ark in Holly, standing on the Mount; the Ribs a little damaged for want of Water.

A Pair of *Maidenheads* in Firr, in great forwardness.

The Guardian, No. 173.

Tuesday, September 29, 1713.

THE
NARRATIVE
OF

Dr. *Robert Norris,*

Concerning the ſtrange and deplorable

FRENZY

OF

Mr. JOHN DENN---

An Officer of the *Cuſtom-houſe* :

Being an exact Account of all that paſt
betwixt the ſaid Patient and the Doctor till this preſent Day ; and a full
Vindication of himſelf and his Proceedings from the extravagant Reports of the ſaid Mr. *John Denn*—

——*excludit ſanos Helicone Poetas*
Democritus—— — —— Hor.

London : Printed for *J. Morphew* near *Statio-
ners-Hall,* 1713. Price 3 *d.*

THE

NARRATIVE

OF

Dr. *ROBERT NORRIS*,

Concerning the Strange and Deplorable Frenzy of
Mr. *JOHN DENN[IS]* an Officer of the Custom-
house.

IT is an acknowledg'd Truth, that nothing is so
dear to an honest Man as his good Name, nor
ought he to neglect the just Vindication of his
Character, when it is injuriously attack'd by any
Man. The Person I have at present Cause to complain of, is indeed in very melancholy Circumstances, it having pleas'd God to deprive him of his
Senses, which may extenuate the Crime in Him. But
I should be wanting in my Duty, not only to my
self, but also to him who hath endu'd me with Talents for the benefit of my Fellow-Creatures, shou'd
I suffer my Profession or Honesty to be undeservedly aspers'd. I have therefore resolv'd to give the Publick an account of all that has past between that unhappy Gentleman and my self.

On the 20*th* instant, while I was in my Closet pon-
dering the Case of one of my Patients, I heard a

Knocking at my Door; upon opening of which enter'd an old Woman with Tears in her Eyes, and
told me, that without my Assistance her Master
would be utterly ruin'd. I was forc'd to interrupt her
Sorrow by enquiring her Master's Name and Place
of Abode. She told me he was one Mr. *Denn*[*is*] an
Officer of the Custom-house, who was taken ill of a
violent Frenzy last *April*, and had continu'd in those
melancholy Circumstances with few or no Intervals.
Upon this I ask'd her some Questions relating to his
Humour and Extravagancies, that I might the better know under what Regimen to put him, when the
Cause of his Distemper was found out. Alass, Sir,
says she, this Day fortnight in the Morning a poor
simple Child came to him from the Printer's; the
Boy had no sooner enter'd the Room, but he cry'd
out *the Devil was come*. He often stares ghastfully,
raves aloud, and mutters between his Teeth the
Word *Cator*, or *Cato*, or some such thing. Now, Doctor, this *Cator* is certainly a *Witch*, and my poor
Master is under an evil Tongue; for I have heard
him say *Cator* has bewitch'd the whole Nation. It
pitied my very Heart, to think that a Man of my
Master's Understanding and great Scholarship, who,
as the Child told me, had a Book of his own in Print,
should talk so outragiously. Upon this I went and
laid out a Groat for a Horse-shoe, which is at this
time nail'd on the Threshold of his Door; but I don't
find my Master is at all the better for it; he perpetually starts and runs to the Window when any one
knocks, crying out, *S'death! a Messenger from the
French King! I shall die in the* Bastile.

Having said this, the old Woman presented me
with a Viol of his Urine; upon Examination of which
I perceiv'd the whole Temperament of his Body to
be exceeding hot. I therefore instantly took my Cane
and my Beaver, and repair'd to the Place where he
dwelt.

When I came to his Lodgings near *Charing-cross*,
up three Pair of Stairs, (which I should not have
publish'd in this manner, but that this Lunatick con-
ceals the Place of his Residence on purpose to prevent the good Offices of those charitable Friends and
Physicians, who might attempt his Cure) when I
came into the Room, I found this unfortunate Gentleman seated on his Bed, with Mr. *Bernard Lintott*,
Bookseller, on the one side of him, and a grave elderly Gentleman on the other, who, as I have since
learnt, calls himself a Grammarian, the Latitude of
whose Countenance was not a little eclips'd by the
Fullness of his Peruke. As I am a black lean Man of
a pale Visage, and hang my Clothes on somewhat
slovenly, I no sooner went in but he frown'd upon
me, and cry'd out with violence, *S"Death*, a *French-
man!* I am betray'd to the Tyrant! who cou'd have
thought the Queen wou'd have deliver'd me up to
France in this Treaty, and least of all that you, my
Friends, wou'd have been in a Conspiracy against
me?——Sir, said I, here is neither Plot nor Conspiracy, but for your advantage. The Recovery of your
Senses requires my Attendance, and your Friends
sent for me on no other account. I then took a particular Survey of his Person, and the Furniture and
Disposition of his Apartment. His Aspect was fur-

ious, his Eyes were rather fiery than lively, which he roll'd about in an uncommon manner. He often open'd his Mouth, as if he wou'd have utter'd some Matter of Importance, but the Sound seem'd lost inwardly. His Beard was grown, which they told me he would not suffer to be shav'd, believing the modern Dramatick Poets had corrupted all the Barbers in the Town to take the first Opportunity of cutting his Throat. His Eye-brows were grey, long, and grown together, which he knit with Indignation when any thing was spoken, insomuch that he seem'd not to have smoothed his Forehead for many Years. His Flannel Night Cap, which was exceedingly begrim'd with Sweat and Dirt, hung upon his Left Ear; the Flap of his Breeches dangled between his Legs, and the Rolls of his Stockings fell down to his Ankles.

I observ'd his Room was hung with *old Tapestry*, which had several Holes in it, caus'd, as the Old Woman inform'd me, by his having cut out of it the Heads of divers *Tyrants*, the Fierceness of whose Visages had much provoked him. On all sides of his Room were pinned a great many Sheets of a Tragedy called *Cato*, with Notes on the Margin with his own Hand. The Words *Absurd*, *Monstrous*, *Execrable*, were every where written in such large Characters, that I could read them without my Spectacles. By the Fire-side lay Three-farthings-worth of Smallcoal in a *Spectator*, and behind the Door huge Heaps of Papers of the same Title, which his Nurse inform'd me she had convey'd thither out of his sight, believing they were Books of the Black Art; for her Master never read in them, but he was either quite

mop'd, or in raving Fits: There was nothing neat in
the whole Room, except some Books on his Shelves
very well bound and gilded, whose Names I had
never before heard of, nor I believe are any where
else to be found; such as *Gibraltar, a Comedy*; *Remarks on Prince Arthur*; *the Grounds of Criticism in
Poetry*; *an Essay on publick Spirit*. The only one I
had any Knowledge of was a *Paradise Lost*, inter-
leav'd. The whole Floor was cover'd with Manuscripts, as thick as a Pastry Cook's Shop on a Christ-
mas Eve. On his Table were some Ends of Verse and
of Candles; a Gallipot of Ink with a yellow Pen in
it, and a Pot of half-dead Ale cover'd with a *Longinus*.

As I was casting my Eyes round on all this odd
Furniture with some Earnestness and Astonishment,
and in a profound Silence, I was on a sudden surpriz'd to hear the Man speak in the following manner:

'Beware, Doctor, that it fare not with you as with
your Predecessor the famous *Hippocrates*, whom the
mistaken Citizens of *Abdera* sent for in this very
manner to cure the Philosopher *Democritus*; he return'd full of Admiration at the Wisdom of that Person whom he had suppos'd a Lunatick. Behold, Doctor, it was thus *Aristotle* himself and all the great
Antients spent their Days and Nights, wrapt up in
Criticism, and beset all around with their own Writings. As for me, whom you see in the same manner,
be assur'd I have none other Disease than a Swelling
in my Legs, whereof I say no more, since your Art
may further certify you.'

I thereupon seated my self upon his Bed-side, and

placing my Patient on my Right Hand, to judge the better in what he affirm'd of his Legs, felt his Pulse.

For it is *Hippocrates*'s Maxim, that if the Pulse have a Dead Motion, with some unequal Beatings, 'tis a Symptom of a Sciatica, or a Swelling in the Thigh or Leg; in which Assertion of his this Pulse confirm'd me.

I began now to be in hopes that his Case had been misrepresented, and that he was not so far gone, but some timely Medicines might recover him. I therefore proceeded to the proper Queries, which with the Answers made to me, I shall set down in Form of Dialogue, in the very Words they were spoken, because I would not omit the least Circumstance in this Narrative; and I call my Conscience to witness, as if upon Oath, that I shall tell the Truth without addition or diminution.

Doct. Pray, Sir, how did you contract this Swelling?

Denn. By a Criticism.

Doct. A Criticism! that's a Distemper I never read of in *Galen*.

Denn. S'Death, Sir, a Distemper! It is no Distemper, but a Noble Art. I have sat fourteen Hours a Day at it; and are you a Doctor, and don't know there's a Communication between the Legs and the Brain?

Doct. What made you sit so many Hours, Sir?

Denn. *Cato*, Sir.

Doct. Sir, I speak of your Distemper, what gave you this Tumor?

Denn. *Cato*, *Cato*, *Cato*.

Old Wom. For God's sake, Doctor, name not this evil Spirit, 'tis the whole Cause of his Madness: Alass, poor Master's just falling into his Fits.

Mr. *Lintott.* Fit's! Z—— what Fits? A Man may well have Swellings in his Legs, that sits writing fourteen Hours in a Day. He got this by the *Remarks.*

Doct. The *Remarks!* what are those?

Denn. S'Death! have you never read my Remarks? I will be damn'd if this Dog *Lintott* ever publish'd my Advertisements.

Mr. *Lint.* Z——! I publish'd Advertisement upon Advertisement; and if the Book be not read, it is none of my fault, but his that made it. By G—, as much has been done for the Book, as cou'd be done for any Book in Christendom.

Doct. We do not talk of Books, Sir; I fear those are the Fuel that feed his *Delirium*; mention them no more. You do very ill to promote this Discourse.

I desire a Word in private with this other Gentleman, who seems a grave and sensible Man: I suppose, Sir, you are his Apothecary.

Gent. Sir, I am his Friend.

Dr. I doubt it not. What Regimen have you observ'd since he has been under your Care? You remember, I suppose, the Passage of *Celsus*, which says, if the Patient, on the third Day, have an Interval, suspend the Medicaments at Night; let Fumigations be used to corroborate the Brain; I hope you have upon no Account promoted Sternutation by Hellebore.

Gent. Sir, no such matter, you utterly mistake.

m

Dr. Am I not a Physician? and shall an Apothecary dispute my *Nostrums*—You may perhaps have
fill'd up a Prescription or two of *Ratcliff*'s, which had
chance to succeed, and with that very Prescription
injudiciously prescrib'd to different Constitutions,
have destroy'd a Multitude. *Pharmacopola componat,*
Medicus solus prescribat, says *Celsus.* Fumigate him,
I say, this very Evening, while he is relieved by an
Interval.

Denn. S'Death, Sir, my Friend an Apothecary! a
base Mechanic! He who, like my self, professes the
noblest Sciences in the Universe, Criticism and Poetry. Can you think I would submit my Writings to
the Judgment of an Apothecary? By the Immortals,
he himself inserted three whole Paragraphs in my
Remarks, had a Hand in my *Publick Spirit,* nay, assisted me in my Description of the Furies, and infer-
nal Regions in my *Appius.*

Mr. *Lintott.* He is an Author; you mistake the
Gentleman, Doctor; he has been an Author these
twenty Years, to his Bookseller's Knowledge, and no
Man's else.

Denn. Is all the Town in a Combination? Shall
Poetry fall to the ground? Must our Reputation be
lost to all foreign Countries? O Destruction! Perdi-
tion! *Opera! Opera!* As Poetry once rais'd a City,
so when Poetry fails, Cities are overturn'd, and the
World is no more.

Dr. He raves, he raves; Mr. *Lintott,* I pray you
pinion down his Arms, that he may do no Mischief.

Denn. O I am sick, sick to Death!

Dr. That is a good Symptom, a very good Symptom. To be sick to Death (say the modern Physicians) is an excellent Symptom. When a Patient is sensible of his Pain, 'tis half a Cure. Pray, Sir, of what are you sick?

Denn. Of every thing, Of every thing. I am sick of the *Sentiments*, of the *Diction*, of the *Protasis*, of the *Epitasis*, and the *Catastrophe*—— Alas, what is become of the *Drama*, the *Drama?*

Old Wom. The *Dram*, Sir? Mr. *Lintott* drank up all the Geneva just now; but I'll go fetch more presently!

Denn. O shameful Want, scandalous Omission! By all the Immortals, here is no *Peripœtia*, no Change of Fortune in the Tragedy; Z—— no Change at all.

Old Wom. Pray, good Sir, be not angry, I'll fetch Change.

Dr. Hold your Peace, Woman, his Fit increases; good Mr. *Lintott* hold him.

Mr. *Lintott.* Plague on't! I am damnably afraid they are in the right of it, and he is mad in earnest, if he should be really mad, who the Devil will buy the *Remarks?*

(*Here Mr.* Lintott *scratched his Head.*)

Dr. Sir, I shall order you the cold Bath to morrow ——Mr. *Lintott*, you are a sensible Man; pray send for Mr. *Verdier's* Servant, and as you are a Friend to the Patient, be so kind as to stay this Evening whilst he is cupp'd on the Head. The Symptoms of his Madness seem to be desperate; for *Avicen* says, that if Learning be mix'd with a Brain that is not of a Contexture fit to receive it, the Brain ferments till it be totally exhausted. We must eradicate these undigested Ideas out of the *Perecranium*, and reduce the Patient to a competent Knowledge of himself.

Denn. Caitiffs stand off; unhand me, Miscreants! Is the Man whose whole Endeavours are to bring the Town to Reason mad? Is the Man who settles Poetry on the Basis of Antiquity mad? Dares any one assert there is a *Peripætia* in that vile Piece that's foisted upon the Town for a Dramatick Poem? That Man is mad, the Town is mad, the World is mad. See *Longinus* in my right Hand, and *Aristotle* in my left; I am the only Man among the Moderns that support them. Am I to be assassinated? and shall a Bookseller, who hath liv'd upon my Labours, take away that Life to which he owes his Support?

Gent. By your Leave, Gentlemen, I apprehend you not. I must not see my Friend ill treated; he is no more affected with Lunacy than my self; I am also of the same Opinion as to the *Peripætia*—— Sir, by the Gravity of your Countenance and Habit, I should conceive you to be a graduate Physician; but by your indecent and boisterous Treatment of this Man of Learning, I perceive you are a violent sort of *Person*, I am loth to say *Quack*, who, rather than his Drugs should lie upon his own Hands, would get rid of them, by cramming them into the Mouths of others: The Gentleman is of good Condition, sound Intellectuals, and unerring Judgment: I beg you will not oblige me to resent these Proceedings.

THESE were all the Words that pass'd among us at this Time; nor was there need for more, it being necessary we should make use of Force in the Cure of my Patient.

I privately whisper'd the old Woman to go to *Verdier*'s in *Long Acre*, with Orders to come immediately with Cupping Glasses; in the mean time, by the Assistance of Mr. *Lintott*, we lock'd his Friend into a Closet, (who 'tis plain from his last Speech was likewise toucht in his Intellects) after which we bound our Lunatick Hand and Foot down to the Bedsted, where he continued in violent Ravings, notwithstanding the most tender Expressions we could use to perswade him to submit to the Operation, till the Servant of *Verdier* arriv'd. He had no sooner clap'd half a dozen Cupping Glasses on his Head, and behind his Ears, but the Gentleman abovemention'd bursting open the Closet, ran furiously upon us, cut Mr. *Denn[is's]* Bandages, and let drive at us with a vast Folio, which sorely bruis'd the Shin of Mr. *Lintott*; Mr. *John Denn[is]* also starting up with the Cupping Glasses on his Head, seized another Folio, and with the same dangerously wounded me in the Skull, just above my right Temple. The Truth of this Fact Mr. *Verdier*'s Servant is ready to attest upon Oath, who, taking an exact Survey of the Volumes, found that which wounded my Head to be *Gruterus*'s *Lampas Critica*, and that which broke Mr. *Lintott*'s Shin was *Scaliger*'s *Poetices*. After this, Mr. *John Denn[is]* strengthen'd at once by Rage and Madness, snatch'd up a Peruke-Block, that stood by the Bed-side, and weilded it round in so furious a Manner, that he broke three of the Cupping Glasses from the Crown of his Head, so that much Blood trickled down his Visage—He look'd so ghastly, and his Passion was grown to such a prodigious Height, that my self, Mr. *Lintott*, and *Ver-*

dier's Servant, were oblig'd to leave the Room in all the Expedition imaginable.

I took Mr. *Lintott* home with me, in order to have our Wounds drest, and laid hold of that Opportunity of entering into Discourse with him about the Madness of this Person, of whom he gave me the following remarkable Relation:

That on the 17th of *May*, 1712. between the Hours of 10 and 11 in the Morning, Mr. *John Denn*[*is*] enter'd into his Shop, and opening one of the Volumes of the *Spectator*, in the large Paper, did suddenly, without the least Provocation, tear out that of N° [40] where the Author treats of Poetical Justice, and cast it into the Street. That the said Mr. *John Denn*[*is*] on the 27th of *March*, 1712. finding on the said Mr. *Lintott*'s Counter a Book called an *Essay on Criticism*, just then publish'd, he read a Page or two with much Frowning and Gesticulation, till coming to these two Lines;

Some have at first for Wits, then Poets past,
Turn'd Criticks next, and prov'd plain Fools at last.

He flung down the Book in a terrible Fury, and cried out, *By G— he means Me.*

That being in his Company on a certain Time, when *Shakespear* was mention'd as of a contrary Opinion to Mr. *Denn*[*is*] he swore the said *Shakespear* was a *Rascal*, with other defamatory Expressions, which gave Mr. *Lintott* a very ill Opinion of the said *Shakespear*.

That about two Months since, he came again into the Shop, and cast several suspicious Looks on a

Gentleman that stood by him, after which he desired some Information concerning that Person. He was no sooner acquainted that the Gentleman was a new Author, and that his first Piece was to be publish'd in a few Days, but he drew his Sword upon him, and had not my Servant luckily catch'd him by the Sleeve, I might have lost one Author upon the spot, and another the next Sessions.

Upon recollecting all these Circumstances, Mr. *Lintott* was entirely of Opinion, that he had been mad for some Time; and I doubt not but this whole Narrative must sufficiently convince the World of the Excess of his Frenzy. It now remains, that I give the Reasons which obliged me in my own Vindication to publish this whole unfortunate Transaction.

In the first place, Mr. *John Denn*[*is*] had industriously caused to be reported that I enter'd into his Room *Vi & Armis*, either out of a Design to deprive him of his Life, or of a new Play called *Coriolanus*, which he has had ready for the Stage these four Years.

Secondly, He hath given out about *Fleetstreet* and the *Temple*, that I was an Accomplice with his Bookseller, who visited him with Intent to take away divers valuable Manuscripts, without paying him Copy-Money.

Thirdly, He hath told others, that I am no Graduate Physician, and that he had seen me upon a Mountebank Stage in *Moorfields*, when he had Lodgings in the College there.

Fourthly, Knowing that I had much Practice in the City, he reported at the *Royal Exchange, Custom-*

house, and other Places adjacent, that I was a foreign Spy, employ'd by the *French* King to convey him into *France*; that I bound him Hand and Foot; and that, if his Friend had not burst from his Confinement to his Relief, he had been at this Hour in the *Bastile.*

All which several Assertions of his are so very extravagant, as well as inconsistent, that I appeal to all Mankind whether this Person be not out of his Senses. I shall not decline giving and producing further Proofs of this Truth in open Court, if he drives the Matter so far. In the mean time I heartily forgive him, and pray that the Lord may restore him to the full Enjoyment of his Understanding: So wisheth, as becometh a Christian,

Robert Norris, M.D.

From my House on
  Snow-hill, July
  the 30th.

God Save the Queen.

The Dedication

OF

The RAPE of the LOCK

1714

TO

Mrs. *ARABELLA FERMOR*

MADAM,

IT will be in vain to deny that I have some Value for this Piece, since I Dedicate it to You. Yet You may bear me Witness, it was intended only to divert a few young Ladies, who have good Sense and good Humour enough, to laugh not only at their Sex's little unguarded Follies, but at their own. But as it was communicated with the Air of a Secret, it soon found its Way into the World. An imperfect Copy having been offer'd to a Bookseller, You had the Good-Nature for my Sake to consent to the Publication of one more correct: This I was forc'd to before I had executed half my Design, for the *Machinery* was entirely wanting to compleat it.

The *Machinery*, Madam, is a Term invented by the Criticks, to signify that Part which the Deities, Angels, or Dæmons, are made to act in a Poem: For the ancient Poets are in one respect like many modern Ladies; Let an Action be never so trivial in it self, they always make it appear of the utmost Importance. These Machines I determin'd to raise on a very new and odd Foundation, the *Rosicrucian* Doctrine of Spirits.

I know how disagreeable it is to make use of hard Words before a Lady; but 'tis so much the Concern of a Poet to have his Works understood, and particularly by your Sex, that You must give me leave to explain two or three difficult Terms.

The *Rosicrucians* are a People I must bring You acquainted with. The best Account I know of them is in a French Book call'd *Le Comte de Gabalis*, which both in its Title and Size is so like a *Novel*, that many of the Fair Sex have read it for one by Mistake. According to these Gentlemen, the four Elements are inhabited by Spirits, which they call *Sylphs, Gnomes, Nymphs*, and *Salamanders*. The *Gnomes*, or Dæmons of Earth, delight in Mischief; but the *Sylphs*, whose Habitation is Air, are the best-condition'd Creatures imaginable. For they say, any Mortals may enjoy the most intimate Familiarities with these gentle Spirits, upon a Condition very easie to all true *Adepts*, an inviolate Preservation of Chastity.

As to the following Canto's, all the Passages of them are as Fabulous, as the Vision at the Beginning, or the Transformation at the End; (except the Loss of your Hair, which I always name with Reverence.) The Human Persons are as Fictitious as the Airy ones; and the Character of *Belinda*, as it is now manag'd, resembles You in nothing but in Beauty.

If this Poem had as many Graces as there are in Your Person, or in Your Mind, yet I could never hope it should pass thro' the World half so Uncensured as You have done. But let its Fortune be what it will, mine is happy enough, to have given me this Occasion of assuring You that I am, with the truest Esteem,

Madam,
Your Most Obedient
Humble Servant,
A . P O P E .

A

KEY

TO THE

LOCK.

OR,

A TREATISE proving, beyond all Contradiction, the dangerous Tendency of a late Poem, entituled, *The RAPE of the LOCK.*

TO

GOVERNMENT and RELIGION.

By ESDRAS BARNIVELT, Apoth.

𝔗𝔥𝔢 𝔖𝔢𝔠𝔬𝔫𝔡 𝔈𝔡𝔦𝔱𝔦𝔬𝔫.

To which are added commendatory Copies of Verſes, by the moſt Eminent Political Wits of the Age.

LONDON:

Printed for J. ROBERTS near the *Oxford-Arms* in *Warwick-Lane,* 1715.

THE
Epistle Dedicatory to Mr. *POPE*.

THOUGH *it may seem foreign to my Profession, which is that of making up and dispensing salutary Medicines to his Majesty's Subjects, (I might say my Fellow-Subjects, since I have had the Advantage of being naturalized) yet cannot I think it unbecoming me to furnish an Antidote against the Poyson which hath been so artfully distilled through your Quill, and conveyed to the World through the pleasing Vehicle of your Numbers. Nor is my Profession as an Apothecary so abhorrent from yours as a Poet, since the Ancients have thought fit to make the same God the Patron of Both. I have, not without some Pleasure, observ'd the mystical Arms of our Company, wherein is represented* Apollo *killing the fell Monster* Python; *this in some measure admonishes me of my Duty, to trample upon and destroy, as much as in me lies, that Dragon, or baneful Serpent,* Popery.

I must take leave to make you my Patient, whether you will or no; though out of the Respect I have for you, I should rather chuse to apply Lenitive than Corrosive Medicines, happy, if they may prove an Emetic sufficient to make you cast up those Errors, which you have imbibed in your Education, and which, I hope, I shall never live to see this Nation digest.

Sir, I cannot but lament, that a Gentleman of your acute Wit, rectified Understanding, and sublimated Imagination, should misapply those Talents to raise ill Humours in the Constitution of the Body Politick, of which your self are a Member, and upon the Health whereof your own Preservation depends. Give me leave to say, such Principles as yours would again reduce us to the fatal Necessity of the Phlebotomy of War, or the Causticks of Persecution.

In order to inform you of this, I have sought your Acquaintance and Conversation with the utmost Diligence; for I hoped in Person to persuade you to a publick Confession of your Fault, and a Recantation of these dangerous Tenets. But finding all my Endeavours ineffectual, and being satisfied with the Conscience of having done all that became a Man of an honest Heart and honourable Intention; I could no longer omit my Duty in opening the Eyes of the World by the Publication of this Discourse. It was indeed written some Months since, but seems not the less proper at this Juncture, when I find so universal [an] Encouragement given by both Parties to the Author of a libellous Work that is designed equally to prejudice them both. The uncommon Sale of this Book (for above 6000 of 'em have been already vended) was also a farther Reason that call'd aloud upon me to put a stop to its further Progress, and to preserve his Majesty's Subjects, by exposing the whole Artifice of your Poem in Publick.

Sir, to address my self to so florid a Writer as you, without collecting all the Flowers of Rhetorick, would be an unpardonable Indecorum; *but when I speak to the World, as I do in the following Treatise, I must use a simple Stile, since it would be absurd to prescribe an universal Medicine, or* Catholicon, *in a Language not universally understood.*

As I have always professed to have a particular Es-

teem for Men *of Learning, and more especially for your self, nothing but the Love of Truth should have engaged me in a Design of this* Nature. Amicus Plato, Amicus Socrates, sed magis Amica Veritas.   *I am*

Your most Sincere Friend,
and Humble Servant,
E. Barnivelt.

n

To my much Honoured and Esteemed *Friend,* Mr. E. BARNIVELT, *Author of the* Key to the Lock. *An* ANAGRAM *and* ACROSTICK. *By* N. CASLETON, *A Well-willer to the Coalition of Parties.*

BARNIVELT.

Anagram,

UN BAREL IT.

B ARRELS conceal the Liquor they contain,
A nd Sculls are but the Barrels of the Brain.
R ipe Politicks the Nation's Barrel fill,
N one can like thee its Fermentation still.
I ngenious Writer, lest thy Barrel split,
V nbarrel thy just Sense, and broach thy Wit.
E xtract from *Tory* Barrels all *French* Juice, ⎫
L et not the *Whigs* Geneva's Stumm infuse, ⎬
T hen shall thy Barrel be of gen'ral Use. ⎭

N. CASLETON.

To the Ingenious *Mr*. E. BARNIVELT.

HAIL, dear Collegiate, Fellow-Operator,
   Censor of Tories, President of Satyr,
   Whose fragrant Wit revives, as one may say,
The stupid World, like *Assa fetida*.
How safe must be the King upon his Throne,
When *Barnivelt* no Faction lets alone.
Of secret Jesuits swift shall be the Doom,
Thy Pestle braining all the Sons of *Rome*.
Before thy Pen vanish the Nation's Ills,
As all Diseases fly before thy Pills.
Such Sheets as these, whate'er be the Disaster,
Well spread with Sense, shall be the Nation's Plaister.

                    HIGH GERMAN DOCTOR.

To my Ingenious Friend, the Author of the Key to the
Lock.

THO' many a Wit from time to time has rose
    T' *inform* the World of what *it better knows,*
    Yet 'tis a Praise that few their own can call,
To tell Men things they never *knew at all.*
This was reserv'd, Great *Barnivelt,* for Thee,
To save this Land from dangerous Mystery.
But thou too gently hast laid on thy Satyr;
What awes the World is Envy and ill Nature.
Can Popish Writings do the Nations good?
Each Drop of Ink demands a Drop of Blood.
A Papist wear the Lawrel ! is it fit?
O *Button!* summon all thy Sons of Wit!
Join in the common Cause e'er 'tis too late;
Rack your Inventions some, and some *in time* tran-
    late.
If all this fail, let Faggot, Cart, and Rope,
Revenge our Wits and Statesmen on a *Pope.*

The GRUMBLER.

To the most Learned Pharmacopolitan, and Excellent Politician, Mr. ESDRAS BARNIVELT.

By Sir JAMES BAKER, *Knt.*

THE *Spaniard* hides his Ponyard in his Cloke,
The Papist masques his Treason in a Joke;
But ev'n as Coughs thy *Spanish* Liquorish heals,
So thy deep Knowledge dark Designs reveals.
Oh had I been Ambassador created,
Thy Works in *Spanish* shou'd have been translated,
Thy Politicks should ope the Eyes of *Spain*,
And, like true *Sevil* Snuff, awake the Brain.
Go on, Great Wit, contemn thy Foe's Bravado,
In thy defence I'll draw *Toledo*'s Spado.
Knighthoods on those have been conferr'd of late,
Who save our Eyesight, or wou'd save our State,
Unenvy'd Titles grace our mighty Names,
The learn'd Sir *William*, or the deep Sir *James*,
Still may those Honours be as justly dealt,
And thou be stil'd Sir *Esdras Barnivelt*.

               JAMES BAKER, Knt.

A KEY to the *LOCK*

SINCE this unhappy Division of our Nation into Parties, it is not to be imagined how many Artifices have been made use of by Writers to obscure the Truth, and cover Designs, which may be detrimental to the Publick; in particular, it has been their Custom of late to vent their Political Spleen in Allegory and Fable. If an honest believing Nation is to be made a Jest of, we have a Story of *John Bull* and his Wife; if a Treasurer is to be glanced at, an *Ant* with a *white Straw* is introduced; if a Treaty of Commerce is to be ridiculed, 'tis immediately metamorphosed into a Tale of Count *Tariff*.

But if any of these Malevolents have never so small a Talent in Rhime, they principally delight to convey their Malice in that pleasing way, as it were, gilding the Pill, and concealing the Poyson under the Sweetness of Numbers. Who could imagine that an *Original Canto* of *Spencer* should contain a Satyr upon one Administration; or that *Yarhel's Kitchin*, or the *Dogs of Egypt*, should be a Sarcasm upon another.

It is the Duty of every well designing Subject to prevent, as far as in him lies, the ill Consequences of such pernicious Treatises; and I hold it mine to warn the Publick of the late Poem, entituled, the *RAPE of the LOCK;* which I shall demonstrate to be of this nature. Many of these sort of Books have been bought by honest and well-meaning People purely for their

Diversion, who have in the end found themselves insensibly led into the Violence of Party Spirit, and many domestick Quarrels have been occasioned by the different Application of these Books. The Wife of an eminent Citizen grew very noisy upon reading *Bob Hush*; *John Bull*, upon *Change*, was thought not only to concern the State, but to affront the City; and the Poem we are now treating of, has not only dissolved an agreeable Assembly of Beaus and Belles, but (as I am told) has set Relations at as great a distance, as if they were married together.

It is a common and just Observation, that when the Meaning of any thing is dubious, one can no way better judge of the true Intent of it, than by considering who is the Author, what is his Character in general, and his Disposition in particular.

Now that the Author of this Poem is professedly a *Papist*, is well known; and that a Genius so capable of doing Service to that Cause, may have been corrupted in the Course of his Education by *Jesuits* or others, is justly very much to be suspected; notwithstanding that seeming *Coolness* and *Moderation*, which he has been (perhaps artfully) reproached with, by those of his own Profession. They are sensible that this Nation is secured with good and wholesome Laws, to prevent all evil Practices of the Church of *Rome*; particularly the Publication of Books, that may in any sort propagate that Doctrine: Their Authors are therefore obliged to couch their Designs the deeper; and tho' I cannot averr that the Intention of this Gentleman was directly to spread Popish Doctrines, yet it comes to the same Point, if he touch the Government: For the Court of *Rome* knows very well, that the Church at this time is so firmly founded on the State, that the only way to shake the one is by attacking the other.

What confirms me in this Opinion, is an accidental Discovery I made of a very artful Piece of Management among his Popish Friends and Abettors, to hide this whole Design upon the Government, by taking all the Characters upon themselves.

Upon the Day that this Poem was published, it was my Fortune to step into the *Cocoa Tree*, where a certain Gentleman was railing very liberally at the Author, with a Passion extremely well counterfeited, for having (as he said) reflected upon him in the Character of *Sir Plume*. Upon his going out, I enquired who he was, and they told me, a *Roman Catholick Knight*.

I was the same Evening at *Will*'s, and saw a Circle round another Gentleman, who was railing in like manner, and shewing his Snuff-box and Cane, to prove he was satyrized in the same Character. I asked this Gentleman's Name, and was told, he was a *Roman Catholick Lord*.

A Day or two after I was sent for, upon a slight Indisposition, to the young Lady's to whom the Poem is dedicated. She also took up the Character of *Belinda* with much Frankness and good Humour, tho' the Author has given us a Key in his * Dedication, that he meant something further. This Lady is also a *Roman Catholick*. At the same time others of the

---

* *The Character of* Belinda (*as it is here manag'd*) *resembles you in nothing but in Beauty.*   Dedication to the *Rape of the Lock*.

Characters were claim'd by some Persons in the Room; and all of them *Roman Catholicks.*

But to proceed to the Work it self.

In all things which are intricate, as Allegories in their own Nature are, and especially those that are industriously made so, it is not to be expected we should find the Clue at first sight; but when once we have laid hold on that, we shall trace this our Author through all the Labyrinths, Doublings and Turnings of this intricate Composition.

First then let it be observed, that in the most demonstrative Sciences, some *Postulata* are to be granted, upon which the rest is naturally founded. I shall desire no more than one *Postulatum* to render this obvious to the meanest Capacity; which being granted me, I shall not only shew the Intent of this Work in general, but also explain the very *Names*, and expose all his fictitious *Characters* in their true Light; and we shall find, that even his *Spirits* were not meerly contrived for the sake of *Machinary.*

The only Concession which I desire to be made me, is, that by the *Lock* is meant

The Barrier Treaty.

I. First then I shall discover, that Belinda represents Great Britain, or (which is the same thing) her late Majesty. This is plainly seen in his Description of her.

On her white Breast a sparkling Cross she bore.

Alluding to the antient Name of *Albion*, from her

white Cliffs, and to the *Cross*, which is the Ensign of *England*.

II. The BARON, who cuts off the Lock, or Barrier Treaty, is the E[arl] of O[*xfor*]*d*.

III. CLARISSA, who lent the Scissars, my Lady M[*ashe*]*m*.

IV. THALESTRIS, who provokes *Belinda* to resent the Loss of the Lock or Treaty, the D[uches]s of M[*arlborou*]*gh*.

V. SIR PLUME, who is mov'd by *Thalestris* to re-demand it of *Great Britain*, P[rin]ce *Eu*[*ge*]*ne*, who came hither for that purpose.

There are other inferior Characters, which we shall observe upon afterwards; but I shall first ex-plain the foregoing.

The first Part of the *Baron*'s Character is his being *adventrous*, or enterprizing, which is the common Epithet given the E[arl] of O[*xfor*]*d* by his Ene-mies. The Prize he aspires to is the T[reasur]y, in order to which he offers a Sacrifice.

———————————————— *an Altar built*
Of twelve vast French *Romances neatly gilt.*

Our Author here takes occasion maliciously to in-sinuate this Statesman's *Love to France*; representing the Books he chiefly studies to be vast *French Ro-mances.* These are the vast Prospects from the Friend-ship and Alliance of *France*, which he satyrically calls *Romances*, hinting thereby, that these Promises and Protestations were no more to be relied on than those idle Legends. Of these he is said to build an Altar; to intimate, that all the Foundation of his Schemes and Honours was fix'd upon the *French Romances* above-mentioned.

A Fan, a Garter, Half a Pair of Gloves.

One of the Things he sacrifices is a *Fan*, which both for its *gaudy Show* and *perpetual Flutt'ring*, has been made the Emblem of *Woman.* This points at the Change of the *Ladies* of the *Bedchamber*; the *Garter* alludes to the Honours he conferr'd on some of his Friends; and we may without straining the Sense, call the Half Pair of Gloves, a *Gauntlet*; the Token of those Military Employments, which he is said to have sacrificed to his Designs. The Prize, as I said before, means the T[reasur]y, which he makes it his Prayers *soon to obtain,* and *long to possess.*

The Pow'rs gave ear, and granted half his Pray'r,
The rest the Winds dispers'd in empty Air.

In the first of these Lines he gives him the T[reasur]y, and in the last suggests that he should not long possess that Honour.

That *Thalestris* is the D[uches]s of *M[arlborou]gh,* appears both by her Nearness to *Belinda,* and by this Author's malevolent Suggestion, that she is a Lover of War.

To Arms, to Arms, the bold Thalestris *cries.*

But more particularly in several Passages in her Speech to *Belinda,* upon the cutting off the Lock, or Treaty. Among other Things she says, *Was it for this you bound your Locks in Paper Durance?* Was it for this so much Paper has been spent to secure the Barrier Treaty?

> *Methinks already I your Tears survey,*
> *Already hear the horrid Things they say;*
> *Already see you a degraded Toast.*

This describes the Aspersions under which that good Princess suffer'd, and the Repentance which must have followed the Dissolution of that Treaty, and particularly levels at the Refusal some People made to drink Her M[ajest]y's Health.

Sir Plume (a proper Name for a Soldier) has all the Circumstances that agree with P[rin]ce *Eu[ge]ne.*

> Sir Plume *of Amber Snuff-box justly vain,*
> *And the nice Conduct of a clouded Cane,*
> *With earnest Eyes* ——

'Tis remarkable, this General is a great Taker of Snuff as well as Towns; his Conduct of the clouded Cane gives him the Honour which is so justly his due, of an exact Conduct in Battle, which is figured by his Truncheon, the Ensign of a General. His earnest Eye, or the Vivacity of his Look, is so particularly remarkable in him, that this Character could be mistaken for no other, had not this Author purposely obscur'd it by the fictitious Circumstance of a *round, unthinking Face.*

Having now explained the chief Characters of his *Human Persons* (for there are some others that will hereafter fall in by the by, in the Sequel of this Discourse) I shall next take in pieces his *Machinary,* wherein his Satyr is wholly confined to Ministers of State.

The SYLPHS and GNOMES at first sight appeared to me to signify the two contending Parties of this Nation; for these being placed in the *Air*, and those on the *Earth*, I thought agreed very well with the common Denomination, HIGH and LOW. But as they are made to be the first Movers and Influencers of all that happens, 'tis plain they represent promiscuously the *Heads of Parties*, whom he makes to be the Authors of all those Changes in the State, which are generally imputed to the Levity and Instability of the *British* Nation.

> *This erring Mortals Levity may call,*
> *Oh blind to Truth! The Sylphs contrive it all.*

But of this he has given us a plain Demonstration; for speaking of these Spirits, he says in express Terms,

> —— *The chief the Care of Nations own,*
> *And guard with Arms Divine the* British *Throne.*

And here let it not seem odd, if in this mysterious way of Writing, we find the same Person, who has before been represented by the *Baron*, again described in the Character of *Ariel*; it being a common way with Authors, in this fabulous Manner, to take such a Liberty. As for instance, I have read in the *English St. Evremont*, that all the different Characters in *Petronius* are but *Nero* in so many different Appearances. And in the Key to the curious Romance of *Barclay's Argenis*, that both *Poliarchus* and *Archombrotus* mean only the *King* of *Navarre*.

We observe in the very Beginning of the Poem, that *Ariel* is possess'd of the Ear of *Belinda*; therefore it is absolutely necessary that this Person must be the Minister who was nearest the Queen. But whoever would be further convinc'd, that he meant the late T[reasure]r, may know him by his Ensigns in the following Line.

He rais'd his Azure Wand.————

His sitting on the Mast of a Vessel shows his presiding over the *S[ou]th S[e]a* Tr[a]de. When *Ariel* assigns to his *Sylphs* all the Posts about *Belinda*, what is more clearly described, than the Tr[easure]r's disposing all the Places of the Kingdom, and particularly about her M[ajest]y? But let us hear the Lines.

———— *Ye Spirits to your Charge repair,*
The flutt'ring Fan be Zephyretta's *Care;*
The Drops to thee, Brillante, *we consign,*
And, Momentilla, *let the Watch be thine:*
Do thou, Crispissa, *tend her fav'rite Lock.*

He has here particularized the Ladies and Women of the Bed-Chamber, the Keeper of the Cabinet, and her M[ajest]y's Dresser, and impudently given Nicknames to each.

To put this Matter beyond all Dispute, the *Sylphs* are said to be *wond'rous fond of Place,* in the Canto following, where *Ariel* is perched uppermost, and all the rest take their Places subordinately under him.

Here again I cannot but observe, the excessive Malignity of this Author, who could not leave this Character of *Ariel* without the same invidious Stroke which he gave him in the Character of the *Baron* before.

> *Amaz'd, confus'd, he saw his Power expir'd,*
> *Resign'd to Fate, and with a Sigh retir'd.*

Being another Prophecy that he should resign his Place, which it is probable all Ministers do with a Sigh.

At the Head of the *Gnomes* he sets *Umbriel*, a dusky melancholy Spright, who makes it his Business to give *Belinda* the Spleen; a vile and malicious Suggestion against some grave and worthy Minister. The Vapours, Fantoms, Visions, and the like, are the Jealousies, Fears, and Cries of Danger, that have so often affrighted and alarm'd the Nation. Those who are described in the House of Spleen, under those several fantastical Forms, are the same whom their Illwillers have so often called the *Whimsical*.

The two fore-going Spirits being the only considerable Characters of the Machinary, I shall but just mention the *Sylph* that is wounded with the Scissars at the Loss of the Lock, by whom is undoubtedly understood my L[or]d *To[wnshen]d*, who at that Time received a Wound in his Character for making the Barrier Treaty, and was cut out of his Employment upon the Dissolution of it: But that Spirit reunites, and receives no Harm; to signify, that it came to nothing, and his L[o]rdsh[i]p had no real Hurt by it.

But I must not conclude this Head of the Characters, without observing, that our Author has run through every Stage of Beings in search of Topicks for Detraction; and as he has characteriz'd some Persons under Angels and Men, so he has others under Animals, and Things inanimate. He has represented an eminent Clergy-man as a Dog, and a noted Writer as a Tool. Let us examine the former.

—*But* Shock, *who thought she slept too long,*
Leapt up, and wak'd his Mistress with his Tongue.
'Twas then, Belinda, *if Report say true,*
Thy Eyes first open'd on a Billet-doux.

By this *Shock,* it is manifest he has most audaciously and profanely reflected on Dr. *Sach[evere]ll,* who leap'd up, that is, into the Pulpit, and awaken'd *Great Britain* with his *Tongue,* that is, with his *Sermon,* which made so much *Noise;* and for which he has frequently been term'd by others of his Enemies, as well as by this Author, a Dog: Or perhaps, by his *Tongue,* may be more literally meant his *Speech* at his *Trial,* since immediately thereupon, our Author says, her Eyes open'd on a *Billet-doux; Billets-doux* being Addresses to Ladies from Lovers, may be aptly interpreted those Addresses of Loving Subjects to her M[ajest]y, which ensued that Trial.

The other Instance is at the End of the third Canto.

Steel did the Labours of the Gods destroy,
And strike to Dust th' Imperial Tow'rs of Troy.
Steel could the Works of mortal Pride confound,
And hew Triumphal Arches to the Ground.

Here he most impudently attributes the Demolition of *Dunkirk,* not to the Pleasure of her M[ajest]y, or her Ministry, but to the frequent Instigations of his Friend Mr. *Steel*; a very artful Pun to conceal his wicked Lampoonery!

Having now consider'd the general Intent and Scope of the Poem, and open'd the Characters, I shall next discover the Malice which is covered under the Episodes, and particular Passages of it.

The Game at *Ombre* is a mystical Representation of the late War, which is hinted by his making Spades the Trump; Spade in *Spanish* signifying a Sword, and being yet so painted in the Cards of that Nation; to which it is well known we owe the Original of our Cards. In this one Place indeed he has unawares paid a Compliment to the Queen, and her Success in the War; for *Belinda* gets the better of the two that play against her, the Kings of *France* and *Spain*.

I do not question but ev'ry particular Card has its Person and Character assign'd, which, no doubt, the Author has told his Friends in private; but I shall only instance in the Description of the Disgrace under which the D[uke] of *M[arlborou]gh* then suffer'd, which is so apparent in these Verses.

Ev'n mighty Pam, *that* Kings *and Queens o'erthrew,*
And mow'd down Armies *in the Fights of* Lu,
Sad Chance of War! now destitute of Aid,
Falls undistinguish'd ——

That the Author here had an Eye to our modern Transactions, is very plain from an unguarded Stroke towards the End of this Game.

o

And now, as oft in some distemper'd State,
On one nice Trick *depends the gen'ral Fate.*

After the Conclusion of the War, the publick Rejoicings and *Thanksgivings* are ridiculed in the two following Lines.

The Nymph exulting, fills with Shouts the Sky,
The Walls, the Woods, and long Canals reply.

Immediately upon which there follows a malicious Insinuation, in the manner of a Prophecy, (which we have formerly observ'd this seditious Writer delights in) that the Peace should continue but a short Time, and that the Day should afterwards be curst which was then celebrated with so much Joy.

Sudden these Honours shall be snatch'd away,
And curst for ever this victorious Day.

As the Game at *Ombre* is a satyrical Representation of the late War; so is the Tea-Table that ensues, of the Council-Table and its Consultations after the Peace. By this he would hint, that all the Advantages we have gain'd by our late extended Commerce, are only Coffee and Tea, or Things of no greater Value. That he thought of the Trade in this Place, appears by the Passage where he represents the *Sylphs* particularly careful of the *rich Brocade*; it having been a frequent Complaint of our Mercers, that *French Brocades* were imported in too great Quantities. I will not say, he means those Presents of rich Gold Stuff Suits, which were said to be made her M[ajest]y by the K[ing] of *F[rance]*, tho' I cannot but suspect, that he glances at it.

Here this Author, as well as the scandalous *John Dunton*, represents the Mi[nist]ry in plain Terms taking frequent Cups.

And frequent Cups prolong the rich Repast.

Upon the whole, it is manifest he meant something more than common Coffee, by his calling it,

Coffee that makes the Politician *wise.*

And by telling us, it was this Coffee, that

Sent up in Vapours to the Baron's *Brain*
New Stratagems ———

I shall only further observe, that 'twas at this Table the Lock was cut off; for where but at the Council Board should the Barrier Treaty be dissolved?

The ensuing Contentions of the Parties upon the Loss of that Treaty, are described in the Squabbles following the Rape of the Lock; and this he rashly expresses, without any disguise in the Words.

All side in Parties ———

Here first you have a Gentleman who sinks beside his Chair: A plain Allusion to a Noble Lord, who lost his Chair of Pre[side]nt of the Co[unci]l.

I come next to the *Bodkin,* so dreadful in the Hand of *Belinda*; by which he intimates the *British Scepter,* so rever'd in the Hand of our late August Princess. His own Note upon this Place tells us he alludes to a Scepter; and the Verses are so plain, they need no Remark.

The same (his ancient Personage to deck)
Her great great Grandsire wore about his Neck
In three Seal Rings, which, after melted down,
Form'd a vast Buckle for his Widow's Gown;
Her Infant Grandame's Whistle next it grew,
The Bells she gingled, and the Whistle blew,
Then in a Bodkin grac'd her Mother's Hairs,
Which long she wore, and now Belinda *wears.*

An open Satyr upon *Hereditary Right.* The three
Seal Rings plainly allude to the three Kingdoms.

These are the chief Passages in the Battle, by
which, as hath before been said, he means the Squab-
ble of Parties. Upon this Occasion he could not end
the Description of them, without testifying his malignant Joy at those Dissentions, from which he forms
the Prospect that *both* should be disappointed, and
cries out with Triumph, as if it were already accom-
plished.

Behold how oft ambitious Arms are crost,
And Chiefs contend till all the Prize is lost.

The Lock at length is turn'd into a *Star,* or the
Old Barrier Treaty into a new and glorious *Peace;*
this no doubt is what the Author, at the time he
printed his Poem, would have been thought to mean,
in hopes by that Complement to escape Punishment
for the rest of his Piece. It puts me in mind of a Fellow, who concluded a bitter Lampoon upon the
Prince and Court of his Days, with these Lines.

God save the King, the Commons, and the Peers,
And grant the Author long may wear his Ears.

Whatever this Author may think of that Peace, I imagine it the most *extraordinary Star* that ever appear'd in our Hemisphere. A Star that is to bring us all the Wealth and Gold of the *Indies*; and from whose Influence, not Mr. *John Partridge* alone, (whose worthy Labours this Writer so ungenerously ridicules) but all true *Britains* may, with no less Authority than he, prognosticate the Fall of *Lewis*, in the Restraint of the exorbitant Power of *France*, and the Fate of *Rome* in the triumphant Condition of the Church of *England*.

We have now considered this Poem in its Political View, wherein we have shewn that it hath two different Walks of Satyr, the one in the Story it self, which is a Ridicule on the late Transactions in general; the other in the Machinary, which is a Satyr on the Ministers of State in particular. I shall now show that the same Poem, taken in another Light, has a Tendency to Popery, which is secretly insinuated through the whole.

In the first place, he has conveyed to us the Doctrine of Guardian Angels and Patron Saints in the Machinary of his *Sylphs*, which being a Piece of Popish Superstition that hath been endeavoured to be exploded ever since the Reformation, he would here revive under this Disguise. Here are all the Particulars which they believe of those Beings, which I shall sum up in a few Heads.

1*st*. The Spirits are made to concern themselves with all human Acts in general.

2dly. A distinct Guardian Spirit or Patron is assigned to each Person in particular.

> *Of these am I, who thy Protection claim,*
> *A watchful Sprite* ———

3dly. They are made directly to inspire Dreams, Visions, and Revelations.

> *Her Guardian Sylph prolong'd her balmy Rest,*
> *'Twas he had summon'd to her silent Bed*
> *The Morning Dream* ———

4thly. They are made to be subordinate, in different Degrees, some presiding over others. So *Ariel* hath his several Under-Officers at Command.

> *Superior by the Head was Ariel plac'd.*

5thly. They are employed in various Offices, and each hath his Office assigned him.

> *Some in the Fields of purest Æther play,*
> *And bask and whiten in the Blaze of Day.*
> *Some guide the Course,* &c.

6thly. He hath given his Spirits the Charge of the several Parts of Dress; intimating thereby, that the Saints preside over the several Parts of Human Bodies. They have one Saint to cure the Tooth-ach, another cures the Gripes, another the Gout, and so of all the rest.

> *The flutt'ring Fan be Zephyretta's Care,*
> *The Drops to thee, Brillante, we consign,* &c.

7thly. They are represented to know the Thoughts of Men.

As on the Nosegay in her Breast reclin'd,
He watch'd th' Ideas rising in her Mind.

8*thly*. They are made Protectors even to Animals and irrational Beings.

Ariel *himself shall be the Guard of* Shock.

So St. *Anthony* presides over Hogs, *&c.*

9*thly*. Others are made Patrons of whole Kingdoms and Provinces.

Of these the chief the Care of Nations own.

So St. *George* is imagined by the *Papists* to defend *England:* St. *Patrick, Ireland:* St. *James, Spain,* &c. Now what is the Consequence of all this? By granting that they have this Power, we must be brought back again to pray to them.

The *Toilette* is an artful Recommendation of the *Mass,* and pompous Ceremonies of the *Church of Rome.* The *unveiling* of the *Altar,* the *Silver Vases* upon it, being *rob'd* in *White,* as the Priests are upon the chief Festivals, and the *Head uncover'd,* are manifest Marks of this.

A heav'enly Image in the Glass appears,
To that she bends ———

Plainly denotes *Image-Worship.*

The *Goddess,* who is deck'd with *Treasures, Jewels,* and the *various Offerings of the World,* manifestly alludes to the Lady of *Loretto.* You have Perfumes breathing from the *Incense Pot* in the following Line.

And all Arabia *breaths from yonder Box.*

The Character of *Belinda*, as we take it in this third View, represents the Popish Religion, or the Whore of *Babylon*; who is described in the State this malevolent Author wishes for, coming forth in all her Glory upon the *Thames*, and overspreading the Nation with Ceremonies.

Not with more Glories in th' ætherial Plain,
The Sun first rises o'er the purple Main,
Than issuing forth the Rival of his Beams,
Launch'd on the Bosom of the Silver Thames.

She is dress'd with a *Cross* on her Breast, the Ensign of Popery, the *Adoration* of which is plainly recommended in the following Lines.

On her white Breast a sparkling Cross *she wore,*
Which Jews might kiss, and Infidels adore.

Next he represents her as the *Universal Church*, according to the Boasts of the Papists.

And like the Sun she shines on all alike.

After which he tells us,

If to her Share some Female Errors fall,
Look on her Face, and you'll forget them all.

Tho' it should be granted some Errors fall to her Share, look on the pompous Figure she makes throughout the World, and they are not worth regarding. In the Sacrifice following soon after, you have these two Lines.

For this, e'er Phœbus *rose, he had implor'd*
Propitious Heav'n, and ev'ry Pow'r ador'd.

In the first of them, he plainly hints at their *Matins*; in the second, by adoring ev'ry Power, the *Invocation of Saints.*

Belinda's Visits are described with numerous *Wax-lights*, which are always used in the Ceremonial Parts of the *Romish* Worship.

——*Visits shall be paid on solemn Days,*
When num'rous Wax-lights in bright Order blaze.

The *Lunar Sphere* he mentions, opens to us their *Purgatory*, which is seen in the following Line.

Since all Things lost on Earth are treasur'd there.

It is a Popish Doctrine, that scarce any Person quits this World, but he must touch at Purgatory in his Way to Heaven; and it is here also represented as the *Treasury* of the *Romish Church.* Nor is it much to be wonder'd at, that the *Moon* should be *Purgatory*, when a Learn'd Divine hath in a late Treatise proved *Hell* to be in the *Sun.**

I shall now before I conclude, desire the Reader to compare this Key with those upon any other Pieces, which are supposed to be secret Satyrs upon the State, either antient or modern; as with those upon *Petronius Arbiter*, *Lucian*'s true History, *Barclay*'s *Argenis*, or *Rablais*'s *Garagantua*; and I doubt not he will do me the Justice to acknowledge, that the Explanations here laid down, are deduced as naturally, and with as little Force, both from the general Scope and Bent of the Work, and from the several Particulars, and are every Way as consistent and un-

* *The Reverend Dr.* Swinden.

deniable as any of those; and ev'ry way as candid as any modern Interpretations of either Party, on the mysterious State Treatises of our Times.

To sum up my whole Charge against this Author in a few Words: He has ridiculed both the present Mi[nist]ry and the last; abused great Statesmen and great Generals; nay the Treaties of whole Nations have not escaped him, nor has the Royal Dignity it self been omitted in the Progress of his Satyr; and all this he has done just at the Meeting of a new Parliament. I hope a proper Authority may be made use of to bring him to condign Punishment: In the mean while I doubt not, if the Persons most concern'd would but order Mr. *Bernard Lintott*, the Printer and Publisher of this dangerous Piece, to be taken into Custody, and examin'd; many further Discoveries might be made both of this Poet's and his Abettor's secret Designs, which are doubtless of the utmost Importance to the Government.

FINIS.

The Dignity, Use and Abuse of
Glass-Bottles.

Set forth in A

SERMON

Preach'd to an

Illustrious Assembly,

And now Publish'd for the Use of the

Inferiour CLERGY.

By the Author of the T A L E of a T U B.

L O N D O N :

Printed, and Sold by the Booksellers of
London and *Westminster.* 1715.

THE
PREFACE

SERMONS and Glass-Bottles (*says a Sour Fellow*) what Incongruities have we here? This is *Ludere cum Sacris*, or I have lost my Understanding.—*You should first have convinc'd us you ever had any. Cannot a Man be Serious without a stiff Mode of Speech, contracted Brows, and distorted Features? Does Gravity consist in Grimace? Doubtless, then, the Ass gave himself very agreeable Airs, when Mumbling the Thistles. Sermonizing and Bottlelizing will not appear such Opposites, if you consider how many (had they the Ingenuity to be Grateful to their Benefactors) would confess, that the most beautiful Flowers of their Pulpit-Rhetorick, came out of Bottles. Is not Man brightest when his Heart is Glad? And does not the Scripture say, that Wine was given for that Purpose? Can it then be prov'd a Heresie to Bottle it?* Bezaleel *and* Aholiah were fill'd with the Spirit in Wisdom and Understanding, in Knowledge to find out Curious Works, *&c. Now, Questionless the Invention of the Bottle was the first Discovery, being so essential an Assistant to all other Discoveries: Nay, the Concavity of it appears the very Womb where they are conceiv'd, while the Spirit contain'd within, midwifes them into the World. But, says another Dogmatical Pedant,* Who ever heard

of a Sermon without a Text? *And pray before that
Custom begun, who ever heard of One with a Text?
Had the Art commenc'd without it, it had been as
prepost'rous now to have us'd it; and what is all this
but* Custom? *Custom, which has involv'd us in fifty
Errours for every single Truth it has produc'd, and
doubtless very worthy then to be maintain'd. But further, Has not a Potter absolute Power over his Clay,
to make a Vessel of Honour or Dishonour of it, and shall
a Learn'd and Illuminated Author be more restrain'd,
than a Scurvy Dirt-moulding Potter? It is enough he
tells you, his Theam is* Bottles, *which every Body understands; whereas many take a Text which no Body understands, insomuch that the Preacher is forc'd to spend
half his Time, in informing us what he would be at.
Thus much for all I think can be objected against his irregular Motions; he who would discover more, must take
a Bottle beyond the Author, and so lose the Argument
by the very Means of maintaining it. Methinks I hear
some fleering Puppies say,* however our Clergy dress
up their Modulations the grand Topick they all go
upon is *Preferment. And are our Author's deviatory
Measures, Means to mend his Fortune? Why not?
Mayn't an* Arch-Wagg *expect the Favour of an* Arch-
B——, *when* B—— *and* Wagg *have the same Epithet
to distinguish them from Inferiour Dignities? And it is
not in the Nature of a true* German *to neglect a true
Bottle-Man, they being, in a manner, Synonymous
Terms. For further Illustration of the Matter, we need
only add, that lately a* Print, *a meer Shadow of a Man,
composed of Bottles and Vials, under the Title of the*
German Doctor, *took such a Run, that it brought in*

far more Money than wou'd be given for the real *Author of a Paper under the same Title, were he slash'd, season'd, and serv'd up in a* Ragoo. *If all this Mathematical Demonstration gains not an absolute Ascendant over your Faith, we must give you over for lost Men; but to my Comfort, I see a Shoal of our Inferiour Clergy approaching, with Addresses of Thanks (pinn'd in their Hats like their Mistresses's Favours) for this Essay so* apropos *to their Gusts; I read their Convictions (in Ruby Characters) in their Countenances, that if they miss being Dignify'd and Distinguish'd elsewhere, they cannot be disappointed in the* Bottle, *since Two at any Time make a* Doctor, *and the Third an* Arch-B——, *the same can mount to no proportion under Five; for whose Conversation I may at present take my leave of my Reader.* Vale.

A

SERMON

Preach'd to a

CONGREGATION

O F

Glass-Bottles, &c.

MY Beloved, yea, most dearly Beloved Vessels of Election! I call not upon you to open your Ears, since for the most part Ears you have none, or only such as the Prophet speaketh of, *Ears which do not hear*; but I rejoice to behold you with open Mouths, gaping as it were, and thirsting for the Word of the Lord. It has been long a Pious and Praiseworthy Custom, among the Children of Men, to listen to Godly Exhortations with open Mouths, as well as Ears; but they, alas! like Hounds in pursuit of Game, often open their Mouths, yet do not comprehend; but it is your happy Property to retain whatever is pour'd into you; whereas, Men, on the contrary, are before Hand so tainted with the Tincture of Prejudice, that as one of the Ancients has it, *Quodcunque infundis, adhæsit.*

Did not *Ezekiel* Preach to dry Bones? Did not St. *Francis* and St. *Anthony* hold forth to Birds and Fishes, and the Holy Saints of divers Convents to

Calves? I doubt not, but you will Profit as much by my Discourse; and I hold myself in this, happier than they, that I am to Preach (O ye Bottles of Glass) to a most Illustrious Audience, whose Capacity and Comprehension none can doubt of.

The Subject I propose to treat of, is such as may seem most suitable to this Assembly; for the Gravest Philosophers have determin'd, That the Knowledge, most useful to all People is that of themselves; and therefore I conceive nothing so proper to be address'd to Bottles, as a Discourse of Bottles.

This Discourse I will divide into Three Parts. *First*, I shall declare the Dignity of Bottles. *Secondly*, The Use of Bottles. *Thirdly*, The Abuse of them; together with an Application to all Bottles in general, and Advice to you in particular.

Part I. *The Dignity of Bottles shewn from the Matter.*

The Dignity of Bottles arises from Two Things. From the Matter and from the Form. The Matter of Bottles is not exactly distinguish'd by the Vulgar, who (mistaken in this as in most other Things) will talk of Leathern and Stone-Bottles, with the same Impropriety as they do of Glass-Inkhorns: But That Glass alone is the proper Matter of all true and genuine Bottles, is to the Learned as clear and perspicuous as Glass itself. To manifest the Excellency of which, it might suffice to mention, what all Conversant in the Holy Fathers, must have read in *Petronius Arbiter*; I mean, the Answer of *Julius Cæsar* to a certain *Roman*, who proposed to make Glass Mal-

p

leable, (that is to say, to endure the Hammer;) I dare
not permit, said *Cæsar*; for, were it once so, Gold and
Silver would no longer be valued. But what need we
insist on this, when the Beloved Apostle prefers you
at once, to all the precious Stones in the World; for,
in the 21st Chapter of the *Revelations*, describing the
exceeding Glory and Magnificence of the Heavenly
Jerusalem, after he has told us, That the First Foundation was the *Jasper*; the Second the *Sapphire*; the
Third the *Calcedonus*; (observe, I beseech you, the
Gradation of each) the Fourth the *Emerald*; the Fifth
the *Sardonix*, and so on to the Twelfth; losing us, as
it were, in the Blaze of Glory. Often he has told us,
as still more Wonderful, That every Gate was of One
several Pearl; and what was more possible to be
added? And yet after all, he adds, The Streets of the
City was; What was it? (Mark my dear Auditors!) It
was, as it were, *Transparent Glass*.

It was not without much Mistery, our wise Ancestors invented this Composition, which is Symbolical
of that of the great Master-piece of Nature, *Man*, to
whom, tracing both from the First Principle, I will
now compare, O my beloved, and most worthy to be
beloved Bottles. *First*, In the Manner. *Secondly*, In
the Form. And *Thirdly*, In the End of your Creation.

1. *From your Manner of being made.*

Even as Man who is said in Holy Writ to be, *Tan-
quam Vasculus in manu teguli*, was once meer Dust,
till inspired with the Breath of Life, he was raised up
to their Graceful Fabrick; so you (O ye Bottles) were
at first vile Ashes; but, no sooner was the informing

Breath blown into you, but your loose Atoms assum'd a Shape, and on a sudden appear'd with fair
long Necks and goodly round Bellies. And again,
like as Man, when he seems to perish and is dissolved
into Ashes, is purg'd, refined and elevated into a new
Life of Brightness and Purity, even so, when the
Trace, which liv'd, is reduc'd to Ashes; from those
very Ashes is raised up (by means of purging Fire, as
we are taught by the Holy Mother, the Church) the
new and more glorious Body of Glass. Which has
manifestly the chief Properties of a Glorious Body,
that is to say, Clarity. This was the Opinion of the
blessed Bishop *Gregory*, who (*Lib.* 18. *Moral. Cap.*
2.) has these Words; *The heavenly State is liken'd to
Glass on account of the Purity, Clarity and Resplen-
dency of the Glorified Bodies, where one Man's Body,
Conscience and Thoughts are presented to another, as
Corporeal Objects in this Life are beheld thro' Glasses.*

Secondly, *The Form.*

To proceed to the Form of all Forms. Saith *Plato*,
the most excellent of all Forms is the Circular. How
nearly Bottles approach to this is visible to every Eye;
whilst Man makes but an irregular, forked Figure,
neither so uniform, compact, or standing so firm as
you: The heaviest Parts of him (of all which his Head
is many times the heaviest) are placed above, and the
weakest are Legs unable to support 'em; directly contrary to all good Rules of Architecture. What he
values himself most upon, is his having (as the Poet
expresses it) *Os sublime*, which literally translated, as
Things of that Consequence ought to be, is a Mouth

erect towards Heaven. Now, how much more up-
right are your Mouths, O ye Vessels of Glass, is too
manifest to need any Proof. With good reason therefore did that ancient *Epicurean* Philosopher make it
his Wish (being studious of the Improvement of his
Form) to have a Neck like a Crane's, and a Belly
twice as large as other Mortals. For what was this,
but the perfect Form of yourselves, *O most compleat
Bottles?*

Thirdly, *From the End for which they were made.*

The End for which Bottles were made was to contain, according to their Capacity, what is entrusted
to their Custody; and of which a Return is expected.
Where it is to be noted, that of Bottles there are divers Sorts; some Quarts, some two Quarts, and others
Gallon Bottles. *To whom much is given* (saith the
Scripture) *of such much is required.* And it is even
thus with Men: They are, as it were, so many Reser-
vers and Vessels of Grace, which the Lord has put
into them, more or less according to different Capacities, and which he expects there to Work and Improve and Refine; every One living being accountable only, forasmuch as he has received. And Oh!
That Men in general were but as faithful Preservers
of this Heavenly Infusion, as you O Bottles! How
few are there of you that fly, and how few of them
that hold!

Part II. *The Use of Bottles.*

I come now to the Second Division, *The Use of Bottles*, which is two-fold; the natural and common Use of Bottles, and the mystical and allegorical Use: Which last being not so generally known as the former, but a kind of Occult Science, I shall in the First Place endeavour to lay it open unto you. The Wise and Learned *Panurge* (as we may read in the Works of that most Reverend Doctor *Rablais*) being about to enter on an Affair of the highest Importance, resolv'd first to consult the Oracle of the Bottle; and it were well if the same prudent Method was used by all Divines, Politicians and Men of Morals. The first of these might discern in a good Bottle, the lively Figure of a good Divine, who has ever been compar'd to a Vessel from the First Ages of Christianity down to this Present. Was not *Paul* in those Days stiled by the Scripture itself, a Vessel of Election; and in our time has not the most Learned of our Universities given to a large Mugg, the Name of *Bellarmine?* Now a Vessel of Election is the same Thing in the *Hebrew*, as a chosen Vessel: and how doth the Lord choose his Vessels, that is to say, his Preachers? Even as a wise Man chooseth his Bottles; such, I mean, as have not only the largest Capacity to contain what is infused, but likewise the properest Mouths to vent it freely to others. It was therefore with more Propriety of Speech than may at first be imagined, that St. *Paul* said of himself, *I am pour'd forth in the Service of the Brethren.* To conclude then, Divines are liken'd unto Bottles, because they ought to be pure and without Deceit, for it is said, there is no deceit in a full Bottle. Now, as for Politicians, how can they better set before us the Submission we owe to Government, than by the Example of good and sound Bottles which remain peaceable and quiet under the Limitation of such Corks as are establish'd and set over them, while those who fly out into rebellious Workings, do not only expose their Corks, but also lose their Liquor. 'Tis likewise granted on all Hands, that the most useful Knowledge of such as govern, is the Knowledge of Mankind, which is not to be attain'd by Conversation, without the Company and Concurrence of you, O Bottles: 'Tis by your Means that Men have the most frequent Opportunities of observing the Instability of each other, and the many Slips and false Steps they make. For which Reason the wisest Kings of Old have made use of your Assistance in the Choice of their Counsellours, as One (in his Days famous for Sermons) has exprest it;

Reges dicuntur Multis urgere culullis,
Et torquere mero, quem perspexisse laborant,
An sit Amicitiæ dignus?

Let the Kings of the Earth seek Truth, says *Solomon*, and where shall they find it; the Sage *Grecian* answers, Οἴνῳ Ἀλήθεια, *in Vino veritas.*

For the Moral Man there are so many Precepts exhibited to him by you (most conspicuous Auditors) that, to avoid being tedious, I shall only touch on a few. And First, the Liberality of Bottles in general, which only receive that they may bestow; But

narrow-soul'd Men, like narrow-neck'd Bottles, hold
much but give little, nay, and that little too with
much Difficulty and murmuring; for it may be justly
observ'd of such, that the less they bestow, the more
Noise they make about it. Against Pride and Anger
you afford us a most notable Caution; for as Bottles
are destroyed by bouncing and cracking, even so are
Men. Are we to choose Friends, you are to assist us
in the Scrutiny; O beloved Bottles, you are to sound
and fathom their Minds, till they become as clear to
be seen thorough as your selves. Are we to take a
Wife, 'tis by your mirrour we must contemplate her,
and learn to manage her: The sacred Text comparing Woman to you, calls her the weaker Vessel; and
'tis observable to the nice Inspeƈtors in Nature, that
your very Form bears some Allusion to that Part
which distinguishes the Sex; your Neck most aptly
represents what the Anatomists call the *Vagina Uteri*,
your wider Space the *Sinus*, and that Part which returning inwards swells almost to the middle of the
Vacuity seems a Figure of that which the learned
Soranas (*Epist. ad Cheap*) calls the *Landica*: There
are, moreover two Properties common to both Bottles and Women; the One, that how much soever is
pour'd into 'em, there will still, by means of the
Part I last mention'd, remain a Vacancy at Bottom;
and the Other, that neither of 'em will be quiet or
silent, but in a continual Motion and Ferment, unless they be extremely well stopt.

Secondly, *Natural Use of Bottles.*

Having shewn how useful, the silent, the allegorical Doctrine of Bottles may be to Men in a spiritual Sense, I need but just touch upon the natural and most obvious Use thereof, that is, First, to be filled; and Secondly, to be emptied; than which nothing can be more great and generous. Ask the Sun, the Moon and the Stars, (those glorious and transparent Bottles of Light) ask why they are fill'd therewith, and they will answer, 'tis to be emptied for the Use and Advantage of the World, and even so may you, O you Bottles.

Part III. *Abuse of Bottles.*

But from the Use of Bottles, I am naturally led to the Abuse of them; in these evil Days the Generality of Men by the Instigation of Satan seize you (as one may say) by the Throat, and force you from your peaceable Repositories in Cellars to the noisy Tables of Drunkards, where often those barbarous Wretches serve you innocent Vessels as ravenous Wolves do harmless Sheep, first suck your Blood, and then destroy your Carcases; they compel you to assault even your own Relations, the Windows (who may be said to be Glass of your Glass) and send flint Glasses to encounter with flint Stones. It were endless to enumerate all the Outrages committed by these Bottles of Flesh to the Bottles of Glass.

It will more than suffice to mention unto you one, but that a most dreadful Example.

A dreadful Example *of the* Abuse *of* Bottles.

In this very Kingdom of *Albion*, and even in the great and famous Metropolis thereof, not long since lived and may still live a most wicked and heathenish Mortal, who not only inherited from his Ancestor Falstaff a most prodigious and Bottle-like Rotundity of Belly, but likewise his evil and pernicious Faculty of draining, desolating and destroying many of you, Bottles; divers of you had he spurn'd under his Feet, divers had he cast over his own Head, and manifold others at the Heads of others. But what I am about to relate, is far more horrible; being at a Time in company with other Bottles (and those of much better Credit and Fashion than himself) after having seemingly carest and embrac'd one of them a considerable time and exhausted it of all it was worth, he did—my Beloved, alas what did he? What will make your empty Bowels to yearn, and the full ones to foam with Indignation. He put, in the most scornful and insulting Manner, the very worst and filthiest Part of him in the (till now unpoluted Neck of that) most miserable Bottle, and replenish'd it, even to the Top, with his most ungrateful Urine. *O Tempora! O Mores!* An Usage so barbarous might have made a Stone speak, much more a Bottle; which had this, for the Horrour of those vile Miscreants been permitted to do, might it not have arose in the midst of them, and, opening its Mouth, have spoke in this Manner? 'Men and Brethren, answer unto me, was it for this I have lain in Cobwebs and Dust and obscure Places so many Months? For which of the good things I have done for Thee, am I thus rewarded? Was it not unto us, Bottles, that Thou owest all thy new Systems of Divinity, thy strange Definitions of Faith, thy unheard of Discoveries in Arts and Sciences? Was it not we that furnish'd Thee with Excuse for all thy Brutalities and Absurdities? If Thou didst blaspheme the Lord or his Priests, if Thou abusedst thy Friends, if Thou didst ravish thy Maid-Servants, was it not immediately alledg'd, he had his Bottle too much? It was his Bottle? Other Indignities from Thee and thy Mates I and my Fellows have born with Patience: Nay, tho' we have been call'd by a Name, at which the very Children are taught to spit; a Name, the most ignominious, most detestable, to all Christian Bottles, that is to say, Devils; after ye have insatiably squeez'd from us all our Virtue, ye cry out with Fury, Here, Drawer, away with these Devils. Miserable Bottle that I am! Would I had suffer'd any Ignominy rather than this! Better I had been tied to the Tail of a mangey and masterless Dog, than to thine, O Varlet! Sweeter had my Scituation been, and I less resented the Application!'

Consolation and advice to Bottles.

But cease, ah cease, O Thou most justly complaining Vessels! 'Tis I, thy Preacher, who will unto thee,

Pudet hæc opprobria nobis
Et dici potuisse, et non potuisse refelli !

Which for thy Ease (Dear British Bottles) is thus interpreted, It shameth me that these Disgraces may be charged upon us Men, and it cannot be denied. Yet consider (for thou lookest like a considerable and conscientious Bottle) consider, I say, that, what Thou sufferest from Man, is proceeding from God, who hath set him over thee, as thy Lord and Master endued with absolute and supreme Power, to which you owe an unconditional Obedience, and not to resist on any Pretence whatsoever. 'Tis true, he may be a Tyrant, yet is he accountable to Heaven alone, and you Bottles (if you will be Christian Bottles) are to submit. What if Providence (whose Workings and Ways are not to us accountable) had made you Urinals, not Bottles; Receptacles of Water, not of Ale? What if you had not been made Christian, but *Turkish, Indian* or *Mahometan* Bottles? Confess the signal Favour of Heaven, which has not only made you Bottles, but *Europæan* Bottles; not only *European* Bottles, but *British* Bottles: You are not born Slaves to *French* Wines and *French* Brandies, but enjoy the most sweet and gentle Power of *English Ale* and *German Mum*. *Aldermen* shall embrace you; *Common-Council-Men* shall drink of you; The Ministers of the Lord himself shall encourage their Texts with you, and every of you, O most Illustrious Bottles of the Lord! Forsake then, O for ever forsake the lewd and dangerous Assemblies of ungodly Drunkards; open not your Corks unto them: But, when Two or Three Zealous Divines are gather'd together, come amidst them, O ye Bottles, come all of you, come speedily to those who will soberly and carefully empty you, (as many as may be) in the Fear of the Lord. I will therefore now give the finishing Stroke, and close, or, as I may say, cork up my Discourse with a most fervent and hearty Prayer both for you, and for us.

Grant, Good Lord, unto these Bottles that they may never fall into the Hands of such Miscreants who make of Vessels of Election, Vials of Indignation, and unto us that we may never be fill'd with the Wines and Brandies of Drunkenness and Madness, but may ever continue sound and faithful Vessels of the true aqua vitæ *of Righteousness. Amen.*

FINIS

The Preface

TO

The Iliad

1715

THE

PREFACE

TO

The Iliad

HOMER is universally allow'd to have had
the greatest Invention of any Writer whatever. The Praise of Judgment *Virgil* has justly contested with him, and others may have their
Pretensions as to particular Excellencies; but his Invention remains yet unrival'd. Nor is it a Wonder if
he has ever been acknowledg'd the greatest of Poets,
who most excell'd in That which is the very Foundation of Poetry. It is the Invention that in different
degrees distinguishes all great Genius's: The utmost
Stretch of human Study, Learning, and Industry,
which masters every thing besides, can never attain
to this. It furnishes Art with all her Materials, and
without it Judgment itself can at best but *steal wisely:*
For Art is only like a prudent Steward that lives on
managing the Riches of Nature. Whatever Praises
may be given to Works of Judgment, there is not
even a single Beauty in them but is owing to the Invention: As in the most regular Gardens, however
Art may carry the greatest Appearance, there is not
a Plant or Flower but is the Gift of Nature. The first
can only reduce the Beauties of the latter into a more

obvious Figure, which the common Eye may better take in, and is therefore more entertain'd with. And perhaps the reason why most Criticks are inclin'd to prefer a judicious and methodical Genius to a great and fruitful one, is, because they find it easier for themselves to pursue their Observations through an uniform and bounded Walk of Art, than to comprehend the vast and various Extent of Nature.

Our Author's Work is a wild Paradise, where if we cannot see all the Beauties so distinctly as in an order'd Garden, it is only because the Number of them is infinitely greater. 'Tis like a copious Nursery which contains the Seeds and first Productions of every kind, out of which those who follow'd him have but selected some particular Plants, each according to his Fancy, to cultivate and beautify. If some things are too luxuriant, it is owing to the Richness of the Soil; and if others are not arriv'd to Perfection or Maturity, it is only because they are overrun and opprest by those of a stronger Nature.

It is to the Strength of this amazing Invention we are to attribute that unequal'd Fire and Rapture, which is so forcible in *Homer*, that no Man of a true Poetical Spirit is Master of himself while he reads him. What he writes is of the most animated Nature imaginable; every thing moves, every thing lives, and is put in Action. If a Council be call'd, or a Battle fought, you are not coldly inform'd of what was said or done as from a third Person; the Reader is hurry'd out of himself by the Force of the Poet's Imagination, and turns in one place to a Hearer, in another to a Spectator. The Course of his Verses resembles that of the Army he describes,

Οἱ δ' ἄρ' ἴσαν, ὡσεί τε πυρὶ χθὼν πᾶσα νέμοιτο.

They pour along like a Fire that sweeps the whole Earth before it. 'Tis however remarkable that his Fancy, which is every where vigorous, is not discover'd immediately at the beginning of his Poem in its fullest Splendor: It grows in the Progress both upon himself and others, and becomes on Fire like a Chariot-Wheel, by its own Rapidity. Exact Disposition, just Thought, correct Elocution, polish'd Numbers, may have been found in a thousand; but this Poetical *Fire*, this *Vivida vis animi*, in a very few. Even in Works where all those are imperfect or neglected, this can over-power Criticism, and make us admire even while we dis-approve. Nay, where this appears, tho' attended with Absurdities, it brightens all the Rubbish about it, 'till we see nothing but its own Splendor. This *Fire* is discern'd in *Virgil*, but discern'd as through a Glass, reflected, and more shining than warm, but every where equal and constant: In *Lucan* and *Statius*, it bursts out in sudden, short, and interrupted Flashes: In *Milton*, it glows like a Furnace kept up to an uncommon Fierceness by the Force of Art: In *Shakespear*, it strikes before we are aware, like an accidental Fire from Heaven: But in *Homer*, and in him only, it burns every where clearly, and every where irresistibly.

I shall here endeavour to show, how this vast *Invention* exerts itself in a manner superior to that of

q

any Poet, thro' all the main constituent Parts of his Work, as it is the great and peculiar Characteristick which distinguishes him from all other Authors.

This strong and ruling Faculty was like a powerful Planet, which in the Violence of its Course, drew all things within its *Vortex*. It seem'd not enough to have taken in the whole Circle of Arts, and the whole Compass of Nature; all the inward Passions and Affections of Mankind to supply his Characters, and all the outward Forms and Images of Things for his Descriptions; but wanting yet an ampler Sphere to expatiate in, he open'd a new and boundless Walk for his Imagination, and created a World for himself in the Invention of *Fable*. That which *Aristotle* calls the *Soul of Poetry*, was first breath'd into it by *Homer*. I shall begin with considering him in this Part, as it is naturally the first, and I speak of it both as it means the Design of a Poem, and as it is taken for Fiction.

Fable may be divided into the *Probable*, the *Allegorical*, and the *Marvelous*. The *Probable Fable* is the Recital of such Actions as tho' they did not happen, yet might, in the common course of Nature: Or of such as tho' they did, become Fables by the additional Episodes and manner of telling them. Of this sort is the main Story of an Epic Poem, *the Return of* Ulysses, *the Settlement of the* Trojans *in* Italy, or the like. That of the *Iliad* is *the Anger of* Achilles, the most short and single Subject that ever was chosen by any Poet. Yet this he has supplied with a vaster Variety of Incidents and Events, and crouded with a greater Number of Councils, Speeches, Battles, and

Episodes of all kinds, than are to be found even in those Poems whose Schemes are of the utmost Latitude and Irregularity. The Action is hurry'd on with the most vehement Spirit, and its whole Duration employs not so much as fifty Days. *Virgil*, for want of so warm a Genius, aided himself by taking in a more extensive Subject, as well as a greater Length of Time, and contracting the Design of both *Homer*'s Poems into one, which is yet but a fourth part as large as his. The other Epic Poets have us'd the same Practice, but generally carry'd it so far as to superinduce a Multiplicity of Fables, destroy the Unity of Action, and lose their Readers in an unreasonable Length of Time. Nor is it only in the main Design that they have been unable to add to his Invention, but they have follow'd him in every Episode and Part of Story. If he has given a regular *Catalogue* of an *Army*, they all draw up their Forces in the same Order. If he has funeral Games for *Patroclus*, *Virgil* has the same for *Anchises*, and *Statius* (rather than omit them) destroys the Unity of his Action for those of *Archemorus*. If *Ulysses* visit the Shades, the *Æneas* of *Virgil* and *Scipio* of *Silius* are sent after him. If he be detain'd from his Return by the Allurements of *Calypso*, so is *Æneas* by *Dido*, and *Rinaldo* by *Armida*. If *Achilles* be absent from the Army on the Score of a Quarrel thro' half the Poem, *Rinaldo* must absent himself just as long, on the like account. If he gives his Heroe a Suit of celestial Armour, *Virgil* and *Tasso* make the same Present to theirs. *Virgil* has not only observ'd this close Imitation of *Homer*, but where he had not led the way, supply'd the

Want from other *Greek* Authors. Thus the Story of *Sinon* and the *Taking of Troy* was copied (says *Macrobius*) almost word for word from *Pisander*, as the Loves of *Dido* and *Æneas* are taken from those of *Medæa* and *Jason* in *Apollonius*, and several others in the same manner.

To proceed to the *Allegorical Fable*: If we reflect upon those innumerable Knowledges, those Secrets of Nature and Physical Philosophy which *Homer* is generally suppos'd to have wrapt up in his *Allegories*, what a new and ample Scene of Wonder may this Consideration afford us? How fertile will that Imagination appear, which was able to cloath all the Properties of Elements, the Qualifications of the Mind, the Virtues and Vices, in Forms and Persons; and to introduce them into Actions agreeable to the Nature of the Things they shadow'd? This is a Field in which no succeeding Poets could dispute with *Homer*; and whatever Commendations have been allow'd them on this Head, are by no means for their Invention in having enlarg'd his Circle, but for their Judgment in having contracted it. For when the Mode of Learning chang'd in following Ages, and Science was deliver'd in a plainer manner, it then became as reasonable in the more modern Poets to lay it aside, as it was in *Homer* to make use of it. And perhaps it was no unhappy Circumstance for *Virgil*, that there was not in his Time that Demand upon him of so great an Invention, as might be capable of furnishing all those Allegorical Parts of a Poem.

The *Marvelous Fable* includes whatever is supernatural, and especially the Machines of the Gods. If

Homer was not the first who introduc'd the Deities (as *Herodotus* imagines) into the Religion of *Greece*, he seems the first who brought them into a System of *Machinery* for Poetry, and such an one as makes its greatest Importance and Dignity. For we find those Authors who have been offended at the literal Notion of the Gods, constantly laying their Accusation against *Homer* as the undoubted Inventor of them. But whatever cause there might be to blame his *Machines* in a Philosophical or Religious View, they are so perfect in the Poetick, that Mankind have been ever since contented to follow them: None have been able to enlarge the Sphere of Poetry beyond the Limits he has set: Every Attempt of this Nature has prov'd unsuccessful; and after all the various Changes of Times and Religions, his Gods continue to this Day the Gods of Poetry.

We come now to the *Characters* of his Persons, and here we shall find no Author has ever drawn so many with so visible and surprizing a Variety, or given us such lively and affecting Impressions of them. Every one has something so singularly his own, that no Painter could have distinguish'd them more by their Features, than the Poet has by their Manners. Nothing can be more exact than the Distinctions he has observ'd in the different degrees of Virtues and Vices. The single Quality of *Courage* is wonderfully diversify'd in the several Characters of the *Iliad*. That of *Achilles* is furious and intractable; that of *Diomede* forward, yet list'ning to Advice and subject to Command: We see in *Ajax* an heavy and self-considering Valour, in *Hector* an active and vigilant one:

The Courage of *Agamemnon* is inspirited by Love of Empire and Ambition, that of *Menelaus* mix'd with Softness and Tenderness for his People: We find in *Idomeneus* a plain direct Soldier, in *Sarpedon* a gallant and generous one. Nor is this judicious and astonishing Diversity to be found only in the principal Quality which constitutes the Main of each Character, but even in the Under-parts of it, to which he takes care to give a Tincture of that principal one. For Example, the main Characters of *Ulysses* and *Nestor* consist in *Wisdom*, and they are distinct in this; the Wisdom of one is *artificial* and *various*, of the other *natural*, *open*, and *regular*. But they have, besides, Characters of *Courage*; and this Quality also takes a different Turn in each from the difference of his Prudence: For one in the War depends still upon *Caution*, the other upon *Experience*. It would be endless to produce Instances of these Kinds. The Characters of *Virgil* are far from striking us in this open manner; they lie in a great degree hidden and undistinguish'd, and where they are mark'd most evidently, affect us not in proportion to those of *Homer*. His Characters of Valour are much alike; even that of *Turnus* seems no way peculiar but as it is in a superior degree; and we see nothing that differences the Courage of *Mnestheus* from that of *Sergesthus*, *Cloanthus*, or the rest. In like manner it may be remark'd of *Statius*'s Heroes, that an Air of Impetuosity runs thro' them all; the same horrid and savage Courage appears in his *Capaneus*, *Tydeus*, *Hippomedon*, &c. They have a Parity of Character which makes them seem Brothers of one Family. I believe when the Reader is led into this Track of Reflection, if he will pursue it through the *Epic* and *Tragic* Writers, he will be convinced how infinitely superior in this Point the Invention of *Homer* was to that of all others.

The *Speeches* are to be consider'd as they flow from the Characters, being perfect or defective as they agree or disagree with the Manners of those who utter them. As there is more variety of Characters in the *Iliad*, so there is of Speeches, than in any other Poem. *Every thing in it has Manners* (as *Aristotle* expresses it) that is, every thing is acted or spoken. It is hardly credible in a Work of such length, how small a Number of Lines are employ'd in Narration. In *Virgil* the Dramatic Part is less in proportion to the Narrative; and the Speeches often consist of general Reflections or Thoughts, which might be equally just in any Person's Mouth upon the same Occasion. As many of his Persons have no apparent Characters, so many of his Speeches escape being apply'd and judg'd by the Rule of Propriety. We oftner think of the Author himself when we read *Virgil*, than when we are engag'd in *Homer*: All which are the Effects of a colder Invention, that interests us less in the Action describ'd: *Homer* makes us Hearers, and *Virgil* leaves us Readers.

If in the next place we take a View of the *Sentiments*, the same presiding Faculty is eminent in the Sublimity and Spirit of his Thoughts. *Longinus* has given his Opinion, that it was in this Part *Homer* principally excell'd. What were alone sufficient to prove the Grandeur and Excellence of his Sentiments in general, is that they have so remarkable a Parity with those of the Scripture: *Duport*, in his *Gnomologia Homerica*, has collected innumerable Instances of this sort. And it is with Justice an excellent modern Writer allows, that if *Virgil* has not so many Thoughts that are low and vulgar, he has not so many that are sublime and noble; and that the *Roman* Author seldom rises into very astonishing Sentiments where he is not fired by the *Iliad*.

If we observe his *Descriptions*, *Images*, and *Similes*, we shall find the Invention still predominant. To what else can we ascribe that vast Comprehension of Images of every sort, where we see each Circumstance and Individual of Nature summon'd together by the Extent and Fecundity of his Imagination; to which all things, in their various Views, presented themselves in an Instant, and had their Impressions taken off to Perfection at a Heat? Nay, he not only gives us the full Prospects of Things, but several unexpected Peculiarities and Side-Views, unobserv'd by any Painter but *Homer*. Nothing is so surprizing as the Descriptions of his Battels, which take up no less than half the *Iliad*, and are supply'd with so vast a Variety of Incidents, that no one bears a Likeness to another; such different Kinds of Deaths, that no two Heroes are wounded in the same manner; and such a Profusion of noble Ideas, that every Battel rises above the last in Greatness, Horror, and Confusion. It is certain there is not near that Number of Images and Descriptions in any Epic Poet; tho' every one has assisted himself with a great Quantity out of him: And it is evident of *Virgil* especially, that he has scarce any Comparisons which are not drawn from his Master.

If we descend from hence to the *Expression*, we see the bright Imagination of *Homer* shining out in the most enliven'd Forms of it. We acknowledge him the Father of Poetical Diction, the first who taught that *Language of the Gods* to Men. His Expression is like the colouring of some great Masters, which discovers itself to be laid on boldly, and executed with Rapidity. It is indeed the strongest and most glowing imaginable, and touch'd with the greatest Spirit. *Aristotle* had reason to say, He was the only Poet who had found out *Living Words*; there are in him more daring Figures and Metaphors than in any good Author whatever. An Arrow is *impatient* to be on the Wing, a Weapon *thirsts* to drink the Blood of an Enemy, and the like. Yet his Expression is never too big for the Sense, but justly great in proportion to it: 'Tis the Sentiment that swells and fills out the Diction, which rises with it, and forms itself about it. For in the same degree that a *Thought* is warmer, an *Expression* will be brighter; and as That is more strong, This will become more perspicuous: Like Glass in the Furnace which grows to a greater Magnitude, and refines to a greater Clearness, only as the *Breath* within is more powerful, and the *Heat* more intense.

To throw his Language more out of Prose, *Homer* seems to have affected the *Compound-Epithets*. This was a sort of Composition peculiarly proper to Poetry, not only as it heighten'd the *Diction*, but as it assisted and fill'd the *Numbers* with greater Sound and

Pomp, and likewise conduced in some measure to thicken the *Images*. On this last Consideration I cannot but attribute these to the Fruitfulness of his Invention, since (as he has manag'd them) they are a sort of supernumerary Pictures of the Persons or Things they are join'd to. We see the Motion of *Hector*'s Plumes in the Epithet Κορυθαίολος, the Landscape of Mount *Neritus* in that of Εἰνοσίφυλλος, and so of others; which particular Images could not have been insisted upon so long as to express them in a Description(tho' but of a single Line)without diverting the Reader too much from the principal Action or Figure. As a Metaphor is a short Simile, one of these Epithets is a short Description.

Lastly, if we consider his *Versification*, we shall be sensible what a Share of Praise is due to his Invention in that also. He was not satisfy'd with his Language as he found it settled in any one Part of *Greece*, but search'd thro' its differing *Dialects* with this particular View, to beautify and perfect his Numbers: He consider'd these as they had a greater Mixture of Vowels or Consonants, and accordingly employ'd them as the Verse requir'd either a greater Smoothness or Strength. What he most affected was the *Ionic*, which has a peculiar Sweetness from its never using Contractions, and from its Custom of resolving the Diphthongs into two Syllables; so as to make the Words open themselves with a more spreading and sonorous Fluency. With this he mingled the *Attic* Contractions, the broader *Doric*, and the feebler *Æolic*, which often rejects its Aspirate, or takes off its Accent; and compleated this Variety by altering some Letters with the License of Poetry. Thus his Measures, instead of being Fetters to his Sense, were always in readiness to run along with the Warmth of his Rapture; and even to give a farther Representation of his Notions, in the Correspondence of their Sounds to what they signify'd. Out of all these he has deriv'd that Harmony, which makes us confess he had not only the richest Head, but the finest Ear in the World. This is so great a Truth, that whoever will but consult the Tune of his Verses even without understanding them (with the same sort of Diligence as we daily see practis'd in the Case of *Italian Opera's*) will find more Sweetness, Variety, and Majesty of Sound, than in any other Language or Poetry. The Beauty of his Numbers is allow'd by the Criticks to be copied but faintly by *Virgil* himself, tho' they are so just to ascribe it to the Nature of the *Latine* Tongue. Indeed the *Greek* has some Advantages both from the natural *Sound* of its *Words*, and the Turn and *Cadence* of its *Verse*, which agree with the Genius of no other Language. *Virgil* was very sensible of this, and used the utmost Diligence in working up a more intractable Language to whatsoever Graces it was capable of, and in particular never fail'd to bring the Sound of his Line to a beautiful Agreement with its Sense. If the *Grecian* Poet has not been so frequently celebrated on this Account as the *Roman*, the only reason is, that fewer Criticks have understood one Language than the other. *Dionysius* of *Halicarnassus* has pointed out many of our Author's Beauties in this kind, in his Treatise of the *Composition of Words*, and others will be taken notice of in the Course of the Notes. It suffices at present to observe of his Numbers, that they flow with so much ease, as to make one imagine *Homer* had no other care than to transcribe as fast as the *Muses* dictated; and at the same time with so much Force and inspiriting Vigour, that they awaken and raise us like the Sound of a Trumpet. They roll along as a plentiful River, always in motion, and always full; while we are born away by a Tide of Verse, the most rapid, and yet the most smooth imaginable.

Thus on whatever side we contemplate *Homer*, what principally strikes us is his *Invention*. It is that which forms the Character of each Part of his Work; and accordingly we find it to have made his Fable more *extensive* and *copious* than any other, his Manners more *lively* and *strongly marked*, his Speeches more *affecting* and *transported*, his Sentiments more *warm* and *sublime*, his Images and Descriptions more *full* and *animated*, his Expression more *rais'd* and *daring*, and his Numbers more *rapid* and *various*. I hope in what has been said of *Virgil* with regard to any of these Heads, I have no way derogated from his Character. Nothing is more absurd or endless, than the common Method of comparing eminent Writers by an Opposition of particular Passages in them, and forming a Judgment from thence of their Merit upon the whole. We ought to have a certain Knowledge of the principal Character and distinguishing Excellence of each: It is in *that* we are to consider him, and in proportion to his Degree in *that* we are to admire him. No Author or Man ever excell'd all the World in more than one Faculty, and as *Homer* has done this in Invention, *Virgil* has in Judgment. Not that we are to think *Homer* wanted Judgment, because *Virgil* had it in a more eminent degree; or that *Virgil* wanted Invention, because *Homer* possest a larger share of it: Each of these great Authors had more of both than perhaps any Man besides, and are only said to have less in Comparison with one another. *Homer* was the greater Genius, *Virgil* the better Artist. In one we most admire the *Man*, in the other the *Work*. *Homer* hurries and transports us with a commanding Impetuosity, *Virgil* leads us with an attractive Majesty: *Homer* scatters with a generous Profusion, *Virgil* bestows with a careful Magnificence: *Homer* like the *Nile*, pours out his Riches with a sudden Overflow; *Virgil* like a River in its Banks, with a gentle and constant Stream. When we behold their Battels, methinks the two Poets resemble the Heroes they celebrate: *Homer*, boundless and irresistible as *Achilles*, bears all before him, and shines more and more as the Tumult increases; *Virgil* calmly daring like *Æneas*, appears undisturb'd in the midst of the Action, disposes all about him, and conquers with Tranquillity: And when we look upon their Machines, *Homer* seems like his own *Jupiter* in his Terrors, shaking *Olympus*, scattering the Lightnings, and firing the Heavens; *Virgil* like the same Power in his Benevolence, counselling with the Gods, laying Plans for Empires, and regularly ordering his whole Creation.

But after all, it is with great Parts as with great Virtues, they naturally border on some Imperfection; and it is often hard to distinguish exactly where the

Virtue ends, or the Fault begins. As Prudence may sometimes sink to Suspicion, so may a great Judgment decline to Coldness; and as Magnanimity may run up to Profusion or Extravagance, so may a great Invention to Redundancy or Wildness. If we look upon *Homer* in this View, we shall perceive the chief *Objections* against him to proceed from so noble a Cause as the Excess of this Faculty.

Among these we may reckon some of his *Marvellous Fictions*, upon which so much Criticism has been spent as surpassing all the Bounds of Probability. Perhaps it may be with great and superior Souls as with gigantick Bodies, which exerting themselves with unusual Strength, exceed what is commonly thought the due Proportion of Parts, to become Miracles in the whole; and like the old Heroes of that Make, commit something near Extravagance amidst a Series of glorious and inimitable Performances. Thus *Homer* has his *speaking Horses*, and *Virgil* his *Myrtles distilling Blood*, without so much as contriving the easy Intervention of a Deity to save the Probability.

It is owing to the same vast Invention that his *Similes* have been thought too exuberant and full of Circumstances. The Force of this Faculty is seen in nothing more, than its Inability to confine itself to that single Circumstance upon which the Comparison is grounded: It runs out into Embellishments of additional Images, which however are so manag'd as not to overpower the main one. His Similes are like Pictures, where the principal Figure has not only its proportion given agreeable to the Original, but is also set off with occasional Ornaments and Prospects. The same will account for his manner of heaping a Number of Comparisons together in one Breath, when his Fancy suggested to him at once so many various and correspondent Images. The Reader will easily extend this Observation to more Objections of the same kind.

If there are others which seem rather to charge him with a Defect or Narrowness of Genius, than an Excess of it; those seeming Defects will be found upon Examination to proceed wholly from the Nature of the Times he liv'd in. Such are his *grosser Representations* of the *Gods*, and the vicious and *imperfect Manners* of his *Heroes*, which will be treated of in the following* *Essay*: But I must here speak a word of the latter, as it is a Point generally carried into Extreams both by the Censurers and Defenders of *Homer*. It must be a strange Partiality to Antiquity to think with Madam *Dacier*, 'that† those Times and Manners are so much the more excellent, as they are more contrary to ours.' Who can be so prejudiced in their Favour as to magnify the Felicity of those Ages, when a Spirit of Revenge and Cruelty reign'd thro' the World, when no Mercy was shown but for the sake of Lucre, when the greatest Princes were put to the Sword, and their Wives and Daughters made Slaves and Concubines? On the other side I would not be so delicate as those modern Criticks, who are shock'd at the *servile Offices* and *mean Employments* in which we sometimes see the Heroes of

* *See the Articles of* Theology *and* Morality, *in the third Part of the* Essay [in *The Iliad,* vol. i. 1715].   † *Preface to her* Homer.

Homer engag'd. There is a Pleasure in taking a View of that Simplicity in Opposition to the Luxury of succeeding Ages; in beholding Monarchs without their Guards, Princes tending their Flocks, and Princesses drawing Water from the Springs. When we read *Homer*, we ought to reflect that we are reading the most ancient Author in the Heathen World; and those who consider him in this Light, will double their Pleasure in the Perusal of him. Let them think they are growing acquainted with Nations and People that are now no more; that they are stepping almost three thousand Years backward into the remotest Antiquity, and entertaining themselves with a clear and surprizing Vision of Things no where else to be found, and the only authentick Picture of that ancient World. By this means alone their greatest Obstacles will vanish; and what usually creates their Dislike, will become a Satisfaction.

This Consideration may farther serve to answer for the constant Use of the same *Epithets* to his Gods and Heroes, such as the *far-darting Phœbus*, the *blue-ey'd Pallas*, the *swift-footed Achilles*, &c. which some have censured as impertinent and tediously repeated. Those of the Gods depended upon the Powers and Offices then believ'd to belong to them, and had contracted a Weight and Veneration from the Rites and solemn Devotions in which they were us'd: They were a sort of Attributes that it was a Matter of Religion to salute them with on all Occasions, and an Irreverence to omit. As for the Epithets of great Men, Mons. *Boileau* is of Opinion; that they were in the Nature of *Sir-Names*, and repeated

as such; for the *Greeks* having no Names deriv'd
from their Fathers, were oblig'd when they mention'd any one to add some other Distinction; either
naming his Parents expressly, or his Place of Birth,
Profession, or the like: As *Alexander* Son of *Philip*,
Herodotus of *Halicarnassus*, *Diogenes* the *Cynic*, &c.
Homer therefore complying with the Custom of his
Countrey, us'd such distinctive Additions as better
agreed with Poetry. And indeed we have something
parallel to these in modern Times, such as the Names
of *Harold Harefoot*, *Edmund Ironside*, *Edward Long-
shanks*, *Edward* the *black Prince*, &c. If yet this be
thought to account better for the Propriety than for
the Repetition, I shall add a farther Conjecture.
Hesiod dividing the World into its Ages, has plac'd a
fourth Age between the Brazen and the Iron one, of
*Heroes distinct from other Men, a divine Race, who
fought at* Thebes *and* Troy, *are called Demi-Gods,
and live by the Care of* Jupiter *in the Islands of the
Blessed.** Now among the divine Honours which
were paid them, they might have this also in common
with the Gods, not to be mention'd without the Solemnity of an Epithet, and such as might be acceptable to them by its celebrating their Families, Actions, or Qualities.

What other Cavils have been rais'd against *Homer*
are such as hardly deserve a Reply, but will yet be
taken notice of as they occur in the Course of the
Work. Many have been occasion'd by an injudicious
Endeavour to exalt *Virgil*; which is much the same,
as if one should think to raise the Superstructure by

* Hesiod, *lib.* i. v. 155, &c.

r

undermining the Foundation: One would imagine by the whole Course of their Parallels, that these Criticks never so much as heard of *Homer*'s having written first; a Consideration which whoever compares these two Poets ought to have always in his Eye. Some accuse him for the same things which they overlook or praise in the other; as when they prefer the Fable and Moral of the *Æneis* to those of the *Iliad*, for the same Reasons which might set the *Odysses* above the *Æneis*: as that the Heroe is a wiser Man; and the Action of the one more beneficial to his Countrey than that of the other: Or else they blame him for not doing what he never design'd; as because *Achilles* is not as good and perfect a Prince as *Æneas*, when the very Moral of his Poem requir'd a contrary Character. It is thus that *Rapin* judges in his Comparison of *Homer* and *Virgil*. Others select those particular Passages of *Homer* which are not so labour'd as some that *Virgil* drew out of them: This is the whole Management of *Scaliger* in his *Poetices*. Others quarrel with what they take for low and mean Expressions, sometimes thro' a false Delicacy and Refinement, oftner from an Ignorance of the Graces of the Original; and then triumph in the Aukwardness of their own Translations. This is the Conduct of *Perault* in his *Parallels*. Lastly, there are others, who pretending to a fairer Proceeding, distinguish between the personal Merit of *Homer*, and that of his *Work*; but when they come to assign the Causes of the great Reputation of the *Iliad*, they found it upon the Ignorance of his Times, and the Prejudice of those that followed. And in pursuance of this Principle, they make those Accidents (such as the Contention of the Cities, *&c.*) to be the Causes of his Fame, which were in Reality the Consequences of his Merit. The same might as well be said of *Virgil*, or any great Author, whose general Character will infallibly raise many casual Additions to their Reputation. This is the Method of Mons. *de la Motte*; who yet confesses upon the whole, that in whatever Age *Homer* had liv'd he must have been the greatest Poet of his Nation, and that he may be said in this Sense to be the Master even of those who surpass'd him.

In all these Objections we see nothing that contradicts his Title to the Honour of the chief *Invention*; and as long as this (which is indeed the Characteristic of Poetry itself) remains unequal'd by his Followers, he still continues superior to them. A cooler Judgment may commit fewer Faults, and be more approv'd in the Eyes of *One Sort* of Criticks: but that Warmth of Fancy will carry the loudest and most universal Applauses which holds the Heart of a Reader under the strongest Enchantment. *Homer* not only appears the Inventor of Poetry, but excells all the Inventors of other Arts in this, that he has swallow'd up the Honour of those who succeeded him. What he has done admitted no Encrease, it only left room for Contraction or Regulation. He shew'd all the Stretch of Fancy at once; and if he has fail'd in some of his Flights, it was but because he attempted every thing. A Work of this kind seems like a mighty Tree which rises from the most vigorous Seed, is improv'd with Industry, flourishes, and produces the finest Fruit; Nature and Art have conspir'd to raise it; Pleasure and Profit join'd to make it valuable: and they who find the justest Faults, have only said, that a few Branches (which run luxuriant thro' a Richness of Nature) might be lopp'd into Form to give it a more regular Appearance.

Having now spoken of the Beauties and Defects of the Original, it remains to treat of the Translation, with the same View to the chief Characteristic. As far as that is seen in the main Parts of the Poem, such as the *Fable*, *Manners*, and *Sentiments*, no Translator can prejudice it but by wilful Omissions or Contractions. As it also breaks out in every particular *Image*, *Description*, and *Simile*; whoever lessens or too much softens those, takes off from this chief Character. It is the first grand Duty of an Interpreter to give his Author entire and unmaim'd; and for the rest, the *Diction* and *Versification* only are his proper Province; since these must be his own, but the others he is to take as he finds them.

It should then be consider'd what Methods may afford some Equivalent in our Language for the Graces of these in the *Greek*. It is certain no literal Translation can be just to an excellent Original in a superior Language: but it is a great Mistake to imagine (as many have done) that a rash Paraphrase can make amends for this general Defect; which is no less in danger to lose the Spirit of an Ancient, by deviating into the modern Manners of Expression. If there be sometimes a *Darkness*, there is often a *Light* in Antiquity, which nothing better preserves than a Version almost literal. I know no Liberties one ought

to take, but those which are necessary for transfusing
the Spirit of the Original, and supporting the Poetical Style of the Translation: and I will venture to
say, there have not been more Men misled in former
times by a servile dull Adherence to the Letter, than
have been deluded in ours by a chimerical insolent
Hope of raising and improving their Author. It is
not to be doubted that the *Fire* of the Poem is what a
Translator should principally regard, as it is most
likely to expire in his managing: However it is his
safest way to be content with preserving this to his
utmost in the Whole, without endeavouring to be
more than he finds his Author is, in any particular
Place. 'Tis a great Secret in Writing to know when
to be plain, and when poetical and figurative; and it
is what *Homer* will teach us if we will but follow
modestly in his Footsteps. Where his Diction is bold
and lofty, let us raise ours as high as we can; but
where his is plain and humble, we ought not to be
deterr'd from imitating him by the fear of incurring
the Censure of a meer *English* Critick. Nothing that
belongs to *Homer* seems to have been more commonly mistaken than the just Pitch of his Style: Some of
his Translators having swell'd into Fustian in a proud
Confidence of the *Sublime*; others sunk into Flatness,
in a cold and timorous Notion of *Simplicity*. Methinks I see these different Followers of *Homer*, some
sweating and straining after him by violent Leaps
and Bounds, (the certain Signs of false Mettle) others
slowly and servilely creeping in his Train, while the
Poet himself is all the time proceeding with an unaffected and equal Majesty before them. However of

the two Extreams one could sooner pardon Frenzy than Frigidity: No Author is to be envy'd for such Commendations as he may gain by that Character of Style, which his Friends must agree together to call *Simplicity*, and the rest of the World will call *Dulness*. There is a *graceful* and *dignify'd* Simplicity, as well as a *bald* and *sordid* one, which differ as much from each other as the Air of a *plain* Man from that of a *Sloven*: 'Tis one thing to be tricked up, and another not to be dress'd at all. Simplicity is the Mean between Ostentation and Rusticity.

This pure and noble Simplicity is no where in such Perfection as in the *Scripture* and our Author. One may affirm with all respect to the inspired Writings, that the *Divine Spirit* made use of no other Words but what were intelligible and common to Men at that Time, and in that Part of the World; and as *Homer* is the Author nearest to those, his Style must of course bear a greater Resemblance to the sacred Books than that of any other Writer. This Consideration (together with what has been observ'd of the Parity of some of his Thoughts) may methinks induce a Translator on the one hand to give into several of those general Phrases and Manners of Expression, which have attain'd a Veneration even in our Language from their use in the *Old Testament*; as on the other, to avoid those which have been appropriated to the Divinity, and in a manner consign'd to Mystery and Religion.

For a farther Preservation of this Air of Simplicity, a particular Care should be taken to express with all Plainness those *Moral Sentences* and *Proverbial*

Speeches which are so numerous in this Poet. They have something Venerable, and as I may say *Oracular*, in that unadorn'd Gravity and Shortness with which they are deliver'd: a Grace which would be utterly lost by endeavouring to give them what we call a more ingenious (that is a more modern) Turn in the Paraphrase.

Perhaps the Mixture of some *Græcisms* and old Words after the manner of *Milton*, if done without too much Affectation, might not have an ill Effect in a Version of this particular Work, which most of any other seems to require a venerable *Antique* Cast. But certainly the use of *modern Terms* of *War* and *Government*, such as *Platoon, Campagne, Junto*, or the like (which some of his Translators have fallen into) cannot be allowable; those only excepted, without which it is impossible to treat the Subjects in any living Language.

There are two Peculiarities in *Homer*'s Diction that are a sort of *Marks* or *Moles*, by which every common Eye distinguishes him at first sight: Those who are not his greatest Admirers look upon them as Defects, and those who are seem pleased with them as Beauties. I speak of his *Compound-Epithets* and of his *Repetitions*. Many of the former cannot be done literally into *English* without destroying the Purity of our Language. I believe such should be retain'd as slide easily of themselves into an *English-Compound*, without Violence to the Ear or to the receiv'd Rules of Composition; as well as those which have receiv'd a Sanction from the Authority of our best Poets, and are become familiar thro' their use of them; such as

the *Cloud-compelling Jove, &c.* As for the rest, whenever any can be as fully and significantly exprest in a
single word as in a compounded one, the Course to
be taken is obvious. Some that cannot be so turn'd as
to preserve their full Image by one or two Words,
may have Justice done them by Circumlocution; as
the Epithet εἰνοσίφυλλος to a Mountain would appear
little or ridiculous translated literally *Leaf-shaking*,
but affords a majestic Idea in the *Periphrasis: The
lofty Mountain shakes his waving Woods*. Others that
admit of differing Significations, may receive an Advantage by a judicious Variation according to the
Occasions on which they are introduc'd. For Example, the Epithet of *Apollo*, ἑκηβόλος, or *far-shooting*, is
capable of two Explications; one literal in respect of
the Darts and Bow, the Ensigns of that God, the
other allegorical with regard to the Rays of the Sun:
Therefore in such Places where *Apollo* is represented
as a God in Person, I would use the former Interpretation, and where the Effects of the Sun are describ'd,
I would make choice of the latter. Upon the whole,
it will be necessary to avoid that perpetual Repetition
of the same Epithets which we find in Homer, and
which, tho' it might be accommodated (as has been
already shewn) to the Ear of those Times, is by no
means so to ours: But one may wait for Opportunities of placing them, where they derive an additional
Beauty from the Occasions on which they are employed; and in doing this properly, a Translator may
at once shew his Fancy and his Judgment.

As for *Homer*'s *Repetitions*; we may divide them
into three sorts; of whole Narrations and Speeches,

of single Sentences, and of one Verse or Hemistich.
I hope it is not impossible to have such a Regard to
these, as neither to lose so known a Mark of the Author on the one hand, nor to offend the Reader too
much on the other. The Repetition is not ungraceful
in those Speeches where the Dignity of the Speaker
renders it a sort of Insolence to alter his Words; as in
the Messages from Gods to Men, or from higher
Powers to Inferiors in Concerns of State, or where
the Ceremonial of Religion seems to require it, in
the solemn Forms of Prayers, Oaths, or the like. In
other Cases, I believe the best Rule is to be guided
by the Nearness, or Distance, at which the Repetitions are plac'd in the Original: When they follow
too close one may vary the Expression, but it is a
Question whether a profess'd Translator be authorized to omit any: If they be tedious, the Author is to
answer for it.

It only remains to speak of the *Versification*. *Homer* (as has been said) is perpetually applying the
Sound to the Sense, and varying it on every new Subject. This is indeed one of the most exquisite Beauties of Poetry, and attainable by very few: I know
only of *Homer* eminent for it in the *Greek*, and *Virgil*
in *Latine*. I am sensible it is what may sometimes
happen by Chance, when a Writer is warm, and fully
possest of his Image: however it may be reasonably
believed they design'd this, in whose Verse it so
manifestly appears in a superior degree to all others.
Few Readers have the Ear to be Judges of it, but
those who have will see I have endeavour'd at this
Beauty.

Upon the whole, I must confess my self utterly in-capable of doing Justice to *Homer*. I attempt him in no other Hope but that which one may entertain without much Vanity, of giving a more tolerable Copy of him than any entire Translation in Verse has yet done. We have only those of *Chapman*, *Hobbes*, and *Ogilby*. *Chapman* has taken the Advantage of an immeasurable Length of Verse, notwithstanding which there is scarce any Paraphrase more loose and rambling than his. He has frequent Interpolations of four or six Lines, and I remember one in the thirteenth Book of the *Odysses*, *ver.* 312, where he has spun twenty Verses out of two. He is often mistaken in so bold a manner, that one might think he deviated on purpose, if he did not in other Places of his Notes insist so much upon Verbal Trifles. He appears to have had a strong Affectation of extracting new Meanings out of his Author, insomuch as to promise in his Rhyming Preface, a Poem of the Mysteries he had revealed in *Homer*; and perhaps he endeavoured to strain the obvious Sense to this End. His Expression is involved in Fustian, a Fault for which he was remarkable in his Original Writings, as in the Tragedy of *Bussy d'Amboise*, &c. In a word, the Nature of the Man may account for his whole Performance; for he appears from his Preface and Remarks to have been of an arrogant Turn, and an Enthusiast in Poetry. His own Boast of having finish'd half the *Iliad* in less than fifteen Weeks, shews with what Negligence his Version was performed. But that which is to be allowed him, and which very much contributed to cover his Defects, is a daring

fiery Spirit that animates his Translation, which is
something like what one might imagine *Homer* himself would have writ before he arriv'd to Years of Discretion. *Hobbes* has given us a correct Explanation of
the Sense in general, but for Particulars and Circumstances he continually lopps them, and often omits
the most beautiful. As for its being esteem'd a close
Translation, I doubt not many have been led into
that Error by the Shortness of it, which proceeds not
from his following the Original Line by Line, but
from the Contractions above-mentioned. He sometimes omits whole Similes and Sentences, and is now
and then guilty of Mistakes which no Writer of his
Learning could have fallen into, but thro' Careles-
ness. His Poetry, as well as *Ogilby*'s, is too mean for
Criticism.

It is a great Loss to the Poetical World that Mr.
Dryden did not live to translate the *Iliad*. He has left
us only the first Book and a small Part of the sixth;
in which if he has in some Places not truly interpreted the Sense, or preserved the Antiquities, it ought
to be excused on account of the Haste he was obliged
to write in. He seems to have had too much Regard
to *Chapman*, whose Words he sometimes copies, and
has unhappily follow'd him in Passages where he
wanders from the Original. However had he translated the whole Work, I would no more have attempted *Homer* after him than *Virgil*, his Version of
whom (notwithstanding some human Errors) is the
most noble and spirited Translation I know in any
Language. But the Fate of great Genius's is like that
of great Ministers, tho' they are confessedly the first

in the Commonwealth of Letters, they must be envy'd and calumniated only for being at the Head of
it.

That which in my Opinion ought to be the Endeavour óf any one who translates *Homer*, is above all
things to keep alive that Spirit and Fire which makes
his chief Charaćter. In particular Places, where the
Sense can bear any Doubt, to follow the strongest
and most Poetical, as most agreeing with that Charaćter. To copy him in all the Variations of his Style,
and the different Modulations of his Numbers. To
preserve in the more aćtive or descriptive Parts, a
Warmth and Elevation; in the more sedate or narrative, a Plainness and Solemnity; in the Speeches a
Fulness and Perspicuity; in the Sentences a Shortness and Gravity. Not to neglećt even the little Figures and Turns on the Words, nor sometimes the
very Cast of the Periods. Neither to omit or confound any Rites or Customs of Antiquity. Perhaps
too he ought to include the whole in a shorter Compass, than has hitherto been done by any Translator
who has tolerably preserved either the Sense or Poetry. What I would farther recommend to him, is to
study his Author rather from his own Text than from
any Commentaries, how learned soever, or whatever
Figure they make in the Estimation of the World.
To consider him attentively in Comparison with *Virgil* above all the Ancients, and with *Milton* above all
the Moderns. Next these the Archbishop of *Cam-
bray*'s *Telemachus* may give him the truest Idea of
the Spirit and Turn of our Author, and *Bossu*'s admirable Treatise of the Epic Poem the justest No-

tion of his Design and Conduct. But after all, with whatever Judgment and Study a Man may proceed, or with whatever Happiness he may perform such a Work; he must hope to please but a few, those only who have at once a Taste of Poetry, and competent Learning. For to satisfy such as want either, is not in the Nature of this Undertaking; since a meer Modern Wit can like nothing that is not *Modern*, and a Pedant nothing that is not *Greek*.

What I have done is submitted to the Publick, from whose Opinions I am prepared to learn; tho' I fear no Judges so little as our best Poets, who are most sensible of the Weight of this Task. As for the worst, whatever they shall please to say, they may give me some Concern as they are unhappy Men, but none as they are malignant Writers. I was guided in this Translation by Judgments very different from theirs, and by Persons for whom they can have no Kindness, if an old Observation be true, that the strongest Antipathy in the World is that of Fools to Men of Wit. Mr. *Addison* was the first whose Advice determin'd me to undertake this Task, who was pleas'd to write to me upon that Occasion in such Terms as I cannot repeat without Vanity. I was obliged to Sir *Richard Steele* for a very early Recommendation of my Undertaking to the Publick. Dr. *Swift* promoted my Interest with that Warmth with which he always serves his Friend. The Humanity and Frankness of Sir *Samuel Garth* are what I never knew wanting on any Occasion. I must also acknowledge with infinite Pleasure the many friendly Offices as well as sincere Criticisms of Mr. *Congreve*, who had led me the way in translating some Parts of *Homer*, as I wish for the sake of the World he had prevented me in the rest. I must add the Names of Mr. *Rowe* and Dr. *Parnell*, tho' I shall take a farther Opportunity of doing Justice to the last, whose Good-nature (to give it a great Panegyrick) is no less extensive than his Learning. The Favour of these Gentlemen is not entirely undeserved by one who bears them so true an Affection. But what can I say of the Honour so many of the *Great* have done me, while the *First Names* of the Age appear as my Subscribers, and the most distinguish'd Patrons and Ornaments of Learning as my chief Encouragers. Among these it is a particular Pleasure to me to find, that my highest Obligations are to such who have done most Honour to the Name of Poet: That his Grace the *Duke* of *Buckingham* was not displeas'd I should undertake the Author to whom he has given (in his excellent *Essay*) the finest Praise he ever yet receiv'd.

Read Homer once, *and you can read no more;*
For all things else appear so mean and poor,
Verse will seem Prose: yet often *on him look,*
And you will hardly need another Book.

That the Earl of *Halifax* was one of the first to favour me, of whom it is hard to say whether the Advancement of the Polite Arts is more owing to his Generosity or his Example. That such a Genius as my Lord *Bolingbroke*, not more distinguished in the great Scenes of Business than in all the useful and entertaining Parts of Learning, has not refus'd to be the

Critick of these Sheets, and the Patron of their Writer. And that so excellent an Imitator of *Homer* as the noble Author of the Tragedy of *Heroic Love*, has continu'd his Partiality to me from my writing Pastorals to my attempting the *Iliad*. I cannot deny my self the Pride of confessing, that I have had the Advantage not only of their Advice for the Conduct in general, but their Correction of several Particulars of this Translation.

I could say a great deal of the Pleasure of being distinguish'd by the *Earl* of *Carnarvon*, but it is almost absurd to particularize any one generous Action in a Person whose whole Life is a continued Series of them. The Right Honourable Mr. *Stanhope*, the present Secretary of State, will pardon my Desire of having it known that he was pleas'd to promote this Affair. The particular Zeal of Mr. *Harcourt* (the Son of the late Lord Chancellor) gave me a Proof how much I am honour'd in a Share of his Friendship. I must attribute to the same Motive that of several others of my Friends, to whom all Acknowledgments are render'd unnecessary by the Privileges of a familiar Correspondence: And I am satisfy'd I can no way better oblige Men of their Turn, than by my Silence.

In short, I have found more Patrons than ever *Homer* wanted. He would have thought himself happy to have met the same Favour at *Athens*, that has been shewn me by its learned Rival, the University of *Oxford*. If my Author had the *Wits* of After-Ages for his Defenders, his Translator has had the *Beauties* of the present for his Advocates; a Pleasure too great to be changed for any Fame in Reversion. And I can hardly envy him those pompous Honours he receiv'd after Death, when I reflect on the Enjoyment of so many agreeable Obligations, and easy Friendships which make the Satisfaction of Life. This Distinction is the more to be acknowledg'd, as it is shewn to one whose Pen has never gratify'd the Prejudices of particular *Parties*, or the Vanities of particular *Men*. Whatever the Success may prove, I shall never repent of an Undertaking in which I have experienc'd the Candour and Friendship of so many Persons of Merit; and in which I hope to pass some of those Years of Youth that are generally lost in a Circle of Follies, after a manner neither wholly unuseful to others, nor disagreeable to my self.

The Iliad, Vol. I, 1715.

A FULL and TRUE

ACCOUNT

OF A

𝕳𝖔𝖗𝖗𝖎𝖉 𝖆𝖓𝖉 𝕭𝖆𝖗𝖇𝖆𝖗𝖔𝖚𝖘

REVENGE by POISON,

On the Body of

Mr. *EDMUND CURLL*, Bookfeller;

With a faithful Copy of his

Laſt WILL and TESTAMENT.

Publiſh'd by an Eye Witneſs.

So when Curll's *Stomach the ſtrong Drench o'ercame,*
(Infus'd in Vengeance of inſulted Fame)
Th' Avenger ſees, with a delighted Eye,
His long Jaws open, and his Colour fly ;
And while his Guts the keen Emeticks urge,
Smiles on the Vomit, and enjoys the Purge.

Sold by *J. Roberts*, *J. Morphew*, R. *Burleigh*, *J. Baker*, and *S. Pop-ping.* Price Three Pence.

A Full and True

ACCOUNT

Of a Horrid and Barbarous

REVENGE by POISON,

On the Body of Mr. *Edm. Curll*, &c.

HISTORY furnishes us with Examples of many Satyrical Authors who have fallen Sacrifices to Revenge, but not of any Booksellers that I know of, except the unfortunate Subject of the following Papers; I mean Mr. *Edmund Curll*, at the *Bible* and *Dial* in *Fleetstreet*, who was Yesterday poison'd by Mr. *Pope*, after having liv'd many Years an Instance of the mild Temper of the *British* Nation.

Every Body knows that the said Mr. *Edmund Curll*, on Monday the 26th Instant, publish'd a Satyrical Piece, entituled *Court Poems*, in the Preface whereof they were attributed to a *Lady of Quality*, Mr. *Pope*, or Mr. *Gay*; by which indiscreet Method, though he had escaped one Revenge, there were still two behind in reserve.

Now on the Wednesday ensuing, between the Hours of 10 and 11, Mr. *Lintott*, a neighb'ring Bookseller, desir'd a Conference with Mr. *Curll* about settling the *Title Page* of *Wiquefort*'s *Ambassador*, inviting him at the same Time to take a Whet together. Mr. *Pope*, (who is not the only Instance how Persons of bright Parts may be carry'd away by the Instigations of the Devil) found Means to convey himself into the same Room, under pretence of Business with Mr. *Lintott*, who it seems is the Printer of his *Homer*. This Gentleman with a seeming Coolness, reprimanded Mr. *Curll* for wrongfully ascribing to him the aforesaid Poems: He excused himself, by declaring that one of his Authors (Mr. *Oldmixon* by Name) gave the Copies to the Press, and wrote the *Preface*. Upon this Mr. *Pope* (being to all appearance reconcil'd) very civilly drank a Glass of Sack to Mr. *Curll*, which he as civilly pledged; and tho' the Liquor in Colour and Taste differ'd not from common Sack, yet was it plain by the Pangs this unhappy Stationer felt soon after, that some poisonous Drug had been secretly infused therein.

About Eleven a Clock he went home, where his Wife observing his Colour chang'd, said, *Are you not Sick, my Dear?* He reply'd, *Bloody Sick*; and incontinently fell a vomiting and straining in an uncommon and unnatural Manner, the Contents of his vomiting being as Green as Grass. His Wife had been just reading a Book of her Husband's printing, concerning *Jane Wenham*, the famous Witch of *Hartford*, and her Mind misgave her that he was bewitch'd; but he soon let her know that he suspected *Poison*, and recounted to her, between the Intervals of his Yawnings and Reachings, every Circumstance of his Interview with Mr. *Pope*.

Mr. *Lintott* in the mean Time coming in, was extremely afrighted at the sudden Alteration he observed in him: *Brother* Curll, says he, *I fear you have got the vomiting Distemper, which* (*I have heard*) *kills in half an Hour. This comes from your not following my Advice, to drink old Hock as I do, and abstain from Sack.* Mr. *Curll* reply'd, in a moving Tone, *Your Author's Sack I fear has done my Business.* Z——ds, says Mr. *Lintott, My Author!*——*Why did not you drink old Hock?* Notwithstanding which rough Remonstrance, he did in the most friendly Manner press him to take warm Water; but Mr. *Curll* did with great Obstinacy refuse it; which made Mr. *Lintott* infer, that he chose to die, as thinking to recover greater Damages.

All this Time the Symptoms encreas'd violently, with acute Pains in the lower Belly. *Brother* Lintott, says he, *I perceive my last Hour approaching, do me the friendly Office to call my Partner, Mr.* Pemberton, *that we may settle our Worldly Affairs.* Mr. *Lintott*, like a kind Neighbour, was hastening out of the Room, while Mr. *Curll* rav'd aloud in this Manner, *If I survive this, I will be revenged on* Tonson, *it was he first detected me as the Printer of these Poems, and I will reprint these very Poems in his Name.* His Wife admonish'd him not to think of Revenge, but to take care of his Stock and his Soul: And in the same Instant, Mr. *Lintott* (whose Goodness can never be enough applauded) return'd with Mr. *Pemberton.* After some Tears jointly shed by these Humane Booksellers, Mr. *Curll*, being (as he said) in his perfect Senses though in great bodily Pain, immediately proceeded to make a verbal Will (Mrs. *Curll* having first put on his Night Cap) in the following Manner.

GENTLEMEN, in the first Place, I do sincerely pray Forgiveness for those indirect Methods I have pursued in inventing new Titles to old Books, putting Authors Names to Things they never saw, publishing private Quarrels for publick Entertainment; all which, I hope will be pardoned, as being done to get an honest livelihood.

I do also heartily beg Pardon of all Persons of Honour, Lords Spiritual and Temporal, Gentry, Burgesses, and Commonalty, to whose Abuse I have any, or every way, contributed by my Publications. Particularly, I hope it will be considered, that if I have vilify'd his Grace the Duke of *M[arlborou]gh*, I have likewise aspers'd the late Duke of *O[rmon]d*; if I have abused the honourable Mr. *W[alpo]le*, I have also libell'd the late Lord *B[olingbro]ke*; so that I have preserv'd that Equality and Impartiality which becomes an honest Man in Times of Faction and Division.

I call my Conscience to Witness, that many of these Things which may seem malicious, were done out of Charity; I having made it wholly my Business to print for poor disconsolate Authors, whom all other Booksellers refuse: Only God bless Sir *Richard Bl[ackmo]re*; you know he takes no Copy Money.

The Book of the *Conduct* of the *Earl of N[ottingha]m*, is yet unpublished; as you are to have the Profit of it, Mr. *Pemberton*, you are to run the Risque of the Resentments of all that Noble Family. Indeed I caused the Author to assert several Things in it as Facts, which are only idle Stories of the Town; because I thought it would make the Book sell. Do you pay the Author for Copy Money, and the Printer and Publisher. I heartily beg God's, and my L[or]d N[ottingha]m's Pardon; but all Trades must live.

The second Collection of Poems, which I groundlesly called Mr. *Prior*'s, will sell for Nothing, and hath not yet paid the Charge of the Advertisements, which I was obliged to publish against him: Therefore you may as well suppress the Edition, and beg that Gentleman's Pardon in the Name of a dying Christian.

The *French Cato*, with the Criticism, showing how superior it is to Mr. *Addison*'s, (which I wickedly inscribed to Madam *Dacier*) may be suppress'd at a reasonable Rate, being damnably translated.

I protest I have no Animosity to Mr. *Rowe*, having printed Part of his *Callipædia*, and an incorrect Edition of his Poems without his Leave, in Quarto. Mr. *Gildon*'s *Rehearsal*; or *Bays the Younger*, did more harm to me than to Mr. *Rowe*; though upon the Faith of an honest Man, I paid him double for abusing both him and Mr. *Pope*.

Heaven pardon me for publishing the *Trials of Sodomy* in an *Elzevir* Letter; but I humbly hope, my printing Sir *Richard Bl[ackmo]re*'s Essays will attone for them. I beg that you will take what remains of these last, which is near the whole Impression, (Presents excepted) and let my poor Widow have in Exchange the sole Propriety of the Copy of Madam *Mascranny*.

Here Mr. Pemberton *interrupted, and would by no Means consent to this Article, about which some Dis-*

pute might have arisen, unbecoming a dying Person, if Mr. Lintott *had not interposed, and Mr.* Curll *vomited.*

What this poor unfortunate Man spoke afterwards, was so indistinct, and in such broken Accents, (being perpetually interrupted by Vomitings) that the Reader is intreated to excuse the Confusion and Imperfection of this Account.

Dear Mr. *Pemberton,* I beg you to beware of the Indictment at *Hicks's-Hall,* for publishing *Rochester*'s bawdy Poems; that Copy will otherwise be my best Legacy to my dear Wife, and helpless Child.

The Case of Impotence was my best Support all the last long Vacation.

In this last Paragraph Mr. Curll*'s Voice grew more free, for his Vomitings abated upon his Dejections, and he spoke what follows from his Close-stole.*

For the Copies of Noblemen's and Bishop's *Last Wills and Testaments,* I solemnly declare I printed them not with any Purpose of Defamation; but meerly as I thought those Copies lawfully purchased from *Doctors Commons,* at *One Shilling* a Piece. Our Trade in Wills turning to small Account, we may divide them blindfold.

For Mr. *Manwaring*'s *Life,* I ask Mrs. *Old*[*fiel*]*d*'s Pardon: Neither *His,* nor my Lord *Halifax*'s Lives, though they were of great Service to their Country, were of any to me: But I was resolved, since I could

not print their Works while they liv'd, to print their
Lives after they were dead.

While he was speaking these Words, Mr. *Oldmixon*
enter'd. *Ah! Mr.* Oldmixon (said poor Mr. *Curll*) *to
what a Condition have your Works reduced me! I die a
Martyr to that unlucky Preface. However, in these my
last Moments, I will be just to all Men; you shall have
your Third Share of the* Court Poems, *as was stipu-
lated. When I am dead, where will you find another
Bookseller? Your* Protestant Packet *might have supported you, had you writ a little less scurrilously, There
is a mean in all things.*
　　Then turning to Mr. *Pemberton*, he told him, he
had several *Taking Title Pages* that only wanted
Treatises to be wrote to them, and earnestly entreated, that when they were writ, his Heirs might have
some Share of the Profit of them.
　　After he had said this he fell into horrible Grip-
ings, upon which Mr. *Lintott* advis'd him to repeat
the Lord's Prayer. He desir'd his Wife to step into
the Shop for a Common-Prayer-Book, and read it by
the Help of a Candle, without Hesitation. He clos'd
the Book, fetch'd a Groan, and recommended to Mrs.
Curll to give Forty Shillings to the Poor of the Parish of St. *Dunstan*'s, and a Week's Wages Advance to
each of his Gentlemen Authors, with some small
Gratuity in particular to Mrs. *Centlivre*.
　　The poor Man continued for some Hours with all
his disconsolate Family about him in Tears, expecting his final Dissolution; when of a sudden he was

surprizingly relieved by a plentiful fœtid Stool, which obliged them all to retire out of the Room. Notwithstanding, it is judged by Sir *Richard Bl[ackmor]e*, that the Poyson is still latent in his Body, and will infallibly destroy him by slow Degrees, in less than a Month. It is to be hoped the other Enemies of this wretched Stationer, will not further pursue their Revenge, or shorten this small Period of his miserable Life.

FINIS.

GOD's Revenge

AGAINST

PUNNING

1716

GOD's Revenge

AGAINST

PUNNING.

Shewing the miserable Fates of Persons addicted to this Crying Sin, in Court and Town.

MANIFOLD have been the Judgments which Heav'n from Time to Time, for the Chastisement of a Sinful People, has inflicted on whole Nations. For when the Degeneracy becomes Common, 'tis but Just the Punishment should be General: Of this kind, in our own unfortunate Country, was that destructive Pestilence, whose Mortality was so fatal, as to sweep away, if Sir *William Petty* may be believ'd, Five Millions of Christian Souls, besides Women and Jews.

Such also was that dreadful Conflagration ensuing, in this famous Metropolis of *London*, which Consumed, according to the Computation of Sir *Samuel Morland*, 100000 Houses, not to mention Churches and Stables.

Scarce had this Unhappy Nation recover'd these Funest Disasters, when it pleased God to suffer the Abomination of Play-houses to rise up in this Land: From hence hath an Inundation of Obscenity flow'd from the Court, and overspread the Kingdom: Even Infants disfigured the Walls of holy Temples with exorbitant Representations of the Members of Generation; nay, no sooner had they learnt to Spell, but they had Wickedness enough to Write the Names thereof in large Capitals; an Enormity, observ'd by Travellers, to be found in no Country but *England*.

But when Whoring and Popery were driven hence by the Happy *Revolution*; still the Nation so greatly offended, that *Socinianism*, *Arianism*, and *Whistonism* triumph'd in our Streets, and were in a manner become Universal.

And yet still, after all these Visitations, it has pleased Heaven to visit us with a Contagion more Epidemical, and of consequence more Fatal: This was foretold to Us, First, By that unparallel'd Eclipse in 1714: Secondly, By the dreadful Coruscations in the Air this present Year: And Thirdly, By the Nine Comets seen at once over *Soho-Square*, by Mrs. *Katherine Wadlington*, and Others; a Contagion that first crept in amongst the First Quality, descended to their Footmen, and infused itself into their Ladies; I mean, the woful Practice of PUNNING. This does occasion the Corruption of our Language, and therein of the Word of God translated into our Language; which certainly every sober Christian must Tremble at.

Now such is the Enormity of this Abomination, that our very Nobles not only commit *Punning* over Tea, and in Taverns, but even on the *Lord's-Day*, and in the King's Chapel: Therefore to deterr Men from this evil Practice, I shall give some True and Dreadful Examples of God's Revenge against *Punsters*.

The Right Honourable————(but it is not safe to

insert the Name of an eminent Nobleman in this Paper, yet I will venture to say that such a one has been seen; which is all we can say, considering the largeness of his Sleeves:) This young Nobleman was not only a flagitious *Punster* himself, but was accessary to the Punning of others, by Consent, by Provocation, by Connivance, and by Defence of the Evil committed; for which the Lord mercifully spared his Neck, but as a Mark of Reprobation wryed his Nose.

Another Nobleman of great Hopes, no less guilty of the same Crime, was made the Punisher of himself with his own Hand, in the Loss of 500 Pounds at Box and Dice; whereby this unfortunate young Gentleman incurr'd the heavy Displeasure of his Aged Grandmother.

A Third of no less illustrious Extraction, for the same Vice, was permitted to fall into the Arms of a *Dalilah*, who may one Day cut off his curious Hair, and deliver him up to the *Philistines*.

Colonel *F[rowde]*, an ancient Gentleman of grave Deportment, gave into this Sin so early in his Youth, that whenever his Tongue endeavours to speak Common Sense, he Hesitates so as not to be understood.

Thomas Pickle Gentleman, for the same Crime, banish'd to *Minorca*.

Muley Hamet, from a healthy and hopeful Officer in the Army, turn'd a miserable Invalid at *Tilbury*-Fort.

Eustace Esq; for the Murder of much of the King's *English* in *Ireland*, is quite depriv'd of his Reason, and now remains a Lively Instance of Emptiness and Vivacity.

Poor *Daniel Button*, for the same Offence, depriv'd of all his Wits.

One *Samuel* an *Irishman*, for his forward Attempt to *Pun*, was stunted in his Stature, and hath been visited all his Life after with Bulls and Blunders.

George Simmons, Shoemaker at *Turnstile* in *Holborn*, was so given to this Custom, and did it with so much Success, that his Neighbours gave out he was a Wit. Which Report coming among his Creditors, no body would Trust him; so that he is now a Bankrupt, and his Family in a miserable Condition.

Divers eminent Clergymen of the University of *Cambridge*, for having propagated this Vice, became great Drunkards and Tories.

A *Devonshire* Man of Wit, for only saying, in a jesting manner, *I get Up—Pun a Horse*, instantly fell down, and broke his Snuff-box and Neck, and lost the Horse.

From which Calamities, the Lord in his Mercy defend us All. So Prayeth the Punless *and* Penyless

J. Baker, *Knight.*

L O N D O N:
Printed for J. R o b e r t s, at the *Oxford-Arms* in *Warwick-Lane.* 1716.
[Price 2*d.*]

A FURTHER

ACCOUNT

Of the moſt

Deplorable Condition

O F

Mr. *EDMUND CURLL*,

Bookseller.

Since his being POISON'D on the
28th of *March*.

To be publiſh'd Weekly.

LONDON

Printed, and Sold by all the Pub-
liſhers, Mercuries, and Hawkers,
within the Bills of Mortality.
1716.

A FURTHER

ACCOUNT

Of the most

Deplorable Condition

Of Mr. *EDMUND CURLL,*

Bookseller.

THE Publick is already acquainted with the Manner of Mr. *Curll*'s Impoisonment, by a faithful, tho' unpolite, Historian of *Grub-street.* I am but the Continuer of his History; yet I hope a due Distinction will be made, between an un-dignify'd Scribler of a Sheet and half, and the Au-thor of a Three-Penny stitcht Book, like my self.

Wit (saith Sir *Richard Blackmore*) *proceeds from a Concurrence of regular and exalted Ferments, and an Affluence of Animal Spirits rectify'd and refin'd to a degree of Purity.* On the contrary, when the igneous Particles rise with the vital Liquor, they produce an Abstraction of the rational Part of the Soul, which we commonly call *Madness.* The Verity of this Hy-pothesis, is justify'd by the Symptoms with which the unfortunate Mr. *Edmund Curll*, Bookseller, hath been afflicted ever since his swallowing the Poison at the *Swan* Tavern in *Fleetstreet*. For tho' the *Neck* of his *Retort*, which carries up the Animal Spirits to the Head, is of an extraordinary Length, yet the said Animal Spirits rise muddy, being contaminated with the inflammable Particles of this uncommon Poison.

The Symptoms of his Departure from his usual Temper of Mind, were at first only *speaking civilly to his Customers*, taking a Fancy to *say his Prayers, singeing a Pig with a new purchas'd Libel*, and *refusing Two and Nine Pence for Sir* R[ichard] B[lackmore]'*s Essays*.

As the poor Man's Frenzy increas'd, he began to *void his Excrements in his Bed, read* Rochester'*s bawdy Poems to his Wife*, gave *Oldmixon* a *slap* on the *Chops*, and wou'd have kiss'd Mr. *Pemberton*'s A—— *by Violence*.

But at last he came to such a pass, that he wou'd *dine upon nothing but Copper Plates*, took a *Clyster for a whipt Syllabub*, and eat a *Suppository* for a *Raddish* with *Bread* and *Butter*.

We leave it to every tender Wife to imagine how sorely all this afflicted poor Mrs. *Curll*: At first she privately put a *Bill* into several *Churches*, desiring the Prayers of the Congregation for a *wretched Stationer* distemper'd in Mind. But when she was sadly convinc'd that his Misfortune was publick to all the World, writ the following Letter to her good Neighbour Mr. *Lintott*.

A true Copy of Mrs. Curll'*s Letter to* Mr. Lintott.

Worthy Mr. Lintott,

'YOU, and all the Neighbours know too well, the Frenzy with which my poor Man is visited. I never perceiv'd he was out of himself, till that melancholy Day that he thought he was poison'd in a Glass of Sack; upon this, he took a strange Fancy to run a Vomiting all over the House, and in the new wash'd Dining Room. Alas! this is the greatest Adversity that ever befel my poor Man since he lost *one Testicle* at School by the bite of a black Boar. Good Lord! if he should die, where should I dispose of the Stock? unless Mr. *Pemberton* or you would help a distressed Widow; for God knows he never pub lish'd any Books that lasted above a Week, so that if we wanted *daily Books*, we wanted *daily Bread*. I can write no more, for I hear the Rap of Mr. *Curll*'s *Ivory headed Cane* upon the Counter.—Pray recommend me to your *Pastry Cook*, who furnishes you yearly with Tarts in exchange for your Papers, for Mr. *Curll* has disoblig'd ours since his Fits came upon him;—before that, we generally liv'd upon bak'd Meats.—He is coming in, and I have but just time to put his Son out of the way for fear of Mischief: So wishing you a merry Easter, I remain your

most humble Servant,
C. Curll.

'*P.S.* As to the Report of my poor Husband's stealing a *Calf*, it is really groundless, for he always binds in *Sheep*.'

But return we to Mr. *Curll*, who all *Wednesday* continued outragiously Mad. On *Thursday* he had a *lucid Interval*, that enabled him to send a general Summons to all *his Authors*. There was but one Porter who cou'd perform this Office, to whom he gave the following Bill of Directions where to find 'em. This Bill, together with Mrs. *Curll*'s Original Letter, lye at Mr. *Lintott*'s Shop to be perus'd by the Curious.

Instructions to a Porter how to find Mr. Curll's Authors.

' A T a Tallow-chandlers in *Petty France*, half way under the blind Arch: Ask for the *Historian*.

'At the Bedsted and Bolster, a Musick House in *Morefields*, two Translators in a Bed together.

'At the *Hercules* and *Still* in *Vinegar-yard*, a School-Master with Carbuncles on his Nose.

'At a Blacksmiths Shop in the *Friars*, a Pindarick Writer in red Stockings.

'In the Calendar Mill Room at *Exeter* Change, a Composer of Meditations.

'At the Three *Tobacco Pipes* in *Dog* and *Bitch* Yard, one that has been a Parson, he wears a blue Camblet Coat trim'd with black: my best Writer against *reveal'd Religion*.

'At Mr. *Summers* a Thief-catchers, in *Lewkners* Lane, the Man that wrote against the Impiety of Mr. *Rowe*'s Plays.

'At the Farthing Pye House in *Tooting* Fields, the young Man who is writing my new *Pastorals.*

'At the Laundresses, at the Hole in the Wall in *Cursitors* Alley, up three Pair of Stairs, the Author of my *Church History*—if his Flux be over—you may also speak to the Gentleman who lyes by him in the Flock Bed, my *Index-maker.*

'The *Cook's Wife* in *Buckingham* Court; bid her bring along with her the *Similes* that were lent her for her next new Play.

'Call at *Budge Row* for the Gentleman you use to go to in the Cock-loft; I have taken away the Ladder, but his Landlady has it in keeping.

'I don't much care if you ask at the *Mint* for the old Beetle-brow'd Critick, and the purblind Poet at the Alley over against St. *Andrews Holbourn.* But this as you have time.'

All these Gentlemen appear'd at the Hour appointed, in Mr. *Curll*'s Dining Room, two excepted; one of whom was the Gentleman in the Cock-loft, his Landlady being out of the way, and the *Gradus ad Parnassum* taken down; the other happened to be too closely watch'd by the Bailiffs.

They no sooner enter'd the Room, but all of them show'd in their Behaviour some Suspicion of each other; some turning away their Heads with an Air of Contempt; others squinting with a Leer that show'd at once Fear and Indignation, each with a haggard abstracted Mien, the lively Picture of *Scorn, Solitude,* and *short Commons.* So when a Keeper feeds his hungry Charge, of Vultures, Panthers, and of *Lybian* Leopards, each eyes his Fellow with a fiery Glare: High hung, the bloody Liver tempts their Maw. Or as a Housewife stands before her Pales, surrounded by her Geese; they fight, they hiss, they gaggle, beat their Wings, and Down is scatter'd as the Winter's Snow, for a poor Grain of Oat, or Tare, or Barley. Such Looks shot thro' the Room transverse, oblique, direct; such was the stir and din, till *Curll* thus spoke, (but without rising from his Close-stool.)

'*Whores* and *Authors* must be paid beforehand to put them in good Humour; therefore here is half a Crown a piece for you to drink your own Healths, and Confusion to Mr. *Addison,* and all other successful Writers.

'Ah Gentlemen! What have I not done, what have I not suffer'd, rather than the World should be depriv'd of your Lucubrations? I have taken involuntary Purges, I have been vomited, three Times have I been can'd, once was I hunted, twice was my Head broke by a Grenadier, twice was I toss'd in a Blanket; I have had Boxes on the Ear, Slaps on the Chops; I have been frighted, pump'd, kick'd, slander'd and beshitten.——I hope, Gentlemen, you are all convinc'd that this Author of Mr. *Lintott's* could mean nothing else but starving you by poisoning me. It remains for us to consult the best and speediest Methods of Revenge.'

He had scarce done speaking, but the *Historian* propos'd a History of his Life. The *Exeter* Exchange Gentleman was for penning Articles of his Faith. Some pretty smart *Pindarick*, (says the Red-Stocking Gentleman,) would effectually do his Business. But the *Index-maker* said there was nothing like an *Index* to his *Homer*.

After several Debates they came to the following Resolutions.

'*Resolv'd*, That every Member of this Society, according to his several Abilities, shall contribute some way or other to the Defamation of Mr. *Pope*.

'*Resolv'd*, That towards the Libelling of the said Mr. *Pope*, there be a Summ employ'd not exceeding Six Pounds Sixteen Shillings and Nine Pence (not including Advertisements.)

'*Resolv'd*, That Mr. *D[ennis]* make an Affidavit before Mr. *Justice Tully*, that in Mr. *Pope*'s *Homer*, there are several Passages contrary to the establish'd Rules of OUR Sublime.

'*Resolved*, That he has on Purpose in several Passages perverted the true ancient *Heathen* Sense of *Homer*, for the more effectual Propagation of the *Popish* Religion.

'*Resolv'd*, That the Printing of *Homer*'s Battles at this Juncture, has been the Occasion of all the Disturbances of this Kingdom.

'*Ordered*, That Mr. *Barnivelt* be invited to be a Member of this Society, in order to make further Discoveries.

'*Resolv'd*, That a number of effective *Errata*'s be raised out of Mr. *Pope*'s *Homer* (not exceeding 1746.) and that every Gentleman, who shall send in one Error, for his Encouragement shall have the whole Works of this Society *Gratis*.

'*Resolv'd*, That a Summ not exceeding Ten Shillings and Six-pence be distributed among the Members of this Society for *Coffee* and *Tobacco*, in order to enable them the more effectually to defame him in *Coffee-Houses*.

'*Resolv'd*, That towards the further lessening the Character of the said Mr. *Pope*, some Persons be deputed to abuse him at Ladies *Tea Tables*, and that in Consideration our Authors are not *well dress'd* enough, Mr. *C——y* be deputed for that Service.

'*Resolv'd*, That a *Ballad* be made against Mr. *Pope*, and that Mr. *Oldmixon*, Mr. *Gildon* and Mrs. *Centlivre* do prepare and bring in the same.

'*Resolv'd*, That above all, some effectual Ways and Means be found to encrease the Joint Stock of the

Reputation of this Society, which at present is exceedingly low, and to give their Works the greater Currency; whether by raising the Denomination of the said Works by counterfeit Title Pages, or mixing a greater Quantity of the fine Metal of other Authors, with the Alloy of this Society.

'*Resolv'd*, That no Member of this Society for the future mix *Stout* in his *Ale* in a Morning, and that Mr. *B.* remove from the *Hercules* and *Still.*

'*Resolv'd*, That all our Members, (except the *Cook's* Wife) be provided with a sufficient Quantity of the *vivifying Drops*, Or *Byfield's Sal Volatile.*

'*Resolv'd*, That Sir *R[ichard] B[lackmore]* be appointed to endue this Society with a large Quantity of *regular and exalted Ferments*, in order to *enliven* their *cold Sentiments* (being his true Receipt to make Wits.)

These Resolutions being taken, the Assembly was ready to break up, but they took so near a-part in Mr. *Curll's* Afflictions, that none of them could leave him without giving some Advice to re-instate him in his Health.

Mr. *Gildon* was of Opinion, That in order to drive a *Pope* out of his *Belly*, he should get the Mummy of some deceas'd Moderator of the General Assembly in *Scotland*, to be taken inwardly as an effectual Antidote against Antichrist; but Mr. *Oldmixon* did conceive, that the *Liver* of the Person who administred the Poison, boil'd in Broth, would be a more certain Cure.

While the Company were expecting the Thanks of Mr. *Curll*, for these Demonstrations of their Zeal, a whole Pile of *Essays* on a sudden fell on his Head; the Shock of which in an Instant brought back his Dilirium. He immediately rose up, over-turn'd the Close-stool, and beshit the *Essays* (which may probably occasion a *second Edition*) then without putting up his Breeches, in a most furious Tone, he thus broke out to his Books, which his distemper'd Imagination represented to him as alive, coming down from their Shelves, fluttering their Leaves, and flapping their Covers at him.

Now *G—d damn* all *Folio's*, *Quarto's*, *Octavo's* and *Duodecimo's!* ungrateful Varlets that you are, who have so long taken up my House without paying for your Lodging?—Are you not the beggarly Brood of fumbling *Journey-men*; born in *Garrets*, among *Lice* and *Cobwebs*, nurs'd upon *Grey Peas*, *Bullocks Liver*, and *Porter's Ale?*—Was not the first Light you saw, the *Farthing* Candle I paid for? Did you not come before your Time into *dirty Sheets* of brown Paper? —And have not I cloath'd you in double *Royal*, lodg'd you handsomely on *decent Shelves*, lac'd your *Backs* with *Gold*, equipt you with splendid *Titles*, and sent you into the World with the Names of *Persons of Quality?* Must I be *always* plagu'd with you? —Why flutter ye your Leaves, and flap your Covers at me? Damn ye all, ye *Wolves* in *Sheeps Cloathing*; *Rags ye were, and to Rags ye shall return.* Why hold you forth your *Texts* to me, ye paltry *Sermons?* Why

cry ye—at every Word to me, ye *bawdy Poems?*—To
my Shop at *Tunbridge* ye shall go, by *G*—— and
thence be drawn like the rest of your Predecessors,
bit by bit, to the *Passage-House:* For in this present
Emotion of my Bowels, how do I compassionate those
who have great need, and nothing to wipe their
Breech with?

   Having said this, and at the same Time recollecting that his own was yet unwiped, he abated of his
Fury, and with great Gravity, apply'd to that Function the unfinish'd Sheets of the Conduct of the
E[arl] of *N[ottingha]m.*

FINIS.

Prose Pieces

FROM

The Works

1717

THE PREFACE

To *The Works*, 1717.

I AM inclined to think that both the writers of books, and the readers of them, are generally not a little unreasonable in their expectations. The first seem to fancy that the world must approve whatever they produce, and the latter to imagine that authors are obliged to please them at any rate. Methinks as on the one hand, no single man is born with a right of controuling the opinions of all the rest; so on the other, the world has no title to demand, that the whole care and time of any particular person should be sacrificed to its entertainment. Therefore I cannot but believe that writers and readers are under equal obligations, for as much fame, or pleasure, as each affords the other.

Every one acknowledges, it would be a wild notion to expect perfection in any work of man: and yet one would think the contrary was taken for granted, by the judgment commonly past upon Poems. A Critic supposes he has done his part, if he proves a writer to have fail'd in an expression, or err'd in any particular point: and can it then be wonder'd at, if the Poets in general seem resolv'd not to own themselves in any error? For as long as one side despises a well-meant endeavour, the other will not be satisfy'd with a moderate approbation.

I am afraid this extreme zeal on both sides is illplac'd; Poetry and Criticism being by no means the

u

universal concern of the world, but only the affair of idle men who write in their closets, and of idle men who read there. Yet sure upon the whole, a bad Author deserves better usage than a bad Critic; a man may be the former merely thro' the misfortune of an ill judgment, but he cannot be the latter without both that and an ill temper.

I think a good deal may be said to extenuate the fault of bad Poets. What we call a Genius, is hard to be distinguish'd by a man himself, from a strong inclination: and if it be never so great, he can not at first discover it any other way, than by that prevalent propensity which renders him the more liable to be mistaken. The only method he has, is to make the experiment by writing, and appealing to the judgment of others: And if he happens to write ill (which is certainly no sin in itself) he is immediately made an object of ridicule. I wish we had the humanity to reflect that even the worst authors might endeavour to please us, and in that endeavour, deserve something at our hands. We have no cause to quarrel with them but for their obstinacy in persisting, and this too may admit of alleviating circumstances. Their particular friends may be either ignorant, or insincere; and the rest of the world too well bred to shock them with a truth, which generally their Booksellers are the first that inform them of. This happens not till they have spent too much of their time, to apply to any profession which might better fit their talents; and till such talents as they have are so far discredited, as to be but of small service to them. For (what is the hardest case imaginable) the reputation of a man generally depends upon the first steps he makes in the world, and people will establish their opinion of us, from what we do at that season when we have least judgment to direct us.

On the other hand, a good Poet no sooner communicates his works with the same desire of information, but it is imagin'd he is a vain young creature given up to the ambition of fame; when perhaps the poor man is all the while trembling with the fear of being ridiculous. If he is made to hope he may please the world, he falls under very unlucky circumstances; for from the moment he prints, he must expect to hear no more truth, than if he were a Prince, or a Beauty. If he has not very good sense, his living thus in a course of flattery may put him in no small danger of becoming a Coxcomb: If he has, he will consequently have so much diffidence, as not to reap any great satisfaction from his praise; since if it be given to his face, it can scarce be distinguish'd from flattery, and if in his absence, it is hard to be certain of it. Were he sure to be commended by the best and most knowing, he is as sure of being envy'd by the worst and most ignorant; for it is with a fine Genius as with a fine fashion, all those are displeas'd at it who are not able to follow it: And 'tis to be fear'd that esteem will seldom do any man so much good, as illwill does him harm. Then there is a third class of people who make the largest part of mankind, those of ordinary or indifferent capacities; and these (to a man) will hate, or suspect him: a hundred honest gentlemen will dread him as a wit, and a hundred innocent women as a satyrist. In a word, whatever be his fate in Poetry, it is ten to one but he must give up all the reasonable aims of life for it. There are indeed some advantages accruing from a Genius to Poetry, and they are all I can think of: the agreeable power of self-amusement when a man is idle or alone; the privilege of being admitted into the best company; and the freedom of saying as many careless things as other people, without being so severely remark'd upon.

I believe, if any one, early in his life should contemplate the dangerous fate of authors, he would scarce be of their number on any consideration. The life of a Wit is a warfare upon earth; and the present spirit of the world is such, that to attempt to serve it (any way) one must have the constancy of a martyr, and a resolution to suffer for its sake. I confess it was want of consideration that made me an author; I writ because it amused me; I corrected because it was as pleasant to me to correct as to write; and I publish'd because I was told I might please such as it was a credit to please. To what degree I have done this, I am really ignorant; I had too much fondness for my productions to judge of them at first, and too much judgment to be pleas'd with them at last. But I have reason to think they can have no reputation which will continue long, or which deserves to do so: for they have always fallen short not only of what I read of others, but even of my own Ideas of Poetry.

If any one should imagine I am not in earnest, I desire him to reflect, that the Ancients (to say the least of them) had as much Genius as we; and that to take more pains, and employ more time, cannot fail to produce more complete pieces. They constantly apply'd themselves not only to that art, but to that single branch of an art, to which their talent was most powerfully bent; and it was the business of their lives to correct and finish their works for posterity. If we can pretend to have used the same industry, let us expect the same immortality: Tho' if we took the same care, we should still lie under a farther misfortune: they writ in languages that became universal and everlasting, while ours are extremely limited both in extent, and in duration. A mighty foundation for our pride! when the utmost we can hope, is but to be read in one Island, and to be thrown aside at the end of one Age.

All that is left us is to recommend our productions by the imitation of the Ancients: and it will be found true, that in every age, the highest character for sense and learning has been obtain'd by those who have been most indebted to them. For to say truth, whatever is very good sense must have been common sense in all times; and what we call Learning, is but the knowledge of the sense of our predecessors. Therefore they who say our thoughts are not our own because they resemble the Ancients, may as well say our faces are not our own, because they are like our Fathers: And indeed it is very unreasonable, that people should expect us to be Scholars, and yet be angry to find us so.

I fairly confess that I have serv'd my self all I could by reading; that I made use of the judgment of authors dead and living; that I omitted no means in my power to be inform'd of my errors, both by my

friends and enemies; and that I expect not to be excus'd in any negligence on account of youth, want of
leisure, or any other idle allegations: But the true
reason these pieces are not more correct, is owing to
the consideration how short a time they, and I, have
to live: One may be ashamed to consume half one's
days in bringing sense and rhyme together; and what
Critic can be so unreasonable as not to leave a man
time enough for any more serious employment, or
more agreeable amusement?

The only plea I shall use for the favour of the publick, is, that I have as great a respect for it, as most
authors have for themselves; and that I have sacrificed much of my own self-love for its sake, in pre-
venting not only many mean things from seeing the
light, but many which I thought tolerable. I believe
no one qualification is so likely to make a good writer, as the power of rejecting his own thoughts; and
it must be this (if any thing) that can give me a
chance to be one. For what I have publish'd, I can
only hope to be pardon'd; but for what I have burn'd,
I deserve to be prais'd. On this account the world is
under some obligation to me, and owes me the justice in return, to look upon no verses as mine that are
not inserted in this collection. And perhaps nothing
could make it worth my while to own what are really
so, but to avoid the imputation of so many dull and
immoral things, as partly by malice, and partly by
ignorance, have been ascribed to me. I must farther
acquit my self of the presumption of having lent my
name to recommend any Miscellanies, or works of
other men, a thing I never thought becoming a per-

son who has hardly credit enough to answer for his own.

In this office of collecting my pieces, I am altogether uncertain, whether to look upon my self as a man building a monument, or burying the dead?

If time shall make it the former, may these Poems (as long as they last) remain as a testimony, that their Author never made his talents subservient to the mean and unworthy ends of Party or self-interest; the gratification of publick prejudices, or private passions; the flattery of the undeserving, or the insult of the unfortunate. If I have written well, let it be consider'd that 'tis what no man can do without good sense, a quality that not only renders one capable of being a good writer, but a good man. And if I have made any acquisition in the opinion of any one under the notion of the former, let it be continued to me under no other title than that of the latter.

But if this publication be only a more solemn funeral of my Remains, I desire it may be known that I die in charity, and in my senses; without any murmurs against the justice of this age, or any mad appeals to posterity. I declare I shall think the world in the right, and quietly submit to every truth which time shall discover to the prejudice of these writings; not so much as wishing so irrational a thing, as that every body should be deceiv'd, meerly for my credit. However, I desire it may then be consider'd, that there are very few things in this collection which were not written under the age of five and twenty; so that my youth may be made (as it never fails to be in Executions) a case of compassion. That I was never so concern'd about my works as to vindicate them in print, believing if any thing was good it would defend itself, and what was bad could never be defended. That I used no artifice to raise or continue a reputation, depreciated no dead author I was obliged to, brib'd no living one with unjust praise, insulted no adversary with ill language, or when I could not attack a Rival's works, encourag'd reports against his Morals. To conclude, if this volume perish, let it serve as a warning to the Critics, not to take too much pains for the future to destroy such things as will die of themselves; and a *Memento mori* to some of my vain contemporaries the Poets, to teach them that when real merit is wanting, it avails nothing to have been encourag'd by the great, commended by the eminent, and favour'd by the publick in general.

The Works of Mr. *Alexander Pope*, 1717.

A DISCOURSE *on*

PASTORAL POETRY

THERE are not, I believe, a greater number of any sort of verses than of those which are called Pastorals, nor a smaller, than of those which are truly so. It therefore seems necessary to give some account of this kind of Poem, and it is my design to comprize in this short paper the substance of those numerous dissertations the Criticks have made on the subject, without omitting any of their rules in my own favour. You will also find some points reconciled, about which they seem to differ, and a few remarks which I think have escaped their observation.

The original of Poetry is ascribed to that age which succeeded the creation of the world: And as the keeping of flocks seems to have been the first employment of mankind, the most ancient sort of poetry was probably pastoral. 'Tis natural to imagine, that the leisure of those ancient shepherds requiring some diversion, none was so proper to that solitary life as singing; and that in their songs they took occasion to celebrate their own felicity. From hence a Poem was invented, and afterwards improv'd to a perfect image of that happy time; which by giving us an esteem for the virtues of a former age, might recommend them to the present. And since the life of shepherds was attended with more tranquillity than any other rural employment, the Poets chose to introduce their Persons, from whom it receiv'd the name of Pastoral.

A Pastoral is an imitation of the action of a shepherd; the form of this imitation is dramatic, or narrative, or mix'd of both; the fable simple, the manners not too polite nor too rustic: The thoughts are plain, yet admit a little quickness and passion, but that short and flowing: The expression humble, yet as pure as the language will afford; neat, but not florid; easy, and yet lively. In short, the fable, manners, thoughts, and expressions, are full of the greatest simplicity in nature.

The complete character of this poem consists in simplicity, brevity, and delicacy; the two first of which render an eclogue natural, and the last delightful.

If we would copy Nature, it may be useful to take this consideration along with us, that pastoral is an image of what they call the Golden age. So that we are not to describe our shepherds as shepherds at this day really are, but as they may be conceiv'd then to have been; when a notion of quality was annex'd to that name, and the best of men follow'd the employment. To carry this resemblance yet farther, that Air of piety to the Gods should shine thro' the Poem, which so visibly appears in all the works of antiquity: And it ought to preserve some relish of the old way of writing; the connections should be loose, the narrations and descriptions short, and the periods concise. Yet it is not sufficient that the sentences only be brief, the whole Eclogue should be so too. For we cannot suppose Poetry to have been the business of the ancient shepherds, but their recreation at vacant hours.

But with a respect to the present age, nothing

more conduces to make these composures natural,
than when some Knowledge in rural affairs is discover'd. This may be made to appear rather done by
chance than on design, and sometimes is best shewn
by inference; lest by too much study to seem natural,
we destroy the delight. For what is inviting in this
sort of poetry (as *Fontenelle* observes) proceeds not so
much from the Idea of a country life itself, as from
that of its Tranquillity. We must therefore use some
illusion to render a Pastoral delightful; and this consists in exposing the best side only of a shepherd's
life, and in concealing its miseries. Nor is it enough
to introduce shepherds discoursing together, but a
regard must be had to the subject; that it contain
some particular beauty in itself, and that it be different in every Eclogue. Besides, in each of them a
design'd scene or prospect is to be presented to our
view, which should likewise have its variety. This
Variety is obtain'd in a great degree by frequent
comparisons, drawn from the most agreeable objects
of the country; by interrogations to things inanimate; by beautiful digressions, but those short; sometimes by insisting a little on circumstances; and lastly
by elegant turns on the words, which render the
numbers extremely sweet and pleasing. As for the
numbers themselves, tho' they are properly of the
heroic measure, they should be the smoothest, the
most easy and flowing imaginable.

It is by rules like these that we ought to judge of
Pastoral. And since the instructions given for any art
are to be deliver'd as that art is in perfection, they
must of necessity be deriv'd from those in whom it is

acknowledg'd so to be. 'Tis therefore from the practice of *Theocritus* and *Virgil*, (the only undisputed
authors of Pastoral) that the Criticks have drawn the
foregoing notions concerning it.

Theocritus excells all others in nature and simplicity. The subjects of his *Idyllia* are purely pastoral,
but he is not so exact in his persons, having introduced Reapers and fishermen as well as shepherds.
He is apt to be long in his descriptions, of which that
of the Cup in the first pastoral is a remarkable instance. In the manners he seems a little defective, for
his swains are sometimes abusive and immodest, and
perhaps too much inclining to rusticity; for instance,
in his fourth and fifth *Idyllia*. But 'tis enough that all
others learn'd their excellencies from him, and that
his Dialect alone has a secret charm in it which no
other could ever attain.

Virgil who copies *Theocritus*, refines upon his original: and in all points where Judgment has the principal part, is much superior to his master. Tho' some
of his subjects are not pastoral in themselves, but only
seem to be such; they have a wonderful variety in
them which the *Greek* was a stranger to. He exceeds
him in regularity and brevity, and falls short of him
in nothing but simplicity and propriety of style; the
first of which perhaps was the fault of his age, and
the last of his language.

Among the moderns, their success has been greatest who have most endeavour'd to make these ancients their pattern. The most considerable Genius
appears in the famous *Tasso*, and our *Spenser*. *Tasso*
in his *Aminta* has as far excell'd all the Pastoral wri-

ters, as in his *Gierusalemme* he has outdone the Epic
Poets of his country. But as this piece seems to have
been the original of a new sort of poem, the Pastoral
Comedy, in *Italy*, it cannot so well be consider'd as a
copy of the ancients. *Spenser*'s *Calender*, in Mr. *Dryden*'s opinion, is the most complete work of this kind
which any Nation has produc'd ever since the time
of *Virgil*. Not but he may be thought imperfect in
some few points. His Eclogues are somewhat too long,
if we compare them with the ancients. He is sometimes too allegorical, and treats of matters of religion
in a pastoral style as *Mantuan* had done before him.
He has employ'd the Lyric measure, which is contrary to the practice of the old Poets. His Stanza is
not still the same, nor always well chosen. This last
may be the reason his expression is sometimes not
concise enough: for the Tetrastic has oblig'd him to
extend his sense to the length of four lines, which
would have been more closely confin'd in the Couplet.

In the manners, thoughts, and characters, he comes
near *Theocritus* himself; tho' notwithstanding all the
care he has taken, he is certainly inferior in his Dialect: For the *Doric* had its beauty and propriety in
the time of *Theocritus*; it was used in part of *Greece*,
and frequent in the mouths of many of the greatest
persons; whereas the old *English* and country phrases
of *Spenser* were either entirely obsolete, or spoken
only by people of the basest condition. As there is a
difference betwixt simplicity and rusticity, so the expression of simple thoughts should be plain, but not
clownish. The addition he has made of a Calendar to
his Eclogues is very beautiful: since by this, besides

that general moral of innocence and simplicity, which is common to other authors of pastoral, he has one peculiar to himself; he compares human Life to the several Seasons, and at once exposes to his readers a view of the great and little worlds, in their various changes and aspects. Yet the scrupulous division of his Pastorals into Months, has oblig'd him either to repeat the same description, in other words, for three months together; or when it was exhausted before, entirely to omit it: whence it comes to pass that some of his Eclogues (as the sixth, eighth, and tenth for example) have nothing but their Titles to distinguish them. The reason is evident, because the year has not that variety in it to furnish every month with a particular description, as it may every season.

Of the following Eclogues I shall only say, that these four comprehend all the subjects which the Critics upon *Theocritus* and *Virgil* will allow to be fit for pastoral: That they have as much variety of description, in respect of the several seasons, as *Spenser*'s: That in order to add to this variety, the several times of the day are observ'd, the rural employments in each season or time of day, and the rural scenes or places proper to such employments; not without some regard to the several ages of man, and the different passions proper to each age.

But after all, if they have any merit, it is to be attributed to some good old Authors, whose works as I had leisure to study, so I hope I have not wanted care to imitate.

The Works of Mr. *Alexander Pope*, 1717.

A
C L U E
To the COMEDY of the
Non - Juror.

WITH SOME
Hints of Confequence
Relating to that
P L A Y.
IN A
L E T T E R
T O
N. ROWE, Efq;
Poet Laureat to His Majefty.

Quo Mufa tendis? define pervicax
Referre Sermones Deorum——Hor.

L O N D O N:
Printed for *E. Curll,* in *Fleet-ftreet.* 1718.

A CLUE *to the* COMEDY *of*

THE NON-JUROR

With some *Hints* of Consequence
relating to the PLAY.

Dear Mr. *Rowe,*

ENTIRELY agree with you, That there has not of late appear'd in Publick, a more *exquisite Piece of Satire,* than the Comedy call'd the *Non-juror*; or that better deserv'd the Distinction that was shown it, not only by your Self, as His Majesty's Laureat, but by all the Loyal Party in general. I also agree with you, that perhaps there never was a Piece of fine *Drama-Theological Satire,* the true Scope of which has been less understood. I am at a Loss which to admire most, the noble, free Spirit of our Friend the Author; the insensibility of those whom the Satire is *really Aim'd at,* or the ignorant Rage of those *dissaffected Jacobite Wretches* who cry out when they are not hurt. You were pleas'd to desire me, when we met last, to put upon Paper the few Hints I dropt to you in Conversation upon this Subject, and which, I doubt not, are sufficient to make any unprejudic'd Reader of your and my Opinion; namely,

That Dissaffection to the Government is the smallest Immorality which is pointed at by this Play; and which indeed is only introduced to hide a far *deeper Design,* and far *more useful Satire.*

x

In order to set this in it's true Light, I will but barely *point* at the several Figures of the Comedy, and make some short Remarks upon their Attitudes, without the Ill-manners of naming any particular Person, but leaving the free and impartial Reader to draw his own Inferences. Two general Observations only, are necessary to be premised, because every common Judge is not so sensible of them, as we who have been Writers all our Lives.

The *First* is, That when we *Rebuke our Superiours,* the Fable ought to be so couch'd, as to make the Criminal give Judgment against himself before he is aware: (an Art as ancient at least as the Days of *Nathan*) But if the Scene of Action be laid in a Subject not only quite *foreign,* but seemingly *opposite* to the principal Aim of the Satire, the Address will be still the more refined; because by this Method the Author introduceth *Facts* and *Personages* which the guilty will be sure to Condemn; not only from *natural Equity,* but *natural Aversion.* Thus, for Example, To engage a *Tory* to condemn a Piece of Iniquity in the Abstract, one need only lay the Scene among *Whigs,* and so on the contrary. And *Secondly,* I would put the Reader in mind that in Fables of this Nature, it is usual to represent *whole Parties of Men by single Personages.*

This premised, let us observe the principal Figure that presents it self to our View; I mean Dr. *Wolf;* whose Character answers to *Moliere's Tartuffe,* who is known to have represented a *certain puritanical Bishop in France.*

We next are to take Notice, That *Wolf* in the Stile of *Ecclesiastical Allegory* constantly signifies the *Presbyterian Party:* You know it is thus in the *Hind* and *Panther,* and most other Pieces of Controversial Divinity or Poetry. So Dr. *Wolf* is a *Presbyterian.*

Dr. *Wolf* expects for his Services in *Betraying the Church,* great *Ecclesiastical Preferment,* (as Sir *John* expresseth it) (1) *an Office for Life, which, on whatsoever Pretence of Misbehaviour, no Civil Government can deprive him of.* This is Ironically represented afterwards by the *See of Thetford.* So, in short, Dr. *Wolf* is a Bishop.

This *Presbyterian* Bishop has wrote something about the *Case of Schism*; and the *Colonel* tells his Father, *That he* (2) *has read enough of him in the* Daily Courant. What Bishop has publish'd in the *Daily Courant,* is *lippis et tonsoribus notum.*

This Bishop protests great Zeal for the *Church,* at the same Time that he is betraying it: On which the *Colonel* tells Sir *John, Tho'* (3) *I have always honour'd your Concern for the Church, I little thought it was for a Church that is Establish'd no where.* (i.e.) *No visible Church.*

This Bishop is mark'd with another strong Characteristick, managing a Dispute with *Heartly* about *the Nature of Prayer.* That it ought not to be *Tedious*; (4) *outward Expression not so absolutely necessary, since Heaven knew the true Intention of the Heart.** And then he talks of his own *Manual of Devotions.*

(1) Nonjuror, pag. 18.   (2) pag. 3.   (3) pag. 3.
(4) pag. 13.   * pag. 12.

This Bishop also pretends a mighty Regard to *tender Consciences.* He tell's *Heartly,* That we (5) *ought to allure them to what is Good by the gentlest, easiest Means we can,* nor give the least colour of Offence to tender Consciences.

The *Colonel* here urges the *Constitution* against him, and the force of the Laws; and desires him to explain himself; to which this Bishop Answers (6) Sir, *I shall not explain my Self: But make your best of what I've said — But Power perhaps may change it's Hands, and you e're long as little dare to speak your mind, as I do*; viz. *That there may come a Time when this Constitution you talk so much of, may be overturned.*

Sir *John* is fully satisfy'd that the *Doctor* is all this while a (7) *true stanch Member of the* English *Catholick Church*; mark, that is, such a Church as *comprehends all Sects and Parties whatsoever.*

But lest these Lines shou'd not be strong enough, the Author gives the finishing Stroke.

This Bishop is at last discover'd to be a *Jesuit* in Disguise, By whom? By one of his *School-Boys* in whom he had distilled some of his *Jesuitical Principles.* And most remarkable it is what the *Colonel* says on this Occasion. That (8) *Charles* begs *he will not insist upon the Discovery, 'till his Circumstances will allow it*: Almost in the very Stile of some *Letters* that passed, upon a parallel Occasion, between a *Master of a School,* and a *Reverend Doctor.*

At last *Substantial Affadavits* are produced, to prove Dr. *Wolf* to have been Educated a *Jesuit*; by which (as it is usual in Allegorical Writers) *the close Con-*

(5) pag. 13.   (6) pag. 13.   (7) pag. 18.   (8) pag. 47.

junction of a Reverend Prelate *and a certain* Jesuit, is most injuriously and scandalously insinuated.

So here is a *Prelate* and a *Jesuit* and his *Gang*, got into the Family of Sir *John*! Let us next see what they are to do there. Why, they contrive the *Ruin* of his Family, and the *disinheriting* and *expulsion* of his *Children* with so great an Assurance of Success, that the *Doctor* talks of Sir *John* in this manner: (9) *Poor Man! he knows not his own Weakness; he is moulded into any Shape, if you but gently stroke his Humour. I intend to Morrow, to perswade him 'tis for the Interest of our Cause it should be so; and then I have him sure.* Poor Sir *John* indeed!

I must here put you in mind of my second Observation, that by the single Person of Dr. *Wolf*, without any forced Construction, may be understood a whole Sett or Party of Men. To proceed then,

The Play Opens with a Dispute between Sir *John* and his *Daughter*, about the Formality of *Christening*, and Sir *John* is at it again, (*pag* 63) being extremely rejoyced that *Heartly* is *Christ'ned* according to the *Right Form*. There is also mention made of *Searching the Register*, &c.

Next we see Dr. *Wolf* insulting Sir *John*'s *Son* and *Daughter*; he breaks into the *Daughter*'s Bedchamber before she is quite *Up*; and when *she resents it,* he tell's her (10) *Compose your Transport, Madam: I came by your* Father's Desire; *for what I have done, Madam, I had your* Father's Authority, *and shall leave him to answer you.* The *Daughter* replies, (11) *It is false, he gave you no Authority to insult me: What*

(9) pag. 68.   (10) pag. 15.   (11) *Ibid.*

is it you presume upon? your Function! does that exempt you from the Manners of a Gentleman?

At last his foul Behaviour provokes the *Son* to that degree, that he call's him (12) *Villain*, and *Rascal*.

Sir *John* is nettled at this; he tells his *Son* and *Daughter*, (13) *I see your Aim: Your Malice on your own vile Heads: To me it but the more endears him: Either submit and* ask his Pardon *for this Wrong,* — *or this Instant* leave my Sight, *my* House, *my* Family *for ever.*

The *Son* answers, (14) *Tho' I would hazard Life to save you from the Ruin he misleads you to, could Die to Reconcile my Duty to your Favour; yet on the Terms that Villain offers, 'tis Merit to refuse it. I Glory in the Disgrace your Errors give me.*

In short, Sir *John*'s Attachment to Dr. *Wolf* was so great, that there appear'd but small Hopes of ever opening Sir *John*'s Eyes: And remarkable is the Lamentation of the *Son* upon that Occasion; (15) *What horrid Hands is this poor Family fall'n into? How little is my Father like himself, by Nature Open, Just, and Generous? but this vile Hypocrite drives his weak Passions like the Wind; and I foresee, at last, will dash him on his Ruin.*

When Dr. *Wolf* had wrought up the Passion of Sir *John* to this degree, as to turn his *Children out of Doors*; then he interposeth his good Offices, and proposeth a *Reconciliation*.

I beg the Reader to observe the *Terms* of it. *That his Child should be at the sole Disposal of Dr.* Wolf, and do nothing without *his Consent.*

(12) pag. 4.   (13) pag. 44.   (14) pag. 45.   (15) pag. 16.

It must here be observ'd that the Daughter had a Fortune of *her own, independent on the Father,* upon which she seems to value her Self. (17) *Have not I 5000 l. in my own hands? have not I had the full Swing of my own Airs and humours these four years?* Mark the precise time. But she is put in mind by the *Son,* that tho' the Father could not *deprive her of her Fortune, he might abridge* her Equipage; in these words (18) *however a Father's Consent might have clapt a pair of horses more to your Coach.*

But at last he applauds her resolution, and tells her she *speaks with the Spirit of a free-born Englishman.*

Mark now the modesty of Dr. *Wolf;* he proposes, as the Lowest and *last condition, that she should resign the half of this independent fortune* (19) *Is not two thousand pounds worth two Thousand pounds?* Is not *half* better than *nothing?*

Observe next, (good Mr. *Rowe*) how Dr. *Wolf* endeavours to debauch Lady *Woodvill,* and make her Subservient to his Villainous designs: This Lady is described as having a great Ascendant over Sir *John's* Spirit that *She keeps no Assemblys;* that she had been *Poor* and *Beautiful,* while Sir *John* was *Rich* and *Amourous.* This Lady proves honest and trusty; and contributes, in the conclusion, to the discovery of the wicked purposes of Dr. *Wolf.*

Pray take notice too of a very odd Episode that seems to contribute very little to the main Action. That is Dr. *Wolf's* endeavouring to Bring Sir *John* into a *Scheme* of *Church Comprehension;* Referring again to his *Case of Schism,* he tells Sir *John* that (20)

(17) pag. 5.   (18) *Ibid.*   (19) pag. 54.   (20) pag. 25.

differences are not so material as some would represent them. Ah! could we be brought to a Temper, a great many seeming Contradictions might be reconciled. I allow this is a *Comprehension* of a different kind; but I beg leave to remind you and my Readers of my first observation, that the *Circumstances of a Fable* do not determine the *Satire.* But you, Sir, who are intimate with Mr. *Cibber* may examine and know the Truth of this.

Nothing is so plain as the Catastrophe; when Dr. *Wolf* thought himself sure of his Blow, and had brought Sir *John* to believe that his (21) *hot brain'd* Son (as he calls him) had a Design to get his Estate; he instantly makes Sir *John* resolve to repay it in kind by disinheriting him.

But at last, there arises a misfortune from a Corner where the *Doctor* least suspected it. Some of his own Party, whom he thought inviolably attach'd to his interests, discover his wicked purposes. This Sett of Men is represented by *Charles* an ingenious Gentleman, a Servant of Sir *John*'s, a man of Business, a good *Greek* and *Latin* Scholar *&c.* This *Charles* (it seems) highly obliged by the Generous treatment of the *Son* and enamour'd of the good Qualities of the *Daughter*, both reveals, and prevents the whole *mystery of Iniquity*: Upon which Dr. *Wolf* seeing his project dissappointed vents his Rage upon this honest Gentleman; and attempts his Life.

Lastly, Mr. *Cibber* (to obviate all possibility of mistaking his meaning) upon the winding up of the whole design, breaks on a sudden into an open dis-

(21) pag. 24.

course of *Politicks*; talks of *embroiling the Nation*, and *ending Publick disputes* and calls upon King *George,* with abundance more good *Morality* very well worth observing.

Thus, Sir, according to your desire, I have given a short Sketch of the *Fable* and *Characters* of this Play; just enough to enable some person of greater *Sagacity* to find out who are meant by every particular Personage of the *Drama*. I am sure I would not presume so much as to guess.

But one Thing I must observe, which I remember we both took particular notice of: It is, that the Author tho' questionless a great master of Stile, puts *bad English* into the mouths of most of his Personages: So that indeed scarce any of 'em talk at all like *English Folks*; but perpetually make use of an uncorrect, *Foreign, Jargon*. What his drift is in this I cannot imagine; but the Instances of it are obvious to every Reader; and numerous *in every Page*.

I am,

Dear *Mr*. Rowe,

Your, &c.

POSTSCRIPT.

Part of an *EPILOGUE*, Written by *N. Rowe*, Esq; to a Play call'd, *The Cruel Gift*: Or, *The Royal Resentment*; a *TRAGEDY*.*

THE former Part of this *EPILOGUE* turns upon the Plot of the Play, the latter Part is as follows, *viz*,

How many Worthy Gentlemen of late,
Swore to be true to *Mother-Church* and State;
When their *False Hearts* were secretly maintaining
Yon trim King *PEPIN* at *Avignon* Reigning?
Shame on the canting Crew of *Soul Insurers*,
That *Tyburn-Tribe* of *Speech-Making Non-Jurors*.
Who in new fangled Terms, old Truths explaining,
Teach honest *English-men*, damn'd *Double Meaning*.

The great *Loyalty* express'd in these Lines, is so apparent, as not to stand in need of the least Comment.

The Conclusion of this *Epilogue* being the Character of an Illustrious *PERSONAGE*, I refer the Reader to the Play above-mention'd for the Satisfaction of his Curiosity.

FINIS.

* Printed for *E. Curll*. Price 1*s*.

A Strange but True

RELATION

HOW

EDMUND CURLL,

was converted from the Christian Religion . . .
And . . . circumcis'd.

[1720]

A Strange but True

RELATION

HOW

EDMUND CURLL,

of Fleetstreet, Stationer,

Out of an extraordinary Desire of Lucre, went into *Change Alley*, and was converted from the Christian Religion by certain Eminent *Jews*: And how he was circumcis'd and initiated into their Mysteries.

AVARICE (as Sir *Richard* in the Third Page of his Essays hath elegantly observ'd) *is an inordinate Impulse of the Soul towards the amassing or heaping together a Superfluity of Wealth without the least Regard of applying it to its proper Uses.*

And how the Mind of Man is possessed with this Vice, may be seen every Day both in the City and Suburbs thereof. It has been always esteemed by *Plato*, *Puffendorf* and *Socrates*, as the darling Vice of old Age: But now our young Men are turn'd Usurers and Stock-jobbers; and, instead of lusting after the real Wives and Daughters of our rich Citizens, they covet nothing but their Money and Estates. Strange Change of Vice! when the Concupiscence of Youth is converted into the Covetousness of Age, and those Appetites are now become VENAL which should be VENEREAL.

In the first Place, let us shew you how many of the ancient Worthies and Heroes of Antiquity have been undone and ruin'd by this Deadly Sin of Avarice.

I shall take the Liberty to begin with *Brutus*, that noble *Roman*. Does not *Ætian* inform us that he received Fifty Broad Pieces for the Assassination of that renowned Emperor *Julius Cæsar*, who fell a Sacrifice to the *Jews*, as Sir *Edmund Bury Godfrey* did to the *Papists*?

Did not *Themistocles* let in the *Goths* and *Vandals* into *Carthage* for a Sum of Money, where they barbarously put out the other Eye of the famous *Hannibal*? As *Herodotus* hath it in his ninth Book upon the *Roman* Medals.

Even the great *Cato* (as the late Mr. *Addison* hath very well observ'd) though otherwise a Gentleman of good Sense, was not unsully'd by this pecuniary Contagion: For he sold *Athens* to *Artaxerxes Longimanus* for a hundred *Rix-Dollars*, which in our Money will amount to two *Talents* and thirty *Sestertii*, according to Mr. *Demoiver*'s Calculation. *See* Hesiod *in his 7th Chapter of* Feasts *and* Festivals.

Actuated by the same Diabolical Spirit of Gain, *Scylla* the *Roman* Consul shot *Alcibiades* the Senator with a Pistol, and robb'd him of several *Bank Bills* and *Chequer Notes* to an immense Value; for which he came to an untimely End, and was deny'd *Christian* Burial. Hence comes the Proverb *incidat in Scyllam*.

To come near to our own Times, and give you one modern Instance (tho' well known, and often quoted by Historians, *viz. Echard, Dionysius Halicarnassæus, Virgil, Horace*, and others) 'Tis that, I mean, of the famous *Godfrey* of *Bulloigne*, one of the great Heroes of the Holy War, who rob'd *Cleopatra* Queen of *Egypt* of a Diamond Necklace, Ear-Rings, and a

Tompion's Gold Watch (which was given her by *Mark Antony*) all these things were found in *Godfrey*'s Breeches Pocket, when he was kill'd at the Siege of *Damascus*.

Who then can wonder after so many great and illustrious Examples that Mr. *Edmund Curll* the Stationer, should renounce the *Christian Religion* for the *Mammon* of Unrighteousness, and barter his precious Faith for the filthy Prospect of Lucre in the present Fluctuation of *Stocks*.

It having been observ'd to Mr. *Curll* by some of his ingenious Authors, (who I fear are not overcharg'd with any Religion) what immense Sums the *Jews* had got by *Bubbles*, &c. he immediately turned his Mind from the Business in which he was educated, but thriv'd little, and resolv'd to quit his Shop, for *Change Alley*. Whereupon falling into Company with the *Jews* at their Club at the Sign of the *Cross* in *Cornhill*, they began to tamper with him upon the most important Points of the *Christian Faith*, which he for some time zealously, and *like a good Christian obstinately* defended. They promised him *Paradise*, and many other Advantages *hereafter*, but he artfully insinuated that he was more inclinable to listen to *present* Gain. They took the Hint, and promis'd him that immediately upon his Conversion to their Persuasion he should become as rich as a *Jew*.

They made use likewise of several other Arguments, to wit,

That the wisest Man that ever was, and inasmuch the richest, beyond all peradventure, was a *Jew*, videlicet *Solomon*.

That *David*, the Man after God's own Heart, was a *Jew* also. And most of the Children of *Israel* are suspected for holding the same Doctrine.

This Mr. *Curll* at first strenuously deny'd, for indeed he thought them *Roman Catholicks*, and so far was he from giving way to their Temptations, that to convince them of his *Christianity* he call'd for a *Pork-Grisking*.

They now promis'd if he would poison his Wife and give up his *Grisking*, that he should marry the rich *Ben Meymon's* only Daughter. This made some Impression on him.

They then talk'd to him in the *Hebrew* Tongue, which he not understanding, it was observ'd had very great Weight with him.

They, now perceiving that his *Godliness* was only *Gain*, desisted from all other Arguments, and attack'd him on his weak side, namely that of *Avarice*.

Upon which *John Mendez* offer'd him an Eighth of an advantagious Bargain for the *Apostles Creed*, which he readily and wickedly renounced.

He then sold the *Nine and Thirty Articles* for a *Bull*; but insisted hard upon *Black-Puddings*, being a great Lover thereof.

Joshua Perrara engag'd to let him share with him in his *Bottomrye*, upon this he was persuaded out of his *Christian Name*; but he still adher'd to *Black-Puddings*.

Sir *Gideon Lopez* tempted him with *Forty Pound* Subscription in *Ram's Bubble*; for which he was content to give up the *Four Evangelists*, and he was now compleated a perfect *Jew*, all but *Black-Pudding* and

Circumcision; for both of which he would have been glad to have had a Dispensation.

But on the 17th of *March*, Mr. *Curll* (unknown to his Wife) came to the Tavern aforesaid. At his Entrance into the Room he perceived a meagre Man, with a sallow Countenance, a black forky Beard, and long Vestment. In his Right Hand he held a large Pair of Sheers, and in his Left a red hot Searing-Iron. At Sight of this, Mr. *Curll*'s Heart trembled within him, and feign would he retire; but he was prevented by six Jews, who laid Hands upon him, and unbuttoning his Breeches threw him upon the Table, a pale pitiful Spectacle.

He now entreated them in the most moving Tone of Voice to dispense with that *unmanly* Ceremonial, which if they would consent to, he faithfully promis'd that he would eat a Quarter of *Paschal Lamb* with them the next *Sunday* following.

All these Protestations availed him nothing, for they threatned him that all Contracts and Bargains should be void unless he would submit to bear all the *outward* and *visible* Signs of *Judaism*.

Our Apostate hearing this, stretched himself upon his Back, spread his Legs, and waited for the Operation; but when he saw the High-Priest take up the *Cleft Stick*, he roared most unmercifully, and swore several Christian Oaths, for which the *Jews* rebuked him.

The Savour of the *Effluvia* that issued from him, convinced the Old *Levite* and all his Assistants that he needed no present *Purgation*, wherefore without farther *anointing* him he proceeded in his Office;

y

when by an unfortunate Jerk upward of the impatient Victim, he lost five times as much as ever Jew did before.

They finding that he was too much circumcis'd, which by the *Levitical Law* is worse than not being circumcis'd at all, refused to stand to any of their Contracts: Wherefore they cast him forth from their Synagogue; and he now remains a most piteous, woful and miserable Sight at the Sign of the *Old Testament* and *Dial* in *Fleet-street*, his Wife, (poor Woman) is at this Hour lamenting over him, wringing her Hands and tearing her Hair; for the barbarous Jews still keep, and expose at *Jonathan's* and *Garraway's*, the Memorial of her Loss, and her Husband's Indignity.

PRAYER. (*To save the Stamp.*)

KEEP *us, we beseech thee, from the Hands of such barbarous and cruel* Jews, *who, albeit, they abhor the Blood of* Black Puddings, *yet thirst they vehemently after the Blood of* White *ones. And that we may avoid such like Calamities, may all good and well-disposed Christians be warn'd by this unhappy Wretch's woful Example to abominate the heinous Sin of* Avarice, *which sooner or later will draw them into the cruel Clutches of* Satan, Papists, Jews, *and* Stock-jobbers. Amen.

Miscellanies. The Third Volume. 1732.

THE
DEDICATION
of The ILIAD
1720

THE
DEDICATION
of
The ILIAD

I MUST end these Notes by discharging my Duty
to two of my Friends, which is the more an in-
dispensable piece of Justice, as the one of them is
since dead: The Merit of their Kindness to me will
appear infinitely the greater, as the Task they under-
took was in its own nature of much more Labour,
than either Pleasure or Reputation. The larger part
of the Extracts from *Eustathius*, together with several excellent Observations were sent me by Mr.
Broome: And the whole Essay upon *Homer* was written upon such Memoirs as I had collected, by the
late Dr. *Parnell*, Archdeacon of *Clogher* in *Ireland*:
How very much that Gentleman's Friendship prevail'd over his Genius, in detaining a Writer of his
Spirit in the Drudgery of removing the Rubbish of
past Pedants, will soon appear to the World, when
they shall see those beautiful Pieces of Poetry the
Publication of which he left to my Charge, almost
with his dying Breath.

For what remains, I beg to be excus'd from the
Ceremonies of taking leave at the End of my Work;
and from embarassing myself, or others, with any
Defences or Apologies about it. But instead of en-

deavouring to raise a vain Monument to my self, of the Merits or Difficulties of it (which must be left to the World, to Truth, and to Posterity) let me leave behind me a Memorial of my Friendship, with one of the most valuable Men as well as finest Writers, of my Age and Countrey: One who has try'd, and knows by his own Experience, how hard an Undertaking it is to do Justice to *Homer*: And one, who (I am sure) sincerely rejoices with me at the Period of my Labours. To Him therefore, having brought this long Work to a Conclusion, I desire to *Dedicate* it; and to have the Honour and Satisfaction of placing together, in this manner, the Names of Mr. *CONGREVE*, and of

A. POPE.

March 25.
1720.